About the author

Preeti Singh currently lives in Delhi with her diplomat husband, having spent several years in the United States, Egypt and Afghanistan. She studied English Literature in both India and in Washington D.C. and has been a Lecturer/ Reader in the Department of English at the Indraprastha College for Women, Delhi. She is now Editor at the Oxford University Press, New Delhi. Preeti has contributed articles, reviews and short stories to literary magazines before writing her first full-length novel.

Circles of Silence

PREETI SINGH

FLAME
Hodder & Stoughton

First published in Great Britain in 2001 by Hodder & Stoughton
A division of Hodder Headline Ltd
First published in paperback in 2002 by Hodder & Stoughton
A Flame Paperback

A CIP catalogue record for this title is available from the British Library.

ISBN 0 340 82028 4

Printed and bound in Great Britain by
Mackays of Chatham plc, Chatham, Kent

Hodder and Stoughton
A division of Hodder Headline Ltd
338 Euston Road
London NW1 3BH

For my father, Ram Nath Chopra, in remembrance.

ACKNOWLEDGEMENTS

This book was begun in Cairo, furthered in Houston, and completed in New Delhi. In the long and lonely journey of writing, I received extended support and wish to thank all those who believed in me: Swash, my husband without whose faith, support and creative suggestions I could never have written a word; Kabir, my son, for his patience, and for deeming me a 'typer' of stories when he was only five; my mother Usha Chopra, for endowing me with the gift of narrative; Steve Alter in whose creative writing classes in the AUC Cairo I honed my writing skills; Venkatesh Kulkarni who showed me that I already had a novel in my head; Bapsi Sidhwa who told me that I should give myself a chance; to Harpal, Meena, Neelu and Kitty, my consultants and first readers; and last but not least, Urshilla, a dear friend and colleague, for her spontaneous lucidity.

I would also like to thank Anil, in whose lovely gardens I met Ralph Richards who, quite miraculously, took my book into the wider world. Thank you Ralph. Special thanks also to my agent, Ros Edwards — and everyone at Edwards Fuglewicz — with whom it was a pleasure to work, who found me a publisher, and with whom I look forward to a long association. Finally, many thanks also to Sue Fletcher and Swati Gamble at Hodder & Stoughton, for their professionalism and courtesy.

CONTENTS

Part One

Prophecy   3
Ennui   15
Sahayata   25
Two Women, Sour and Sweet   37
The Nether World   51
A Walk through the Door   55
A Woman Dead   71

Part Two

Nalini on the Nile   85
Letters from Home   99
An English Breakfast   113
A Scar in Cairo   127
Meeting under a Flag   137
Kasr-El-Nil   151

Part Three

A Letter Delivered   171
Shadow Play   179
Panna the Fakir Revisited   197
Afloat in a Felucca   213
The Festival of Lights   227

Part Four

A Dip in the River   249
The Red Serviettes   259
Single Parent   271
Convalescence   281
Commitment   301

Part Five

Snowflakes in Garhwal   311

Cafeteria Confusions   317

Two Friends in Cairo   335

Heart to Heart   351

Sons and Mothers   359

Part Six

From the Floors of Memory   379

Adrift on the Nile   393

The Tombs of the Dead   411

The Aftermath   425

A Truth Told   437

The Meeting   455

In the Shadow of the Pyramids   469

Glossary of Indian Words   489

PART ONE

Prophecy

When Rattan was born on a cold January night in 1960, one of the first things done in celebration of his arrival was to have his *janam patri* made. His paternal grandmother always made sure that Panna – a *fakir* long known to the Malhotras – blessed every single newborn in the large extended family. A tall broad-shouldered man, with thick wavy hair, a long flowing beard, and a deep myopic stare, Panna the Fakir was particular about signs and stars. He always insisted that to know the time, hour, or second of any birth was not enough: the baby must be brought before him. And, as soon after the birth as possible.

'We must take the baby today. Panna the Fakir is waiting,' old Mrs Malhotra said imperiously to her daughter-in-law.

Rattan's mother, Pammi, a rather large woman from one of Delhi's well-to-do families, was furious. Much had depended on Rattan's birth, and it was only two days after. The labour had been a prolonged affair. After seeing Pammi through twenty-seven hours of it, the doctor had decided to do a Caesarean section. Mother and child were still in the nursing home, and though Pammi was a strong woman, she was exhausted. And the stitches still hurt.

Pammi heard her mother-in-law in silent amazement. How could this simple enough looking woman be so cold and unfeeling? She had never liked her mother-in-law, an old superstitious (and suspicious) woman given to wearing dull, beige silk saris even in summer, and who ran her household with an iron hand. Everybody had to do what she decided they had to, and whenever she said so. But everyone also – including Sultan, the large Alsatian watch dog tied to the gates of her Old Delhi *haveli* – bristled and howled resentfully in secret, helpless.

So far, Pammi – already twenty-eight years old – had been doing the same, too.

When old Mrs Malhotra saw her grandson Rattan for the first time in the hospital nursery, she immediately noticed a small, darkened patch on the baby's right shoulder.

'*Hari Om, Narayan,*' she said loudly in shock, moving a step backwards from the cot in which he lay. Her mouth had formed a large, wide O. Four fingers of her right hand had lifted involuntarily in reflex, and rested heavily on her rounded lips. Her eyebrows had risen too, touching the prominent widow's peak high on her forehead, forcing wrinkles to bunch up in heavy, multiplying grooves.

'A birthmark on the right shoulder! And one as big, and as dark as that! *Arre baap re!* This is of some terrible significance ... Panna the Fakir should see the baby quickly.'

Pammi had seen the patch too, but had made nothing of it. She had noticed rather, as all anxious mothers of newborns do, the shape and colour of Rattan's face, the thick shock of his jet-black hair, his fine pointed nose, and his long tapering fingers. Pleased with what she saw, she was savouring a tremendous sense of accomplishment. Rattan was a huge baby, almost 3.8 kilograms; and was, as far as she could tell, doing well. And, she did not think it right that he should be taken out so soon, on such a cold January morning, just to have his *janam patri* made by some old fakir.

When the hue and cry about the birthmark temporarily died down, she decided to reason with her husband. The trip to the fakir was, as she looked at it, most unnecessary. But when told this on his evening visit to the hospital, Rattan's father, Noni Malhotra, a tall man given to looking elsewhere when spoken to, had his mind full of a new business venture in which an American firm was going to be a partner. He was sitting hunched at the edge of the bed, trying unsuccessfully to get one of Rattan's fingers to go around his own, bigger ones. He was impatient, even somewhat distant in his response.

'Just do what she says, will you, please?' he told his wife, wanting all this to be over with as soon as possible. 'How the hell does it matter? You know how Ma is! It means a lot to her.' He avoided looking at Pammi as he spoke.

Pammi had no choice but to agree. But she insisted that they wait till she was out of the nursing home, had taken the baby home, and her stitches were healed.

'OK! OK! I'll tell her that,' said Noni impatiently. 'Is there anything else?'

There was nothing else, then. Pammi gave her husband an exasperated look. But before she could say any more, Rattan let out a loud cry. Noni moved away hurriedly. He and wailing babies did not go together. Pammi got on with mothering, and Noni left for the day. There was no more talk of birthmarks. Or fakirs.

But once home, it all began again. Old Mrs Malhotra began her insistent, superstitious reminders. Ten days later, the young parents, resigned to their nagging fate, did as the older woman instructed. At seven thirty a.m., when one of Delhi's infamous winter morning fogs hovered densely over the *haveli* – and over Majnu ka Tila where Panna the Fakir had his hut – mother-in-law, mother, son, and baby grandson squeezed themselves into the old blue Austin driven by the family driver. Sultan barked after them as they drove out of the gates, frightening Rattan and making him cry.

Even though the visibility was low, the drive did not take long. Majnu ka Tila was not very far from the house. So fully was her mind on the safety of her baby that Pammi did not notice anything of her surroundings, either during the drive or at her destination. Mercifully, Rattan had fallen asleep, swaddled in baby blankets straight from London; and had not woken when his mother moved him to a more secure position in the crook of her elbow before stepping out of the car. The foursome hurried along the winding pathway leading to the fakir's hut. Placing the bundled Rattan before the fakir, they unwrapped his cocoon of layered blankets in the not-so-clear light of the thatched, dingy structure.

Panna the Fakir took a careful look at the naked Rattan while his mother turned him upside down. He was silent for a few moments.

'Hmm. Good. It is a good baby ... a good baby. But the birthmark on his shoulder is bad. Very bad. Hmm. Very bad,' he said. There was a pregnant pause. He continued in a voice low and ominous, 'His own will eat him up.'

Everyone present stared at him round-eyed, their jaws dropping in amazement.

After a brief silence – in which the fakir continued to stare at baby Rattan with a narrow, pinched glare – he spoke again.

'Yes. His own will eat him up ... or at least, very nearly. And then he will survive. Yes, survive ... Remind him, he should visit me when he is thirty-six years old. Write it down somewhere, so nobody forgets. He must come.'

The last sentence seemed addressed directly to baby Rattan. But the latter was not impressed. His body gave a small shiver; and, waving a tightly clenched fist in Panna the Fakir's face, he let out a loud wail.

'He is cold, the poor thing!' said Pammi, furious again.

But she had to sit still for at least three more minutes, cross-legged on the freezing floor. She thanked her stars that she had worn *salwar kameez*, and not the sari her mother-in-law was insisting upon. At least the small of her still tender back – exposed to the gusty draughts blowing in through the low doorway behind her – was fully covered by her *kameez*, cardigan and shawl. She watched, grim-faced, as Panna the Fakir tied a thin black thread – with a silver amulet in the shape of a trishul hanging from it – on Rattan's right wrist.

Throughout the proceedings Rattan howled. Maybe, lying in his mother's lap, he noticed the grimacing, seething face of his mother; and just above her head, the dark, intense one of the bearded fakir. Behind them, on one side, stood his solicitous grandmother, wrapped in a beige sari and a white shawl. On the other, stood his father, in a Pierre Cardin suit, and a Rolex watch. While old Mrs Malhotra, the great matriarch, chanted the Gayatri mantra in a loud murmur, Pammi tried to calm Rattan. Noni, the fond father, kept looking at his Rolex, waiting for it all to end.

As soon as he could, Noni slipped two hundred rupees into the waiting hands of Panna the Fakir, and hurried everyone into the car. He ignored his mother's continuing incantations, but held on to Pammi's elbow protectively, pushing her along. It was getting late; and it wouldn't do to keep his American partners waiting.

Still shivering in the early morning cold, Rattan protested all the way home.

Rattan grew up a happy, hyperactive child, looked after fondly by mother, grandmother, ayahs and servants. The Malhotra-Moncrief business partnership had worked out well, and the decade of the 70s saw the family income of the Malhotras multiply. Noni tied up with his American partners in other business ventures, and Pammi became a well-known society woman.

The Malhotras moved out of the Old Delhi family *haveli* in 1975, when Rattan was fifteen years old. In all these years, it had taken constant verbal manoeuvring on Pammi's part to keep her mother-in-law off the subject of Panna the Fakir's prophecy. She was, however, successful in making sure that Rattan did not hear of it from anyone. The day they moved to their new home –

73 Hauz Khas — in New Delhi was one of great celebration and relief for Pammi. With the move disappeared the memory of the prophecy. The *janam patri* — wrapped tightly in its orange and red cloths — was stashed away behind mounds of other documents in the brand new safe installed in Pammi's dressing room. And forgotten.

The birthmark on Rattan's shoulder remained, growing in size, as his body grew bigger and taller. It was often the subject of talk among his friends, especially in the gym or the swimming pool. But it never worried Rattan. In fact, over the years he had begun to see it as a sign of being someone special — as someone marked out by the powers that be. Since nobody told him what Panna the Fakir had said, he did not wonder about it. By the time he was seventeen — a strapping six feet and two inches tall, with dark hair and brows, aquiline features and the wheatish complexion typical of Punjabis — the birthmark was completely forgotten.

At seventeen, Rattan's special interest was computers. This was somewhat surprising, since all through his childhood years Rattan had found it hard to sit still on a chair. All his early school reports complained of a high intelligence and good oral skills, but a complete lack of application where written work was concerned. However, a slight change came over him with his introduction to computers. When they were first introduced in his high school, he was amongst the first in his class to enrol for computer studies.

Soon after, his father bought him his own personal computer from the USA. Rattan was thrilled. His father could not tell him anything about how to use it. This was the first time that Rattan — in awe of his father during most of his childhood — felt some irritation at this most admired figure in his life. But Noni, who had other people to do his computing for him, apologised to his son for his ignorance. However, he encouraged him to learn how to use one himself.

And learn Rattan did. Both mother and father were surprised how, suddenly, their so far hyperactive, gregarious son could stay shut up for hours in his room, staring at a computer screen. In fact, Pammi noted in great surprise that, often, he would forbid his friends from coming to visit, saying that he was busy.

Pammi did not really know her son very well. She did not know that, under his great extrovert exterior, he had a shrewd brain attempting to master all the possibilities offered by the computer world. Every computer game was played and played until the highest level of skill was achieved. In fact, those games that allowed the central computer character to achieve complete and virtual power over the world, universe, or the galaxies, held a special fascination for Rattan. When playing these, his concentration would become fierce. Often, the house would be startled out of its afternoon silence by loud triumphal yells and whoops emanating from his room. Pammi and the servants got quite used to these thudding down on them from the second floor of the house.

Whenever Noni was at home — which was not very often — Rattan's computer triumphs were the subject of conversation between father and son. Never having played a computer game himself, Noni did not often understand what these amounted to exactly. But he would try not to let his son know this. He would praise the young man enthusiastically in loud, bluff tones, and encourage him to 'give it to them'. But in reality, his mind would be on the next business meeting. At the same time, he hoped that his son did not guess his continuing ignorance about computers in general.

When Rattan finished school, it was decided that he should go to university in the USA. It was not a much debated decision, since in the late 70s and early 80s many successful families in New Delhi felt this was the ultimate they could do for their children. Rattan applied to five US schools, and of these chose to study at the University of Boston.

Rattan's undergraduate years went the same way as those

of many other Indian students studying in the USA. The early weeks were hard. Everything and everyone seemed strange to Rattan. More than his mother and father, Rattan missed the comforts of home, especially the cooking of Hari Ram, the family cook. It seemed strange to wake up in the morning and know that you had to fend for yourself. But he soon got into his stride, looking to see – and learn – what the others were doing and how they were doing it.

But more than some of the other inmates in his dorm, he took his classes seriously, making sure that his grades remained high. When he compared himself with fellow foreign students from other Asian countries, he could not help but be thankful for the English he knew. Every semester he did as much in computers as possible, spending hours in the computer laboratory. At the end of his freshman year, he was at the top of his class.

Rattan enjoyed dorm life for two years. But at the beginning of the third, he wrote home to Pammi saying that he wanted to move out to his own apartment. He needed more time to himself than was possible in the noisy dorm where the others were not as motivated as he was. The collective pressures of dorm life were slowing things down for him. Also, he was just a little tired of having most of his room-mate Matt's belongings left almost permanently in his space. At home in New Delhi, he remembered always coming back to a spotless room, the servants in the house making sure that not one thing was out of place. America had taught Rattan how to be tidy, but he could see that not all Americans wanted this.

Rattan really enjoyed the sense of freedom in his own apartment. When Pammi visited in the summer of 1980, she found her son surprisingly grown. At twenty, he seemed energised – to have become a man with a personality who, though lighthearted and full of fun in the old way, had come to see his student life like that of a grown-up doing a job. He could not, as she discovered, wait to finish his undergraduate work. She tried to question Rattan about the change, and about whether there was a girl in his life. But she found him closed on both subjects.

In the two weeks that mother and son were together, they toured the town, ate in different restaurants, and went shopping. But all her attempts at conversation about his personal life met with prevarication and evasion. Ultimately, she could not help but be amused, and a little hurt.

'OK, don't tell me if you don't want to. But remember the family business needs you at home. Your father is growing older and can't be in all places at the same time.'

Rattan looked at her quickly through narrowed warm-brown eyes. He knew exactly what she meant. It was the same old thing – the same as what all Indian parents periodically told their children sent to study in the USA.

'Yes, Ma,' he said impatiently. But since his face was averted, Pammi did not see the expression on his face.

As it happened, future plans were far from Rattan's thoughts. His young-adult heart was on other, more immediately felt things. He had fallen in love. Her name was Meghan McGinnis, and she had been with him in some of his classes in the last four semesters. Tall, slim and brown-haired, Meghan was a swimmer, and was on the team for all inter-college swimming tournaments. Rattan and Meghan first got talking in the swimming pool, where they often found themselves doing lengths in the morning before class. One day, when there were not too many people in the pool, Meghan noticed Rattan's birthmark. In the bright neon lights reflecting in the water, it always stood out darkly on his right shoulder. She did not say anything at that moment, or the next three or four times they found themselves together in the pool.

But one day, when she was still standing at the edge of the pool on the way to the changing rooms, he waved a wet hand out of the water in warm greeting.

'Hi! You're late. Aren't you coming in?'

'Hi! I say, that's a big scar you have on your shoulder.

How did you get it?' she said, plucking up courage to satisfy her curiosity.

Rattan did not reply. Instead he plunged headlong into the water and spoke only when his head emerged. Meghan was still standing at the edge of the pool.

'It's a birthmark. I've had it since I was born ... or so my mother tells me,' said Rattan in a raised voice, somewhat breathless as he trod water.

'Really?' said Meghan. 'Does it mean anything? I'm curious.'

'So was I,' said Rattan, wiping water from his face and pushing back his black hair.

'And ...?' prodded Meghan, wanting to know more.

'My mother would not talk about it whenever I asked her. But one day, when I insisted, she told me that I should forget it. I've always wondered why she was so vehement ... but she never told me. I guess I've just been singled out! But for what, I don't know.'

'Wow!' said Meghan, with wonder in her voice.

And from that day onwards they became friends. Meghan was quite taken by the almost-handsome Indian, whose large brown eyes had this way of looking deep inside everyone he met. She was also fascinated with India. She did not know much about that part of the world, and was full of questions. Often, Rattan was unable to answer her because his own middle class, somewhat westernised, life had not included any overt forms of Indian superstitions or mysticism. Only his grandmother and old ayah, he remembered, would sometimes tell him tales while trying to put him to sleep.

In the months that followed, Rattan and Meghan began to do many things together, especially after he moved into his apartment. By the time Pammi came to visit, others at the university assumed they were serious about each other.

However, for reasons spelt out clearly to no one other than himself, Rattan did not wish Pammi to meet Meghan. A few days before her arrival, he told her to stay away. Meghan was most upset. No amount of argument or reasoning could get Rattan to agree to anything else. Rattan knew he owed her an explanation. But he did not try to give her one.

'I guess I'm just not ready for Mom to know,' he said lamely.

The truth of the matter was that Pammi's impending arrival had forced Rattan to think clearly about his relationship with Meghan. She had been coming over more often in the last few months, often spending the nights with him. Her things were all over the place – and visibly. After some quick thinking, Rattan came to the conclusion that the situation was delicate, and had to be handled carefully but firmly. No false signals should be given to anyone, especially inadvertently. How, for instance, would he introduce Meghan to his mother, out for the first time from India? Such friendships were not the norm in New Delhi.

Also, he did not want Meghan to be misunderstood.

After much thought, he decided that it was best to keep Pammi and Meghan apart.

The day before Pammi's arrival in that May of 1980, he met Meghan in the college cafeteria for dinner. They had spent the last two days clearing out her things from his apartment and returning them to her dorm. It hadn't been very pleasant, with Meghan alternating between anger and tears more than once during the whole process. Now she was quieter than usual, and a hurt look hung around her green-eyed, oval face. Rattan too was rather silent. As she sat down opposite him, Meghan noticed that he was not eating much, his fork merely re-mashing mashed potatoes in their gravy, a look of quiet determination about his face.

Realising suddenly that all this did not augur well for her, she decided to take things into her own hands.

'I am going home for the weekend,' she said before he could speak, her voice unnaturally cheerful. 'And then I go off to see my grandmother in Virginia. I'll see you later, sometime.'

She picked up her handbag and jacket and was gone before Rattan could even think. He found himself sitting still, frozen into immobility, watching her retreat out of the restaurant. His first feeling was one of pique at having been seen through by Meghan. However, on subsequent pondering, he was relieved that she had not reopened the subject, and was, in a vague sort of way, grateful to her for sparing him a tough moment.

Even though there was still a year to go before graduation, that day Rattan realised that he would eventually return to India, and work with his father in the family business.

As far as he could see, Meghan could not have any place in these plans.

As for Meghan, though she appeared jaunty and careless as she walked away, she was quite distraught. More than distraught, she was angry. As she swung into the driver's seat of her red, two-door Ford Mustang in the parking lot outside the college cafeteria, she spoke out loud for all to hear. Her tones were viciously bitter.

'Damn Rattan ... No wonder these Indians are born with scars!'

Ennui

Even though – in that summer of 1992 – the two air-conditioners under the windows had been switched on to 'high cool' four hours before the arrival of the guests, the temperature at noon was still above comfort range in the large, silk-curtained living room of 73 Hauz Khas. A pocket of warm air swirled dizzily under the fan in the centre of the room, enveloping all beneath in its claustrophobic hold. Already the flowers – double gladioli in pinks and reds and the fragrant ivory-white *rajnigandha* bought especially from the florist for the event – were beginning to wilt in Pammi Malhotra's crystal vases. Every piece of silver, and other *objets d'art* scattered tastefully on the fine teak tables, stood in mute sufferance of the northern hemisphere's longest day of the summer – the 21st of June – waiting for it to end.

For a while the inevitable, oven-like heat did not make any difference to the gathering of women playing cards. They were engrossed, their minds elsewhere. The women were in two circles around separate tables, set close to each other in the centre of the room. One had six women playing rummy with two packs, and was led by Usha Chib. The other had seven around it, and was led by the hostess herself. It was at *teen patti*. The rummy players were quieter, their concentration fierce. The *teen patti* players, however, often cursed loudly at the cards fate delivered them.

The loudest protests came from Urmil, a buxom fifty-year-old, whose long, dangling earrings gave her a falsely youthful air.

It was she who broke the silence.

'My God, Pammi! What's happened to your air-conditioners?' she said, dumping her cards face down on the table, and lifting her sticky hair off the back of her neck. 'Aren't they working? It really is so hot!'

'They're working all right. But it is very hot today. It is nearly the end of June, and the rain still far away,' said Pammi calmly, as if prepared that such complaints would come her way. It was always difficult to entertain in June. But she was not one to be cowed down by the heat, or give in to carping about it. 'Why don't you have something to drink? That will cool you down.'

By this time the others were listening too, and the rummy wallahs decided that they were also thirsty.

'Ram Singh?' said Pammi, calling out towards the kitchens in a loud, peremptory voice. A tall, uniformed man in white appeared in the doorway.

'Bring something cold for everybody. It should be really chilled, with lots of ice. Everybody is very hot.'

'Yes, memsahib,' said Ram Singh, with a slight bow – more a nod of the head – and retreated from the room.

Ram Singh was the second servant in the Malhotra household. The first was, officially, the cook, whose name was Hari Ram. A small, mild-mannered man, who even slept in his thick-lensed spectacles, Hari Ram loved to cook, do what he was told, stay largely in the kitchen, and leave everything else to everybody else. It was Ram Singh, really, who functioned as the first servant for the Malhotras. And Pammi liked it this way. No doubt, this was because he had been with them for a long time. But it was also because, over the years, he had displayed a bearing even more regal than Noni Malhotra, his employer. Ram Singh had been in the army in an armoured regiment, but had had to retire prematurely because of an injury to his right arm in the Indo-Pakistan war of 1965.

The Malhotras had employed him soon after he was discharged. He was then only twenty-nine. Now, in 1992, his fifty-six years sat well on him. Tall, even handsome, in the brawny kind of way so typical of ex-soldiers from the north, he did full justice to the white *bandgala* coat and trousers his employers insisted he wear. He was a source of awe to first-time visitors at the Malhotra residence. It was an effect immediately appreciated by Pammi, who saw it as yet another symbol of their growing success in society.

Ram Singh re-entered Pammi's living room in a few minutes with a large tray in his hands. It was loaded with glasses of chilled *nimbu pani*, each full of ice. He had obviously anticipated the demands of his mistress by making sure that Hari Ram the cook had prepared four jugs of the cooling liquid to be available as soon as it was asked for. The sight of Ram Singh's laden tray gave rise to a few oohs and aahs.

'Let's take a break. It's only twelve o'clock,' said Pammi, knowing that the concentration needed for rummy and *teen patti* was broken. 'There's no hurry is there?'

'No, none at all,' said Urmil loudly, jerking her head so that her shoulder-length curls moved away from her face, and her long diamond-and-pearl earrings could glitter visibly. She picked up her glass, took a long sip, and stood up from the card table. Slowly, she walked over the marble floors and Persian carpets towards the windows, which spanned the full width of Pammi's large, well-appointed living room along the front of the house. Fanning herself with the edges of the *pallav* of her *mithai* pink crepe sari, she peered out through the half-drawn curtains.

'I say, Pammi,' she said, 'you have new neighbours!'

'Yes, we do,' said Pammi, also standing up and wiping her rather large forehead with a white, lace-edged handkerchief. She moved under the chandeliers towards the windows, and pulled the curtains fully back on both ends. Through the shining glass panes, her well-manicured garden was visible. On the right was the spotlessly swept driveway, and beyond that the gate. On the other side of the low boundary wall, the driveway of the neighbouring house ran parallel, reaching out to its own gate.

A large truck stood on the road beyond the adjacent gates, and from this distance at the window, it seemed to be blocking the entrance of both houses. It was full of rather tattered furniture – chairs and tables, a couple of wooden *almirahs* (one of whose doors swung open drunkenly), and some beds. One of these had its *newar* hanging loose, and was repeatedly getting caught in the rough edges of the truck as it was lowered to the ground. A short, stout man in a once-white *kurta* pyjama stood supervising the proceedings under the hot midday sun. A large, reddish handkerchief fluttered from his hands as he frequently mopped heavy perspiration from his dark, unshaven face.

The labourers, employed on daily wages, were moving slowly, even reluctantly.

'Get a move on,' the man yelled. 'We have to be done by one o'clock, you fools! We have another load for two o'clock.'

But his yelling was half-hearted. It was hot. Nobody could move faster in this heat.

The ladies in the living room heard the man shouting over the purr of the struggling air-conditioners, but pretended they hadn't. Pammi moved away from the windows, her diamond solitaires glinting under the light. She was a handsome woman, tall and statuesque in her mushroom-and-peach-coloured crepe sari, and elegantly coiffured hair.

'Yes, we have new neighbours,' she repeated disgustedly, her voice plunging into the silence that had followed the shouting man outside. 'You'll never guess who they are – or rather, what they are. They are not a family as you and I know it . . .'

She let her sentence peter out as she swung around, suddenly, to pull the curtains with vicious energy. As the fabric slid smoothly along the rails, the bright light from the outside receded, leaving the room in cool darkness.

'Oh, don't, please,' said Urmil loudly, her earrings jerking again and her eyebrows meeting in a protesting frown. 'Let me see . . . "they are not a family as you and I know it"? What does that mean, exactly?'

As she said this, she looked around the room, winking one eye suggestively.

Pammi saw her friend's rude winking, but chose to ignore it.

'Well,' she said, in a flat voice as she moved the curtains halfway open. The expression on her wheat-complexioned face was deliberately deadpan. 'It's not a family that is moving in but a women's outfit . . . you know the kind that helps women in distress . . . counselling, and all that?'

'Really?' said Urmil, as loudly as before, expecting Pammi to continue.

But Pammi refused to be drawn. 'Yes. Their name is, literally, *Sahayata*. Have you heard of it?'

'*Sahayata*?' Urmil said vaguely, once again assuming that Pammi was addressing only her.

Before Pammi could reply, however, Nina Singh, a younger wife – very good at rummy but new to the group – spoke out quickly. It was hard to get a word in once Urmil began talking.

'Yes, I have heard of *Sahayata*. I read about it in *Femina* recently. It has been the subject of many articles in the newspapers, and other magazines too. It was put together by a group of women. They run this organisation to help destitute women . . . and others too . . . you know, the ones with marriage problems and things . . .'

'Really?' said Urmil again, and went up to peer out of the window.

She pulled the curtains away to the very edges again, once again letting in the bright light, and making everyone squint. Pammi winced. She wanted to say something sharp, but refrained. Though Urmil was supposed to be her good friend, she was really being horrid. What was with her today?

On her part, Urmil was not-so-secretly enjoying this richer-than-herself friend's moments of discomfiture. It was rarely that circumstances did not work out to Pammi Malhotra's liking. This was the one time they had, and Urmil was tickled by her all too apparent dislike of her new neighbours.

'Now isn't that interesting, ladies?' said Urmil, addressing herself to all present in her callous, tea-party manner. 'Pammi will have to be careful. It's like having a police station next door! Now she and Noni will have to fight only in low tones, or else they'll hear everything and come poking around to find out what is happening!'

At this, all the women laughed, albeit in nervous embarrassment.

'I've got nothing to hide,' said Pammi, immediately defensive. In her effort to ignore the nasty edge in her friend's comments, her own voice emerged neutral and stiff. 'I do wish, though, there was a law banning such institutions in residential neighbourhoods,' she continued. 'They shouldn't be allowed here. We'll have all kinds of vague people loitering around the gates at odd hours. But we can't do anything about it. I suppose people can rent their houses to whomever they like.'

'Whose house is it anyway?' asked Mini Chandra, a petite woman with short hair who always wore trousers to card parties, much to the envy of the others who felt they could not do so because they were too fat, and would not look half as nice. Pammi liked her because she always spoke to the point, and refrained from unnecessary criticism of others.

'It belongs to a slightly eccentric woman named Miss Nanavati,' said Pammi. 'She's now about ninety, but is supposed to have been a great one for women's liberation. She never married, and wore a lot of khaddar in her youth.'

'I think I've heard of her,' said Mini.

'You must have heard of her,' said Pammi. 'She led the

women's contingent in the Independence Movement in Lahore. There were many like her in those years. Ugly as hell, they couldn't find husbands to marry, and so spent their energies helping the cause of women.'

Pammi said this matter-of-factly, and her guests seemed to accept her description as it was rendered.

'So what's all this got to do with the house next door?' asked Urmil firmly, annoyed that the tenor of the conversation had bypassed her quite neatly.

'Well, *Sahayata* needed larger premises, and they went and asked Miss Nanavati for the house. She agreed. She's given it to them really cheap. When I think of this neighbourhood and the money she could make only on rent ...'

Pammi paused, a little breathless. She hadn't really wanted to tell all this to the women gathered in her living room, but found that she was doing so anyway. Why was she talking so much? It was not as if the others — apart from Urmil of course — were showing more than a casual interest. Deliberately, Pammi tried to change the subject.

'We tried to buy the house. For Rattan, you know. But she didn't agree to sell. Instead she's given it to the *Sahayata* women.'

'Ah! Rattan!' said Urmil, sensing another prey. 'How is he?'

'He's fine,' Pammi replied, relief in her voice.

But it took her only a few seconds to realise that though the subject of conversation had changed, Urmil would find her son even more interesting.

'And where is Rattan's wife? Your new daughter-in-law?' asked Urmil smoothly, homing in on her target.

'She's here,' said Pammi shortly.

'Really? I thought we would see her today. What was her name? I've forgotten ...'

'Her name is Tanvi,' said Pammi. Her voice was bland and off-hand.

'Ah yes, of course. Tanvi. She made such a pretty bride. Are the young couple back from their honeymoon?' asked Urmil, looking for more details.

'Yes,' said Pammi, noting and ignoring Urmil's feigned ignorance. Pammi could not help thinking that Urmil was really quite a small-minded, vicious woman even though she (and her husband) always pretended they were very good friends.

'They returned about two months ago,' she said aloud, her face completely expressionless. 'I asked Tanvi to join us, but she doesn't play cards, so I didn't force her. She's gone to her mother's.'

'Now isn't that interesting, ladies?' said Urmil, stopping a minute to swallow the last mouthful of her tepid *nimbu pani*. Her bright pink sari sparkled brightly in the shadows of Pammi's living room. 'We must remember this. We must remember that we are not young any more. We are all going to be mothers-in-law soon. You're the first amongst our group, aren't you, Pammi?'

'I suppose so,' said Pammi, somewhat distantly.

'But the rest of us still have a long way to go. Isn't that so, ladies?' said Urmil, pushing her point and concluding her sentence with a little giggle to which none of the others responded.

They had watched the battle and decided not to enter it. Those standing looked for their chairs; those already sitting turned their attention to the packs of cards lying on the table.

For a few seconds there was silence in the room.

The firm but strident words of a young woman coming from some distance broke it. They sliced through the lull in the room, ringing out clearly over the steady hum of the air conditioners.

'That's enough. That's what the deal was, and that's what you'll get. There is no need for an argument . . .' she was saying in a firm, steely voice.

The women in Pammi's living room turned, once again, to

the windows. The truck with the furniture had been unloaded. Near it stood a young woman in a white *salwar kameez* and a red *bandhej dupatta*. Only a little over five feet tall, she had her back to the Malhotra house. No one in the room could see her face. Long, black wavy hair, slightly dishevelled, hung down her back. A largish, brown leather handbag swung from her left shoulder. As she finished speaking, she pressed some rupee notes into the hands of the man supervising the unloading. The man accepted them, but it was apparent that he was unhappy at what he had been given. The woman, however, ignored him; bending slightly to her left, she was attempting to button up the clasp of her handbag. As soon as she was done, she turned around sharply and began to walk up the driveway of the neighbouring house.

In a moment she had disappeared. The man with the red handkerchief, and all the others working for him, were left staring at her retreating back. Soon, they piled on to the truck, and after a few jerky starts, it drove off.

'My God,' said Urmil. 'She was some woman!'

'Yes, wasn't she?' said Pammi. 'That's the way they come these days. Who'll marry them, I wonder!'

'She was so loud,' said Urmil. The others exchanged telling glances, but nodded in seeming agreement. Pammi went to the windows and pulled the curtains firmly to a close. It was getting near one o'clock. They could play a few more rounds before lunch was served.

'Should we begin again, ladies?'

Everyone agreed. This time both the tables decided they wanted to play *teen patti*, and so *teen patti* it was.

Sahayata

In the house next door, Maneka Saxena, the young woman in the white *salwar kameez* and red *dupatta*, spent what seemed like an age supervising the unloading of the furniture from off the truck. She stood in the foyer of the empty 74 Hauz Khas, issuing crisp instructions: the beds upstairs ('put them anywhere in the rooms'); the tables and chairs downstairs; the cupboards upstairs ('put them along the walls'). When all the furniture was unloaded, she walked out to the truck to make sure nothing was left behind. She stood a while at the gate to pay the supervisor. By the time this was done, it was almost one o'clock, and by God, she was hot.

Walking briskly up the driveway and into the house, Maneka found she was also quite tired. Her round, strong-chinned face was damp with sweat, and her forehead twisted in an unhappy frown. It had been a long morning. She had woken at 5.30 a.m., and not had much to eat. As she walked, she reached for one end of her red *dupatta* and mopped her face. Stepping into the porch, she stood still for a moment, relieved to be out of the clutches of the demon sun. She looked around the hallway – at the newly whitewashed walls, and the splotched white spills that dotted the floor along them. All the windowpanes were streaked with the foggy lines of a dirty cloth. The same scene awaited her in the other rooms of the ground floor. There was so much to be done, but at least now *Sahayata* had larger premises. She walked towards the back of the house, to the kitchen and the adjoining pantry. The floor and the kitchen sinks were filthy. In spite of the newly painted kitchen cabinets, a strong smell of stale food hung in the air.

Outside the kitchen, a cat meowed plaintively near the back door. 'Somebody must have been feeding it,' thought Maneka, seeing it trying to peer in through the wire meshing of the door. She realised suddenly that she herself was also hungry. Jabbingly hungry. And, also, very angry. Why hadn't any of the others come? Why was she here alone, in the malevolent heat of June's longest day, dealing with a truckful of furniture with just about enough money to pay for the delivery? There wasn't even a fan anywhere — because the electricity hadn't been connected yet.

'And neither is there any water in the taps!'

Maneka did not mean to say this aloud, but found that she had done so. Her statement echoed faintly as it wafted up the staircase of the empty house. In the distance the cat meowed again. She walked into the living room and sat down tiredly on one of the chairs. For a busy, residential neighbourhood, the street was strangely silent, and the hot, oppressive breeze flowing through the open doorway added to the still, prickling heat.

It had always been like this, thought Maneka dispiritedly, allowing herself the luxury of a weak moment. The deep lines on her broad forehead had become troughs for sweat to collect in, and no amount of wiping would keep them dry. Her large kohl-lined eyes, always alert to injustices in the world, drooped in fatigue. She thought of all those others who had promised to be there with her. But nobody had come. Nobody wanted to do the dirty work. They only wanted their names in the newspapers when people like her had done all the hard work. Had her best friend Nalini been in New Delhi, she would surely have been there with her. She would have overcome all her inhibitions and reservations, found the time and been there to help her. But Nalini was far away, and she had to make do with all the others. Where was that Arti Chug? And Manju? Tomorrow Manju would come up and say she was very sorry she couldn't make it because she had been held up. 'It was because of Anil,' she would say as surely as night follows day, and expect everybody to believe it.

Making herself more comfortable in the half-broken chair in the so-called living room of 74 Hauz Khas, Maneka remembered a brief conversation she had had about the subject of Anil with Manju recently.

'No really, Maneka, Anil is not like that. He leaves me free to do whatever I want. Really!'

Really. Little did she know. Anil would never like it. He would never like his wife spending time with 'unhappy women who got together and cursed men'. That's what Anil thought they all did at *Sahayata* anyway. Manju would be controlled long before realising it. Already he was preventing her from keeping her appointments, and soon would stop her coming completely. No doubt, she would then come crying to *Sahayata* – not to help, but to be helped. Maneka knew quite clearly what she would tell her then: that she was their first client, and that they would inaugurate their new premises by counselling her. And all because of Anil.

Anil, Anil, Anil. Manju was so moony-eyed about him! How long would it take her to realise that her husband-of-three-months would never like his wife's involvement in *Sahayata*? She would have to decide – and sooner rather than later – whether she would continue to work for it. But Manju was nowhere near capable of such strong decision-making.

'Oh, how I hate men!' said Maneka aloud.

As her words reverberated through the empty house once again, dark eyes flashed in her tanned face and her lips pursed together mutinously. She pushed back her thick, dark, waist-length wavy hair impatiently and walked to the windows overlooking the driveway. On the right was what must have been a small garden. Today, it was unkempt and full of weeds dying in the sun. What a contrast to the smooth green grass on the other side of the low wall! Her eyes scanned further, to the left. Along the length of the unswept driveway, the heat shimmered in waves. She was sure it was at least 45 degrees Celsius. It really was no time to be out of doors.

Outside, the cat meowed again, its plaintive tones only adding to Maneka's sense of restless dissatisfaction. There was silence for a while.

The more Maneka thought about her current predicament, the more agitated she became. Suddenly she stood up. Taking off her *dupatta* in an angry movement, she hung it carelessly along the back of her chair. She was hungry and should eat. Maybe that would make her feel a little better. She turned to her large, brown handbag. She fumbled around in its depths and soon brought out a small round stainless-steel tin. Inside were two *paratha* rolls stuffed with *alu methi*. Meera the maid had packed them for her before she left the house in the morning. As she bit on the first one, she heard the cat meow from not too far away. She looked around, and found that it had entered the house through the front door and was walking towards her.

'I have nothing of interest for you,' she said aloud. The cat sniffed her feet for a while, then moved away. It sat down at a distance, and began watching her.

Maneka Saxena was twenty-nine years old, a divorcee and a single parent, with the custody of a five-year-old boy. Ahmer was a delicate child, small of build and prone to catching all of childhood's unsparing infections. He was also a difficult child, his large brown eyes always looking at the world with outraged accusation writ large in them. Or so it seemed to his mother, who always felt inadequate whenever he was around. She looked at her watch. It was almost two o'clock. Ahmer would be back from school – and be fussing as usual, she was sure. She felt it quite unfair of the Gods to have given her such a handful when all the other mothers of her acquaintance seemed to have children that sat around quietly in corners, doing their own thing. Ahmer was just the opposite, always poking around and demanding attention.

'He is just like his father,' she said, immediately denying her own conclusions.

The cat looked up in surprise, and Maneka found she had spoken aloud again.

Bhasker Saxena had been Maneka's contemporary in Hindu College in the University of Delhi. Of slight build and medium height, with a shock of startlingly black wavy hair falling romantically over his brow, he was a charismatic personality, given to wearing *kurta* pyjamas in ethnic khaddar. His friendship with Maneka had begun in their second year, when they had both acted in a joint college production of Shakespeare's *Hamlet*. Bhasker had been Hamlet, and Maneka his Ophelia. While Bhasker had donned the mantle of tragic hero quite easily in the very first rehearsals, Maneka had found it more difficult to become a tragic heroine. The source of her resistance lay in her ideological beliefs. It was not in her to enact the pathetic female, plucking flowers – and counting them – all in the name of a madness brought on by a typically indifferent male. In the initial rehearsals she had chafed, stopped halfway through her lines, and begun complaining. She had accused Shakespeare of being a male chauvinist who always showed women's lives controlled by hard-hearted, self-centred men.

At first, she had quite an audience for her conclusions, making the rehearsing gang laugh at all she had to say. However, she soon stopped voicing her objections against the Bard when she found that the director was thinking of finding another woman for the role. This Maneka would not have. In the rehearsals that followed, she worked hard to efface her own strong personality and put on a different persona. She ended by making a good Ophelia to Bhasker's scintillating Hamlet.

The romance of Bhasker and Maneka was the talk of Hindu

College and Miranda House. Those in Delhi University in the early 80s would remember seeing them together everywhere. They were known as an intelligent duo, very keen on Economics. They were also radical in their views. If you were anywhere in their vicinity, Marxian ideas could be heard all the time. It was in these years that Maneka also became an active participant in the feminist wave that was passing through Delhi University. She became a member of the Women's Empowerment Centre set up by a group of dedicated women in response to the growing number of incidents of wife battering and dowry burnings in Delhi.

Student-run extension wings of the WEC undertook special projects in the consciousness-raising, empowerment – and some-times even protection – of women in the slum areas and lower middle-class neighbourhoods surrounding the different colleges of the University of Delhi. Maneka was chosen leader of her group of seven girl students going out in a band to trouble-point areas after college hours, and soon became a well-known student activist on women's issues on the university campus. All through her post-graduate years, she continued to attend rallies and seminars, and even began to give talks and lectures. Later, she published articles on the different aspects of women and patriarchy in newspapers and journals.

Bhasker and Maneka decided to marry after they had finished their Master's degrees from the Delhi School of Economics. Though he did better than her in the final examinations, it was she who found a job first. The Indira Gandhi Memorial College for Women – not far from her alma mater – gave her a position as a Lecturer in Economics two months after the results of the MA examinations were declared. Bhasker, meanwhile, was still deciding. He didn't want to teach. 'He who can, does; he who cannot, teaches,' was something he said often, always flamboyantly disparaging about the academic profession. He was made for better, proactive things. He did not wish to join the Civil Services either. 'Be a part of the Establishment?

Never ...' he would often declare, his dark wavy hair moving definitively in a flick over his brows.

Public Sector companies, naturally, were completely out.

The worst, in his view, was the corporate world. His sympathies lay with the employees and the workers in the factories rather than with their exploiting management cadres. In any case, he could not see himself in a tie, ever. Never.

Two years after their marriage, Bhasker became a trade union leader who was heard everywhere but had no fixed place of work. Neither did he earn much. He often found himself deeply frustrated, having got into trouble once or twice with the police. The last time he led a protest march by workers of a factory making spare parts for heavy machinery, he had been the first to be beaten up by the lathi-charging police. And, it had not been very pleasant for Maneka to rescue him.

Even years after her divorce, Maneka could never define exactly when her marriage with Bhasker Saxena began to sour. Very early on, she had begun to feel that the burden of providing for the family unit had begun falling on her, too much on her. She paid the rent, the electricity and water bills, the servants, and ran the kitchen. She found herself giving Bhasker money for his cigarettes and, after the first few weeks, even for his whisky.

At first she didn't mind. In fact, she joined him in late-night orgies of eating, drinking and smoking – each illuminated by the bright attractive light of grand solutions – with a close group of friends. Every one of those evenings was glorified in her eyes by the fact that they and their friends were going to solve India's problems. Marxian ideals seemed imminently to prevail as seen through the haze of cigarette smoke, fumes of whisky, and generous helpings of chicken biryani, mutton korma and ice cream grandiosely sent for from the nearest *dhaba*. Not for them staid, bourgeois parties in which people sat on sofas, ate off fine china, and everyone said good bye at 11 p.m. sharp.

'No socialite gossipy conversation for us,' the Saxenas and

their guests would say to each other. Their gatherings were serious business.

Such evenings, however, began to have odd consequences. Afterwards, Maneka could never get over how predictable these became, even discounting the fact that many lofty Marxian, even feminist ideas were thrown around in the debris of the morning-after. It always came down to asking and wondering who would clean up, who would take Ahmer to school because he had missed the bus to his play school (who could get up on time after all that thought?), and who would pay the bills? All those bills.

Not the friends who had been present the night before, deciding the fate of the sub-continent.

It was in 1990 that the Saxenas decided to separate for good. It was Maneka who filed for divorce. And, because it was she who had a permanent job, got custody of Ahmer. That was two years ago. The separation had been bitter. Bhasker did not want to let go, but Maneka was adamant. The worst part was the division of the household. But since Maneka was paying the rent anyway, she had the upper hand. It was Bhasker who moved out, finding with great difficulty a single-room for himself somewhere on the outskirts of the town.

Maneka's real friends lamented the divorce, but saw its inevitability. It was Maneka's mother, Mrs Mahajan, a small wisp of a woman always in a hurry, who was the most upset. She had not approved of Maneka's choice of marriage partner. However, tired as she was with long years of single parenting as a widow, she had given in. And now, she had to accept the terrible disgrace of a divorced daughter. What would her colleagues at the government school say? They said a lot, in snide asides, and she could do nothing about it.

The divorce increased Maneka's activist feminism. Her job as a lecturer left her with much free time in the late afternoons and evenings. She had always been interested in Arti Chug's efforts at establishing *Sahayata*. A few weeks after the court settlement, Maneka committed herself to volunteering fixed hours to work there every week. Its causes absorbed the emptiness of the long, hot evenings even as they soothed her sense of being wronged. The first summer vacations after the divorce found her fully involved in its programmes. It was she who negotiated with Miss Nanavati about the house for *Sahayata*. Afterwards, all her friends acknowledged that it was her sincerity and passion that had been responsible for persuading the older woman to give it to them.

Two years of being on her own had changed Maneka. They had given her otherwise productive personality an unnecessarily hard edge. If ever her determined chin and a definite unpainted mouth gave her a more arrogant air than her medium build, work-a-day *salwar kameezes* and brown matter-of-fact sandals warranted, today this effect was more enhanced. Maneka was a woman who was usually right about most things. A real woman of substance — except that the substance had taken over, often leaving no room for the small daily moments of *lehaaz* most people made for the shortcomings and compromises of their fellow men and women.

Today she was hot and aggrieved, and in no mood to forgive the absence of the companions who had let her down.

It took Maneka all of ten minutes to finish eating her *parathas*, close the round tiffin box carefully, and tuck it away in a corner of her handbag. She looked around for the bathroom, walked in, and found it filthy. They would really have to work on this place, she mused, combing out her thick wavy hair with a large comb in front of a spotted mirror. *Sahayata* would never be swanky, but it could at least be clean and tidy. She thought of the floor upstairs, and mentally made space for sixteen beds to be spread out in the four large bedrooms. That was quite a lot ... at least sixteen women could turn to this place when they had nowhere else to go for a temporary roof over their heads.

As she moved out of the bathroom, she looked around the hallway again. It would make a large enough reception area. The room across the hall could become the counselling room. Maybe they could have a regular doctor and lawyer come in once a week . . .

Maneka looked at her watch. It was way past three o'clock. God, she was thirsty! She would have liked a drink of water before setting off for home. But of course, there was no water in the taps. She gave a last look around, and picking up the lock and key from the table in the hallway, proceeded to close up. In a minute she was walking down the driveway towards the gate.

The road outside was surrounded by cars. The neighbours seemed to be having a party. Somewhat irritated, she negotiated the spaces between the cars (some of them with waiting drivers sleeping in the driver's seats) crowding the road in front of 73 Hauz Khas. She wondered if she would have to walk all the way to the main road to find a three-wheeler rickshaw to take her home. She was sure she would, for no one – surely no one – would need a rickshaw in this posh neighbourhood. She might just be lucky, though. It would save her a hot walk to the end of the street.

She hadn't realised that she had been standing in front of the neighbouring gates while scanning the road in search of her rickshaw. Behind her were the two houses, as different from each other as earth from sky. Number 73 Hauz Khas looked new, its front facade standing tall over three floors, its decorative balconies graced with tall palms, the door and window frames a tanned, polished teak. The walls were painted in spanking white Snowcem, shining proudly in the hot June glare. Number 74 was a short, dejected, two floors – its walls and wooden frames desperately in need of repairs and a coat of paint. It was, undoubtedly, the older and shabbier poor relative living permanently next door.

As Maneka stood a moment looking up and down the road for a rickshaw, a car drove up, stopping right next to her. A petite figure stepped out of the back. Maneka found herself face to face with a small-built young woman, with a simple yet attractive oval face. She must have been nineteen or twenty. Her shiny black hair was cut stylishly short, and she was dressed casually in figure-hugging blue jeans, a smart white blouse, and high heels. In her arms were five or six large brown paper bags full of shopping.

Maneka looked at her in distaste, and her glance was cold. The younger woman did not seem to notice.

'Hi!' she said. Almond eyes looked straight at Maneka from under light, blue-shadowed lids. 'Are you moving in next door?'

'Yes,' said Maneka. 'In a manner of speaking.'

'Oh, good,' she said a little breathlessly, seeming not to notice anything odd in Maneka's statement. 'Welcome to the neighbourhood! We'll be seeing you then . . .'

And she was gone, walking up the driveway with a small wave of her hand. Behind her, a deferential chauffeur followed with more parcels and paper bags in one hand, and the latest issues of *Femina*, *Stardust* and *Filmfare* in the other. He had given Maneka a cursory glance, but did not greet her or say *namaste*.

How inane these little rich women were, with nothing to do other than look pretty, thought Maneka, and shuddered inwardly. She resumed her unsuccessful search for a rickshaw.

By the time she got home it was almost 5.30 p.m. Ahmer had already gone to play with his friends. As she unlocked the door, all Maneka could do was hope that Meera had held his hand tightly when they had crossed the road through the traffic to the park on the other side.

Two Women, Sour and Sweet

The card party in 73 Hauz Khas wound up rather late that day. Much later than it ever had before. Pammi's guests were still in the dining room sipping coffee and tea when the kitchen clock showed four o'clock. Ram Singh twirled his moustache in disgust. No time for today's afternoon nap. But he did not let the irritation show on his face. When one worked in the houses of the rich, there were other compensations. In any case, sahib was not in town, and Rattan sahib and *choti* memsahib were going out for dinner.

The prospect of a relatively free evening made a small, satisfied smile cross Ram Singh's face. It made him extra solicitous in providing his mistress with a cup of tea. As was to be expected, she was the last to be served. But he made sure it was just as she liked it – lightly flavoured, no milk, and only half a spoon of sugar. And the first cup out of a freshly made pot. When it was ready, he looked around for her. She was standing near the tea trolley on the other side of the dining room. Though many of the women seemed to be surrounding her, Ram Singh noticed immediately that she was really by herself, standing alone and surveying the scene.

So it seemed to Ram Singh, who thought he knew his mistress rather well. He did know her rather well, just as he knew the whole Malhotra household rather well. But he would have been surprised to know what she was really thinking at that point in time.

Pammi Malhotra was taking a break. A small, unobtrusive break from the very party she had taken so much trouble to organise. Why had she suddenly stopped enjoying the afternoon? Why did it seem to be going on and on? She had won a lot of the hands, and the pile of rupees before her had kept increasing. In contrast, it had been a bad morning for Urmil who had lost almost every round.

That should make me happy, Pammi had told herself more than once.

But it hadn't. She looked around for Urmil, and spotted her at the far end of the dining room, deep in private conversation with Nina Singh. She must be at it again, thought Pammi. Tearing someone's name to shreds. The thought made her sick. Why had she become friends with people like Urmil? Why was she doing all this? She looked at the dessert on her plate – expensive Tiramisu on special order from the Taj Palace Hotel – and it tasted like mush in her mouth. She put the plate down on the tea trolley near her with a slight clatter. Nobody noticed. They were busy eating and talking. They seemed obviously to be enjoying themselves. Why wasn't she doing the same?

'This is hardly a time for introspection,' she told herself firmly, and shook her head surreptitiously.

But unbidden thoughts came, nevertheless – flooding through her and leaving her awash at precisely that moment when she was completely unprepared to deal with them. Where was Noni? Why was he not in town? Why did he have to go away for such long stretches, leaving her to do her own thing for days at a time? And what did this amount to? Play rummy or *teen patti*? And win? Surely there was more to life than this?

From above the heads of the ladies, Pammi saw Ram Singh coming towards her with a cup of tea in his hand. She could do with one – especially now that her left temple had begun to throb.

Maybe she should have worked harder to persuade Noni to allow her to work. To do a job, or start a business of her own. A boutique maybe? But she did not have the money. She was a rich man's wife with money to spend, but not enough to begin something. She knew deep inside her that Noni would never help her. Give her money to invest in a project? Never. 'You don't need to work,' he had said repeatedly, and warned her against playing the poor little rich wife. There were plenty in the country that needed to work, and he wished them the best of luck. But there was no need for his wife – the wife of the famous Noni Malhotra – to go out of his home into the market place.

'I suppose I should, even now, take matters into my own hands ... and do something about it,' she told herself silently, the slow burn of her unhappiness turning her insides into molten lead. She sighed deeply, cursing herself for having thought this a million times before and yet been unable to do anything about it.

By this time Ram Singh had reached her. She took the steaming cup gratefully from his hand, and took a small sip. He pulled forward one of the dining chairs for her to sit on.

'Have you made sure everyone has had a cup?' she asked, looking up at him briefly.

'Yes, memsahib,' he replied. 'There was a phone call from Noni sahib. He is in Frankfurt and said his return would be delayed. He will only be able to return on Monday night.'

'Oh,' said Pammi blankly, a spasm of pain crossing her face. She recovered instantly, and cast a glance at Ram Singh. He was standing still, quietly deferential, his eyes on the ground and his hands folded behind his back. She didn't say anything, but put out her right hand to touch his arm briefly.

'Thank you,' she said.

But her voice emerged cracked and broken. Ram Singh for a second looked directly into her eyes. Was there a hint of tears in them? He could not tell, and knowing he was dismissed for the moment, moved away quickly.

In the late 40s, when Pammi's mother was worrying about the future of her daughter, life was different. The Chopras of Lahore never thought that their life would be affected by the politics of the time. Pammi's father, Mantosh Chopra, was a physician who had his own flourishing practice in one of Lahore's fashionable suburbs. Tall and broad-shouldered even as a girl, Pammi was his favourite child. She remembered her father once standing her before him and saying, 'I must find a proper boy for you. He must be nothing but the best. A maharaja, maybe, so that you will be a maharani.'

Only twelve then, Pammi had laughed and vehemently shaken her head — with its swinging, shoulder-length black hair — from side to side.

'No, Papa, no. I want to be a doctor like you. I don't want to marry, and just run the kitchen . . . and have babies,' she had said, shocking her little, mild-mannered mother hovering around.

'Sh, sh, *beti*, how can you talk so in front of your father? Girls should not talk this way,' she had reprimanded, but with love in her voice.

'I'm not a child any more,' Pammi remembered replying, a little defiantly. Her father had agreed with her.

'We'll see,' he had said, diffusing an imminently difficult moment between mother and daughter. 'Finish school first.'

Pammi finished her eighth grade in the summer of 1947 when the political situation began to get worse and worse, and then became completely out of hand. All the Hindus of Lahore began to worry about their safety. As Nehru, Jinnah, and Mountbatten went about their confabulations about the future of the sub-continent, so the families on either side of the Hindu/Muslim divide went about theirs. Some did not feel that the situation was at all dangerous. Politics was always politics and rarely, as far as they knew, affected godfearing, respectable citizens in their homes. But when, that July, the riots, the looting in the bazaars, the arson and the killings began, even the most fearless sat up.

Among these was Mantosh Chopra.

'This is really going too far! Whoever heard of the town's loafers and *goondas* invading the homes of people like us? They should be shot, and put behind bars. Whatever is the government up to ...?' he said angrily, rushing home one afternoon after being forced to shut down his clinic right in the middle of the busiest part of Out Patient day.

'Maybe there isn't any,' his wife replied in a small, meek voice.

It was not usual for Shakuntala Chopra to have political opinions, or indeed dare to contradict her husband when he was so obviously upset. But she had her sources; and had been talking of nothing else but the rising communal tension with her neighbours across the compound wall on both sides of the house. She had also talked at length to all the servants living in the quarters at the far end of the garden. In fact, she had a better sense of what was going on in the street than her husband who, besides being given to idealistic theories about how the situation was not being handled by the authorities, was hardly at home for long hours in the day.

It was she who told him a week later that even if he was not afraid for both of them, he should at least think of Pammi.

'You know she is now almost fifteen, and growing up to be a very attractive woman,' she said, the words almost choking in her throat. To see one's daughter as attractive to potential murderers and rapists in this hideous way had made her frantic with apprehension.

'OK, OK! So what do you want me to do?' Mantosh Chopra asked irritably.

'Can't we send her away?' said Shakuntala, busily putting

away freshly ironed clothes into the cupboards lining the walls of their bedroom. Her face was turned away from her husband.

'Where?' asked Mantosh Chopra.

'To the other side. To Delhi. To Harsh *Bhai* Sahib and Usha *bhabi*, maybe?' said his wife, daring to mention her brother and his wife in front of her strong-minded husband.

A small grunt was all the reply Shakuntala received. There was silence for a while. Shakuntala finished hanging up five shirts, two suits, and three saris in the closets. All the while she was wondering whether it was wise to say more.

'I'll think about it,' said Mantosh Chopra dismissively.

But for once Shakuntala felt she should have the last word.

'Yes do, and soon,' she said, shutting the door of the cupboard with a decisive click, even as she began walking towards the door. 'The situation is really dangerous. We have to act quickly.'

The last words of her statement were uttered just before leaving the room. Mantosh Chopra looked at the retreating back of his wife in some surprise. She was really quite worried! Maybe it was a good idea to send both mother and daughter off to Delhi. For a few weeks ... or at least until the situation cleared. The problem, however, was that he did not really like his in-laws. He did not want to be indebted to them.

But, that is precisely where Pammi was dispatched before the week was out. That evening, an unruly crowd of lathi-wielding, slogan-shouting men, young and old, swept down Metcalfe Road. It was lucky for those living on the street that the violent mob's destination was a temple, two blocks away. The stream of unkempt males, with their hatred-darkened faces and loud, abusive shouting, frightened the normally peaceful residents of the neighbourhood. However, the hordes were gone before the residents understood what was happening. They heard afterwards that the temple had been ransacked, and the resident *pujari* hacked to death.

Violence had entered the peaceful suburbs of Lahore.

* * *

Pammi, just fifteen when she went away, stayed with the Malhotras for almost three years. In contrast to the Chopras and the many others fundamentally affected, the Malhotras were lucky. As Hindus they had found themselves living on the right side of the new borders dividing the sub-continent. Their business interests were spread out more towards the east — in Bihar and Assam — and their lives were not much changed by the partition of the country. In fact, they were among the few who benefited from it, their business expanding greatly in the years following Partition as they diversified into sugar products and chemicals. By the early 1950s, the Malhotra business empire was becoming difficult to deal with single-handed. All their friends had felt the injustice of the Malhotras having only the one child, Noni, to help them — which he eventually did in 1949.

When Pammi came to stay in the Malhotra household, Noni was in the last year of his undergraduate programme at the nearby St Stephen's College. If Pammi at that time was tall and attractive, so too was Noni. Even taller, at six feet and two inches, he did not have the fair complexion so typical of Punjabis. This was a source of great embarrassment for old Mrs Malhotra, who always felt her son was disadvantaged for having a darker-than-most skin. But rather than the colour of his skin, a long, aquiline nose, a strong jaw, and sharp, alert eyes were what most people noticed when they first met him. Noni enjoyed the company of his cousin. It was quite unusual having someone his own age — never mind a young girl growing into womanhood — around the house. It was only inevitable that this enjoyment soon became more than friendship. The Malhotras could see their son falling in love with the refugee from Pakistan, but could do nothing about it.

Pammi and Noni were married in the winter of 1952. Pammi was just over nineteen. By this time the Chopras too, had been forced to flee Lahore with as many of their belongings as they could pack into the old family Chevrolet. They chose to settle in Delhi not far from their daughter, now Mrs Noni Malhotra.

All that was years ago. Harsh Malhotra was dead, having succumbed to a massive heart attack on the golf course. Already well into the management of the family business, Noni became its sole inheritor after his father's death. Foreign collaborations helped in a gradual expansion of the Malhotra businesses. Pammi's youthful plans of becoming a doctor sank into history. However, she took to married life with some enthusiasm. In the early years, she and Noni made a loving enough couple, and within eight years had two children: Nisha, the elder, who died of diphtheria when she was four years old; and Rattan, born in 1960, since then the only child of the Malhotras.

Noni made a fond but preoccupied father to his son, and an attentive enough husband. But at some point after the first ten years of his marriage to Pammi, he had begun to wonder if he had not been in too much of a hurry to marry. Pammi was a dutiful mother to Rattan – perhaps too dutiful – but was she not also much too strong, even overbearing . . . ?

In fact, over the years Noni found himself typically caught in the ongoing battle between his wife and his mother. Old Mrs Malhotra had never really liked Pammi's mother, her husband's sister. The threatened turmoil of 1947 had, however, made it difficult to refuse her sister-in-law's plea for help regarding a safe home for her daughter. Once Pammi was in her house, she saw her as bold and headstrong, and all too ready to ensnare her only son into marriage. She also resented the fact that society had not forgiven the impropriety of her son marrying his first cousin. Matrimony between cousins so closely related was a singularly 'Muslim' thing to do; and the larger family and the old-standing network of friends and acquaintances never allowed her to forget this.

Every instance of difference between mother-in-law and daughter-in-law would eventually end in loud arguments in which the older woman would accuse the younger of being an interloper; of being a 'sister' who had never understood what being 'sisterly' was; of being an incestuous pervert who had been sent from across enemy borders to pollute and disfigure a fledgling nation. All efforts on the part of Pammi to say that Noni, too, had been a willing participant in their decision to marry, was lost on the deaf ears of the fond mother. For many years, old Mrs Malhotra would have the last word in such quarrels, and after flinging one final, parting shot at the defiant Pammi, she would withdraw into her bedroom, draw all the curtains, and refuse to eat.

Often Rattan, the only male grandchild, and heir to the Malhotra millions, would find himself right in the middle of such battles. In his early years, he would immediately run out of the room and hide in ayah's lap. As he grew older, he would shout 'stop fighting, you two' disgustedly, and shut himself in his room with his computer. At these moments, old Mrs Malhotra would remember Panna the Fakir. Though she never mentioned him directly, she would shriek barbs and innuendoes at her ill-omened daughter-in-law and grandson. Pammi and her son would silently swear at the absent Noni, away on a business trip, for leaving them so stuck and helpless.

The quarrels between both women were made worse by Noni's successes at work. Noni seemed to have less and less time for large family gatherings in which his mother could preside as the venerated matriarch in the old way. Instead, there was a substantial increase in business dinners in which Noni would invite his guests to one of New Delhi's posh hotels or restaurants. Old Mrs Malhotra was rarely invited to them. It was Pammi who played hostess to her son's guests.

The more frequently this happened, the more old Mrs Malhotra would feel that the kitchen, the centre of her world and the household, was slipping out of her grasp. It would make her insecure and vicious, leading to differences of opinion over the most petty things between herself and her daughter-in-law.

These would have odd consequences. Every evening both women would await the return of Noni from work, and attempt to explain their point of view to him. The outcome would depend on who got to tell him first. At first, young as he was, Noni did not realise that he was being centred in this way. It was hard for him to tell his mother anything that suggested that his wife could be right, or that she should be left alone. Conversely, any attempts to defend his mother would result in a long-lasting quarrel between husband and wife, and they would not speak to each other for days. Soon, Noni began staying away. This would make Pammi sullen and withdrawn, and Noni impatient and angry. So when business deals called for travel abroad, Noni would go in relief, secretly glad to be spared the tension-filled evenings with his wife in the bedroom.

About ten years into her marriage, Pammi began to tell Noni that they needed to move to South Delhi. The first decade after Independence had seen Lutyens' capital expand southwards. Also, the centre of the business world was no longer in the Old City or around Kashmiri Gate and Darya Ganj. For the Malhotra household, the furthest south they had, traditionally, ever ventured was to Connaught Circus and Janpath (originally 'The Queen's Way') for shopping. The day Noni invested money in acquiring newer and larger space for his office in Loknayak Bhavan behind Khan Market, Pammi began to insist that they also move house to the more open and stylish suburbs of New Delhi. It would save so much of Noni's commuting time, and they would become a much more integral part of South Delhi's newly establishing social circles.

Not once did Pammi openly say that her desire for a home in New Delhi had anything to do with her wanting to get away from old Mrs Malhotra and her old-fashioned friends. Had she done so, her whole argument for a move southwards would have blown up in her face. Noni could see nothing in the situation at home that called for such drastic measures. After all, it wasn't as if the old house was small. In fact, it was spacious. It was amazing, Noni had often pointed out sarcastically, how two women and one child found it so difficult to live happily in seven thousand square feet of space in a home that held so many memories for him! There was no answer to this. Pammi thought it best to keep silent then, and think of other ways to persuade her husband to move.

Thus, Pammi presented her argument for shifting house by appealing to her husband's sense of success at work. This time, Noni had to concede the truth of Pammi's arguments. Gradually, he began exploring the possibilities of buying a plot of land with a view to building a house. When 73 Hauz Khas came up for sale, he consulted his friends. On their advice he bought it.

Whenever she looked back over those years, Pammi could never pinpoint precisely when she began to sense that Noni was drifting away from her and their marriage. Did this coincide with their move to Hauz Khas, or had it begun much earlier when a house in South Delhi was a distant dream? There was no doubt, however, that the move southwards saw her husband travel more and more frequently to Europe and the USA, and the number of unaccounted-for days in their life together increase. In the last few years, especially after Rattan left for university in the USA, Noni became more and more detached, more and more elusive. Recently, he seemed to feel that if he gave Pammi sufficient money at the beginning of the month to run the house and her own personal expenses, his duties by her and his household were absolved.

Needless to say, Pammi rebelled. And fought strongly. But her quarrels with her husband did not lead anywhere. When pressed into answering her questions about whether there were other women in his life, Noni would begin shouting, accuse Pammi of having a suspicious mind, and walk out of the room. Once or twice their quarrels turned violent, and Pammi found herself slapped hard across the face and pushed spinning out of the room. Noni would accuse her of being stubborn and demanding, of always finding some reason or other to badger him, of being a woman incapable of finding peace and contentment no matter how much she was given.

'Don't I always return to you, to this house ... after every trip?' he asked her once, just after Pammi had accused him of becoming uninterested and detached. But only a few weeks later she realised that his loudly avowed returns to home sweet home did not alter anything. In fact, they only made things worse, since telltale signs of involvements with other women began to appear. There were odd phone calls which could not be explained; business dinners to which Pammi could not go; secret weekend trips to nearby resorts which Pammi would get to know of, inadvertently, days later.

By the mid 80s, Pammi knew she had lost Noni. The feelings between them had turned to complete indifference on his part. His pointed – and repeated – references to always returning home had become merely the facade of normality he needed to preserve in the eyes of the world. Pammi knew he would never desert her. She would always be his wife at home, and be 'Papa' for Rattan. And he would, also, always be the Sahib of the house in the eyes of all of them, the servants, and the world.

Everything had changed. But outwardly, everything was there as it was.

It was a truth Pammi found hard to accept. In practical terms, all it had come to mean was finding ways to fill her time with something, anything. Frenetic social activity had come to mark her daytime hours, and long hours of waiting in the evenings. Both made for increasing frustration and unhappiness. These were magnified by Noni's longer and longer trips abroad, and made worse by dreaded last-minute messages about delayed arrivals and changes in programme.

The latter upset Pammi the most, and it took a lot out of her to hide her feelings of rejection and hurt from the rest of the world. The strain had given her face a stony, bitter look, and her demeanour a stern toughness that was intimidating to those meeting her for the first time.

If Ram Singh's disclosure about Noni's changed programme on the afternoon of the card party disconcerted Pammi, it was not visible to her friends in the drawing room. They were full of the headiness of *teen patti* and the good food on her table. She played more rounds of *teen patti* with them after lunch with great determination and as if nothing had happened. At last, they decided to call it a day. As the late afternoon sun beat mercilessly on the windows facing south, the women picked up their handbags and dark glasses in preparation for departure. The room was filled with 'thank-yous' and 'good-byes' even as Ram Singh walked quietly around the rooms clearing the plates and glasses and straightening the chairs.

Suddenly, above the sound of the women's voices was heard the jingling of the doorbell. Quickly setting down a pile of plates on the dining table, Ram Singh hurried out to the front door.

He opened it to the return of a breathless Tanvi, her hair slightly windblown, and her arms filled with brown paper parcels.

The first to notice her arrival was Urmil.

'Is this Tanvi, Pammi?' she cooed, in her loudest society manner.

'Yes,' replied Pammi, walking forward to greet her daughter-in-law by kissing her stylishly on both cheeks.

Tanvi stepped forward. But, nervous as she always was about facing her mother-in-law and meeting her friends, she tripped on the doormat in her high heels. Her greetings were cut short by a soft 'ouch', and she stumbled forward, straight into the arms of the waiting Urmil.

'Hello, auntie,' she said, her face worried in confusion.

'How are you, *beti*?' Urmil smiled through her dark glasses and gave the new bride a hug. 'It's good to see you. Why didn't you play cards with us?'

Tanvi blushed pink in embarrassment. 'I am so sorry! You see, I don't know how to play ...' she said apologetically, clutching her parcels tightly in her hand.

'Never mind, we will teach you. Won't we, ladies?' said Urmil, not to be refused. 'The next card session is to be in my house. You absolutely must come with Pammi,' she continued and, squeezing Tanvi to her once more, kissed her on both cheeks.

'I will ... thanks so much ...' said Tanvi breathlessly, stepping backwards to get out of her way.

The other women, not to be outdone, took turns to kiss Tanvi, the new young bride in the house. By the time they were finished, her cheeks were sore. She felt she had been taken over — been punched and pummelled by a strange mixture of sweat and French perfume into becoming somebody other than herself. When they had gone, she was so overpowered that she said a hurried 'I'll just be back!' to her mother-in-law, and ran upstairs to her room.

The Nether World

An hour later, just as the clock showed ten minutes after five o'clock in the evening, Ram Singh entered one of the servants' quarters located above the garage. It was a small room, and contained two beds arranged along the walls on either side. Opposite the door were two small windows which let in some of the late evening light. The room was hot and very stuffy, with a strong smell of perspiration hanging in the air. The ceiling fan was doing its best, but all it accomplished was to make the half dead houseflies hanging about windowpanes whir around in dizzy circles.

On one of the beds, Hari Ram the cook was already sprawled out in his underwear, having taken off his shirt and trousers because of the heat. He seemed to be asleep, his spectacles slightly askew over his nose. Ram Singh looked around and – as he had been given to doing quite often lately – screwed up his nose in disgust. When was Pammi memsahib going to find some other place for him to sleep in? And keep his things in? She had repeatedly promised that she would make alternative arrangements for his living quarters, but had done nothing about it. He had argued that sharing a room with Hari Ram was hardly appropriate. And she had agreed. Now he was getting impatient. Really impatient.

Hari Ram heard Ram Singh enter, and very pointedly turned over on his side, facing the wall. Since his glasses got in the way, he took them off and placed them beside his pillow. The old cook wanted to sleep, but knew that he would not be able to until Ram Singh had said his few sentences as overbearingly as possible. He hoped that if he seemed to be asleep, Ram Singh would refrain.

'It's so hot,' grumbled Ram Singh just as Hari Ram had expected. 'I'm going to tell the memsahib that there should be no parties in summer. I really get tired giving those women drink after drink.'

'Go to sleep,' Hari Ram mumbled. 'There is time only for a brief nap before the bell will be rung for the tea tray . . . unless there is a call for you before that.'

'*Oi*, don't you say anything about that, you bastard,' said Ram Singh over his shoulder in a mildly threatening voice. He was taking off his white *bandgala* and draping it carefully on a hanger. Soon he had tucked it away in a built-in cupboard along the wall.

Hari Ram did not respond except to say that he wanted to sleep and did not want to be disturbed. Ram Singh growled an 'okay' in reply, and walked across to one of the windows. He removed a small spotted mirror from off a conveniently placed nail on the wall, and peered into it. In the dull light creeping in through the dirty panes, he contemplated his face for a few seconds. He smoothed down his moustache in a stroking gesture typical of him. He felt his cheeks with the tips of his fingers and examined the state of his shave. It wouldn't really do. He looked at his watch, a Diwali gift from Pammi memsahib – one a little more special than the others distributed to all the servants. It was barely five thirty. Time enough for a quick shower.

'You never know,' he told himself, and moved towards the door.

He picked up a towel and entered the small shower room he shared with Hari Ram. He shaved again, and bathed quickly in the tepid water trickling out of the tap into an old plastic bucket. He was back in the room in twenty minutes. Hari Ram was fast asleep. Ram Singh dragged his bed as quietly as he could under the ceiling fan in the middle of the room, and lowered himself down on it. 'It wouldn't do to be sweaty,' he said to himself, his face twisting in a slight smile. He lay in bed a while, thinking of this and that, but mainly of the poor memsahib upstairs. She had had a bad deal in life, poor thing. He was glad he was not a woman. Yes, by God, he was glad he was not a woman.

In his mind's eye he tried to see himself as he might appear to her. What he saw was a tall, darkishly handsome man with a striking moustache, a flat stomach, and a strong body on which a spotlessly white *bandgala* uniform sat well. Feeling generally good about himself, Ram Singh smiled at the flies in the window.

It was exactly six fifteen when the call bell rang in the room. Two short rings, and one long one. But Ram Singh had heard them both in his head seconds before they actually rang. Before the last one had ended in silence, he was already moving towards the cupboard, and reaching for his *bandgala* coat.

As he did so, he smiled to himself. It was always like that on days when the sahib called from abroad to say that his return was delayed. How could he help but be prepared! He moved down the spiral outside staircase swiftly, and in a second, had entered the kitchen from the back door. He moved into the hallway, glancing into the living and dining rooms where the ladies had gathered that morning. Spying a forgotten glass under one of the chairs, he loped across to pick it up. There were plenty of crumbs scattered on the floor. He would have to make sure that the cleaning woman did a thorough job tomorrow.

As he passed the oval, gold-framed mirror in the foyer, he paused for a few seconds, and was quite pleased with what he saw. It took him only a few seconds to climb the stairs, to the first floor of the house. The doors to all three rooms on the floor were shut. Pammi memsahib's was the last one, at the end of the corridor. Ram Singh stood a while outside it, listening. He could hear Pammi moving. He knocked softly, waited a few seconds, opened the door.

He found his mistress lying on the sofa at one end of the room, away from the large king-sized bed covered smoothly with a handsome bedspread in rich burgundy silk. The sofa and its two matching arm chairs in patterned upholstery were arranged along the flowing lines of matching silk curtains closing off long, deeply recessed windows on the right of the bed. A glass-topped coffee table ran along the length of the sofa, and at a certain angle in the dim light reflected Pammi's tall frame lying prone on the sofa. Her head was resting on two cushions. Her thick long hair, highlighted with the deep red of henna, was unpinned, and made a sharp contrast to the mushroom-coloured raw silk cushions under her head. She was wearing a black paisley-printed dressing gown in silk. A lamp, standing tall above silver-framed pictures of the family on a round table adjacent to the arm of the sofa, glowed above her head. Otherwise the room was in darkness, the heavy silk curtains shutting out completely the last rays of the sun setting outside.

For a second Ram Singh stood where he was, quite taken aback. Never before had he found Pammi memsahib like this. She looked pale, almost ill, but very attractive. She turned her head slowly, and looked at him for a few seconds. Suddenly she spoke.

'Don't just stand there. Come over here.'

'Yes, memsahib,' he said, his head bowing low.

In a minute he had reached her.

A Walk through the Door

In the newly constructed second floor of 73 Hauz Khas, the distant ringing of the call bell — at fifteen minutes after six o'clock — pierced Tanvi's sleep. She stirred a little, and turned over onto her back. As she faced the ceiling, a network of red lines — where her skin had squashed against the white pillow — was clearly visible. In the large double bed she seemed small, almost fragile. Her heart-shaped face in repose seemed childlike — certainly not more than that of a girl of eighteen or twenty.

A new bride. A very young bride for the well-travelled Rattan Malhotra, now almost thirty-two years old.

On the bedside table at Tanvi's left stood a large framed photograph of herself and her husband dressed as bride and groom. Next to it was a smaller one of Rattan, beaming at the camera with confidence. His eyes were sparkling with energy and a visible impatience — as if saying there was so much to accomplish and this photography et cetera was wasting his time. Not that Tanvi noticed all this. Very fond of the photograph, she only saw Rattan as a romantic figure — as romantic as the handsome outsider of legend, riding a white stallion and dashing through the white mists of the heroine's waiting life. He had returned from the USA to marry *her*, a simple soul who had barely finished her BA.

Though she lay quietly for a few minutes in her bed, the

call bell had woken Tanvi. She looked at her watch, and was surprised to find that it was so late. She hadn't meant to fall asleep because she knew that she had to go out for dinner that evening with Rattan. She had to bathe, do her face and hair – *and* wear a sari. This latter process she absolutely dreaded. It took her so long to get everything just right. All those difficult pleats, and the *pallav* . . . and the high heels!

She wondered what the party would be like. It would probably be a big one – in one of the new five-star hotels – and with lots of people.

So different from the gatherings she had known at home.

By 'home' Tanvi meant her mother's house. It would be years before she could begin to feel comfortable enough in this large fashionable one at 73 Hauz Khas and call it 'home'. Three months after her marriage, it still seemed huge, almost hotel-like. In fact, it was very similar to the places she had stayed in on her honeymoon in Europe. At certain moments it seemed positively frightening, making her want to tiptoe down its corridors so as not to disturb its ghosts.

Tanvi firmly believed that all houses had their secrets, and that you could only eliminate them by filling out the corners with your own. So far, she did not think she had done so, feeling a complete stranger on this newly added second floor – with its suite of two huge bedrooms, attached bathroom, and a bar-cum-sitting room – in which she and Rattan could entertain their friends.

One of the first things that Tanvi noticed when she came to 73 Hauz Khas as a bride was that all the rooms in the house opened into a hallway, and that each room always had its door tightly shut. There was no such thing as moving freely from room to room. As you left a room, you shut the door behind you, only to come face to face with another shut door in front of you. It was perhaps this feature that gave the house the air of a cold, impersonal hotel.

Tanvi had said as much to her mother earlier that afternoon, as they had eaten lunch together. Mrs Madan had been thrilled at having her sorely missed daughter all to herself as in old times. In her early fifties — and given to dressing in crisply starched cotton saris — Mrs Madan was one of those overly protective middle-class women who sentimentalised her role as 'a girl's mother', inevitably having to — quite heart-wrenchingly — give away her daughter in *kanyadan* at the time of marriage. The brief twenty years her only daughter spent in her custody was clearly a time earmarked for indulgence. As for Tanvi — she had enjoyed every minute of being spoiled and cosseted by her parents even as she had realised, quite unconsciously, that marriage would automatically put an end to such things. In this sense, Tanvi was quite typical of other girls of her age and station in life. They saw marriage as a rite of passage to a life of responsibility and giving.

However, as a typical 'girl's mother', Mrs Madan also knew that new, married roles were not immediately understood by ones so young and hitherto protected. The first few months were crucial — even difficult — for an Indian bride. They could make or mar any marriage.

And Tanvi had been married barely three months.

Mrs Madan had awaited her daughter's arrival for lunch that morning with hidden apprehension. Today could be the day when she as a mother would know instinctively whether her daughter was really happy in her new marriage. All her friends had told her what to look out for, and what advice to give a daughter who had left her home to live in the home of her husband and his family. She wondered whether she would be able to remember all those things, and whether they would be adequate to answer the specific problems of her daughter.

She was very doubtful. Very, very doubtful.

The match between Tanvi and Rattan had happened all so quickly. Too quickly. As she was at cards in New Delhi's well-known Gymkhana Club one evening, a mutual friend had told Mrs Madan about the return of Rattan Malhotra from the

USA. The word had spread that his mother was on the look-out for a bride for him, and wouldn't he be a good match for Tanvi? Mrs Madan had been sceptical. She wasn't going to throw away her only innocent daughter on an America-returned young man who, almost definitely, would have a 'wife' in the USA anyway. How could one be sure that she had been left behind for good? Or, maybe, he would not like India at all – and think of returning to the USA? That would mean that Tanvi would have to go with him into the unknown. That Mrs Madan did not want at all. She had heard too many stories of ill-fated Indian wives hauled all the way across the oceans only to be dumped unceremoniously for American ones.

How could she ever risk any such thing with her one-and-only beloved Tanvi!

However, one Sunday morning a few weeks later – as she and her friend were returning books to the Club library – Mrs Madan met the young man himself. He was with his mother, Pammi Malhotra. They all stopped and exchanged pleasantries. Mrs Madan liked what she saw, because besides being eligible, Rattan's thirty-two years sat well on him. He looked particularly relaxed that morning, standing more than six feet tall with his hands in his pockets, the warm January sun in his face, and his dark hair still wet from a late shower. Fashionable dark glasses covered his eyes. As a concession to the cool season, he had chosen to wear a white V-necked cricket sweater, which sat stylishly on his broad shoulders. He appeared cool and laid back, secure in the knowledge that he would be viewed as different (and therefore interesting), especially by women – and even their mothers.

When introduced to Mrs Madan, he bowed politely and, taking off his glasses, offered his hand to her. More used to being greeted with the traditional *namaste*, Mrs Madan was somewhat taken aback. But she recovered quickly and shook his hand firmly.

'Nice to meet you,' he said, his slow American drawl

distinctly out of place in the post-colonial ambiance of New Delhi's Gymkhana Club. But its effect on Mrs Madan was mesmerising. While Pammi and Mrs Madan talked, Rattan stood aside, listening politely. He did not replace his dark glasses, allowing Mrs Madan to see clearly the complete profile of his face. Thick dark brows and lazy brown eyes stood above a thick but straight nose. A strong jaw and even teeth completed the picture of an affable young man confident of the world at his feet. At the first convenient pause in the conversation, she turned to Rattan.

'How is it that you did not find a pretty young wife for yourself in the USA?'

If Rattan was embarrassed by the sudden directness of the question, he did not show it. In fact, he behaved as if he had expected it. His reply was cool and measured. But it was spoken in a lighthearted way.

'I always wanted to return and join Dad in his business. I couldn't see an American girl making it even in the India of the 1990s. So, I figured that it would be better if I did not bring one back with me. That's about it!'

Everybody laughed, and the conversation moved to other things. But Mrs Madan was impressed. In fact, she was quite taken in by the aura of distant American shores that hung about the young man from Boston. She went home and told her husband about the encounter with Rattan. Mr Madan remained unruffled; but it was obvious to his wife that he was interested. However, they both decided it would not do to seem too eager, so they schooled themselves not to do anything about it for a few weeks. Luckily for them, however, Pammi Malhotra was making her own round of inquiries, and by the end of the month, had short-listed two or three young ladies whom she felt would be appropriate for her son.

Heading the list was Tanvi.

Pammi phoned Mrs Madan's friend, and requested her help in establishing more serious contact with the Madans. Once that was done, things had moved quickly. Pammi insisted that they meet as fast as possible, by implication assuming that the Madans would never say no to so good a proposal for their daughter. But Mrs Madan was a little uneasy about this, and said as much to her friend.

'Why are they in such a hurry?' she asked.

'No, they are not in a hurry. It's just that there does not seem to be any reason to delay things. They've completed the second floor of the house, and Rattan wants to settle down. That's all there is to it.'

There was nothing Mrs Madan could say to this. It was true that the Malhotras had finished the construction of the third floor in preparation for receiving a daughter-in-law. In fact, she had heard that they had spent a lot of money and renovated the whole house. It was obvious to everyone that the Malhotras' businesses were prospering, and now that their only son had returned to join his father, they could only expand.

All this information Mrs Madan gleaned from her friends. In the general opinion of everyone, Tanvi was considered a lucky girl for being so chosen. After all, the Malhotras were rich people. Rattan was a smart young man, and Tanvi would never want for anything.

There was not much more that the Madans could say to all these recommendations. Put together, they squashed any remaining scepticism on their part. In fact, the more the Madans thought about it, the more Rattan Malhotra came to resemble a positively good 'catch' for their daughter.

Tanvi was married to Rattan exactly six weeks after the day the Madans accepted the Malhotra proposal of marriage. And the day the ceremonies were completed, Tanvi moved from her mother's house to live with her husband and his family at 73 Hauz Khas. It took a few days for Tanvi to understand the geography of the huge building rising up three floors: the ground floor had the public areas of the kitchen, living rooms and dining room; the suite of rooms on the first floor was inhabited by her in-laws, Pammi and Noni; and the second floor was meant only for Rattan and herself.

'It's a huge house, Ma,' said Tanvi, removing her high-heeled pumps as she sat down in her favourite chair in her mother's home. In the brief silence that followed, she wiggled her toes in the open air. 'I really feel so lost in it!' she continued.

Mrs Madan looked at her daughter protectively. Tanvi was such an innocent. She still did not realise how lucky she was in having married the only heir of such a prosperous Delhi family!

'Don't compare that house with ours, *beti*,' counselled Mrs Madan weightily. 'We are ordinary middle-class people. Your father is a government servant, and could hope to live only a comfortable but not very stylish life. Your in-laws are rich people – much more affluent than us – and you will have to get used to it.'

By now Tanvi was sitting curled up in her chair and she was staring out of the window. However, she was listening carefully to what her mother was saying.

'You are probably right, Ma,' she said at last. 'But I do so hate those shut doors.'

There was silence in the room.

'Do you know what I think?' said Mrs Madan brightly, as if a truth had dawned on her suddenly. 'The doors are always shut because of the air-conditioning. If you have air-conditioning through window units, you have to shut *all* the doors!'

It was a simple explanation, but it did not satisfy Tanvi. She knew that her mother was making light of her statements to dispel her fears. She did not know how to tell her mother that her new home was opulent but not comfortable; that the furniture, the upholstery and the *objets d'art* were in the best of taste, but dwarfed her. They made her feel that she was not good enough for them. They made her want to hide in the corners – or else, melt into the corridors and walls, and disappear.

What a contrast, thought Tanvi silently, to this living room with its pale cream emulsioned walls, the shabby green rug, and the once-matching curtains! And no air-conditioners. This was the way houses should be – taking on the character of the people who lived in them rather than of the objects displayed in them. But Tanvi's mother would never understand. She seemed suddenly to be at a great distance from her. Looking at the expression on her face, Tanvi realised with shock that her mother was more taken in by her daughter's new and glittering life than the daughter herself.

It was no use trying to explain.

Shaking her head quickly to clear it of dark fears, Tanvi stood up and crossed the room to where her mother was sitting on the sofa.

'I love you so, Ma,' she said softly, even sadly, as she gave her a tight hug. It was a hug that said many things, but not all of them were understood by the older woman. Mother and daughter sat a while in silence. Both knew that the other's eyes were moist with unshed tears, and so gave each other a moment of stillness.

'It is always like that for us women,' said Mrs Madan after a pause. Her voice was gentle and low.

To Tanvi, still with her head buried in her mother's shoulder, it seemed to come from very far away.

'It takes a long time to get used to your real home. Now 73 Hauz Khas is your "real" home; not this one in which you sit today. That is why they use so much rice in Hindu weddings. The fate of a grain of rice is similar to the fate of women, *beti*. Rice is first planted in one field, and then transplanted into another. It is the same with us. You have been "transplanted" into your new home now! In fact, you are lucky. Pammi Malhotra allows you to visit us as often as you like. I doubt that rice grains are allowed this much . . .'

Mrs Madan laughed – albeit somewhat feebly – at her attempt to lighten the mood. Tanvi did not respond. She sat by her mother's side looking pensively into the distance. It was after a distinct pause that she said, 'I suppose so ...' in tones so faint and doubtful that her mother began to look concerned.

'What is the matter, *beti*? Aren't they good to you? Isn't Rattan a nice young man?'

'Oh, yes. He's wonderful,' said Tanvi, her face lighting up for the first time since her arrival. 'He's so gentle and kind. He's always so concerned about me and my feelings. You know, Ma, he made sure it didn't hurt ... I mean, the first time ...'

She stopped, embarrassed, and blushing a deep red looked away from her mother's intense gaze. Mrs Madan was most relieved, and from that day onwards, her love for her son-in-law increased a hundredfold. Her instinctive judgement of the young Rattan had been proved correct.

'You are lucky, Tanvi *beti*. Rattan is really a most eligible young man. Not only does he come from a well-to-do family, but he also has good BA and MBA degrees to his credit. And both from American universities. He could just as easily have been a rich *kakaji*, a spoilt rotten good-for-nothing young fellow, expecting to live off his father's money. He even worked hard in the USA for so many years. And, I have heard that they gave him very good recommendations. You really must try and be a good wife to him.'

It was a long and breathless speech, full of praise, advice, and admonition. Tanvi felt its full force surround her.

'Yes, Ma. You are right,' said Tanvi, over awed. 'I will try my best.'

Mrs Madan did not realise that such praise of her new son-in-law was intimidating rather than reassuring to her daughter. By the end of the conversation, the playful, somewhat rest-less Rattan that she had known during her honeymoon was transformed in Tanvi's mind into a tough-talking boardroom decision-maker, whose drive and ambition could have no room for silly feelings of inadequacy in a wife to whom he was bringing so much. Tanvi began to feel small, even foolish, for having such misgivings. But she could not tell her mother all this. Mrs Madan was in her own world, in her own understanding of what she thought the reality of her daughter's life was, and should be. She was continuing to speak in her own inimitable way.

'I used to worry so much about whom you would eventually marry!' she said, genuine feelings of self-satisfaction giving her voice a slightly pompous edge. 'Your father is such a recluse. Even though he is a member of the best clubs, he doesn't like to socialise. That was one of the reasons I began playing cards. If it weren't for my card circle we would have been nowhere ...'

'That may be,' said Tanvi suddenly, unashamedly cutting her mother short. 'But you must *not* play cards with her any more,' she continued so vehemently that Mrs Madan was startled.

'With whom?' asked Mrs Madan, completely perplexed.

'My mother-in-law, Ma!' said Tanvi, the first hints of exasperation showing in her voice.

'Why?' asked Mrs Madan.

'No. You will not. You *cannot* play cards with your daughter's mother-in-law. It is just not done,' said Tanvi adamantly.

Mrs Madan was surprised. Her daughter sounded like a well-seasoned society woman, speaking to her as an equal.

'If you say so, my dear,' the mother said, suddenly meek. 'I suppose you are right ...'

'I am right,' said Tanvi determinedly. 'And neither am I going to play with her, and her horrid friends.'

'Why? Has anything happened?' worried Mrs Madan.

'No. Nothing has happened ... In fact, she is very nice to me ... gives me lots of presents. But ...' said Tanvi, finding it difficult to complete what she was saying.

'But what?' asked Mrs Madan.

'Nothing. Nothing really ... The truth is, I don't really like her. In fact, I am afraid of her,' said Tanvi.

The last part of her sentence came out in a rush – as if she had just understood in her own mind the exact nature of her apprehension.

'Afraid of her? Why? Has she said something? Or done anything?' asked Mrs Madan, in panic.

'No, no. It's nothing really ... But I don't like her. She is so huge, and tall, and big, and has such hard eyes,' said Tanvi, in a flat voice. 'Even Rattan does not talk to her much. He told me the other day that he does not feel that he knows his parents very well. He was away for over ten years.'

'There is nothing wrong with that,' said Mrs Madan brusquely. It would not do to encourage Tanvi in her fears. 'What is there to know? Parents are parents!'

Tanvi did not speak. She was looking at her mother, her large eyes wide, listening intently.

'Pammi Malhotra has always been a woman with a presence, but she is not bad at heart. You think I would have married you to her son if she wasn't that way?' said Mrs Madan firmly.

'I suppose not,' said Tanvi, melting somewhat, and wanting desperately to believe her mother. She looked at the older woman fondly – at least she had a mother she could talk to. So many of her friends still in college did not. She looked at her watch. It was almost half past four. She should be thinking of leaving.

'I must go. The car must have come to fetch me. I have to stop at the tailor's on the way back. My *salwar kameezes* are ready. And so also are my mother-in-law's blouses. I am supposed to collect them ...' said Tanvi, looking reluctantly for her shoes.

And then, as if a truth had dawned, she spoke again.

'See,' she said, smiling stoically. 'I am already running errands for her!'

'Good for you,' said Mrs Madan, and gave her daughter a tight, approving hug.

By this time Tanvi had put on her high heels, and was taking out a comb from her handbag. Soon each strand of her smartly styled hair fell into place, neatly framing her face. She took out a small compact from her handbag, and began applying lipstick.

When she was done, she seemed transformed, looking smartly chic. And modern.

'We are going out later tonight, Rattan and I, and I would like to take a small nap before he returns from work. I'm not yet used to sleeping so late in the night ...' said Tanvi, a faint blush spreading over her face. She hoped that her mother had not noticed it.

'Yes, go, *beti*. Go and relax ...' said the fond mother, giving her daughter a farewell squeeze. 'And don't worry about Pammi Malhotra. She's not a bad sort. But she is your mother-in-law, of course, and you must be careful. A mother-in-law is always a mother-in-law – this relationship is like that. In the early years especially, every daughter-in-law must know her place.'

'Yes, Ma,' said Tanvi, dutifully. And left.

Lying in bed after her short nap, Tanvi relived the afternoon visit to her mother. 'Ma read me quite a lecture,' she thought pensively, and wondered what she meant by her 'knowing her place'. Perhaps she was trying to tell her that she should help in the house, and do things to please her mother-in-law. Tanvi wondered what she could do to help in a house where there were so many servants anyway. She got out of bed and straightened the bedclothes. Nearby, on a cherry-brown, highly lacquered table stood a new music system. She moved towards it, and inserted a CD of one of the latest Hindi films. The romantic words of a current hit filled the room. Tanvi had heard the song before, and hummed along as she moved around the room tidying things. We should see the film, Rattan and I, she told herself.

And then remembered that Rattan did not like Bollywood films at all.

'He's such an *angrez*,' thought Tanvi fondly. 'He only likes films from Hollywood.'

Did this mean that she would not be able to see any more

of the latest films from Bombay? Or did it mean that she would have to go alone?

Such definitive questions and decisions were only vaguely on the mind of the new bride. She was still finding her feet in her new home; still savouring her new status and her new relationship with the young man from Boston. As Tanvi finished tidying the bed, she looked around. Her eyes rested on the television, making her walk over to straighten the Rajasthani embroidery draped over it. They moved next towards the sitting arrangement on one side of the room. On the main sofa stood the pile of brown paper bags full of clothes from the tailor. She separated those bags that contained her mother-in-law's newly stitched blouses, and stacked them in one of the armchairs. Her own she carried to the bed. Soon, she had emptied them all onto the bedspread.

'I really feel guilty about these,' thought Tanvi, holding up her new *kameezes* and inspecting each carefully even as she began humming louder the song that was playing on the CD player. 'I have so many new clothes in my trousseau that I still haven't worn. And yet I've had new ones made! I feel so guilty! What will Rattan think?'

Nevertheless, she felt pleased with herself. Clothes were Tanvi's passion, and every new outfit gave her satisfaction that lasted a long time. The tailor seemed to have done a good job. Maybe she could wear one of these new ones that very evening!

It took Tanvi about fifteen minutes to admire and carefully hang up the four new *salwar kameez* sets in the cupboard. When she was done, she glanced at the parcels still lying in the armchair near the sofa and looked at her watch. She knew that the card party had ended, and all the guests had left long ago. There was time for a quick visit downstairs. With her mother's instructions fresh in her mind, she decided that she might as well deliver the blouses to her mother-in-law. She quickly gathered all the parcels in her arms and moved towards the door, hoping all the while that the tailor had done as good a job with them as he had done with her own clothes. She moved out onto the landing, shutting the door of her room behind her.

The wall-to-wall carpet on the second-floor landing muffled her footsteps until she reached the stairs. As she descended these, her heels clicked loudly down the twenty marble steps to the first floor. The carpet on the landing of the first floor muffled her footsteps once again. Humming softly, Tanvi moved towards the door of her mother-in-law's room. Somewhere at the back of her mind she remembered that her father-in-law was out of the country. She knocked on the door, and without really waiting for permission to enter, turned the handle and passed into the room.

Upstairs, in the bridal suite, a quiet, almost eerie in its totality, overwhelmed everything. The drone of the air-conditioner did not drown it; neither did the hum of the two bedside lamps. The CD still played on, the purring romantic lyrics combining with the other sounds in the room. If Tanvi had always felt that every house had its ghosts, today she could have confirmed that every room had its own ghosts too. The ones in this first abode of the new bride were certainly there – under the bed; behind the whatnot filled with wedding presents of fancy ceramics and imported cut glass; among the roses in the vase trying to survive their second day; in the music system by the sofa trying to carve out space for a new film tune. All the objects in this second-floor room of 73 Hauz Khas were new – new to each other, and new to the occupants of the room.

Rattan and Tanvi, also new to each other.

It was at that moment in that evening of the 21st of June 1992 – when Tanvi went downstairs, dutifully punctual, to deliver the newly tailored blouses to her mother-in-law – that all the recently put-together objects in her room melded together tangibly to take on what would become the ghostlike memories of a new but short-lived marriage. Tanvi had hardly been gone a few minutes when there was a momentary fluctuation in the electricity. The music from the CD paused a moment in its rhythms, and the air-conditioner tripped briefly – seemingly in warning to the door to be ready for a sudden opening.

Open it did, hastily, to the return of Tanvi, who faced her room as white as a sheet – as if she had seen a world full of ghosts. Maybe she really had. Those in the room couldn't tell. Entering at a run, she closed the door confusedly behind her. And stopped. The parcels she was carrying slipped from her fingers to the floor, and her hands covered her face. She stood absolutely still for a few seconds, her stomach all a-churn, and her breath catching in her throat.

When she opened her eyes, they were wild with terror. Her mouth opened in horror.

'Oh God!' she said, her eyes closing tightly again and her hands scraping her burning cheeks.

'Oh God,' she said again, walking forward without seeing although her eyes were now wide open. In a minute the bed received her hot flushed face into itself.

'Oh God, my dear, dear God! I hope they didn't; I hope they didn't; I hope they didn't ... see me. What should I do? What should I do? Oh God ...' she said, and continued mumbling incoherently.

All in the room – the bed, the walls, the ceiling, and the sofa – knew in that moment that something had happened. The clock on the bedside table could have told, if asked, that it was exactly forty minutes after six p.m. that Tanvi returned tumultuously to the room; and that it was precisely two and a half minutes later that she, bride of three months, picked up the phone on the bedside table and attempted to dial a number. Her fingers were so out of control that she only got through after many, disoriented, attempts.

It was the fifth one that at last got her talking to her mother – her dearly beloved mother with whom she had spent the day.

'Ma?' everything in the room heard her say in quavering panic. 'Ma? It's me, Tanvi. I have to tell you something . . . and you have to tell me what to do. Something has happened . . . something dreadful has happened . . .'

A Woman Dead

At the moment when Tanvi returned petrified to her bedroom on the second floor of 73 Hauz Khas, her dearly beloved husband was sitting in his Maruti 1000, stuck in a traffic jam. It was at the infamous crossroads before the All India Institute of Medical Sciences on the Ring Road. The time was 6.40 p.m. and in the late June evening, the sun was still making the heat rise up in transparent waves. They glistened hotly between the rows and rows of impatient cars, buses, cyclists and motor cyclists eager to reach home. Rattan Malhotra was glad for the air-conditioning in his car which kept the world at bay, and him cooler than most of the others around him. It also saved him from inhaling the deadly monoxide fumes that, besides polluting the air, added to the heat.

A beggar rattled at the window, peering myopically through the darkened panes to gauge whether he would be lucky and be given something. At the other window, a woman dressed in a flowing Rajasthani *ghagra* in red and yellow and suckling a naked child, tried to sell him a packet of fragrant *agarbatti*. A man riding a two-wheeler scooter scraped the side of the car in order to squeeze ahead. He seemed to belong to another, extra-terrestrial world, his face invisible in a monstrous, ape-man helmet.

It was at times like these that Rattan wondered whether he had been wise to return to India. Had he stayed on in the USA, at least the fumes could have been avoided. And much else as well – the great struggle to get everything moving, effectively and efficiently at home and in the office. The new economic liberalisation programmes were beginning to make many things easier. But the quality of the basic systems of Indian life – their penchant for holding on to the comfortably familiar yet anachronistic norms, customs and habits – still left much to be desired. The policies had no doubt changed, but only on paper. The mindset of those putting them into practice and the basic ways of doing things, had not. This was all too evident outside the stationary car, reverberating to the efficient combined hum of the Maruti Suzuki engine and the air-conditioning. Too many automobiles and too narrow a road. And other vehicles of all kinds – cycles, scooters, rickshaws, carts, and tempos – jostling each other for space.

Merely a foot away from his window, Rattan saw a middle-aged man on a bicycle. His lined face, shining with the wet glow of perspiration in the light of the all-too-bright evening, looked exhausted. As he leaned over onto one side, a foot on the tarmac, his face was fairly close to Rattan's, sitting as he was in the rear seat on the left-hand side of a chauffeur-driven car. Through the dark panes of the window separating them, Rattan noted that, despite the potential danger that surrounded him by way of larger-than-him vehicles, there was an air of impatient expectancy in the rider's eyes. Rattan wondered idly what it could be. All he knew was that this expectancy would translate into the man on the bicycle being the first to move when the lights changed from red to green. He had seen this many times before, and each time was amazed. Cyclists would often be more prepared to begin moving at changing light signals than drivers of four-wheeled cars (and buses and trucks) which needed precious seconds to change from neutral to first gear in stick shift transmissions. But of course, the victory of a quicker start would only be a short-lived affair. Once the engines got going, the cyclist would soon be left far behind.

This was going to happen again, Rattan was sure, and shuddered in apprehension for the physical safety of the rider.

Speaking suddenly into the silence in the car, he told Kishore, the chauffeur, to watch out for him.

'They always do that,' said Kishore curtly, not at all sympathetic. 'Do they think they can win that they even bother to try?'

'Maybe he is in a hurry . . . Maybe he wants to get home soon, to his wife and children . . .' said Rattan evenly.

But Kishore did not think so.

'What wife and children? They'll be living somewhere in some *jhuggi*. Maybe they won't even be here in Delhi. Maybe they'll be back home, in a village far away . . .'

Rattan could not help wondering why Kishore was always so hard on others who had somewhat less than him. It was only recently that he himself had been able to make a pukka house for his family. In fact, his wife and two-year-old son had joined him in Delhi barely two years ago. But this only made him less, rather than more, understanding of others less successful than himself.

Rattan thought that some day he would ask why this was so. He thought of his own recent marriage, and his new life in a freshly renovated house, 73 Hauz Khas. And there now was his wife, Tanvi. Also new. And young. And somewhat unknown. But quite a sweet thing. Somewhere deep inside him something stirred, making him shift his position on the seat. He wanted, suddenly, to be with her; to hold her fresh, sweet body close to him; to make love to her, then and there, in this hot June evening. It was a pity he was not going home right away. He would have liked to surprise her with an earlier than usual return – and maybe even get her to agree to a quick round of love-making. In the shower, maybe?

The thought was inspiring and the desire already there, nicking his insides with intensity.

But there was no way in which he could ask Kishore to turn the car around the other way and head towards Hauz Khas when he had a business appointment with an associate in the Taj Hotel on Mansingh Road. The meeting would take at least forty minutes; even more maybe, if a round of drinks got included. Rattan looked at his watch impatiently. Almost seven o'clock. He could never be home before 8.30 p.m. That would certainly make them — him and Tanvi — late for that big dinner with the partners. And leave no time for possibilities.

'I haven't yet got myself into the workday mode after the honeymoon,' Rattan told himself, and thought of his three-month bride with some fondness. She was a sweet soul, so giving and trusting, and always making him feel so responsible for her. In fact, responsibility was what he felt most strongly when he was with Tanvi, and couldn't help thinking that none of this had figured in his relationship with Meghan, or any of the other women he had known in the USA. The women there had been so different. They were so sure of themselves, and knew exactly what they were looking for in their relationships with men. This seemed to be so even when they were only students in high school.

Tanvi was completely the opposite. Rattan smiled to himself at the thought of her and other men. He was sure she had known none other than him. The thought made him happy, but also a little uneasy. A small wrong step this way or that, and she would see him as an unfeeling cad. And that would not be good; either for him or for her. This is what arranged marriages were about: two people unknown to each other being asked to succeed at the most intimate and responsible of all relationships. He knew that Tanvi was looking to him for the lead in most things. And so far he had taken it. In fact, she was quite acquiescent. But occasionally he had seen a spark flash in her eyes that suggested that she was no yes-person.

'I wonder how long it will be before I see the other side of her. Not too long, I hope . . . And then, I hope it won't be something too dramatic either!'

Rattan smiled to himself at the prospect of a good and proper quarrel with Tanvi. It hadn't happened yet. He should enjoy every moment of this new relationship before the cynical calls of the workday world put pressures on it. He looked outside the window. Kishore was just negotiating the roundabout near the gates of the Taj Hotel on Mansingh Road. Soon he had turned into its steep driveway, coming to a halt outside the hotel's gleaming doors. As Rattan stepped out of the car, he looked at his watch. It was almost 7.30 p.m. No chance of being home before 9 p.m. Reason enough for a first quarrel with Tanvi, considering he had told her to be dressed and ready to leave by 7.30 p.m.! But business was business, however long it took. He decided to phone her from the foyer to let her know that he would be late.

But as soon as he entered the doors, his secretary accosted him from the office. Balraj was looking anxious and relieved.

'Thank God you have come, sir,' Balraj said breathlessly, and turned around to introduce Rattan to the visitor from the USA. In the apologies that followed, and in the general sense that it was late enough already, Rattan forgot the phone call to Tanvi. In fact, the meeting with the American went on till well after 8.45 p.m. Rattan left his visitor to wash and freshen up before they met again for dinner.

It was 9.15 p.m. when Kishore drove up to 73 Hauz Khas. It was a dark night, but the neon lights of street lamp-posts cast a silvery glow on the newly done road. The *chowkidar* hurried to open the gates, shut every evening to prevent stray cows – returning homewards at sunset – from wandering into the driveway. As the Maruti slid under the porch, the light from the lamp-posts receded. Rattan noticed vaguely that none of the outside lights – not those at the gate or the one in the porch – had been switched on. In fact, the entrance to the house stood in almost complete darkness.

He was really very late. 'Tanvi will be angry,' thought Rattan as he moved up the four steps towards the front door. He turned the handle but was surprised to find that it didn't move. He tried again but the door did not open.

'Where is everybody?' he asked of no one in particular.

Behind him, Kishore was the only one who heard him but did not reply. He had opened the boot of the car, and was collecting all of Rattan's papers and briefcase in order to carry them inside.

'Someone should be there! Why are they not opening the door?' said Rattan, impatiently.

By now Kishore had shut the boot and had come up behind him. Assuming that the question was not addressed to him, he still did not say anything.

Rattan reached out to the bell on the side of the door and rang it twice or thrice. For a few seconds master and chauffeur stood in silence, listening for the sound of footsteps moving inside. At last they heard them. They heard the click of the door unlock and saw it being opened slowly, even tentatively. Behind the half-opened door stood Hari Ram the cook, peering to see who it was in the dark porch. He had, obviously, taken his time walking up from the kitchen at the back of the house. He stood there, squinting up through his glasses at Rattan. Opening the front door to callers was not something Hari Ram usually did. Ram Singh almost always performed this role.

'Why did no one switch on the porch light? Where is Ram Singh?' asked Rattan, annoyed at having had to wait.

'Memsahib sent him to the bazaar. He must have left in a hurry . . . to get there before the shops close, I suppose. He must have forgotten to put on the lights,' said Hari Ram turning away and beginning to walk down the corridor towards the kitchen, his rightful domain.

'But it is past nine o'clock now . . .' protested Rattan, speaking to the back of the old cook.

Hari Ram did not respond.

Rattan looked at his retreating back and was going to say something sharp and chiding, but decided not to. There was no point in getting at Hari Ram who was growing old and who had always been happy at being invisible in the kitchen as the cook of the family.

'Where is memsahib?' he asked into the silence. As he expected, he did not receive a reply. He turned towards Kishore, and collected his papers and briefcase from him. This was also something Ram Singh did every evening.

'She has gone out in the car,' said Hari Ram in a seeming after-thought. Now that he had almost reached the kitchen door, he was barely audible.

Rattan smiled a little and did not say any more. As he began to climb the stairs, he told Kishore to wait outside. He would be downstairs shortly with the *choti* memsahib, and they would proceed for dinner. Kishore went out into the porch, shutting the door behind him. Hari Ram disappeared into the back of the house.

Rattan climbed up the stairs as quickly as he could. It was really late, and he hoped that Tanvi was dressed. In fact, he hoped that she would be ready to leave within the next three minutes. He doubted this, because it still took her ages to leave, especially when she had to wear a sari and get its folds just the way she wanted them. If she had her way, she would always be in blue jeans! This was fine by him, but blue jeans didn't always work when things got serious.

'She's going to be angry because I'm late. I made her wait, and I didn't call . . .' thought Rattan, thinking of how he could placate her as well as hurry her departure.

By this time Rattan had finished his climb up two floors. His briefcase felt heavy in his hands. He told himself he really should, in the next available free time, go through it and remove unwanted paper and bills. There was no point in carrying unnecessary weight around with him. He moved towards the door of their bedroom, stopping a minute to put his briefcase down on the floor so he could turn the knob. It turned easily, and he swung it open quickly.

'I'm so sorry, darling . . .' he began, turning around to pick up his briefcase from the floor where he had placed it before entering the dimly lit room.

'. . . but I couldn't help it. The traffic was bad, and everything ran late today. I tried to call but . . .' he continued, and turned to face the room.

Only to stop, suddenly, tripping over the edge of the dark

red Bukhara rug on the floor, his words dying in his mouth. His eyes widened in complete disbelief, and his breath caught in his throat in a harsh, hoarse whimper.

He saw her then, his Tanvi, with her head hanging to the side, and her short pixie-cut hair hanging outwards over her left ear. Her hands hung limply by the sides of her sleeveless cream silk shirt – the one that she had bought in London on their honeymoon – and, below her snug-fitting blue jeans, were her feet, their pink soles looking down at Rattan as he moved into the room. Around her neck was a pink chiffon *dupatta*, knotted tightly, its loose ends wound around the ceiling fan from where she hung, swaying slightly.

'My God . . .' said Rattan, his mouth hanging open and head tilting upwards as he looked at his bride of three months. The files and papers in his numb left hand slipped silently to the floor, making a jumbled heap near his feet. And the briefcase fell to the ground with a muffled thud, as the grip of his right hand around it loosened involuntarily.

'Oh my God . . .' he said again, as he moved up closer under her. It was her . . . it was her . . . his Tanvi! For a second he stood absolutely still, feeling a tight, painful constriction in his chest which seemed to move downwards to his feet, leaving them as cold as ice. His vision seemed for a second to blur into blindness. He shut his eyes even as his hands clenched into tight fists which – he realised afterwards – dug into his thighs with a strength he did not imagine he possessed. The purr of the air-conditioner was loud, and the air inside the room felt cold – like the insides of a refrigerator.

He shook his head slightly and opened his eyes. She was still there, hanging from one of the two ceiling fans in the room. As he took a step forward, he could see that her eyes were wide open – the whites bulging out as they hid the pupils which had slid downwards into the lower eyelids – looking blankly into the distance. Her mouth was slightly open. And, from its left side saliva dribbled downwards, making a wet patch on the material of her shirt at her left breast.

For a few seconds Rattan stood there, staring upwards in horror. It was terrible . . . a terrible, terrible sight! He wondered frantically about what to do. What should he do? My God, what could he do? What could he do?

Suddenly he knew. He should get her down. Quickly. He should untie her, and lay her on the bed. Quickly. Quickly! Maybe she was alive. Maybe she could be resuscitated. But he must be quick, very quick, because there wasn't time. Wasn't any time . . .

He jumped onto the bed. Suddenly she seemed within his reach. He could touch her. Her feet were in his face. How did she get up there? So high up? She must have used something . . . something to stand on . . . Quickly. Quickly.

He saw it immediately, right next to the side of the bed. It was an upturned stool, its four legs gaping wantonly towards anyone who wished to use it. It was the one that matched her dressing table at the far corner of the room. He rushed to pick it up, and place it on the disordered bedclothes. It wobbled on the ruffled bedspread hunched in the middle of the bed. Rattan knew that he would have to smooth it down somewhat, before he could get the stool to balance at all. Quickly. Quickly. Oh my God. Quickly. Please God . . . don't let her be dead. Don't let her be dead, he prayed silently, saliva rising hysterically in his throat. Where was everybody? 'I should call Ma . . . and Ram Singh . . . and Hari Ram. Quickly. I should get her down first . . .'

It was not easy to untie the knot. Her whole weight pulled at it downwards, stretching the bunched ends tightly together. Rattan moved right under her, understanding suddenly that to take the weight off the knot he would have to hold her up with his own body. Already unsteady, the stool moved slightly, its four legs sinking a little deeper into the Dunlop mattress. His hands fumbled at first, trying to get around Tanvi's — his beloved wife Tanvi's — head. His fingers searched for the direction that the ends of the *chunni* had taken.

Ah, yes. The left hand first. And then the right. Hurry. Hurry.

Once the first round was untied, the second was easy. Easy. Easy. Her complete descending weight would have to be handled, though. Slowly. Carefully . . . so that he . . . and she . . . would not fall off the stool. He held her body tightly against his, her head hanging heavily over his left shoulder. Slowly he put down one leg, searching for a firm foothold on the bedclothes. And then the other. When he had found a firm foothold, he stepped back a little with her against him, and kicked the stool off the bed with one foot. The action almost made him lose his balance, so he stood a moment trying to steady himself — and Tanvi, leaning heavily on him.

Slowly he laid her down on the bed.

She was dead. Completely dead. He had known this the moment he had held her weight in his arms, and seen that her head had dangled loosely on his shoulder. Now that he had laid her down, he was doubly sure. He stared at her blankly, unseeing, and then sat at the edge of the bed, his head in his clammy hands. What did he have to do next? He could feel her presence behind him: her left side was touching his back, solid and dead. He put an arm out behind him and found her hand. It was limp and cold.

There she was, his wife Tanvi, lying dead behind him. Limp, and cold, and dead.

He turned around to look at her. Her eyes were still open, staring and ugly. He put his hand out, and tried to shut them, moving her eyelids downward in a soft, caressing gesture. With her eyes closed, she seemed asleep. He remembered how once earlier, not too long ago, he had stared at her sleeping deeply on the bed beside him. It had been in the hotel on their honeymoon in London. He had woken earlier than her one morning, and watched her lying beside him. Her body had moved rhythmically, in cadence to her even, soft breathing.

It was a bit like that day; he tried to tell himself.

But of course, it wasn't.

'It isn't like that at all ... it isn't ... it isn't ...' he said aloud, the taste of earth on his tongue. His words came out of his throat in racking sobs.

'She's dead ... my God ... she is dead ...'

Rattan stood up slowly. And stared at the inert body on the bedclothes. What had he to do now? He had better tell somebody. He could hardly sit there for ever. He wished, suddenly, that his father were in town. Couldn't he do something? Anything? Maybe he should call a doctor to confirm the fact that she was really dead. Maybe he should call Tanvi's mother, Mrs Madan. And tell her ... tell her what? That he had found her daughter hanging from the ceiling fan? No ... he could never tell her that. Never.

But he could tell Ma. In any case, he had to tell her. For she would know what to do.

Where was she? He walked out quickly through the door, and ran down the two flights of steps towards her bedroom.

'Ma? Ram Singh? ... Hari Ram? Hurry ... *jaldi aao ... jaldi aao!*' he shouted as he ran.

At that moment he heard a car driving up under the porch outside. Pausing on the first landing, Rattan glanced out of the glass panes of a small window in the stairwell affording a view of the driveway. The car had come to a halt behind the Maruti 1000 in which Kishore sat waiting. As he hurried down the next flight of stairs to the foyer to open the door, he heard the car door slam. A female voice addressed Kishore.

'So, Rattan sahib is back, is he? Why are you so late?'

The voice was Pammi's, who, without waiting for anyone, opened the front door with her personal key. She hurried into the foyer and made straight for the staircase. She met Rattan on the last few steps.

'Thank God you've come, Ma. Something has happened ... something terrible ...' said Rattan, his voice broken.

Pammi did not reply. Neither did she seem to hear him. In fact, she did not really look at her son. She was moving up the steps quickly, and shouting downwards into the inner recesses of the house.

'Ram Singh? . . . Hari Ram? Come quickly.'

Rattan's eyes followed his mother. He heard her shout to the servants, her voice cracking with the effort. Before anyone could say any more, Ram Singh appeared. So he had returned, Rattan found himself thinking, a look of inconsequential and disjointed annoyance crossing his face. That was rather a long trip to the bazaar. He shouldn't really go off like that. He always behaved oddly when Pa was out of town. He should tell Ma to do something about it.

But Pammi was saying other things.

'Bring something cold to drink. It's really hot. Lots of ice . . .' she ordered. 'In my room . . .'

Rattan saw his mother take a quick look around the foyer, walk past him quickly, and begin turning the corner towards the second flight of stairs to the first floor. As she did so, she began talking.

'What a dreadful day! First those ladies, especially that dreadful Urmil . . . then this awful heat . . . and then your awful grandmother. I went all the way to Old Delhi, in this heat, to see her, and she wasn't even grateful . . .'

'Will you stop going on and on . . . and listen to me?' said Rattan, suddenly angry. He had followed her, climbing two steps at a time. By this time they had reached the first floor. Pammi walked quickly towards her bedroom, the pleated folds of her grey sari lifted away from her feet with her right hand.

Before she could enter, Rattan grabbed her by the shoulders and turned her around. His face was ashen and his eyes blazing. His voice was cracked and hysterical.

'We're going upstairs, Ma. Now . . . before everything else. Something has happened . . . something has happened to my Tanvi! And you have to tell me what to do about it . . .'

PART TWO

Nalini on the Nile

Far away from the new world of the new bride, across the sands of Arabia and the waters of the Red Sea, lived another of Tanvi's kind. Similar, yet different. On the same evening in June when Tanvi was found hanging from the ceiling fan in the newly done-up second floor of 73 Hauz Khas, Nalini Thapar sat in the bay window of her room, two thousand miles away. Her long, flowing brown hair was spread thickly across the broad of her back; her chin was resting on raised knees; and her feet were tucked neatly under them. She was looking out, feasting tired eyes on the waters of the Nile in her father's house in Zamalek, the old island suburb of Cairo.

After a long day of staring at the monochromatic colours of a computer monitor two feet away from her nose, the slowly ever-changing Nile offered considerable relief. Even though she had been a whole year in Egypt, the waters of the Nile under her window had not ceased to fascinate. Today, their rippling flow, incandescent in the light of the setting sun, seemed to draw to themselves her feelings of fatigue. Before she knew it, she had been sitting there a good half-hour, watching the waters flow steadily northwards, all the way to Alexandria, where she knew they gave themselves up to the blue Mediterranean.

'*El-Nil el-gameel* . . . the beautiful Nile,' said Nalini softly to herself, attempting to roll off her tongue the first few words of Arabic she had learned in the language class arranged by the Indian Embassy for the families of the officers. As she said them, the waters seemed to shimmer in response, reminding her of what the teacher had explained the day before about verbs in Arabic. Their endings depended on the gender of the noun referred to earlier in the sentence.

'You must not forget that in our language everything is either masculine or feminine. The Nile is always feminine . . .'

Like all of us women, thought Nalini, and smiled to herself at this stretching of a comparison between woman and water. She could not help but go further: the Nile had existed a long time. Over all those billions of years she had found a way to be herself, distinct from all her sisters, by flowing northwards instead of south. That surely made her different! She seemed so sure of herself, defying the pattern. Nalini wished she could be like her – like the waters that flowed definitively and inexorably, not south but northwards.

The breeze from the open bay window was cooling, lifting and restful as it wafted past her face. The last rays of the setting sun lit the moving water with hues of blue-red and orange. In the gauze of dusk just below her window floated a small fishing boat. There was a woman in it. Her head was tied up in a colourful scarf; she was bent over a stove. The boat swayed gently on the water, and Nalini wondered how the woman could cook in a pot that swayed so much. A small girl, her hair an array of shining blonde-brown curls, played at one end of the boat. She moved suddenly, making the boat sway precariously. The mother shouted in shrill Arabic. The little girl said something in reply.

To Nalini, unable to understand, it seemed as if she was protesting it was not her fault. And it wasn't really, because in her arms was a small, wriggling puppy which she was trying to pacify and hold steady. Nalini heard the woman call out some kind of instructions. In response, the little girl bent over, put the puppy down into the bottom of the boat and then sat down herself. Soon the boat had steadied, and was swaying as gently as before.

'I suppose I should sit still for a while too,' Nalini told herself, and moved her eyes away from the window. She stood up and looked for her slippers. She hadn't realised that, behind her, the room was in darkness. But before she could move across the room to switch on a light, there was a knock on the door. It was Mani Ram, one of the two Indian servants who were part of the Thapar household. He had a cup of tea on a tray in his hands. He switched on the light for Nalini, and she decided she would continue to sit in her bay window until she had drunk the tea.

'*Aji* said to have your tea quickly, and begin getting dressed. The guests will arrive at eight thirty. *Aji* said you should be ready by then,' said Mani Ram deferentially.

'Thank you, Mani Ram,' said Nalini. 'Tell *Aji* I shall be downstairs shortly.'

Mani Ram did not say anything, but moved quietly out of the room.

Nalini Thapar was the daughter of India's ambassador to Egypt, and had been in Cairo a year. As she well knew, being the daughter of a diplomat, a year was just about the real beginning of an assignment in a new world capital. It took that long to get to know people, to become familiar with the layout of the new city, to understand how its systems functioned, to find out with whom you could speak in English, and how much you would need of the local language for effective communication. It certainly took that long to settle down at home: first to wait endlessly for the container carrying your luggage, then to unpack your things and arrange them into some semblance of a pattern in which you could live for the next three years.

In other words, to feel settled.

In this latter aspect, the Thapar household would take a while. The Nalini that sat in the bay window of her bedroom trying to draw sustenance from the flowing waters of the Nile was not merely computer-tired. She was trying very hard to accommodate that absolute of Absolutes – the incontrovertible fact of Death. Her mother's death from cancer. Kanta Thapar had died over a year and a half earlier, one chilly November day in Copenhagen, a grey city in northern Europe, with its perpetual cold and elusive sun.

And with her death had changed the lives of each member of the Thapar family.

All through her childhood, Nalini had been a shy, over-protected child, brought up in a series of foreign capitals. One might think that travel almost since birth should have made her gregarious and outgoing. It had not. It was not that Nalini had found her father's periodic moves difficult. In fact, new homes, new schools, and new friends were, for her, exciting options throughout her childhood and school-going years. And she had usually adjusted, as it seemed to everybody, in a remarkably cool way. She was the first among her siblings to know what was expected of her and get her life going, especially in school.

But the moves had taken their toll in other ways. One of these was the unconscious construction of an almost adult, formal, outer shell beyond which no one could penetrate. Not the friends she giggled with in her early childhood, nor those with whom she spent her confiding, adolescent years. Also, although she duly entered the names and addresses of the friends left behind in an all-too-precious diary (and Nalini would take care to write to them all at least once a year), she shed few tears when it was time for partings. She had learned to steel herself against them well in advance. By the time the plane was boarded, Nalini would be looking ahead, wondering about the new city, and what the new house and school would be like. In fact, at these moments she was at her most controlled, shushing up her weeping younger brother and sister in soft, rational tones which left even her mother and father surprised.

When it was time to go to university, it was decided that

Nalini would return to New Delhi. She spent five years in the Miranda House hostel for girls, studying English Literature. It was then that she really let herself go, enjoying the fun-filled harum-scarum freshman year. She tried her hand at everything – debates, theatre, dance and quiz competitions – everything except sports. She became involved in community service. In her second year she joined the same Women's Empowerment Centre of which Maneka Mahajan, her enthusiastic room-mate, was already an active member.

Though she benefited greatly from being exposed to the real plight of Indian women in society through the WEC, its activities did not do much good for the sensitive Nalini. Much against Maneka's advice and exasperated warnings, she would find herself not only getting *too* involved in the plight of individual women but also getting personally affected. 'To be of help effectively is first to have a tough heart', is what Maneka always said. But Nalini found it hard to follow her friend's dictums. She would worry endlessly about the especially desperate cases, think about them day and night, and even begin to lose sleep over them. This not only rendered her hours at WEC ineffective but it also began to affect her academic work. Ultimately – and much to the disgust of Maneka who secretly thought her too squeamish for having lived too rarefied a life – she had to lessen her involvement with the affairs of the WEC.

Such suddenly discovered over-anxiety was not something Nalini was proud of. However, even as Maneka's involvement with women's issues intensified, Nalini self-consciously and deliberately disengaged herself and began to focus on her books. While Maneka continued to regale her daily with details of her interactions with incidents of injustice to women – as well as to rely on her for help on specific WEC tasks, duties and emergencies – Nalini began to take her work seriously.

For this she often became the object of derisive teasing by her friends. Why did she have to write out every single assignment when there was no real necessity to do so? Nalini would not even bother to answer such irrelevant questions. 'You do as you like; I will do as I like,' she would say to them, and tuck herself into one corner of the hostel room. She would request her room-mate, Maneka, not to make a noise, and get on with her assignment.

One could imagine that this might have made her some enemies. It did not. Everyone acknowledged that she had been schooled 'abroad' and that this had made her see things differently.

Nalini really enjoyed her years at university, and what they entailed for a young Indian girl growing up in the New Delhi of the eighties. During her years in foreign schools, India had always been projected as a distant, exotic land – the home of the wild, roaming elephants, hot, spicy food, and the Taj Mahal. Even though vacations with *Naanima* and *Daadima* had proved it not to be so, Nalini had always fallen in with the exotic-only representations of her motherland. But to be actually living and functioning in the bustling, pulsating capital city of New Delhi was to be aware of urban India in all its vivid, struggling, tactile reality.

Nalini learned quickly that living standards of other capitals (especially those in the western world) did not apply in a women's hostel in Delhi. But the close, bonding relationships, and a taken-for-granted sense of belonging more than made up for them. Nalini knew that the friends she made in her years at Miranda House would stay with her, whether she sent them New Year cards or not.

After she finished her Master's programme at Delhi University, Nalini found a job in a local advertising agency. From then on she began to live in one of Delhi's southern neighbourhoods. She had a wide circle of friends. Her erstwhile classmates remained in close touch with her. Some of her girlfriends got married, leaving the metropolis to follow their husbands; others found jobs and stayed with their parents; still others married and set up households in New Delhi. However, they all made it a point to visit Nalini frequently – a single girl who had rooms of her own for which she paid rent, and in whose small kitchen she could cook for herself and them. Nalini felt the significance of becoming financially independent. It was no small thing, considering how hard she had worked at persuading her parents that she was able to take care of herself, that she was sick of living the nomadic life, that she would like to strike roots in New Delhi, India, and do her own thing.

But the unexpected death of her mother changed everything. It meant being thrust suddenly into the role of a surrogate 'lady of the house' – her father's house. 'We would like to have you around, *beti*,' Gautam Thapar had said, looking at his daughter with loving apprehension. 'For a while, at least.' He had tried hard not to take her acquiescence for granted. She, who had just begun to taste the flavours of freedom, was being pulled away by Fate to take on responsibilities for which she was not yet ready, or even willing. But it had taken her only an instant to say, 'Of course, Papa.' And leave everything in New Delhi to move with the family to Cairo.

It was only afterwards, when the deed was done and the choice exercised, that she realised slowly what it would mean to surrender the independent, self-defining life to the needs of a younger brother then fourteen, and an even younger sister, only eight. Ajay and Minti. So innocent, open and carefree, they had taken their mother's death to heart. When homes changed every three years, it was Mother, and each other, who provided the still centre of existence. With her gone, how could any mansion anywhere come to seem like home? Nalini knew this and considered herself lucky that she had had a mother until she had finished growing up.

'You will stay with us in Cairo, won't you, *Didi*?' Minti had said, clutching at her so-much-older sister. 'What will we do without Ma?' Ajay had not said anything. But Nalini had seen him screwing up his mouth in an effort not to cry and to be a man. And when, all these months later, she still often found him lurking sadly in the corners of Bharat Bhavan, the huge mansion of a home on the banks of Cairo's Nile, Nalini knew she had done the right thing.

This did not, of course, help the passing of time, or the restless purposelessness of each continuing day. Sometimes, her feelings of ennui were more vehement, screaming out from within her in strong protest. Mission life had so few young people in it. All school leavers returned to India or went on to universities in the UK or USA. And those done with their education looked for jobs at home or else also in the UK or USA. It was so hard to make friends in a new place, especially within the context of the formalities of diplomatic life and the different language and culture of the country of assignment. 'Life should surely contain more than this,' Nalini would think, and at once feel guilty. Why was she not satisfied? She had everything, didn't she? She had a loving family, every member of which needed her. She lived in a beautiful home. And, she had a good enough job that kept her busy long hours. In fact, she was fortunate to have found it, considering the rules and regulations that governed the families of any Head of Mission abroad.

To help her remember these obvious advantages, she would look at the deep, muddy waters of the Nile as they flowed steadily northwards under her window, and tell herself she should try to follow their example: like the river, she should flow from day to day, even as the forms of life around it survived because of its life-giving bounty.

Taking a sip of the tea Mani Ram had brought, she shook her head to throw her long hair onto her back.

'I'm getting stupidly poetic! And depressed,' she said to herself, and shook her head free of the sudden influx of memories of her days in Delhi University. Ms Dutta, the poetry teacher, would surely have been pleased at her extended metaphoric comparisons between woman and water. Literature and life! In day-to-day living, however, metaphors remained metaphors.

They didn't really add up to much, except to make one wonder at the unrealistic absurdity of them all.

Nalini smiled cynically, and finished her tea. Casting a last look at the waters below, she stood up and moved away from the window even as she twisted her hair behind her head into an untidy but cooling knot. Though standing a clear five feet and six inches tall and blessed with a complexion a little clearer than that of ripened wheat, a longish face and a slender neck, Nalini was no beauty. But with defined dark brows, a clean hairline on a broad forehead, frank eyes and a slim nose, she had grown into a woman noticed even in a large gathering of people. This probably also had to do with the way she carried herself. Always the eldest, and 'Didi' to her siblings, the servants, and all the staff in her father's office, she had acquired a poise that belied her years. She had perfected the art of hiding under a calm surface all intense feelings – of anger, hurt or disquiet.

Also, Nalini did not always know what was expected of her. But she did her best, stepping into her new persona as well as she understood it. It had been hard for her, shouldering responsibilities not usually given to one so young. Moreover, life in a Mission had not helped. Its formality had given her an air of reserve hard to penetrate; and the sense of being a permanent alien in foreign lands often made her appear – quite falsely – snobbish and privileged.

However, when alone in her room Nalini relaxed, unconsciously allowing herself to slip out of the cloak of all her roles and duties. Her bay window reveries were her access to her real feelings, and she indulged them whenever she could. But now it was time she went to see what *Aji* was doing. It was almost 6.30 p.m. and the guests would be there in two hours. Slipping her feet into a pair of old kolhapuri slippers and stuffing a few pins into her coiled hair, she proceeded downstairs.

* * *

The Thapars were having a dinner party that night. For the first time, the Egyptian foreign secretary was visiting Bharat Bhavan, the official residence of the Indian Ambassador in Cairo. Nalini knew that it was an important evening, and wanted to make sure that everything was in order. But she also knew that it would not do much good to say so in the kitchen. *Aji*, the old family cook, would object if there was too much supervision and if too many questions were asked. Tall, sharp-nosed, and stiff-backed, with greying hair and a penchant for white, bordered saris, she had been with the Thapars twenty-one years. She knew the whole routine of party preparation like the lines on her hands. For her, all guests were of equal importance as far as her cooking skills were concerned – to have it otherwise was to admit that her cooking was better on some days, and not so good on others. That could never be, and Nalini knew better than to say anything that would cast doubt on the state of preparations for the evening.

'You've come?' *Aji* said to Nalini, as she entered the large spacious kitchen.

'Yes, dear *Aji*,' said Nalini cajolingly. She glanced around surreptitiously to see if everything was in order. At the same time, she looked for a reason to peep into each of the six or seven pots lined up on the counter without offending the dear old woman.

There was silence for a while.

'Mmm, everything smells so good,' Nalini said finally, looking directly at *Aji*, and daring her to object to her inspection. Smiling broadly, she lifted the lid of the rather large pot nearest her. Mutton korma fit for a king! She could sense *Aji*'s disapproving eyes boring through her back. But before the older woman could say anything sharp, Nalini said pre-emptively: 'I'm so hungry I could eat it all!'

Her words had the desired effect.

'Are you really? Shall I give you some in a plate, you know . . . just a little bit?' said *Aji*, all concern.

'Oh, no. No,' said Nalini looking away, and trying to hide

the smile on her face. 'I had a biggish lunch in the office. I really should not eat anything now. I'll wait till dinner ...'

As she said this, Nalini had looked into three more of the pans. Everything was, like every other time, quite in order. 'I should really inspect the dining and living rooms,' she told herself. The problems always lay there. But there, it was Mani Ram who was in charge. And he was a different entity altogether.

The evening went well. So her father said afterwards, walking tiredly up the winding staircase of Bharat Bhavan. What did 'well' mean? That the ambiance in the living room, dining room and terrace was stylish, and measured well with international standards; that the house's setting on the banks of the Nile was even better; that the food was good and served flawlessly; that the white wine was well chilled; the red, rich and urbane and served carefully at room temperature; and that the conversation, after a slow start, had become more than lively?

Probably. India and the Indians looked good that evening, and Nalini hoped that something worthwhile would emerge out of her father's plans for Indo—Egyptian collaboration on different issues and projects.

It was so quaint, Nalini could not help thinking, that even in the 1990s diplomats should be entertaining like this. She thought of the few 'parties' she had attended among her friends in New Delhi: carelessly put-together affairs, in which you were lucky if you got a plateful, and second helpings were never a viable option. Who wanted to spend hours cooking, when there were so many, other, more interesting things to do? But, of course, if someone did take the trouble, everybody would turn gourmand. Then they would eat till they were more than full, and savour every mouthful. As she had taken her place in the well-laid-out dining room of Bharat Bhavan, she had smiled privately as she looked down the table seating twenty-four of her father's guests.

It had sparkled with the silver and cut glass so lovingly collected by her mother. What would her friends back in New Delhi have thought of all this? She knew the answer all too well: that it was all bourgeois, pretentious, passé, and old fashioned.

And yet, in all the capitals of the world as she had known them, the traditions remained the same. And diplomatic life expected you to conform.

'So, how do you like Cairo?' Mohammed Younous had asked, interrupting Nalini's ruminations. He was the manager of a local bank, and was sitting on Nalini's right.

'Very much. There is a lot to see,' said Nalini politely.

'Have you been around much?'

'Not to all the sights yet. But I have seen some ...'

'Which is your favourite?'

'I suppose I should say the Pyramids. But, I really do like the Nile the best.'

'Ah, yes. The Nile. Our lifeline.'

'Yes it is, isn't it? We have many rivers in India. But I have never lived along the banks of any in the way I do here, and it is quite beautiful.'

'Yes, you're lucky to be here, in a charming house by the Nile. Not all Egyptians have that opportunity. Like your country, we have our share of the poor.'

'I am aware of that ... very much so,' said Nalini hastily, and wondered whether the banker realised that poverty could also lie in the heart.

But such things were not to be said. The banker wanted to know how she passed her days, and if she worked anywhere. Nalini found herself answering these questions for the hundredth time. She told him that she had a position in the offices of the *Al-Ahram Weekly*, and enjoyed her work.

'Have you ever thought of becoming a diplomat yourself?'

'Yes, I have. Dad — and many of his friends — feel that

I would do well. But I have always wanted to do something different. Back home in Delhi I had a job in advertising — I loved it.'

As she said this, Nalini involuntarily lowered her voice. She also glanced sideways, over the dim candlelight and sparkling china, towards where her father was sitting to make sure that he had not heard her. She did not want him to feel that her heart was in New Delhi, in the new-found world she had left behind.

But from the way his mouth tightened and his eyes narrowed, making more pronounced the crows' feet at their corners, Nalini knew that he had. Immediately she wished she had never said any such thing, or ventured into any discussion about the future. Ma's death was too new, too recent, and the wounds of her absence still open and raw.

How insensitive and foolish she had been to have even thought of saying so much. And so selfish, thinking only of her own feelings!

After this, try as she did, Nalini could not eat any more. For the rest of the evening, she moved around like a zombie amongst her father's guests, waiting for the evening to end.

Letters from Home

At the Indian Embassy in Cairo, Sunday was a day of some excitement. It was the first day of the working week (after the Friday and Saturday weekend), when the Diplomatic Bag was opened, and the mail sorted out and distributed among the various families of the Embassy. Along with letters came Indian newspapers and magazines, weeklies and dailies – the most tangible links with home. Sitting at her desk one Sunday morning in the office, two weeks after the party, Nalini wondered what letters awaited her on her return home. Who, of all the people she had written to, had bothered to reply?

Not too many, she was sure, and then chided herself for being so demanding. How often had she written to friends and family living abroad? 'I really should not expect so much,' she told herself. But in this state between exile and foreign travel, every Sunday evening's bundle was sustenance and a potential lifeline with home.

Later that evening, as the Thapar family gathered in the living room of Bharat Bhavan, Nalini opened the bundle of letters tied with the typical ragged string so commonly used in the offices of the Government of India. As she did so, she prepared herself to be forgiving of the silences from New Delhi. Her share of the mail was considerable: there was one letter from her ex-boss; one from her ex-landlady (what did she want now?

She had paid all her dues before leaving, including her share of the electricity bill); one from *Naanima*, her grandmother (who was no doubt wondering how she was getting on without Mummy); one from Rhea Jacob (so she had written, at last); and one from Maneka Saxena, her ex-room-mate and dear friend. This last letter Nalini turned over, looking at it carefully. She examined the address written on the back. South Extension. So Maneka had moved, thought Nalini, and knew that this letter would be long and full of news.

'Not bad for one day,' she said aloud, holding her letters aloft in triumph. 'I've not been forgotten . . .'

Gautam Thapar looked at his daughter fondly, an indulgent smile softening somewhat the habitually heavy expression on his face. He was actuely aware of how difficult it had been for Nalini to wrench herself away from New Delhi, and fill her mother's – quite undesired, he well knew – diplomatic shoes. In this decade of the 90s, many diplomats' spouses who were well qualified and professionals in their own right were chafing under the burden of diplomatic duties, and often refrained from performing them. Not only did Nalini as a daughter do her best to do everything that was required as conscientiously as she could, but she was also very far – unlike many spouses – from complaining about them. She never chose to say – as did so many of the other wives – that her contributions went unrecognised by the Foreign Office back at home, or that she was not paid for what she did. She really was doing a good job of it all . . .

However, the fact remained that all this was also making her serious, even dour. Was this aspect of her personality perhaps the result of her concealing her real feelings? Feelings of a more negative nature which she had chosen, for the time being, not to express? Gautam Thapar wondered about this, but found himself quite helplessly unable to do – or even say – anything about it. The letters from Delhi had, suddenly, changed her mood and his heart lightened at the sight of her smiling after what seemed to be many days. However, before he could remark on this, they were joined by Ajay and Minti who, after making excited inquiries, moved away disappointed that no one had written to them. Father and daughter stood a moment and sorted through the magazines and newspapers. They were divided according to what each preferred, and were exchanged later in the evening.

Nalini bore her quota upstairs, and immediately headed to her favourite place. Quickly, she curled up on the cushions in her bay window. Below it the Nile flowed by, silently, inevitably. But today she had no time for its sunset moods. Today she was going home, to the dusty plains of New Delhi celebrating the arrival of the monsoon. She opened the least important letter first. The one from her ex-boss was pleasantly formal, asking briefly about her welfare and informing her about some benefits accruing. It ended by his saying that her position was open for her if she ever thought of returning to India. The one from the landlady was also short, informing her tersely about her share of a water bill, still unpaid. After all these months? Nalini was surprised, almost sure that she had paid it before leaving. The letter from *Naanima* was warm and loving. She read it slowly and carefully, savouring every word.

> ... *I hope you are looking after yourself also, my dear. Don't be too caring of the others and forget your own needs. You are only young once, and I would not want too many of these years to fly by without you getting something out of them for yourself. Are you enjoying your work? You did not write anything about this in your last letter. In our days, letters were special things, and people used them to express their deepest feelings. I still try and do this in my letters. But you keep yours far away from the real state of things, don't you? I know letter writing is a dying art, but do indulge your Naanima once in a while, especially now that your mother is not around. I still am, you know ... quite unfairly ...*

Dear *Naanima*, thought Nalini, wiping her eyes quickly. A

bitter-sweet letter, evoking memories best forgotten. Nalini folded her grandmother's letter carefully and slipped it back into its envelope. She could see her clearly: a bright-eyed woman in crisp cotton saris whose perky, cheerful ageing had taken a blow with the death of her daughter. Almost eighty years old herself, she felt responsible for Nalini, asked by Fate to leave behind her own life and become a surrogate mother for her younger siblings. 'Nalini is a good girl . . . too good for her own sake,' she had taken to telling her friends. And she should not spend her youth waiting for life in her father's house.

Nalini put away her grandmother's letter and turned to the one from her friend Maneka. The fat envelope took a while to open, for Maneka had double sealed it with gum and scotch tape. At last, the letter was in her hands – pages and pages of it.

'Who said letter writing was a dying art?' asked Nalini aloud, and twisted into a more comfortable position to read through Maneka's news of Delhi.

27th June 1992
Flat no 4, 4th floor
273 South Extension
New Delhi – 110051

My dear Nuns,
This is written in a hurry, so don't look for any clarity. How are you? I hope you are well. I have a lot to tell you. But first things first.
I will be visiting you in my December holidays. I spoke to the Principal about whether I could add on another two weeks before the Christmas vacation, which begins somewhere in the middle of December. She has agreed, and I shall have a whole month to explore Egypt with you. I hope these dates are convenient. Shall let you know the exact date and hour of arrival nearer the time. Egypt Air is giving me a good discount. As you know, they only fly out to Cairo from Bombay. So, I will catch a train from Delhi to Bombay, and fly out from there.

I haven't decided anything about Ahmer yet. Maybe I will leave him with Mummy. Then you and I will be free to talk and see Cairo. I am saving every paisa these days to enjoy my holiday. But I guess I will depend on you and your dad to feed me during my stay with you!

Now for the news.

Sahayata *is getting along well. Thank God for the Miss Nanavatis of this world. 74 Hauz Khas now looks decent. Not that that is the most important thing for the kind of work we are doing. But at least now we have hassle-free water and electricity connections, and things to sit on — all thanks to our rich benefactress. Women have got to know of our changed address, and have started coming in droves. At the moment, we have nine inmates who absolutely refuse to go home to get beaten. Some even fear for their lives, so we have given them temporary shelter. They cook and wash for themselves.*

Our fame is spreading, and all this means a lot of work. We have added a consulting lawyer and doctor, who volunteer free time with us for two hours every alternate day. I have said it often, and I am going to say it again: Delhi really needs such places. When you see the women come in — so thin and emaciated, and totally done in — it makes my blood boil! What rotters men are. One woman could hardly stand upright. She had been sexually abused by her own husband, and probably by other men too — and with his consent, I'm sure. She has no family in Delhi, and did not know who to turn to. She doesn't talk at all — just sits and stares from her corner of the room. The only thing she says clearly is that she will not leave Sahayata. *It's pathetic. She is undoubtedly pregnant and we will soon be landed with a baby.*

We are thinking about what to do. You should see her, Nunni. She makes me so angry. We are so lucky: you all looked after, and protected still; and I economically independent, and on my own ... As for them, I can only say there is so much to be done.

The other thing I have to tell you is that Sahayata *has very 'oomphy' neighbours! Or so you would say when you look at them and their beautifully done-up house. But they turned out to be no different from any other woman-destroying families that seem to abound in New Delhi. Their daughter-in-law of only three months was found dead a few days ago. A young thing — she must have been hardly twenty. A supposed suicide. She was found hanging from the ceiling fan; her neck tied to it with a* chunni. *Supposedly pink in colour. I met her briefly the day we were moving furniture into* Sahayata. *Nice haircut and super clothes — svelte and all, but rather innocent looking. A lot like you (!) though you seem deeper. She said 'Hi!' to me in friendship, but I regret to say that I was rather cold and critical.*

And now she is dead . . .

I was told the next day when I arrived at Sahayata *that her tongue hung out, that the blacks of her eyes had disappeared into the whites, and her jeans were wet in the crotch . . . can you imagine it all? Her neck is supposed to have been broken. Their house was full of people for days afterwards. The cremation was the very next afternoon after her death, and her mother-in-law — an awful, big-busted and big-diamonded woman — went around conducting the proceedings. It was Tanvi's (the girl's name is Tanvi) mother who could not stop crying. In fact, she was hysterical. She kept wailing out strange things — things like 'maar diya, hai mere Ram, maar diya'.*

I have to tell you that, by the afternoon, everyone at Sahayata *got very suspicious. I was too. I sought out her mother and questioned her. But she said that they had been treating her daughter well. It was hard to get a coherent answer from her, but she did say there were no dowry problems either. I asked her about her son-in-law, and she went even more hysterical, saying that he was a gem, and that no one should suspect him of anything. By this time a crowd had gathered around her, asking other questions.*

On the fateful day, the daughter-in-law had spent the morning with her mother — apparently, the mother-in-law had had a card party or something in the afternoon, and the poor girl was too scared to join the old hags. She returned to 73 Hauz Khas only in the evening, after fetching some clothes from the tailor's — her mother-in-law's blouses or something (these rich women and their clothes!) — and that was the last anyone in the house saw of her. She was found dead by her husband when he returned from work late that night.

I must say that the young man, recently returned from America, seems very fishy to me. The dead girl was so much younger than he was — don't you, my dear Nunni, ever get involved with these America-returned guys, and their question-mark pasts! They could be up to anything! He looked quite shaken at the time of the funeral, though. We saw it all, from over the wall. Quite a sight it was — the dead girl, Tanvi, dressed in her bridal sari, and the mother-in-law presiding over the ceremonies. The latter looked haggard (for once without her make-up, I'm sure), and also quite determined — as if she wanted to get it all over with. She really is a huge woman and must have made a frightening mother-in-law. The way she went around ordering everyone!

There was no sign of the father-in-law. He is supposed to have been out of the country. They obviously did not wait for his return to conduct the cremation. This has made all of us very suspicious, and we are investigating. Who knows, but this Tanvi may have been murdered — bumped off. They have not found any suicide note. The police are also investigating. But I am sure they will get away with it. They managed to keep their photos out of the newspapers — none have appeared so far. Even the write-up was just one small paragraph at the bottom of one of the inside pages in some newspapers. Others did not carry it at all. They're rich, you see, and have good old 'influence' . . .

We at Sahayata have seriously thought of filing a public interest litigation on behalf of the dead young thing. But we have not yet found any concrete evidence that it was a dowry death. Also, her parents are proving to be very uncommunicative. It is obvious that they also want the whole affair to be hushed up. 'She is dead now . . . how will any laws or lawsuit bring her back?' is what her mother said when I suggested it the first time. And now she won't talk at all . . .

Oh, God! It makes me so sick!

What's the difference between poor Tanvi and the woman who just sits in the corner at Sahayata and won't talk? Just her hair, smart trousers, and the fact that she is dead . . . completely dead. At least the woman sitting in the corner is alive. Now you see how much we need Sahayata?

I am seriously thinking of giving up my job. The work at Sahayata is more satisfying than teaching those silly, inane, giggling, middle-class girls who join the Economic Honours course with such gusto, but then give it all up within three months. You do know what I mean, don't you? But I can't quit because I need the money. Sahayata does not have much yet. Not enough to pay us for the work we do. If you were here, you could help us too.

Would you, though? I sometimes wonder . . .

So much for news of my so-called life. Ahmer is fine. As you can see, I have moved house. This is so much more convenient, though it is small. I hear that Bhasker is marrying again . . . good for him. And her! Some woman who runs a radical women's magazine. I bet she does not know what she is in for. I, of course, am still 'heart whole and fancy free'!

What of you? Hope you are not moping too much. I will only say 'Please don't' . . . mope, I mean. Other expressions of sympathy etc. sound so trite in letters. But you know what I mean. Maybe it is time you found a nice Egyptian somebody. In the Pharaonic mould, perhaps — except weren't their queens more famous than them, the Pharaohs?!

I have to go now. I'm going to post this on my way to Tanvi's mother. We have decided to ask some questions, now that all the ceremonies are officially completed. Arti Chug is coming with me. Shall keep you posted.

Write soon,

Love,

Maneka

P.S. Manju is fine. She hardly comes to Sahayata. Is still mooning over her Anil. That girl, she gets me . . . And as for Arti Chug: she talks more and does less. Tell me what else you want to know and I will tell all . . . in my next letter.

'Phew,' thought Nalini, pushing back her hair, folding up the five pages and stuffing them back into their envelope with some difficulty. That was some letter! Maneka was Maneka still. Her active involvement with the Women's Empowerment Centre of their college days had become an even more serious business with *Sahayata*. And her broken marriage had certainly not broken her spirit. In fact, on the surface it seemed more animated than before, its strength all too visible in her intense concern for the plight of women that *Sahayata* was trying to rectify. But she had not said much about Bhasker, or even Ahmer. Nalini wondered about her friend's true feelings. The story of the dead woman next door had masked them completely.

She turned the letter over in her hands. She would have to read it again to soak in all the details. That was New Delhi for you – and Maneka always had the knack of being in the middle of things. Had circumstances not changed, so would she herself have been – not here, on the peripheral distances of Cairo, but right there in the centre, where things happened and you were part of them, and what you did was a contribution to the way things were. Nalini felt herself there, on New Delhi's streets, with their throngs of people rushing to and fro, doing all the things they had to do. They were there, in her mind's eye, weaving through perilous traffic, crossing roads, catching buses at chaotic bus stops, walking the pedestrian walkways, stopping at the fruit vendors to pick up the odd banana, orange or guava, singing the latest film songs oblivious of others around, shouting out a *namaste* in greeting to the taxi man sleeping on a cot under the tree, taking a break from the afternoon heat ...

Nalini did not know how long she sat there with her real self back in New Delhi. The sun set slowly over the waters of the Nile, but she was oblivious of its passing. One by one, the evening lights came on until, on the opposite bank across the waters, the festoon of bulbs between lamp-posts, almost invisible during the day, sparkled into life.

Somewhere in the distance, the sounds of Egyptian music hung on the air. They came nearer and nearer, until the noise of singing and laughter seemed right there, just under where Nalini sat in her bay window. It was a group of young revellers in one of Cairo's larger boats, out on the waters of their beloved river, celebrating something of importance. Their gaiety floated over the waves, and pulled Nalini out of her reverie. She looked towards the boat. It was a bridal party. She could see the bride standing with her groom, leaning against what seemed to be the fragile railings of the boat. Suddenly, the cool Mediterranean breezes blowing southwards lifted the bride's white, embroidered veil, making it billow out over the water. There was a squeal of hysterical laughter, which drowned for a few seconds the sounds of the music. Nalini saw the groom and his friends lean outwards and pull the white length to the bride. She turned around, making the long train of white lace netting wind around her. Loud, warning words in guttural Arabic swayed towards her over the water, to be followed, an instant later, by the sounds of relieved laughter. The groom put his arms around his bride, and their faces came close to each other. Nalini knew that that was as far as their embrace would go, given that the couple was surrounded by their friends. But even from as far as she sat, Nalini could sense their longing. A few seconds later they had parted, and all was in control again. The music took over, until its sounds receded as the boat flowed northwards, way beyond the bridge with the railway line, after which it disappeared where Nalini could see it no further.

'*El-Nil gameel*, the beautiful Nile,' said Nalini softly to herself, feeling suddenly restless and ashamed for being so ungrateful to this land where she had dwelt these last months. She saw the river flow past, slowly and silently, seemingly winking at her through the reflections of the myriad of light bulbs hanging along its banks. 'This is home, too, you know ... and has been for many over eons, who have tasted of my waters. And you, who live within my reach, so close ... why yet so far?' it seemed to be saying.

'This is my home now,' she told herself firmly, and picked up the bundle of newspapers recently arrived from New Delhi. After Maneka's letter, reading the Indian newspapers seemed flat and unexciting. Her mind went back to what Maneka had written. The death of ... what was her name? ... Tanvi. The death of Tanvi.

And Nalini found herself worrying about the dead girl much as in old times when she and Maneka had worked in the WEC together. She immediately conjured up a mental picture of an unhappy young girl who had 'chosen' to commit suicide to escape from being continually harassed, even tortured. She herself could identify quite easily with feelings of intense sorrow and unhappiness. But, she found it somewhat harder to imagine so desperate a state of mind that would call for the drastic act of suicide. All the women she remembered having worked with had often thought about putting an end to their lives but had never had the courage to actually carry it out ...

And then there was Maneka's interpretation of the whole affair ... A dowry murder?

Nalini wondered whether any of the newspapers in front of her would contain the account of the death. She looked at the bundle. It contained newspapers only of the last seven days. Surely her death had taken place earlier? Now that she thought of it, Maneka had not mentioned any dates.

She looked through each issue of *The Times of India* carefully, wondering at events and their reportage. Hard news on the front page, with the central photograph; human interest stories inside somewhere, unless overly disastrous when they might make front page. Nalini wondered whether a bride's unexpected death deserved front-page coverage. But then she recalled that the husband's family had been influential – 'oomphy' Maneka had called them – and managed to keep everything out of the focus of the media.

Soon she had finished reading the newly arrived pile. No mention anywhere.

It must have happened earlier, thought Nalini. A few seconds later, she was rifling through old copies of *The Times of India* and *The Hindustan Times* from the stack in the bottom of her cupboard.

A lone death of a young girl. Why was she so interested in this Tanvi? Was it merely the result of an expatriate's Sunday homesickness for life in New Delhi? Or was it the direct outcome of her many dissatisfactions with her own life in Cairo? Or was it, really, because she saw Tanvi's fate as the potentially typical consequence of women's choices exercised under the heavy burdens of obligation? A fatal consequence in this case ... because she had hanged herself from the ceiling with a pink *chunni*; her tongue sticking out; her eyes glazed; and her jeans wet at the crotch ...

Oh God! It was terrible!

Ah! There it was ...

Young bride commits suicide

New Delhi, Wednesday, 22 June: A young woman, named Tanvi Malhotra, aged 20, is reported to have hanged herself from the ceiling fan in her bedroom, in the posh locality of Hauz Khas in South Delhi yesterday. Initial reports have ruled out the possibility of it being a dowry death. The young woman's parents, residents of Vasant Vihar, have denied any estrangement between husband and wife, married only three months ago. The death has baffled both families. Investigations are continuing.

A brief account of a horrendous act tucked away at the bottom of page seven. Just another of those inexplicable deaths that make for human interest stories in a newspaper. Poor Tanvi! And what of her husband? Did he have anything to do with it? And what of her in-laws? Maneka obviously thought them guilty.

As she folded the newspaper and put it away, Nalini wondered idly if the girl's husband had indeed been responsible for his wife's death. Maneka had, naturally, assumed so. She had also suggested that young men like him enjoyed exercises in male power. And it made no difference if they were poor or rich, merely literate or formally educated. Nalini knew that men across the board could be unthinking and cruel. The few times she had volunteered at the fledgling *Sahayata* had shown this to be so. Nevertheless, she found it strangely hard to picture a young man, recently returned from America, sitting somewhere, and gloating over the death of his young Tanvi.

The more she thought about it, the more unlikely it seemed. But then, she told herself, you never could tell. There were, after all, the sordid life-patterns of the rich ... A scene of typically hateful in-laws and unprotesting sons passed through her mind. And she shuddered. As Maneka Saxena had often pointed out to her — 'These men and their mothers!'

An English Breakfast

In the cooler climes of another continent, a mother and a son sat in a hotel room with the remains of a breakfast lying between them. It was not the typically dull Continental one of dry bread rolls — or a half-sweet Danish — and coffee, but the especially ordered English repast of eggs, lightly browned sausages (the Malhotra family did not like bacon in any form), hot buttered toast, followed by a pot of freshly brewed Earl Grey tea. Though all this was invitingly displayed on a tray placed on a round table, and lit by a sunbeam of a weak London sun, not much had been eaten.

Only the teacups had been used. The one held by the mother, Pammi Malhotra, was empty, with a few tea leaves marking the dregs. Rattan's cup was still half full, and sat forlornly on the glass-topped table, slowly getting cold. Rattan himself stood at the window looking out, his tall slim frame wrapped in a dressing gown of warm brown wool. Watching him from where she was sitting upright on the sofa, Pammi noted the burdened stoop of his shoulders and the over-grown hair at the nape of his neck. 'He needs a haircut,' she thought, but knew better than to say this aloud. She could hardly say such things now, though lately she had wanted to more and more. She had to remind herself that, in spite of all that had happened — and all the hurt he, her son, had suffered — Rattan was a grown man who knew what he had to do, and when he had to do it. It had been this way, ever since he had left home and gone to the USA to study and work. And that had been more than a decade ago.

And now it was even more so.

The silence in the room stretched into long minutes. Pammi could not help but keep looking at her son. Her eyes bored through his back in an effort to get him to talk to her. But Rattan refused to turn around, or behave as if he was aware of her presence in the room. At last, when Pammi found that she could bear the silence no longer, she began to speak.

'You didn't eat anything . . .' she said in tones of deliberate neutrality. 'You should, you know . . . and try not to keep thinking of what happened.'

There was no visible response to this from her son. He continued to stand still by the window with his back to her, seemingly engrossed in the weather outside. Under his intent gaze, the already weak sun was soon covered over by a dark cloud, turning what had looked to be a promising day into a wet morning. From his vantage point on the sixteenth floor, Rattan could see London's red buses make their way slowly down the street. There was one, as Rattan noticed with detachment, which had stopped to let off passengers. It stood still for a few seconds, and then began to lumber slowly down the busy street. By the time it had wound its way down to the very end, dark clouds had gathered, and changed the day.

'So it is going to rain after all,' mused Rattan, and waited for the drizzle to begin. Typical English weather, with rain even in July. Under his eyes, the pedestrians quickly opened out their umbrellas, and soon the street was full of upturned black canopies, looping down the pavement. They were all held at an angle, against the blast of a chilly wind, and together gave the pavements on either side of the street a bizarre, lop-sided look. A mother walked her toddler carefully across the street on a zebra crossing. She was having a hard time holding the hand of her little boy in one hand, and with the other, was using her handbag to hold down the front of her flapping raincoat. She seemed young, with short, closely cropped hair, which was dampening in the drizzle.

'Mother and son,' thought Rattan. 'Like me and Ma here . . .' But the parallel made him wince. For the young mother visible from the window had immediately also reminded him of Tanvi, and all that might have been. In the following few moments that he stood at the window of the room, Rattan lived through the entire vista of his short, married life with Tanvi – till the very end, when he had untied her heavy, dead form from the ceiling fan in their bedroom. And shuddered involuntarily.

Whatever he did, and wherever he went, he could not rid his mind of this sight. Even now he could recall vividly the feel of the last cold touch of her face on his . . . And the memory nicked him with a piercing intensity.

As he stood by the window unmoving, he re-lived the morning hours he had spent with Tanvi before leaving for work on that fateful day. They had been amicable enough, with Tanvi having woken a little before him. She had lain still for a full half-hour beside him – 'Watching you wake up,' she had said. And he remembered having remarked, teasingly, that it wasn't possible that she, an interminable fidget, could have lain still in their bed for so long. She had protested that she could, and had done so, and had spent the time watching the dark scar-like birthmark on his right shoulder. She had even touched it gently, he remembered her saying, with fingertips so light that they hadn't woken him. He remembered having pulled her to him on hearing this, feeling suddenly an intense love for his new, little bride . . .

A sudden movement on the sofa behind him brought Rattan back into the present. He breathed in deeply, and prepared himself for his mother's attempt at conversation that he knew would, inevitably, follow.

'Are you sure you won't eat any of this? Shall I ask for it to be cleared away . . . ?' asked Pammi.

And Rattan, loth to enter the unpleasant present, grunted a 'yes' in reply. His voice, as it emerged from his reluctant throat, sounded harsh and dismissive.

Immediately, he felt impatiently ashamed. There really was no need for him to be so rude, he told himself, when all his mother was doing was being solicitous. He turned around, his face dark-ringed and unshaven, to look at her. She had turned to the phone, and was calling Room Service. Her face, at an angle from his line of vision, was gaunt and strained.

He looked at his mother again. She had stood up from the sofa, and was moving around the room, a ghost-like figure in a dull dressing gown in beige silk. Rattan noted that she looked thinner. 'It couldn't have been easy for her too, given everything, especially the standing of the family in society,' thought Rattan, and moved closer to her.

'I must shave and shower,' he said aloud. 'And go out. I can't stay here.'

Pammi looked at her son anxiously, her right hand twitching unconsciously around the knot of her dressing-gown tie at her waist. She felt she should say something, but didn't quite know what. Rattan guessed her difficulty.

'I need to get some cash. I'll be back for lunch,' he continued, his voice softening a little.

'Good,' said Pammi relieved, her wan, un-made-up face matching almost the dullness of her gown. 'By the way, what did you say to your father last night?'

'Nothing. What was there to say? I merely agreed to what he suggested. I have to present myself at the personnel office of the Bechtal Corporation for an interview tomorrow at noon. That's all,' said Rattan in a voice that dug the abyss of bewilderment.

'Oh, good,' said Pammi again. 'I hope you get the job. It will be best for you to live out of India for a few years. Till things settle down. I mean ... you know how people are, and how they talk ...'

'Yes, I know,' said Rattan interrupting bitterly, his

words a rasping staccato. 'Especially women. "There goes Rattan Malhotra," they say. "The one whose wife died on him. Committed suicide, huh?" ... I know they all think I killed her ... was mean to her ... beat her, et cetera. Oh, God! Just let's forget it, shall we?'

As he said this, he disappeared into the bathroom. Pammi was left staring at his retreating back with a look of anguish on her face.

Soon she was enveloped in a dull, lonely silence.

Half an hour later, Rattan was walking the same wet streets he had been watching from the high windows of his hotel room. The wind had risen, and its chill bit into his neck over the collar of his raincoat. To anyone watching, he would have appeared as one of London's innumerable cosmopolitans. But while the others walking the streets seemed to be going about their business purposefully, Rattan Malhotra's tall frame had a bowed, lost appearance. His face was flushed by the chilly wind, his brow puckered by some irresolute anxiety, and his eyes had a faraway, distant look.

Rattan was, indeed, far away – from himself and all the others walking beside him. A variety of cars hissed by on the wet tarmac. As he moved away from the wet edges of the busy street, his mind was walking moodily through the great parade ground of his past. And what a parade it had been! If nothing else, the last two decades of his life had been full of change – of travel, colour, people, and experience. He had had just about two adult years back in India, and now he would have to live outside again. And to think he had ever liked an expatriate existence! He wondered about his interview at the Bechtal Corporation the next day. He was sure that his father had used one of his many 'contacts' in the world of international business. The thought made him smile bitterly.

So it had come to this: it had become too risky to leave

his future only to the strengths of his personal curriculum vitae! And his father must have ensured that the job he found would be one outside India, and the USA. There were too many people who knew him in both places. There they could easily find out about him and his past.

Find out about Tanvi.

As he squelched along London's wet streets, Rattan wondered for the hundredth time what had happened with Tanvi. He tried, in his mind, to re-create every single moment he had shared with her. And, once again, could find no reason for her to have taken so drastic a step. The more he thought about her hanging from the ceiling fan of their bedroom, the more unreal the whole episode seemed to become. What had been on her mind? Why had she done what she had done? He could find no answers. And now, a whole month after the event, he became intensely aware of the possibility that he could not really have known her.

The thought was baffling. And, more than baffling, it was mortifying.

Rattan went back to the beginnings of their relationship. A few conversations and queries in the Gymkhana Club among a small group of women seemed to have decided the match between them. He asked himself for the thousandth time why his mother had been so adamant about Tanvi being the right choice for him. 'She'll suit you nicely,' he remembered her saying, and wondered why he himself had agreed so readily.

This last question worried him more than any other. The only answer he could give himself was that he had probably felt lonely, especially after all the women he had left behind in America. It was so much harder to have female company in India without being misunderstood, or setting up a whole lot of unnecessary expectations which were difficult to deal with. He thought of all the girls he had known in the USA — beginning with Meghan in the early years of his university life – and wondered what they would say if they heard what had happened to him.

He was sure that they would all have laughed. They might even have mocked him for they had always complained that there was a part of him that he never gave them!

He remembered vividly a woman named Cynthia Jackson. She had worked very closely with him on his first job. In one angry moment after their frenzied lovemaking, she had burst out in exasperation: 'You bastard! You'll just go back to that damned country of yours. There is no point in making a commitment to you!'

Rattan remembered protesting loudly and vehemently at the time but admitting, in retrospect, that Cynthia, astute as she was, was right about not finding his denials very convincing. He had always known that he would return to India to live and work, and would never allow anything to seriously distract him from that resolve. He – and probably Cynthia too – knew that he would never marry any of the women he had known in America.

Pulling the collar of his raincoat high behind his neck, Rattan thought of his greatly successful father. He had always been in awe of Noni. But he also saw him as a great sport – as one who had always been encouraging and supportive. He had allowed him, his only son, enough room and time to do his own thing before returning to join the family business. When Rattan thought of other young people like himself (management trainees from the best Indian universities) – of how hard they worked, and how anxious they were to please – he thought himself lucky to have so comfortable a professional niche waiting for him. He could never forget that he had been the same as them in his apprentice years – working hard in the lower rungs of corporate America, and wondering whether, like them, he would ever make it to the top.

Noni Malhotra was already at the top, and had been so for many years.

When he had heard of Tanvi's death, he had dropped

everything, taken the quickest flight back from Frankfurt and returned home as soon as possible. He had been in time for Tanvi's *chautha* ceremonies. From the moment he had landed at the Indira Gandhi International Airport, he had taken over, making sure that the rituals went smoothly, and that the police and the media were dealt with. Rattan knew that persuasion of more than one kind had been resorted to with both, and was grateful that, distraught as he was, he had been spared their merciless probings.

It was only two days after the *chautha*, when all the relatives had gone, and all the ceremonies were over, that his father sat and talked with him. Even then, he had not asked or said much. He had only inquired whether he knew any reason why Tanvi should have wanted to kill herself. Rattan recalled how he had silently shaken his head. His father had looked at him searchingly, not said anything, but had hugged him close.

Later, he had told him quietly to do his best to forget it all.

It had not been easy. Condolence letters and visits from friends and relatives had only made it worse. The most difficult people to face had been Tanvi's parents. When with them, he had remained silent, speaking only once as he had hugged his mother-in-law.

'I loved your daughter, and I did nothing to hurt her. I swear by God, and all that I hold dear ...'

But that was all he had ever said, because Tanvi's mother had begun weeping louder than before, her sobs rising hysterically and drawing the attention of everyone standing around. In fact, every time they had met subsequently, she had always hugged him closely even as she wept uncontrollably.

'Oh my son, my dearest Rattan! What can I say ... whatever can I say ... What should I say to you ...' she would moan repeatedly.

As he walked blindly down Oxford Street, her words echoed in Rattan's ears. They were his most vivid memory whenever he thought of the days following Tanvi's death. As he walked the length of the wet London street, he wondered what exactly Mrs Madan had meant. He always felt, as he did again now, that her words were full of grief, and even pity for him. But they were also faintly accusatory. Of what exactly, he could never really understand. Surely his mother-in-law did not think that he had driven Tanvi to killing herself? He remembered how he had tried to reassure her, to convince her that, as far as he knew, he had done nothing to make her unhappy.

But when he began to do so, she had cut him short.

'My dear *beta*, my dear Rattan! Whatever shall I say to you! What can anyone say? It must be fated . . . and we should accept it . . . Or else, there will be hell to pay . . .' she had said brokenly, and begun crying.

So immersed was Rattan in the still unreal memories of his past, that he quite forgot what he had set out to do. It took him a few more yards of walking to collect himself, and recall what his destination and purpose was. Both came to him ultimately. Soon he was encashing traveller's cheques at the nearest bank. This was quickly done, and a few minutes later, he was back on the streets. The time was sometime after noon, and the rain was still falling. It was too early to return to the hotel, and much too early to face his mother again.

Yes, much too early.

Rattan returned to Oxford Street and began walking again, seemingly intent on window-shopping. But the shining glass panes blurred before his eyes. He thought of his mother waiting for him so they could eat lunch together. She had lost a lot of weight recently, and lived on edge all the time – as if constantly on the alert to face anyone, anything. The entire month they had been in Delhi after Tanvi's death, her insomnia had become a real problem. But not once in those days had she agreed to take any of the sedatives that the doctors had prescribed to calm her nerves.

'I can't afford to just sleep through it all ... through the aftermath,' she had said, more than once.

When Rattan had asked what more she thought would happen now that the worst was over, she had been enigmatic in her reply.

'You never know ... a young, newly wed bride's death is no joke. Anything can happen, especially now that *Sahayata* has moved in next door.'

The thought of the women in *Sahayata* made Rattan flinch in anger. They had certainly not made it easy for him, his mother, or the entire Malhotra household. He thought of the way they had gathered outside the locked front gates and yelled '*Nari hatya nahi chalegi*' as loudly and vehemently as they possibly could. They had also thrown stones, some of which had pelted down the driveway and broken the window-panes of the living room. He remembered his mother having blazed with anger at how their loud shouting had attracted almost the entire neighbourhood to gather in front of 73 Hauz Khas. She called the police, who had worked only half-heartedly to disperse the crowd of shouting gawkers. In fact, the entire Malhotra family had felt that the inspector leading the small posse of constables had been somewhat insolent, barking his instructions in a smirking 'I-know-better' sort of way. He seemed to know the women of *Sahayata* quite well, standing familiarly near them, speaking all the while in low, conspiratorial tones.

All this had suggested an understanding that did not augur well for the Malhotras. And sure enough, the woman with the waist-length hair and arrogant face had shown an antagonism that had been almost visceral. 'You are all like that, you men,' she had screamed. 'You claim to be innocent all the time, but are rotters inside. You see women as sex objects, or else milk them and their parents for dowry ...'

It was only when Rattan had heard the *Sahayata* woman scream out the word 'dowry' so loudly that he realised for the first time that Tanvi's suicide had the potential of being interpreted as a dowry death. Walking down London's Oxford Street a whole month after that awful morning, Rattan could not help but recall his own sense of complete shock at that possibility. Dowry? From Tanvi's parents? From those good, god-fearing, simple people? He looked back over the privileged life he had always lived, and could not believe that anyone could imagine the Malhotras of 73 Hauz Khas being accused of having asked for dowry from the family of a daughter-in-law.

But the bushy-haired, arrogant woman had gone on and on: screaming, swearing and cursing.

Eventually, all this had made his mother angry – so blazingly angry that she had quite lost herself and screamed back. And cursed them repeatedly. In between her curses, she had taken to telling all the interested bystanders present that she had always known that, from the moment it moved in next door, *Sahayata* would make trouble for the neighbourhood. 'Ask Urmil,' she had said repeatedly, addressing no one in particular. 'Ask her if I did not predict it that fateful day when we were playing cards . . .'

Cards?

Even after a month Rattan could not understand what cards had to do with anything. He had only known the fact of his mother's hate-filled face, which, as he recalled, had quite shocked him. She had looked so strong and purposeful in her venom that it had crossed his mind that she could, at that moment, have killed them all.

'No wonder I couldn't tell Mother about the dream I had last night,' thought Rattan as he mopped his face dry from the damp of the fine London drizzle. He had dreamed that he was standing at the gates of 73 Hauz Khas dressed only in his underwear and surrounded on all sides by hordes of women whose faces were indistinguishable. They all wore white saris with faded red borders, and on their feet were kolhapuri *chappals*. Their uncombed hair flowed wildly, and their foreheads gleamed viciously with large red *kumkum* bindis. Their huge, kohl-lined eyes stared unblinkingly at a point somewhere on his right shoulder. In the background, the sounds of *shehnai* floated on the air, until there was a crash of *tabla* sounds interspersed with the ongoing pulsating sounds of the *dholak*. This seemed to continue endlessly until, suddenly, the rhythms changed. For a minute everything was stilled into silence.

And then, as if on cue, everything started playing together in a loud, eerie conglomeration of sounds. In the white mist that seemed mysteriously to have covered them, all the women surrounding him were raising their right arms slowly, as if in cinematic slow motion, pointing their forefingers at his right shoulder. Rattan knew then that they were pointing at the mark that had scarred him from birth. At that moment, he had felt a slight sensation. When he had looked over his right shoulder, he had found his birthmark turning from its typical bluish brown to a flaming red. As it turned redder and redder, the women set up a wailing which slowly grew louder and louder ...

Standing outside Dolcis and looking stupidly at displays of women's summer shoes, Rattan shuddered. Busy recalling the previous night's dreams, he had not realised where he had gone or what he was doing. Even as he stared at a selection of white-strapped sandals in different designs, he recalled how vividly he had felt that the women in his dream had damned him. He remembered how thankful he had been for having it suddenly and inconclusively cut short by the ringing of the telephone at his bedside. 'Seven forty-five, sir! Wake-up call ...' a woman's voice had said. Her voice had silenced the drums and the *dhols* sounding loudly in his head. He had, after a few waking moments, ventured to look downwards at his right shoulder. The birthmark was there, scarring his shoulder. It was its usual bluish brown.

No change at all.

✳   ✳   ✳

Meanwhile, Pammi Malhotra stood framed in the window watching her son walk away from the hotel. She noticed calmly the droop in his shoulders, and that his head was bent at an angle. Whatever she felt inside at this prospect of her unhappy son, she did not let it show on her face – not even in her private moments when she was certain that she was alone in the hotel suite.

'I must be calm, very calm ...' she said to herself. 'I can't afford to be anything else ... not for his sake, or for my own ...'

As the words echoed silently in her head, she moved briskly towards the adjoining room, returning a few minutes later with a small diary in her hand. She had decided to call her husband in Frankfurt. Noni was eating breakfast in the hotel restaurant. His first 'hello' was a cautious affair, for he wanted to make sure who was on the line. When he discovered that it was his wife calling from London, his words became curt and distant.

'It's me, Pammi,' he heard her say.

'Yes? What is it?' he asked briefly.

'I'm worried about Rattan,' she said in a voice as flat and unemotional as his.

'Where is he now?' asked Noni Malhotra.

'He's just gone out to the bank ... to cash traveller's cheques. He's still very upset ...'

'What did you expect? He has to be.' Noni's voice was brusque and impatient.

'Did you make those phone calls?' asked Pammi, ignoring the exasperation in her husband's voice.

'Yes, I did. Macgregor was very reassuring. He'll get the job, I think. But he'll have to live somewhere in the Middle East. Probably in Cairo or Alexandria. Not anywhere in Europe ... or the USA ...'

'Oh, good,' said Pammi, relief in her voice. 'Egypt is quite off the main route of travel by friends and relatives ... Only those interested in history go there ... that will be just perfect ...'

She could have said more, but her husband did not allow her

to be more expansive. Aware of his business companion awaiting him still at the breakfast table at the other end of the restaurant, Noni cut his wife short.

'I have to go now. I won't be able to return to London before his interview. But wish him luck from me. There is no need to say anything ... I mean, to tell him that I have spoken to Macgregor and so on. You know how Rattan is. He wouldn't like it. And also ... be nice to him, OK?'

'What do you mean by "be nice to him"? I'm his mother, remember?' said Pammi quite angry.

'Yes, I know you are his mother ... But I'll still tell you to leave him be. Bye. I'll talk to you later.'

He put the phone down before Pammi could say anything.

'The bastard,' Pammi thought viciously.

'There's not much more that can be done,' she told herself. 'There really isn't ...'

By this time, she was already in the bathroom looking to put on her outdoor clothes. Since she had already showered before breakfast, this did not take her long. Soon, she was fully dressed in a trouser suit in elegant beige suede silk. No saris or *salwar kameez* for Pammi Malhotra when she was out of India, especially when she was travelling anywhere in the West. When she stepped out from the elevator into the hotel foyer – fully made up, and her carefully creased trousers falling gracefully to her feet shod in black high-heeled shoes – only her long, henna-red hair rolled into a smart French knot on the top of her head could have given away that she was Indian.

A Scar in Cairo

When the plane broke through the heavy white clouds on its descent into Egypt a few weeks later, all Rattan Malhotra could see was the desert — brown-yellow, with large boulders of darker brown rock interspersed with sand dunes as huge as hills. It was the beginning of August — the sixth to be exact — and the heat of high summer shimmered outside the Boeing window, distorting somewhat the view of the ground below. This vista continued for a good ten minutes. Squeezing himself sideways to look out and downwards through the small window of the plane, Rattan felt excitement rise in his stomach even as the aircraft slowly began to lose height.

Surely he would see them now?

It was a few more minutes before anything in the landscape changed. Suddenly he saw the river, a striking blue, with parallel lines of fertile green on either side. It was the Nile — with its accompanying narrow lush green valley — flowing northwards until it fanned out, like a hand with five fingers, into the azure Mediterranean Sea. A few far-apart mounds of drab concrete structures became visible, standing out dully amidst the sea of sand. Soon these began to merge into more and more of the same, and a curving snake-like line of buildings began to take shape below. The drab line of square-roofed structures followed the river's winding path at a width of approximately five miles, all the way to the north, until they came to the mouth of the delta where they gathered together to form a large, round-shaped cluster of dwellings.

'That must be Cairo,' thought Rattan, unconsciously heaving a deep sigh at the prospect of landing in this strange new/old metropolis in which he would have to live for the next few years. Totally unknown to him, and yet one of the world's most ancient cities, it sat on the banks of one of the world's most famous rivers. Home to successive civilisations, it was now to receive him, willy nilly, and hide him from the prying eyes of the world until it forgot his shame.

From up there, just below the clouds, Rattan's destination couldn't have been better laid out for him to see. As the Boeing 747 lost height and descended into the sunset, the outline of each high-rise building became more clearly visible. Tinged by the dark shadows of fading light, tall modern buildings stood cheek by jowl with much lower ones. Their uniformly drab colouring reminded him of a huge and ancient anthill settlement that seemed to have existed for eons along the banks of the sustaining waters. In those moments, just before nightfall, Rattan could not help but wonder at Cairo. What secrets of other dubious pasts had been brought here to be buried within its walls and over-lapping foundations? Many had lived, loved, and died here; many a time had the city rebuilt itself, reinvented itself. Surely it would show him how to do the same? Show him how to clean his slate of earlier unwanted writings and begin again?

Rattan was, by nature, not given to philosophising. Nor had he in the past stopped to decipher any patterns in the way events took place around him. He had moved so smoothly from one phase of his life to the other that to pause and wonder at what seemed so given would have been an irrelevance. He had heard of Hinduism's great divisions of every man's life: *bachpan* or childhood; *brahmacharya* or bachelorhood; *grihastha* or the 'householder' years; *vanaprastha* or a forest-like detachment; and, finally, *sanyas* or an ascetic surrender in preparation for transition into the next life. But he had never given them much thought. He had assumed that they would come by in the natural course of things, and he would respect each as he passed through them.

An American professor in his undergraduate years had once told the class that an 'unexamined life was not worth living'. The statement had generated much discussion. Rattan remembered himself sitting silently through it, never once thinking that there was anything serious that he could contribute to the debate. Afterwards, he had decided that 'a much examined life' was hardly worth living either. Cerebration for its own sake was a dry-as-dust affair, not necessarily a useful preparation for the business of living. Life was a spontaneous, decisive thing in which every future moment beckoned with enticing promise. All one had to do was to live it. Too much thought was irrelevant, even destructive.

This interpretation had worked quite well for the young man from Boston even in the two years after he had returned to India. Until, of course, the discovery of Tanvi's suicide. After the initial shock of her death, Rattan had been forced into thinking about many things. Very early after her passing, he had realised that besides what Tanvi had meant to him personally, her death had singularly denied him entry into that longest and most productive of life's phases: that of the householder. It had been all too easy to mock at the fact that such old-fashioned categories still had currency in Indian society with his friends at university. In fact, he had secretly laughed when the pundit, presiding so piously over the ceremonies of his marriage to Tanvi, had spelt them out monotonously for all to hear. 'The great phase of the responsible householder is about to begin,' he had intoned, looking more pointedly at him than at his shy bride. The priest had gone on to enumerate in detail his responsibilities and duties as the potential head of his household. All the elders of the family sitting around had nodded in silent approval. Rattan recalled how he – his head bowed under the weight of the huge, over-poweringly fragrant *jayamala* made of jasmine and tube roses – had felt impatience at such obvious moralising being directed so specifically at him.

But now, he also remembered recognising that his marriage, brief though it had been, had immediately elevated his status in the eyes of the world. This was, perhaps, most true in the family concern. From being an impatient, ready-to-go, all-too-young individual, he came to be seen as The Son with The New Ideas raring to make his father's business grow. 'Two sets of shoulders instead of one,' is what everyone had murmured approvingly. It was a shift in view that even he, still wrapped in the traditional headiness of the newly wedded state, could not help but notice.

Circling over the great metropolis of Cairo, Rattan re-lived the last few disastrous weeks of his life. They had scarred him for ever – scarred him more deeply than any dark birthmark that burned red on his shoulder when he slept through dark dreams. 'I hope Cairo will change this,' he told himself.

It was at this point that Rattan thought to look for them again. Where were those perfectly constructed structures, the Pyramids? Weren't they supposed to stand out against the desert landscape, defying gravity and the destruction of Time? He looked out carefully, but they were nowhere to be seen. A wave of depression passed over him. The Pyramids, one of the Seven Wonders of the World, were not visible from airplanes landing at Cairo airport.

So much for the Pyramids – the absolute symbols of the city in which he was fated to lead the next few years of his life. And he had been denied a view of them. Their invisibility seemed ominous to Rattan, smarting under Fate's mean hand. Would life now consist merely of denials? Of learning to do without everything he had held dear – family, a circle of friends, a wife?

The way things turned out, Rattan did not see the Pyramids for a good few weeks after his arrival in Cairo. Even the sense of deprivation that this denial created was deferred to a later time. In the noise and chatter of ground personnel shouting out to each other in the guttural sounds of unfamiliar Arabic, both receded to the other side of his mind. As he stood around waiting in the Arrivals lounge for his suitcases to be off-loaded from the hold, Rattan was aware of a pulse and a rhythm to life in Cairo which were quite different from London. In fact, they were more similar to those of any international airport in India.

But there was a difference too, as was evident in the pulsating beat of Arab music playing softly in the background over the public address system. Looking around watching strange faces and hearing strange sounds, Rattan was acutely aware that the period of his banishment had begun. This was really and truly the beginning of an exile that would last a long time.

His colleagues had found him an apartment very near the office, in the heart of town – in one of the buildings overlooking Tahrir Square. From the balcony off his bedroom, the mighty Nile could be seen flowing north. It was quite a view, and no doubt equivalent to having an apartment in Bombay overlooking the sea. Tahrir Square itself was a busy crossroads – full of buses, cars and taxis during the day. It seemed to be an important junction for changing bus routes, and the local underground also had a stop there. Rattan soon learned that the roads that branched off from the central square were lined with shops, and were known as the Downtown area of the city.

It took Rattan many days to get used to the noise of the traffic, and to the fact that the three-bedroom apartment on the ninth floor of a high-rise building was going to be his new home. He found it strange to be living in the midst of noise and confusion, especially after the two years he had spent in his parents' home in suburban New Delhi. There was no lawn to walk on here, and not much green to calm tired eyes. All around him were concrete buildings – some new and ugly, and contrasting sharply with the more stylish and ornate older ones, built, no doubt at a time when Egypt was still a colony.

At night, however, the view was breathtaking. When all the neon signs, streetlights, and the decorative lights along the river came on, Cairo's dirty streets and ugly buildings fell away. The area around the Tahrir Bridge and the surrounding corniche came miraculously to resemble a large fairground. The boats and *feluccas* on the river, bejewelled with their own light bulbs, only added to the sense of enchantment. Their reflections in the water would make it shimmer enticingly. Leaning over the railings of the balcony outside his bedroom late at night on the third day after his moving into the apartment, Rattan spent a few moments drinking in the scene. The August evening breeze had lowered the temperature. Even though it was past midnight, the corniche thronged with people and the sounds of Arabic music floated on the air.

Rattan decided that as soon as it was possible he would take a cruise up the Nile all the way to the south of the country to see what wonders stood on its banks.

Not far from Rattan Malhotra's balcony view of the river, Nalini Thapar sat in her window, watching the magical fairyland of the river front. In fact, Bharat Bhavan stood diagonally opposite to the right from the building in which Rattan Malhotra had his apartment. Nalini was the only one awake. She had just turned in after having a quiet dinner with Ajay and Minti. Her father had asked her to accompany him to an official engagement. But she had refused. It had become awkward, even boring, to be talking through long evenings with men and women her father's age.

And to be fair to him, he had understood her difficulty, and not insisted.

Gautam Thapar was, in fact, very worried about his daughter. He had begun wondering, in the last few weeks, about whether he had done the right thing in asking her to leave her job in New

Delhi. Nalini was twenty-five, going on twenty-six, and he knew how difficult it was for her to be without a proper occupation and friends. In fact, what she needed was to have a home and a husband of her own. Before her death, his wife's constant worry had been that Nalini was still not established in her own home. Gautam Thapar knew that, had she not fallen ill, Kanta would most certainly have looked around and found an eligible young man for their daughter. Now that she was gone, he found it hard to undertake the search. Where would he now learn to fulfil this most important domestic duty without the help of a wife? Match-making had always been a woman's business. He could not imagine himself approaching friends and relatives to suggest suitable young men for Nalini. In fact, he had secretly come to hope that Nalini would find her own mate.

However, he also knew that, unless she was very lucky, suitable boys did not exist in postings outside the country.

Driving back from dinner, Gautam Thapar could not help thinking how difficult it was to be responsible for the choice of an appropriate husband for a beloved daughter when one moved every three years. Also, times had changed. Women were no different from men these days. And now that they were educated in co-educational schools, they had come to have definite views about what they wanted out of life, and whom they wanted to marry. When he thought about how Nalini had enjoyed her job in advertising, and how that contrasted unfavourably with the quality of her life in Cairo, he regretted asking her to leave it all and join him, Ajay and Minti.

Maybe, in a few months, he would insist that she return to Delhi – at least she would be with her friends, return to a job she obviously enjoyed and, who knew, even find someone.

As the driver turned the car into the driveway of Bharat Bhavan, he noticed the lighted window of Nalini's room. In the otherwise dark front of the majestic house, it seemed rather forlorn. Even though it was late, he knew she would be up reading. He went straight up to her bedroom and knocked on the door. He found her sitting up in bed, a pile of newspapers and magazines strewn by its side.

'You're still awake?' he asked.

'I was looking through all the newspapers from India,' said Nalini, waving a new issue of a Sunday magazine at her father. 'There's a short story written by a woman I knew in New Delhi.'

'Really?' asked Gautam Thapar. 'Is it any good?'

'Yes, it was rather good,' replied Nalini, a certain excitement in her voice.

'Why don't you try your hand at fiction, *beti*?' said Gautam Thapar, a careful enthusiasm in his voice.

There was a slight pause before Nalini replied.

'Me? Start writing? Never ... I have nothing to write about,' she said with finality.

The definite, somewhat despairing tone of her voice made Gautam immediately regret having made the suggestion. He saw his daughter fold up the magazine and the other newspapers lying by her bed. They rustled loudly in the silence of the night. The father thought desperately of what else he could say that would not fall awry on the moment. He could find nothing.

'You should get some sleep, my dear,' he said, as neutrally as he could. 'Don't forget that we have to be up early tomorrow. Everyone will be here before nine for the flag-hoisting. It's lucky that Independence Day is on a Friday this year, and all the offices – including yours – are closed. Otherwise you would have missed the ceremony.'

'I would have taken the morning off, Dad,' said Nalini reassuringly. 'I'm sure my Egyptian boss would have understood ... *Aji* and I are making sandwiches, green chutney and red ketchup to suggest the Indian tricolour. The samosas and the *gulabjamuns* will arrive at seven thirty. I have told them to bring five hundred pieces each. There will also be tea and cold drinks. And serviettes. That should be enough, shouldn't it?'

'Thank you, my dear. I knew you would organise it all,'

said Gautam Thapar, and wondered how many from the Indian community would come. Last year the attendance had not been very good. But there had been some new arrivals in the community since then.

'We are expecting larger numbers this year,' he warned.

'We're ready,' said Nalini.

'Good!' said the Ambassador of India wryly. 'What we do for the sake of our country and countrymen! But I'm sure there isn't anyone who thinks it worthwhile! Good night, my dear.'

And switching off the lights, he closed the door gently behind him.

Meeting under a Flag

On 15 August, the day of India's Independence, Rattan Malhotra woke up early. He had not set an alarm to wake him, thinking to enjoy the weekly *Jumma* holiday by sleeping in. But suddenly, just before 5.30 a.m. he found himself jolted into an alert wakefulness. It took him a few minutes to register where he was, and what had woken him. He looked blankly around for a few seconds before he realised fully that he was lying in his bed, in his corniche apartment in Cairo. It took him somewhat longer to know that it was the call of the *muezzin* that had woken him.

Allahu Akbar, Allahu Akbar, Allahu Akbar . . .

Rattan had been almost ten days in Cairo, but was still not used to hearing it repeated five times a day. It always sounded like an irritated snarl. Why did they need mechanised loudspeakers to alert the faithful to remember the Almighty? The loudspeakers distorted the human voice, and hardly seemed conducive to the mood of prayer. He was still feeling strange in 'the city of a thousand mosques', and the loud call jangled his nerves, for it always seemed to emanate from somewhere close to him.

As the minutes passed, a dull calm permeated Rattan. The voice on the loudspeaker had not only woken him (at an hour when he would normally be sleeping) but had also, in some way, upset him. It had reminded him of a moment in his life, not so long ago, when he and Tanvi had been jolted awake in the early hours of the morning by a loud, shrill sound not dissimilar to the *muezzin*'s call. It had been on the first night after their marriage. The festivities had continued into the night, and he and Tanvi had been allowed only reluctantly to retire. It was nearly 1 a.m. and, as Rattan recalled, it had been his mother who had shooed all the guests off. It was late, and no doubt the newly wedded couple was tired. 'Tanvi looks ready to drop,' she had said, with a twinkle in her eye that had made him and Tanvi blush a little even as friends and cousins had grinned and giggled. There had been some whispering, and knowing looks were cast around the room as he and Tanvi made to move upstairs.

Rattan remembered having been more amused than embarrassed at the naïve coyness of his cousins, and had almost laughed aloud. But then, he had seen Tanvi's face and noticed an uncomfortable anxiety written all over it. She was not enjoying the teasing at all, and had begun to look pale, and somewhat frightened. He stood up decisively and, with a straight face, said goodnight to everyone. He had escorted his bride into their bedroom, and shut the door behind them. He recalled Tanvi's sudden nervousness, and how he had tried to reassure her as they found themselves, for the first time, away from the rest of the world.

He had walked up the stairs wondering what would be the most appropriate thing to do. He did not want to add to Tanvi's anxiety. His problem had solved itself. As he opened the door to their bedroom, he found Tanvi staring inside it in delight. There were flowers everywhere! Petals of roses in various colours adorned the floor and the bed sheets. The vases were full of lilies, and around the bed hung garlands of orange marigold and white *rajnigandha*. The perfumes and scents mingled in the room, and were quite overpowering. In the soft light of the two lamps on either side of the bed, the room felt sensuous and inviting. Tanvi had been transported. 'It's just like in the movies,' she had said, shyly delighted. And he remembered telling himself that whatever all this meant to him, the bridegroom, was completely beside the point. To his young bride it had meant everything. It certainly set the atmosphere for ease and surrender. Undressing and lovemaking had been made easier, and she had thrown herself into the spirit of the night.

Sleep had come later, much later, almost near dawn. Tanvi had slept first, nestling her head in his shoulder, completely trusting. Rattan remembered himself lying awake a while, thinking of how the day had been, of how he was finally married in the eyes of God and the world, and of how he was to spend the rest of his life with this young girl whom he was just beginning to know.

He remembered having drifted into sleep slowly . . . only to be awakened by a loud, shrill sound.

It seemed to come from somewhere under them, but was also reverberating loudly around the room in urgent summons. It had woken them with a start, frightening Tanvi into sitting upright in bed, clutching the sheets right up under her chin to hide her nakedness. Rattan remembered himself waking all at once to the loud sound even as he had felt Tanvi cling closer.

'Listen,' he had said. 'It sounds like an alarm clock.'

And so it had been, hidden on the floor behind a wooden cupboard on the left of their bed. It had taken some scrambling on both their parts to locate it. It was Tanvi who had found it, scrabbling with beringed hands and bangled wrists in the narrow space between the cupboard and the floor. But she had not known how to switch it off. That Rattan had done; he remembered clearly how he had grabbed it from her, and finding the knob in a few seconds had quickly disconnected the alarm. Only then had the loud shrilling of the wretched thing stopped, but not before it had reduced them both into peals of laughter, arms and legs entangled right there on the floor.

If there had been any inhibitions left between them, they now evaporated. The loving that had followed had been of a different nature from the nervous penetration of a few hours earlier. Perhaps that is what the younger members of his family had intended – a silly prank to break the ice between a man and a woman who had known each other only briefly, and that too between the strict proprieties of an arranged marriage. The early morning light saw them lying quietly on the bed. Tanvi had looked around at all the flowers, and sniffed the lingering smells luxuriously. Even he, otherwise no believer in such extravagant rituals, had felt himself carried along.

Waking into that dawn had been nothing if not magical.

As he saw the Cairene corniche below him wake into life, Rattan felt acutely his utter and complete loneliness. He had not known Tanvi too long, but his marriage to her had become the reason for his defined place in the world of New Delhi. In the absence of pursuing higher education in India, he had no circle of friends and classmates. His school friends had scattered, and those made at university had all been left behind in the USA. When his mother had suggested that he marry, he had thought it a good idea. Of all the girls shown him, he had chosen Tanvi because she had seemed sweet – an untouched flower awaiting the moment of full bloom.

'Maybe I was too arrogant to think that I could have her blossom for me,' thought Rattan as he moved back into his bedroom, listening absently to the slow increase in the sounds of traffic on the road below. 'Obviously, it was something I did – or didn't do – which touched her to death.' The thought made him wince, bringing back intensely the deep ache inside him and reviving memories he could well have done without.

And there was this daily morning call for prayer to deal with. How would he ever get used to it? 'Maybe I should get up early with the rest of Egypt, and pray with them. Or meditate. It might just make me forget the horror,' Rattan told himself, and walked towards the kitchen.

Half an hour later he had drunk a mug of weakly brewed tea,

which he took back to bed and knew he had not really enjoyed. It was not even 6 a.m. The beginning of the weekend. What would he do with the rest of the long day? And the inevitably following next day? Maybe he should shave, bathe, dress, and eat something — eggs maybe? — and go out across town to see the Pyramids. A cab would take him to that other edge of the city. He would spend the morning there, and then eat lunch at one of the many hotels and restaurants that existed in the area.

But all this was not to be, for at that moment the phone rang. It was Vinod Gupta reminding him that it was India's Independence Day, and that most members of the Indian community traditionally gathered at the Chancery building of the Embassy of India for flag-hoisting. Rattan had met Vinod Gupta a few days after his arrival. Another Indian colleague in his office had taken him to a party hosted by the Guptas, and he had been introduced as the new area manager for the Bechtal Corporation. Short of height and stocky in build, Vinod Gupta worked for Proctor and Gamble, and had been the company's area manager based in Cairo for the last two years. Rattan had now met him three times socially and noticed his warm, no-nonsense friendliness. It was obvious to everyone that he had taken to the silent newcomer, and had arrogated to himself the role of friend and chaperone.

Rattan had not really objected to being taken under the Gupta wing, for in the first three days after his arrival he had discovered that to be an expatriate in the USA was one thing, and to be one in Egypt was quite another. Maybe this was because of the language: the relative absence of English in general discourse. It would be a while before he understood Arabic, whether spoken or heard everywhere in song. The Egyptians seemed friendly enough, but to know them and befriend them would take a while. Or, perhaps, the fault lay with himself, unwilling at the moment to reach out and make friends. If Vinod Gupta had chosen to befriend him, he would go along.

'Come on, Rattan! Wake up. We have to go to the Embassy, remember? This is a wake-up call. It's Independence Day . . .'

Vinod's booming voice crackled with high spirits over the telephone line and brought cheer into Rattan's room. Sitting up straight in bed, Rattan's thoughts readjusted themselves to a different set of plans for the morning. A seemingly pointless day suddenly took on a purpose and urgency. 'No Pyramids today,' he told himself. But there was no sense of disappointment. They could be seen another day. They had been there a long time, and would wait for him.

'What time are we to be there?' asked Rattan.

'Nine a.m. And punctual. Madhu and I will pick you up at eight forty-five. From your apartment the Embassy is not far,' Vinod replied.

'Shall be ready,' said Rattan, feeling in some way like a schoolboy getting ready for Speech Day.

'Shall see you then. We have to be good Indians, remember!'

The telephone clicked off. 'Vinod was in quite a mood,' thought Rattan. He wondered what Vinod meant by being 'good Indians'. As far as he knew, he had never thought of himself as having been either a good or a bad Indian, whether at home in New Delhi or in the USA. He was curious to see what form being 'a good Indian' would take when living in a country which was at the crossroads of three continents: Africa, Asia and Europe.

The Guptas were on time, and Rattan met them standing downstairs on the steps of his building. From where he stood, he couldn't see the Nile. All he could see was one corner of Tahrir Square — a little quieter today than usual, on account of the *Jumma* holiday. While he waited, he lit a cigarette. The sun was up, moving swiftly towards its noonday brilliance. It was warm already, and would surely get hotter even before the morning's proceedings began. The glare caught his eyes, and he fumbled in his pocket for his dark glasses. A cab passed by, full of people. Its back seat was bursting with children, and their squeals rent the air for a few moments – and then were gone. As Rattan drew on his cigarette, his mind returned to New Delhi. He remembered another day, not so long ago, full of glare – of the sun, people, and a fire.

It was on a day similar to this, that they had walked with the dead Tanvi to the cremation grounds.

Standing there, on the steps in the sun, a great feeling of weightlessness swept over Rattan. Why was he feeling as if things were proceeding not by his own volition but by someone else's these days? He hadn't really thought of going to this function. And he wasn't even sure that he wanted to participate in this silly display of patriotism which consisted of standing still before a flag. Why was he doing so now? Why had he allowed his new friends to decide for him?

He contemplated saying, 'I say, Vinod, leave me out of this, will you? Just drop me off here, right here. I'll take a walk ...'

But he couldn't bring himself to do it. And the moment passed. Now that the Guptas had taken the trouble to come all the way to fetch him, it would be churlish to fuss about going. It was better to flow with the moment. Fumbling in his pockets, he looked for another cigarette. He found the pack and, extracting one, lit up quickly.

Rattan saw her as soon as he entered the gates of the Chancery building of the Indian Embassy. She was standing there, tall and long-haired, in a cream-coloured cotton sari, wiping the faint layer of perspiration from her nose and upper lip with a white handkerchief. In the brief look that he cast her, he noticed that she was fair and large-eyed, and stood rather stiffly – as if having braced herself for a morning in the public eye. He didn't know who she was – only that she stood there in what seemed to be an informal welcome line, a little behind and on the left of the

Ambassador of India. And yet she seemed to be all by herself, away from the other women – and their husbands – who stood around, on the other side. He didn't realise it then but it was the hint of her separation from others, both men and women, that made him notice her.

'That's just like me,' he told himself in passing, and wondered who she was. She couldn't be the wife. She looked so much younger than the distinguished, grey-haired man standing near her. He thought to ask, but the Guptas were moving on. He greeted her with a quick *namaste*, and shaking hands with the Ambassador, followed them hastily so as not to be left behind. He greeted the others in the line, and entered the crowd gathered beyond, trailing the Guptas who seemed to know everybody. They moved easily from group to slowly growing group. Soon the grounds of the Chancery were bursting with people greeting each other.

The Ambassador moved to his marked place under the flagpole, bringing their warm and spontaneous socialising to an abrupt halt very soon after. Rattan noticed an informal chorus – consisting of young girls – standing on one side of the gathering who seemed to be preparing to sing. At an unspoken signal, they began the '*Jana, gana, mana*'. To his great surprise, Rattan found that the community gathered there joined them enthusiastically. At the end of the national anthem, Gautam Thapar stepped forward and unfurled the Indian flag. Petals of roses and marigold scattered like confetti through the warm Cairene morning and spread themselves out on the freshly mown, lush green grass. After a round of clapping, the President of India's speech was read out to the attentive crowd. A loud, reverberating '*Jai Hind*' concluded the morning's celebrations, and everyone was invited to help themselves to tea and snacks.

The Guptas were a popular couple. Almost everyone came up to greet them. Rattan understood immediately that if he had to live in this city for the next few years, it would be wise to make friends as quickly as possible. He was lucky that he had met the Guptas so soon after his arrival in Cairo, and that they seemed so affable. But Rattan also realised that though they took pleasure in introducing him to everyone they knew, a new arrival in the Indian community in Cairo was not a daily occurrence. To have befriended one seemed to offer some distinction to the Guptas. He felt like the new boy at school being led around by the class captain, and couldn't help being both faintly irritated and amused. But, as he told himself quickly, he could hardly complain since everyone he met seemed bent on making him feel welcome.

The only time he felt really uncomfortable was when one lady asked whether he was married. He was relieved when he found that he was not expected to answer this question. The plump, moon-faced Madhu Gupta, Vinod's wife, answered it. Her large kohl-ringed eyes and big red bindi sparkled in the sun as she spoke.

'No, he is not. He is quite alone. Isn't that nice? We will have to find a nice girl for him,' she said jovially.

Rattan merely smiled, and pretended that he was used to such statements. Inside, he felt acutely the heaviness of all that had been. 'I had better get used to carrying the burden of a secret past,' he told himself. This was what he had come to Cairo for, hadn't he? To hide away from it all, and to begin again, with a clean slate? And yet all he felt was that he was an impostor, lying to all these people who so obviously thought the best of him. Standing there under the trees, with the Nile flowing past unconcerned and this closely knit community of compatriots welcoming him, he tried to imagine what the general reaction would be if they came to know the truth about him ... and shuddered inwardly.

'I didn't really kill her ... I didn't really kill her, you know,' he wanted to cry out – to tell them, in advance, the truth about things. Tell them all, before they got to hear all the untrue rumours about wife beatings and dowry deaths, and before they came to their own wretched conclusions ...

But, of course, he did no such thing. Feeling suddenly very hot and uncomfortable, he moved away from the group he was standing with, and began to search for something cold to drink: a glass of water ... a Coke or a Pepsi ... anything.

He walked to where the tables were laid out along one end of the lawns of the Chancery. Weaving his way amidst the crowds, Rattan saw that glasses of cold drinks had been laid out at one end, near where the tea and coffee were being served. Further up the table was the food, and already a line had formed at the other end, and people were beginning to serve themselves.

Rattan saw her again, then.

She was standing behind the tables along with the waiters, unselfconsciously supervising everything. He watched her remove the coverings of damp cloths from the trays of tricolour sandwiches. He saw her say something in low tones to the waiter standing next to her and then dispatch another man – an Embassy employee? – to run a quick errand. And then, having given a quick comprehensive look down the tables to see that everything was right, she moved away to stand by the Ambassador once again. Rattan noticed that everyone was making it a point to greet her, and that she was responding distantly yet politely. From time to time the handkerchief was out, wiping the sweat from her face.

It was hot; and now that it was almost 11 a.m., the August sun was blazing down on the crowd. As the morning had progressed and the sun had risen in the heavens, everyone had automatically moved to huddle under the lone tree offering some shade. Even so, temperatures were high, and had made standing around dressed in formal suits quite unbearable.

'I've had enough of this,' thought Rattan, and putting his plate away, he fumbled in his pockets for a cigarette. As he moved away from the table, he looked around for Vinod and Madhu. Suddenly, he saw them walking towards him purposefully.

'Come, let me introduce you to the Thapars,' said Vinod,

and holding on to Rattan's arm, bore him along towards where the Ambassador was standing.

'Who is the young woman? Is she the wife?' asked Rattan.

'No, no. Of course not!' replied Vinod, shocked. 'She's not his wife! However did you come to think that? She's his daughter. His wife is dead!'

Rattan did not respond, but felt as if the slightly blurred picture of the group standing around the Thapars had found sudden focus. At its centre was the young woman in the cream-coloured sari who, although in the middle of the picture, seemed quite aloof, even alone.

'Good morning, sir,' Rattan heard Vinod say. 'Please meet Rattan Malhotra, a newcomer to Cairo. He has recently been appointed area sales manager for the Bechtal Corporation.'

'Hello, and welcome,' said Gautam Thapar in a friendly tone and extended his hand to Rattan for a warm handshake.

Rattan hid his half-smoked cigarette behind his back with his left hand and hoped that the smoke recently exhaled would not come between them. He was aware that the young woman standing next to the Ambassador had moved back a step – seemingly to avoid the smoke hovering over the group – and had her eyes on him. But Gautam Thapar did not seem to notice.

'Meet Nalini, my daughter. Nalini, this is . . . ? I'm sorry I did not get your first name?' he said apologetically to Rattan.

'I'm Rattan Malhotra. I'm new here . . .' said Rattan speaking directly to Nalini, and bowing a little formally as he did so. He wondered for a second whether he was expected to bring up both hands to say *namaste* in the traditional way. But he remembered the smoking cigarette in his left hand, and forgetting all about the *namaste*, he quickly put out his right one to shake hands.

Nalini's in response was dry and firm.

'Hi!' Nalini said coolly, a half-smile on her face. 'I guessed, because I hadn't seen you around.'

There was a slight pause, then Nalini spoke again, her voice formal and polite. 'When did you come in?'

'About two weeks ago,' Rattan responded, equally politely. It was his turn to use the formal tone.

But she did not seem to notice. 'Do you like it here?' she asked.

'I'm getting used to it. I can't say I like it yet ...' he said apologetically, moving his face a little away from her as he lifted his hand to inhale the last of his cigarette. But he found, to his chagrin, that his fingers were shaking. Hoping that she hadn't noticed, he hurriedly threw its smoking remains to the ground and stamped them out with his foot.

But she had noticed. 'You're smoking too much,' she said. 'And it isn't doing you much good.'

'No, it isn't, is it?' he said embarrassd, and looked straight into her eyes even as he stopped grinding the smoking butt under his right toe. She met his eyes for a strong, quiet moment, and then looked away.

'You seem a recent addict,' she said.

'How did you know?' asked Rattan, completely surprised.

'I don't know,' said Nalini, a smile in her voice. 'I'm just guessing!'

'Oh,' said Rattan nonplussed, and looked straight at her again. She returned his glance unflinchingly. It was he who looked away.

'I should stop, really ... quit completely before it becomes too late.'

'Perhaps, you should ... but it doesn't really matter ...'

When Nalini Thapar thought about the encounter afterwards, she couldn't help remembering clearly the sudden droop of Rattan Malhotra's shoulders that had followed this point in their conversation. And that when this happened, he seemed suddenly to lose height. His tall frame seemed slowly to bunch itself up as if to support some tremendous burden, and his face turned an ashen grey.

Even at that time she had immediately understood that her comments had fallen awry. Had she caught him unawares? Or, perhaps, touched something vulnerable in him without meaning to? She had felt terrible, immediately chiding herself for rebuking him so. Feeling somewhat flustered and guilty, she had rushed into the silence with inane words that hung forlornly between them.

'I hope you begin to like it here. You will, I assure you, when you have been here a few weeks ... And then maybe the smoking will stop ... I mean ... what I mean is you just won't feel the need any more ...'

By the time she stopped speaking, Nalini had found herself stuttering a little and having an acute feeling that she had overstepped considerably the boundaries of a first conversation with a stranger.

He certainly made her feel that way, for it was a few moments before he had responded. 'Yes. I'm sure you are right,' he had said, formally, his eyes looking away, over her shoulders, into some vague point in the distance.

By this time she was completely embarrassed, and had felt herself go hot in the face. She was quite sure that Rattan Malhotra had not appreciated her all-too-direct criticism of him, and regretted intensely that she had brought up the subject at all. What business had it been of hers to wonder about whether smoking was good or bad for him? She didn't even know him! And she was sure that he had received quite the wrong impression of her, thinking her to be overly judgemental and overbearing.

The rest of their meeting seemed to pass as if in a slow, distended motion in which they were both more observers than participants. Turning away from each other, they listened to the Guptas complete their conversation with Gautam Thapar. While Rattan had his attention focused on the Ambassador of India, Nalini watched Rattan surreptitiously. She heard him, as if from a distance, say a formal good-bye.

She responded equally formally. She saw him move away, grim-faced, to join Vinod and Madhu Gupta who had moved on and were waiting for him to join them. In a minute they were out of sight. But even as she made perfunctory conversation with other guests, her eyes quite involuntarily searched for Rattan Malhotra moving among the crowds. She saw him leave with the Guptas shortly after, his shoulders still bent.

She was also quite sure that that last fumble of his hands in the pockets of his jacket, as he moved through the Chancery gates, had been in search of another, inevitable cigarette.

And the realisation made her feel wretched with remorse.

Kasr-El-Nil

25th August 1992
Bharat Bhavan
Cairo

Dearest Maneka,

Thanks for your letter received a few weeks ago. It was good hearing from you. I feel very far away from it all here in Cairo. Mission life is quite stifling. Thank goodness I have some kind of job — otherwise it would be really awful.

Now that we are well into August, Cairo is getting hot. Independence Day was celebrated as usual (!), and just as well it was all over before noon, or else we would have been baked alive in the dry heat of this place. There are some new Indians in the community. Had the opportunity to meet some of them. No one exciting. One or two young people — but they smoke too much.

How is work? You did not write very much about college, or your teaching schedule. Now that the first semester is in full swing, how much time do you have for Sahayata? Couldn't be very much. I was glad to read of how organised you all have become. Sixteen beds are a lot.

The Egyptians could do with something like that. There's enough wife-battering here too. My Egyptian friend Nayyara (we meet at work every day) tells me it's really quite common, along with male bigamy. Maybe you all at Sahayata should go on to help with resettlement, and also provide match-making services. They really need the latter here. Nayyara is having a hard time finding a husband. She's thirty-five, and still unmarried. She keeps telling me I should hurry up; or else I'll be left in the same position as her! But she really has some strange notions in her head. She wants a man from an old rich family — you know, the 'khandani' kind, with a big house full of European artefacts! I keep telling her she is out of date. In any case, I suppose I am really sceptical about the very rich. Good old middle-class me! One should stay within one's class, don't you think?

By the way, what is the latest about the Tanvi girl and her suicide? I found the press report about her death in the newspapers. Was it really a suicide? Poor girl. When I read about such things, I feel terrible about the fate of women in our country. These wretched men and their clinging families! One can't help becoming a cynic about men in general. Do let me know what the investigations reveal.

I don't know why, but Tanvi really haunts me. It all takes me back to my (limited) days with Sahayata and the WEC earlier. OK! OK! I know what you would say, 'There she goes again . . .' But really, I do wonder a lot about why so young a person would have taken so drastic a step. I guess I have also had my own low moments here in Cairo, which I shall tell you about some other time. However, I can say that the Thapar family is now feeling settled — though Mummy's absence is felt acutely every day. I agonise over whether I will ever be able to soften her loss for Ajay and Minti who feel particularly bereft. As for Daddy, the less said the better. He goes along in his own quiet and dignified way, but I often catch him sitting in his study supposedly reading but actually staring blankly into the distance . . .

Anyway, let's leave all this for now . . . How is Ahmer? Give him my love. He must be growing up fast. Hope he hasn't forgotten his Auntie Nalini. You'd better make sure he doesn't. I think you should bring him along when you come.

Am looking forward to your visit in December. Don't put it off under any circumstance, do you hear? I could do with a breath of fresh air from New Delhi. And don't forget to pick up some new fiction from India — and two saris in silk, of your choice. Evening wear, because I have to go out with Daddy. We'll settle up when you come.

In the meantime, my love to you, and please keep writing.
Affectionately,
Nalini
P.S.: *Please look up* Naanima *before you come. She will be really*
disappointed if you don't.

Nalini wrote this letter to her friend Maneka in her lunch break,
and decided she wouldn't wait for the weekly Diplomatic Bag
to send it on to New Delhi. She would send it by local mail
instead. Maybe it would reach Maneka quicker this way than the
obligatory two weeks when sent by the Bag. She decided to take
a walk and post it.

She looked around the room wondering who would be the
best person to ask about the location of the nearest post office.
Her eyes eventually rested on Gamal Shukri – her partner in the
report she was working on. He was talking on the phone in loudly
exasperated tones, and in what seemed to Nalini to be a rapid
form of angry Arabic, which reverberated around the room. It had
made all the others look up at him in some surprise. Gamal was a
friendly, audacious being, and the life and soul of the small office
shared by six people. With his teasing eyes and infectious smile,
he could lift the weight off the darkest mood of depression.

What was it that had made him so angry as to lose his
habitual cool?

'Allah, what a day! And to think it is only lunchtime yet. I
want to go home!' he said, running both his hands impatiently
through his dark, curly hair.

'Home?' asked Nalini softly. 'You mean to Alexandria?'

This wasn't very fair on Nalini's part, because she knew that
he hated the two-room apartment in Cairo in which he lived
alone. She knew he missed his family very much.

'Yes. I do want to go back to Alexandria today. I can't wait for
the weekend. But how mean of you to tease me about my wretched,
dingy flat in Dokki!' said Gamal, making a deliberately sad face and
pretending he had been wounded to the core.

153

'I am sorry,' said Nalini, immediately contrite. 'I was only teasing . . .'

Gamal looked down at the slim Indian girl. In a mauve *salwar kameez*, and with a matching flowing *dupatta*, she looked like an exotic tropical flower not often seen in arid Cairo.

'You are forgiven,' he said, mockingly serious. 'But why don't you find me that wife you promised? I do need one, you know. Then I won't have to keep running to Alexandria . . . !'

Gamal was always asking Nalini to find him a nice girl to marry. She had told him often enough that she didn't know many Egyptian women who would be suitable, for she had hardly been in Cairo a year.

'But you know that I don't know many . . .' Nalini began to say.

But Gamal cut her short.

'". . . Egyptian girls because I have only been here a year." Yes, I know! You told me that already. But what about a nice Indian girl like you?' he asked, a knowing glint in his eye.

Nalini laughed, turning her eyes away to hide the slight sense of embarrassment she felt when he chose to speak to her in this way.

'For that I would have to take you to India,' she said, after a slight pause.

The prospect made Gamal's face light up in a beatific smile, and Nalini could see that he had conjured up a row of Indian beauties straight out of Bombay films.

'Oh Gamal!' said Nalini, exasperated. 'You are impossible! They won't just be standing there, all beautiful and dressed up on the pavement only for you, an Egyptian from Cairo!'

'Of course they will be,' he retorted, humming snatches of an old Hindi film song. 'Nothing will be impossible when I go to India . . .'

Nalini did not wait until he had finished.

'OK, OK . . .' she said, cutting him short. She decided then that it would be better, and safer, if she changed the subject.

'Do you think you could show me where the nearest post office is, Gamal? I need to post this letter.'

'Yes, of course, my dear!' said Gamal, ever obliging, and all too aware that Nalini had deliberately changed the subject. 'But isn't there anything more that I can do for you?'

Nalini did not respond. Picking up her handbag, she made for the door. Turning around to wink at the others sitting behind their desks, Gamal followed her out of the room.

He liked Nalini, despite her aloof demeanour and the slightly formal air with which she conducted herself. But he knew that if he tried to get closer, she could freeze him out completely.

And that he did not want at all.

The post office was not far — a mere two blocks down the busy street. On their way to the old dusty building that housed it, the two did not talk much. Gamal wondered what Nalini was thinking, and watched her profile surreptitiously as they walked together. She seemed thoughtful and somewhat distant, with some obviously worrisome things playing on her mind. Inside the post office he watched her buy the stamps, lick and stick them on her letter, and then post it in the out-sized red mailbox standing in the corner.

'You write a lot of letters?' Gamal said, not happy at the somewhat serious mood that had continued to hang about them.

Nalini did not reply.

'Who do you write to?' he asked again, grinning an inquisitive smile.

'Oh, to my friends . . . and family,' she said, a trifle defensively as she stepped out from the dingy post office into the bright light of the hot Cairene afternoon.

It was about one o'clock, and right in the middle of the lunch hour. As she joined the throngs of people crowding the streets, she fumbled in her handbag for her dark glasses.

'Do you miss them all a lot?' Gamal asked, pressingly curious, but his voice was gentle.

Nalini knew what he was getting at. 'Yes,' she said bluntly, daring him to make fun of her.

'Well, I wish you wouldn't! I am here. I could be a good friend ... and more ... if only you'd let me. I could make you forget them all,' he continued, teasingly flirtatious.

'Oh, come on, Gamal!' said Nalini firmly, and proceeded to put on her dark glasses.

Gamal knew immediately that nothing would work that day. The moment was gone, and this was her way of stopping him, of shutting him out.

This had happened many times before. But, today, there was something in the air between them that made him respond equally firmly.

'Oh, come on, Nalini,' he said, imitating the inflections of her voice. 'Stop pushing men away, and start living! How long are you going to go on like this? Shutting out life and self-fulfilment? And what about falling in love? ... Yes, Love! Do you ever think about it?'

By the time Gamal had finished speaking, his voice had taken on rough tones quite unusual for him. Nalini was a little taken aback, and noted mentally that this had been the second time his voice had risen that day. But she decided to let his words pass her by. Gamal was a nice person, and she did not want to be rude to him.

'Hey,' she said mildly. 'What is the matter with you today? I don't know what you are talking about!'

Gamal knew that there was no way he could get Nalini to respond to him. At least not today. He would have to find another moment, another way, and try again. He did not reply, but his face, as it turned away, showed the hurt of her deliberate rebuff. Nalini was intensely aware of it, but felt that anything she said in that moment would be false and inadequate.

The two walked together a little way up the street. The

silence between them contrasted sharply with the lunchtime noises of the Downtown streets. As it grew, Nalini knew that Gamal expected her to say something. But what could she say that would explain her situation to him? Should she tell him about the sorrow in her father's house from where she came to work every day? That after her mother's death, the mantle of mothering her younger siblings had fallen on her? That her father did his best to be cheerful for the sake of his children, but would, at the smallest opportunity, leave everyone to withdraw into his study? That he would tell everyone he had to read his newspapers but actually used its peace and quiet to mourn his lost companion? That this upset her more than her own sense of loss?

Nalini looked up at Gamal, but in a glance saw that his mind was elsewhere, his face inscrutable. She realised suddenly that he and she came from different worlds, and they knew very little about each other's pasts. Where could she begin, and how would he understand it all? No, she could not tell all this to Gamal. At least, not yet. She had known him only a few months.

And she certainly could not say all these things to him right in the middle of the street.

By this time they had reached the crossroads of Kasr-El-Nil and Kasr-El-Aini. The lights were red, and the Indian and the Egyptian waited on the pavement together. While Nalini's eyes were on the traffic lights, Gamal's were on her averted face. Nalini hoped that at least today of all days, he would take the hint already given, and leave well alone.

He did. 'I'll see you later in the office. We should go out and have lunch together one afternoon.'

'Yes, we should. I would like that,' said Nalini in a flat but grateful voice. 'I'll be back in the office soon . . . Not much more than half an hour. I have a few errands to run.'

Gamal nodded his head, and waved a hand in farewell. As the lights turned green, he walked away to the left while Nalini crossed the street, and continued straight ahead.

*   *   *

Though Nalini had told Gamal that she had errands to run, she didn't really have any. All she had wanted was a breath of free air in anonymity. She wanted to walk those spaces where no one knew who she was. It wasn't easy to live daily the confining roles of housekeeper and hostess to the Ambassador of India in Egypt. When Mrs Thapar had been alive, Nalini hadn't given this part of her mother's life much thought, since she as a daughter hadn't been asked to do much by way of housekeeping or socialising. But now that all this had fallen solely on her, she felt acutely the burden of public life and responsibility, and did not enjoy it.

'I wasn't ready for it,' she mused, as she stepped carefully on the pavement. 'And I guess, deep in my heart I wish I didn't have to do it.'

But this thought – articulated in her mind so clearly for the first time – immediately made her feel guilty. She also, at that moment, felt herself miss a step, and trip. Her right foot twisted a little and took her weight awkwardly. She steadied herself, silently cursing Cairo's notoriously uneven pavements. As she looked down on the ground, she noted that each shop owner had chosen, typically, to complete the surface in his own style without making sure that his part of the pavement was level with that in front of his neighbour's store.

As Nalini walked past the cleaner-than-the-rest portion in front of the offices of Egypt Air, the national airline, she looked up into its windows. In the first one, a blackboard displayed the price of fares to different destinations of tourist interest within the country. The second window had large posters of the great coral reefs in the Red Sea, of the Karnak Temple in Luxor, and of the golden beaches of Alexandria. The latter even had people in bathing suits enjoying themselves in the water without a care in the world. Each poster was full of colour, and suggested endless opportunity.

'I must get away too . . . and begin living,' thought Nalini, stopping a while to look at them.

Around her the narrow pavement bustled with people, and soon Nalini was borne along with them. Gradually, their cheerful movement infused her with a life and energy she had not known since she had left New Delhi. She looked around, taking in the colours and smells, the sights and sounds. Only a very few Egyptians in this posh Downtown area wore the long flared robes of the traditional *gallabeya*. The well-built, large women brushing past her were dressed in western skirts and blouses. Many of them had their heads covered with white *hijabs*. Nalini had found this combination of western outfits and the traditional *hijab* a little incongruous when she first arrived in Cairo. But now she had become used to the sight. The women jostled around her, walking purposefully on their business. Some of them had children in tow, and they held on to them with firm, fat fingers. Few walked alone. Even the men held hands, their fat stomachs complementing the jollity so obvious in their verbal intercourse. For certainly nobody was quiet. The quick-paced, thick tones of Arabic floated around, vying with the sounds of cars and buses passing a few feet away from the pavement.

The city was with her: its every song, clang and horn an incitement to come alive.

Nalini stopped a few moments outside a shoe store. Above it loomed the upper-floor balconies of an eight-storey building, one over the other. The balcony immediately above the shoe store was festooned with a line of freshly washed household linen hung out to dry. A bedsheet flapped quaintly barely a foot over her head. Moving away from under its shadow, she stood behind a group of three women, and heard them discussing the merits of the shoes displayed in the window. A child tugged impatiently at the skirt of one of them. The mother didn't seem to mind, saying something soothing to calm the four-year-old.

Without knowing exactly when or how, Nalini found herself back in New Delhi. The present blurred away. Only the noise of the crowds remained in her ears, transporting her into a live memory of window-shopping with her friends — Maneka, Arti,

Alka, Jyoti. She was back in their days together in the hostel, and their Saturday afternoon trips in the university special to the shops at Janpath and Connaught Place. The women in front of her today were a little older than they had been. But there was the same noisy talk and laughter – the easy camaraderie among members of the same sex, taking a break from chores.

And the dull ache in her heart returned with an intensity felt as a physical sensation at the pit of her stomach.

She moved away, and walked on. It was hot, but it did not seem to bother the crowds. They were going about the business of the day. She passed a small kiosk selling T-shirts decorated with figures from Egyptian history and mythology. The vendor tried to persuade her to buy one. She declined politely. The open doorway of a *felfela* shop smelled of fried food, and was full of people eating lunch. As she walked past, a blast of cool, air-conditioned air wafted across her face. She paused a moment until a group of young men, busy eating their *felfela* sandwiches in big mouthfuls, moved a little to make way for her. She debated buying a sandwich for herself. But though she was vaguely hungry, she decided against it and walked on.

In front of her were a couple holding hands. This was unusual in the glare of a Cairene afternoon. Most of the time, as Nalini had noticed, hand-holding couples lurked in the shadows of dusk, mainly on the corniches on either side of the Nile. The couple in front of her was young, and the woman was not wearing a *hijab*. Her long and thick, almost waist-length, henna-red hair swung as she walked. The man walked alongside her with proud propriety. Occasionally, he would put his arm around her shoulders, and hug her tightly. The two were deep in conversation, and did not allow passers-by on the narrow pavement to either separate them as they held hands, or interrupt their discussion. In the huge city, made up of narrow criss-crossing streets that served its sixteen million people, the two seemed quite alone, enclosed in their own private world. Nalini walked behind them for a while, quite sure that they hadn't noticed her.

Why was she the only one alone? Nalini shook her head slightly, as if to clear it of dark thoughts. She had to do something about her life. She wondered what her father thought about her future. He hadn't said anything, but she was sure that, like most Indian fathers tradition-bound to see daughters married, he must have been thinking about it. But then, another – different – question crossed her mind. Why did she have to wait for him to do something?

Suddenly she remembered the words of Anju Gupta, an old college classmate. Anju had always teased her about being much too 'goody goody'. 'Stop being such a *devi*! Life will pass you by and you won't even know it,' she had always said in exasperation. In those days, Nalini remembered having dismissed Anju's words as the inevitable views of a girl from a broken home. But today, the young Egyptian couple in front of her made Nalini feel that, perhaps, Anju Gupta had been right after all.

If she wanted change in her life, she was going to have to seek it for herself, and not wait for it to find her.

The realisation made her feel tired, but also light-headed. It was hot. And the thin layer of fine yellow dust glistening all around her in the afternoon sun was beginning to irritate her nose. Over the din of revving engines, she heard the afternoon call to prayer. '*Allahu Akbar, Allahu Akbar*,' screamed the *muezzin* over a loudspeaker that seemed to exist right over her head. Time to get back. With a slight shake of her head, Nalini decided to overtake the young couple in front of her. She did so in a couple of determined strides. That seemed to make her feel a little better . . . a little more energised.

Readjusting the straps of her handbag on her shoulder, she began walking briskly towards the crossroads . . .

. . . Only to find herself face to face with Rattan Malhotra.

He was standing there, at the intersection, having already crossed the road from the opposite side. He had an unlit cigarette in his mouth and a lighter in his hand.

And as usual, his fingers were shaking.

✳   ✳   ✳

Rattan Malhotra had also left his office in his lunch break – not to post letters or to window-shop, but to look for food.

He had barely walked half the length of Kasr-El-Nil when he thought he saw Nalini Thapar weaving in and out of the lunchtime crowds walking towards him. He looked again, bending his head to one side to get a better view. Yes, it was she. In her mauve *salwar kameez*, flowing hair and *dupatta*, she was visible in a way that he knew he was not, dressed in a business suit and tie. He knew that she had not noticed him, and so allowed her to walk almost right up to him before he neatly stepped into her path.

'Hi!' he said. 'Remember me?'

'Yes,' said Nalini, breathlessly coming to a stop. She lifted a hand to remove her dark glasses, and looked directly at him. 'Rattan Malhotra, isn't it? . . . And you are smoking again!'

'How are you?' he asked formally, ignoring her remark about his smoking.

She said that she was fine and asked politely how he was. She was aware of a figure taller than she remembered, and whose dark suit and elegant tie seemed as out of place amongst the shoppers and tourists crowding the pavements as those of other odd business executives looking for lunch or running an errand. Already he seemed more intrinsically a part of Cairo. She was acutely aware that they were standing in the middle of the pavement, blocking the intersection. Not that this made much difference to the stream of people waiting to cross the road: they simply parted into two, and walked by on either side of them. She felt that they should cross over too, or else move to one side. But the lights turned to red again, and before she could say anything, they became part of the crowd gathering around waiting to cross at the next green signal.

'I'm looking for lunch. Is there a place here where one can eat?' asked Rattan, looking sideways at Nalini.

'I haven't really explored the eating places in this part of town yet. But I'm sure there will be a *Felfela* here somewhere, or a Pizza Hut . . .' said Nalini.

'No. No pizza. I've had a slice too many in these last few days,' said Rattan, speaking definitively, and cutting right through her sentence.

His words were slightly accented, and Nalini wondered whether he had ever lived abroad.

'What's *Felfela*?'

'It's a chain of local restaurants serving mainly Egyptian food. *Fuul, tamayya, koshari,* salad and *tahina* . . . and various forms of *kofta,*' said Nalini, looking at his face as she spoke.

'Care to try some with me?' he asked, formally tentative – as if he knew that since he had met her only once before, she would probably not agree.

She didn't.

'I've already eaten,' she said, lying, but with enough regret in her voice to make her refusal sound genuine.

Rattan nodded, indicating that he had known that she would not join him. Nalini felt that this was not quite fair.

'I ate in the office. I only came downstairs to post a letter, and to window shop a bit. I really must get back,' she explained, her voice slightly anxious in her attempts not to sound rude and unfriendly.

'That's too bad,' said Rattan, the accent more pronounced. He dropped his almost fully smoked cigarette to the ground, and stubbed it out. He then removed his dark glasses and, looking directly at her, asked whether her office was near by. She told him it was located a few blocks from Tahrir Square, down Kasr-El-Nil.

'Mine is not far from here,' said Rattan in reply to her unspoken query about his. 'Bechtal has its offices on the first floor of one of the older, fancier buildings on the street.'

'So we are neighbours,' said Nalini.

'Yes . . . in a manner of speaking,' said Rattan.

He said this in an offhand kind of way, adding casually that he also lived near by in an apartment building in Tahrir Square.

'That's very convenient,' said Nalini, feeling suddenly that Cairo's hot sun was beaming all its heat on her head. The lights turned green, and before he spoke again, Rattan indicated that they could cross the road. They set forth, through the shimmering heat waves rising from the ground, in step with the crowds surging forwards to cross the road.

Once on the other side, Rattan spoke first.

'It is convenient ... to be so close to work, I mean. In Delhi, I had to commute long distances. This is good. At least till my car arrives ... How do you get around?'

'I have a car ... a small second-hand Volkswagen Beetle. The only one, perhaps, on the streets of Cairo.'

'That's nice. And you of course don't live far from here. You live in Zamalek,' said Rattan.

'Yes.'

'In your father's house.'

'I really must go,' said Nalini abruptly, turning her face away from him as she spoke.

Immediately Rattan regretted his mention of her father. What a silly thing to have said! Where else did he think she would be living, a temporary foreigner in Egypt? Every other Indian in town must have assumed that she lived with her father. Only he, foolishly, had decided to state the obvious. It must be awkward for her to always be known as the daughter of the Ambassador of India. He looked towards her. She seemed to have withdrawn into her distant, formal self.

'I really must go ...' she said again, more to herself than to him.

There was a pause. The two found themselves walking together. Nalini felt she should say something more, but her mind seemed blanked out, hanging in the sun. She had a sense that all this was unreal; that she and Rattan Malhotra were a pair, suspended together amidst this crowd of loudly speaking strangers who didn't care what happened to them. For a few seconds, she felt that they had been like this for eons, burning together in the heat of an all-exposing sun, inured to its merciless searing. Her vision blurred around the ideas in her head, and before she knew it she had tripped, once again, on Cairo's uneven pavements.

Rattan was walking a little behind, and couldn't really do much to steady her. By the time he had put his hand out to hold her at her elbow, she had already taken a few steps forward. He felt a sense of inadequacy at his slowness. He asked if she had been hurt, but she responded politely that she was fine.

He walked beside her for a few minutes, still holding her by the arm. He could see the tendrils of her hair curl around her neck, circling a pair of dangling silver earrings in a cosy embrace. He caught a whiff of her smell, distant and sweet, and for some reason began to wish that she would turn around and look at him. But she didn't. He wondered whether he should say something that would make her. But he noticed that a faint blush had stained the nape of her neck and chin, giving her profile a luminous glow. That she had felt its spread was obvious from the way she moved away from him. She was embarrassed, he could see. He watched her as she lifted the edge of her *dupatta*, and began wiping her face in the old way.

'It really is very hot,' she said, but her eyes avoided his. 'We should move out of the sun or else we'll die of heat stroke . . .'

Rattan agreed, and watched her lift her long, rich brown hair from the nape of her neck to let some air cool it. It was beautiful, and he wondered, suddenly, what it would look like against the white of a pillowcase. Tanvi's had been a short crop . . .

The thought of his dead wife immediately confused Rattan. What was he thinking? And what was he doing anyway, thinking such things walking the streets of Cairo, on a hot August afternoon, with a woman he had barely met?

She was different from Tanvi – taller, cooler, and more reserved. And also older. He had a sense of someone who kept life at a distance, of someone who wanted to live – to give herself up to it – but seemed all too aware of its perils. A small, bitter sneer made Rattan's mouth curl in disparagement, giving his face a harsh, almost angry look. These women and their safe home environments that had taught them to look at the world askance! It made them so smug, uppity, and complacent.

But then, a small voice niggled at his own insides. Hadn't he too been more or less the same till not so long ago? Hadn't he also assumed that if you took enough care and anticipated things, there was no chance for life to step out of line? Events had proved him wrong, though. They had left him exposed and vulnerable – all his life's successes mocked for ever by that one completely annihilating disaster. And yet, here she was, this Nalini, who seemed to feel that if she wiped her face with the ends of her *dupatta*, she could wipe away other dangers lurking alongside.

Nalini was not aware that her simple action had given rise to such deep conclusions in the mind of her walking companion. Oblivious to Rattan's thoughts, she continued wiping her face. All the while she searched for something to say, but couldn't find anything suitable.

The silence between them gave Rattan time to calm himself, and return to the formalities attending this chance meeting with the daughter of the Ambassador of India.

'We must have lunch together one day. You will, won't you? ... Have lunch with me?' said Rattan in tones so sombre that Nalini could not help but look at him in surprise.

She saw a face darkened with feelings she could not comprehend.

'Yes ...' she said hurriedly, turning to leave, and began walking a little faster to put some distance between them. 'One of these days.'

'We are walking in the same direction, you know,' he said quietly.

Feeling somewhat foolish, she slowed down, and allowed him to walk with her till they came to the square with the statue and the building that housed her office. But along the way she hardly spoke. Neither did Rattan say anything. A few silent steps later, Rattan put his hand in his pocket for his pack of cigarettes. He took one out carefully, lit it and inhaled, taking care to see that no smoke blew in Nalini's face.

'You smoke too much,' said Nalini by way of a good-bye.

'I know,' said Rattan, and tried to hide from her the fact that his fingers were shaking.

There had been two phone calls for Nalini in her absence from the office. One was from Bharat Bhavan, reminding her not to be late returning home from work; the other was a long-distance call from New Delhi.

'From New Delhi? Who could be calling me from New Delhi?' said Nalini a little breathlessly, for her mind was still on her encounter with Rattan Malhotra.

It was Gamal, who, watching her face closely, replied with a wicked glint in his eyes. 'It was some man. He said he was dying to talk with you. That he was missing you, and that he was waiting for your return!'

'I don't know any man like that ...' said Nalini cutting him short in exasperation. 'Will you tell me who it was, please, Gamal?'

'Ah, well,' said Gamal, giving up his teasing. 'It was somebody called Maneka Saxena ... I wrote down her name so that I wouldn't get it wrong. Here it is. You know her?'

'Yes. She's an old college friend of mine. Did she say she would call again?' asked Nalini, her voice full of regret at having missed her friend.

'No. She just said she had called to say "hello", and was sorry to have missed you. See, you should have returned to the office with me, instead of loitering in the streets,' said Gamal, teasing again. The others in the room laughed.

'And she also said to remind you to write,' continued Gamal, thoroughly enjoying this opportunity to get at Nalini.

'I have written,' said Nalini. 'That is the letter I posted today.'

'Ah well, she will receive it soon enough,' said Gamal. 'Why don't you ask her to visit Egypt? We'll get to meet yet another Indian beauty ... one more approachable than you, maybe?'

'Approachable? Maneka Saxena is a divorcee and a feminist. And a strong one at that ... you'd have to watch out!' said Nalini, quite amused.

'But is she pretty?' asked Gamal mischievously.

At this, Nalini read him a lecture about the need to look for other things in a woman besides the merits of her face. Deliberately putting on the demeanour of a schoolteacher giving a lesson in moral science to a class of impatient children, Nalini spoke for a few minutes.

In response, Gamal put on an expression of mock seriousness, and began saying 'yes ma'am, yes ma'am,' to every point she tried to make. This dramatic tableau continued for a few more moments, until Nalini burst out laughing. Gamal was delighted, and turning around to wink at the others, laughed too. Soon the whole room had joined in.

'Now wasn't that fun?' said Gamal. 'At least I got a laugh out of our ice-maiden here! What do you all say to that?'

They all said 'three cheers for Nalini' – first in English, and then in Arabic. Nalini did her best to prevent herself from blushing.

She was the first to stop laughing and asked seriously, 'Was there anything else she said?'

'No,' said Gamal. 'She only asked me to remind you to write.'

'Thanks, Gamal,' said Nalini, a trifle formally.

'*Ayya khidma* ... at your service, ma'am!' he said, with typical Egyptian flourish.

Everyone in the room laughed again, and soon got back to work.

PART THREE

A Letter Delivered

The postman carrying Nalini Thapar's letter to Maneka Saxena in New Delhi was an old man named Shyam Lal. A diminutive figure, he had a dignified face, and was given to tucking away his completely white hair under an old-fashioned Gandhi cap. He had worn the latter ever since he had become a postman, just after Independence. Many of his younger colleagues had laughed at him, pointing out derisively that such caps were things of the past, and no longer in vogue. But he had stuck steadfastly to the choice made in his youth. Over the years, this had given him an air of dignified distinction. 'We came of age in the decade of the great Indian cause,' the man and his cap seemed to say, and by implication also to suggest that the years that had followed the great moment of 1947 had been marked only by a growing insignificance.

He had only a few months left before he retired from the Indian Postal Service in which he had worked for forty-three years. Then he would no longer have to pedal his bicycle long hours down rows and rows of ill-numbered streets, six days a week, to distribute mail. He looked forward to that time, for he hadn't been feeling very well lately. His cough was getting worse by the day and, in these last few weeks, he had had to dismount at least two to three times to rest on the side of the road under the shade of the nearest tree to get his breath back.

At these times, he hated his struggle with broken bicycle pedals, sliding chains, and slippery letters that often broke free from the strings he tied them with.

Still, his department had been kind to him. Besides giving him as many extensions of service as were possible under the rules, they had let him have his choice of streets to deliver mail in. And he had chosen the areas around Hauz Khas, Gulmohur Park and Yusuf Sarai – all suburbs that were close to each other. In these he knew the pattern of the streets like the lines on his hand. He knew where he should begin his rounds every morning: which side of a street he should go down first; which ones he would have to double ride; where the shortcuts to the adjoining suburbs were; and how he could avoid red lights. He also knew who lived where, and the exact number of members in each household – whether it was a single unit family, or a joint family in which the older, middle, and younger generations lived together. He even knew the names of the servants in each household, often having to ferret them out from their residential quarters behind the big houses in order to collect fines for the under-stamped letters they received. He was the first to know when people moved away, and when new ones came to inhabit the houses under his charge.

He was one of the earliest to know of the changed tenants of 74 Hauz Khas. In these last three months, *Sahayata* of 74 Hauz Khas had begun receiving a lot of mail. It consisted of large quantities of Book Post mail that came in from various organisations both within and outside the country. There were letters too, some of an obviously personal nature. Shyam Lal would tie them all in a bundle before leaving the post office in the morning. If it was a big one, he would alter his route somewhat so he could get to 74 Hauz Khas as quickly as possible. By making it his first destination, he would lighten the load on his bicycle. If the letters and parcels were few, he would ride his normal route, and reach it sometime after noon.

One day, early in the September of 1992, Shyam Lal reached

Sahayata shortly after 1 p.m. He took his time dismounting, leaning against his bicycle to mop his face. Although the length of the days seemed to be shortening, it was still warm and quite humid. Shyam Lal was hungry, and a trifle tired. He needed to eat, and take a break from pedalling. He had delivered the mail in the Reception Room of *Sahayata* and was walking down the driveway towards his bicycle parked on the street when he noticed Ram Singh standing by the gates of 73 Hauz Khas. Ram Singh was talking to the two *chowkidars* on duty there.

Ever since the death of Tanvi, the Malhotras had doubled the security around their residence. On the days following the tragic event, many undesirable people had moved in and out of the street, often stopping for long periods to loiter outside the house. Besides the usual neighbourhood riff-raff of inquisitive passers-by, there had been the police and the officers of the CBI, members of the Press, and other social service groups. What the Malhotras came to dread most were not so much the police or the reporters from the Press, but the members of the different women's groups. They had come around in small bands, armed with posters and banners. They would march down the street, hang around the gates of the house, and shout curses against the Malhotra family. This would be followed by a deliberately dramatic wailing in loud tones that gave way, after a pre-decided period of time, to the shouting of slogans. '*Nari hatya nahi chalegi*' and '*Bechari nari, mari gayi, mari gayi*' were the ones most loudly heard. This was sometimes accompanied by the throwing of stones. Once, many windows of the house were broken before the police had come and lathi charged the women into dispersing.

It didn't help the Malhotras when the visiting bands got to know that *Sahayata* existed right next door. The latter allowed them access to their driveway, which made 'the house of the crime' (as Maneka Saxena had come to describe it) open to view from two sides — the front (from the road) and the side (from across the wall where the Malhotra cars stood under the porch).

If such displays of outrage had lessened a little, it was because the Malhotras had immediately ordered high fencing to be erected on all sides of the house, and because the *chowkidars* at the gate repeatedly told everyone who was interested that the house was completely empty – that all of its three inmates were out of the country. It was their job to see that the crowds did not gather, or come anywhere near forcing the gates open and entering the driveway. While nothing could be done to stop the shouting from the street, the *chowkidars* were under strict instructions to call the police if there was any trespassing.

The newly appointed *chowkidars* were cronies of Ram Singh, and often the tall, ex-serviceman would corroborate their firm-voiced denials. With not much to do by way of work in an empty house, Ram Singh would join his friends outside on security duty.

When Shyam Lal came by on his bicycle, Ram Singh was outside with his *chowkidar* companions. They saw the old postman as a friend, one of the very few in the neighbourhood who, after the initial 'tch tch, poor thing', had chosen to remain neutral about the event in 73 Hauz Khas. Suicide or murder? How did it bother him? It was *Kalyug* anyway, and anything could happen any time. In any case, he knew that many things happened quietly in the households of the rich; but it was not his place to have any more than a private opinion about them.

Shyam Lal stood a while, sorting through the letters in the dilapidated basket attached to the handlebars of his bicycle. He separated the letters for 73 Hauz Khas, and handed them over to Ram Singh who had greeted him with a cool '*Namaskar*, Shyam Lal *ji*.'

Shyam Lal returned his greeting in tired tones, and proceeded to wipe his face with his small towel.

'How are you?' asked Ram Singh, his spotless white *bandgala* glinting in the bright afternoon glare.

'I'm fine, thanks. Just a little tired and hungry,' said Shyam Lal. His back, as he stood there, was slightly bent.

'Why don't you come in for a bit? I'll give you some cold water to drink from the refrigerator in the kitchen, and you can have your lunch in comfort. Maybe we can have some tea afterwards?' said Ram Singh.

'Where are the sahib and the memsahib?' asked Shyam Lal a little warily. He did not want to get involved in any trouble or controversy.

'Oh, they are not in the country. They return next month . . . at least the memsahib does. Sahib will return soon after. Or one of these days . . .' said Ram Singh, stopping mid-sentence suggestively, and winking at his *chowkidar* friends.

They said nothing by way of a reply.

'Has he been gone long?' asked Shyam Lal. He had looked away as he asked, his voice studiedly casual.

'The usual. And he will return only when he has to,' continued Ram Singh. 'Our sahib has his heart in the big wide world. It is not confined only here to his home. He's a man, you know — a man of worth and dignity. He's not some ordinary, small-minded, small-hearted person.'

As he said all this, his eyes looked into the distance and his right hand stroked his handlebar moustache with some degree of satisfaction.

Nobody said anything to this. Ram Singh signalled to his *chowkidar* friends that they should stay at the gates while he and Shyam Lal went into the house. He ushered the postman wheeling his bicycle in through the gates, up the driveway, and under the front porch. He paused a little while watching him park his bicycle carefully against the wall, and lock it.

'Don't worry! Your cycle and your letters are quite safe here!'

'I hope so,' said Shyam Lal sceptically. 'You can never tell these days.'

They went around the rear of the house, entering the kitchen through the back door. Inside, Hari Ram was making chapatis on a *tava* on the gas cooktop. When he finished, the three sat down to eat.

'So, have they discovered anything?' asked Shyam Lal, as he finished drinking the last gulp of refrigerated water from a stainless-steel tumbler. His voice was flat, but also carefully curious.

'Discovered what?' asked Ram Singh, his face deadpan.

'Why the new *bahu* of the house killed herself,' said Shyam Lal.

'*Arre*, what will they find out?' said Ram Singh scornfully, smoothing crumbs of food away from his moustache with fingers made wet with the last drops of ice-cold water left at the bottom of his steel tumbler. 'She just killed herself. You can never tell with these young girls these days. She came from an ordinary house, you know ... But I guess she was nice enough. The memsahib chose her with great care, and liked her because she was simple and innocent. What got into her head, who can tell?'

'Yes, I suppose you are right. Nobody can tell,' said Shyam Lal. 'She had everything. So much given her, so much status, such a good family, and such a good husband ...'

Shyam Lal's words and their intonation suggested that he, for one, was always overawed by the eternally mysterious happenings of the current age. He had taken out his towel once again, and was wiping his face, neck, and hands in preparation for departure. So bent was he on his ablutions that he did not notice that Ram Singh's lips had curled a little cruelly, or that his eyes had focused on some point in the distance. It was Hari Ram, so far a pensively silent part of the threesome, who looked up quickly. He only spoke after he had given Ram Singh a warning glance through his thick-lensed spectacles.

'*Arre bhai*, why don't you just drop the subject? It's over, all over. The poor girl is dead, and our boy has gone ... has had to leave. And to think that he just returned last year from such a long stay in the USA. It was no small thing for the Malhotras that their son returned to them from that country. In today's day and age, who comes back from America? All the young people want to go there ... and stay there. Even marry there!'

Having said all this, and as if aware of the rarity of his own eloquence, Hari Ram immediately turned his back on the other two in the kitchen and walked towards the sink. He began washing the plates, spoons and tumblers used in the meal.

Ram Singh looked at Hari Ram in surprise. He had spoken a lot for the quiet person he always was. He looked at the old cook's back speculatively for a minute. 'That is very true. Rattan *baba* did come back, and his return upset a lot of things in this household. We were getting along so well before he returned! But ... it might just have been that girl, you know! She must have had a bad horoscope. I told the memsahib that she should check it out. But she only laughed, and said that she was a "modern" woman and didn't believe in such things. I told her that being "modern" was all right, but where the *khandan* was concerned, one always had to be careful. The daughter-in-law of a house has to be chosen carefully. Her *karma* can affect the *kismet* of the whole household ...'

'Sh, sh,' said Shyam Lal, moving towards the kitchen door. 'Don't say that. She was nice enough ... and was the same age as my daughter ...'

'Yes,' said Hari Ram suddenly in a loud tone. He was still at the sink and had his back to the other two. 'Be careful about what you say, Ram Singh. There is *Sahayata* next door, remember? And all those screaming women. Especially that Maneka Saxena, and that Arti Chug. I have warned you many times, Ram Singh. But you never listen to me. You will get into trouble one day ...'

'Now, why should I get into any trouble?' asked Ram Singh aggressively.

But Hari Ram did not answer. He only gave his co-worker in the house a speaking look and began putting away washed plates and tumblers in the open cupboards before him. It was Shyam Lal, quite unaware of the exact nature of Hari Ram's warnings, who spoke into the ominous, and slightly mysterious, silence.

'Yes, one should be careful. And now I had better go. I have just delivered letters next door. And one of them was for the Maneka Saxena you spoke of. It had a foreign postmark . . .'

'Really?' said Ram Singh. But his response was automatic. He was not really interested. Following Shyam Lal outside, he stood around watching him unlock his bicycle and leave. A few minutes later, he had made himself comfortable on one of the old chairs at the gates of the house and resumed his lazy afternoon chats with the security guards.

Shadow Play

Ever since the day she had run into Rattan Malhotra on the pavements of Downtown Cairo, Nalini Thapar found herself thinking about him often. His tall, morose frame would float before her mind's eye at the most unexpected moments, and leave her restless and dissatisfied. Every time there was a mention of the Bechtal Corporation, she would think of him sitting behind a desk in a posh office, looking through files and issuing orders through a haze of smoke, his dark eyes serious in concentration. She wondered what exactly his work entailed, and whether he enjoyed it. Such questions would give rise to others – and still others – until she would ask herself in exasperation why she was wasting her time on thinking about someone she hardly knew. However, in her search for that one reason which would help her dismiss him from her mind, she could come up with none other than the fact that he smoked. And that, she told herself repeatedly, was (surely?) absolutely unacceptable. She was allergic to cigarette smoke and would therefore have nothing to do with even thinking about him.

But of course, however much she tried, she could not rid her mind of his image. Her lunchtime walk with him through the streets of Cairo stayed vivid in her imagination. Every time she thought about it, she could not help regretting her refusal to have lunch with him. She came to this conclusion after fighting a hidden battle with herself. One part of her said she had done the right thing; the other chided herself for losing an opportunity that, as time had shown, was hardly likely to come by again. She thought once or twice about calling him – 'just to say hello and ... and ...' But that was where it rested. If she did call, what would she say to him? That she found him interesting? That she wished they could meet again?

Nalini need not have despaired. The Indian expatriate community was not that large after all, and the inevitable socialising brought her together with Rattan soon enough. This happened innocuously one evening at the end of September when the Guptas decided to throw a party. Its main purpose was to extend a long-overdue invitation to the Ambassador and his family. It was Madhu's idea – she had never invited the Thapars to her home, and had begun to feel socially behind the others who had already done so. She goaded her husband into choosing a day and issuing an invitation. When it was accepted by Gautam Thapar, she invited her friends. Before she knew it, twenty-one couples had accepted.

When Gautam Thapar told Nalini about the Gupta invitation to dinner, her first reaction was one of refusal. She had not been in the mood to go out much lately; and her father – loth to force her each time – had not insisted. But that had also meant Nalini spending too many evenings at home all by herself. Her father did not like this growing tendency of withdrawal from society. The chances of some younger people being present at the Guptas were high enough. It would do her good to spend time with them.

'You must come with me, *beti*. You know Madhu Gupta is a cheerful sort of person. And, in any case, it is going to be an informal evening,' he said not agreeing to her excuses this time.

Nalini immediately cast a quick look at her father's face and saw concern in it. 'Yes, Daddy,' she said meekly, regressing deliberately to being a mischievous schoolgirl in front of a loved father. She would agree to his desire this one time.

'Good girl,' said the father, turning to go in relief.

Nalini smiled. She had made her father happy.

But she also knew that they were indulging each other. And also, that both knew this.

The Gupta living room was full of people when Nalini and her father arrived, somewhat later than the others. Everyone stood up deferentially to greet them. However, Gautam Thapar immediately indicated that, as far as he was concerned, it was going to be an informal relaxed evening. After greetings and introductions, Nalini found herself sitting next to a recently married couple named Rashmi and Rohit Gopal who had been in Cairo only a few months. They had just moved into an apartment two blocks away from the Guptas, and were rejoicing in the fact of having their first decent home. Nalini found herself listening passively, not asking too many questions. She did not really need to, for Rashmi was full of details about unpacking and the search for furnishings.

The host made sure that everyone was served drinks. Soon Madhu came around, accompanying a waiter with a tray full of *kebabs* and *pakoras*. The atmosphere was light and friendly, with conversation flowing freely, and the silks of the women glowing warmly in the discreet light of lamps placed strategically in the corners of the large living room. Indian expatriate managers did well for themselves in Cairo. They worked hard and were paid well for it.

Nalini moved away from the Gopals to join another group of women. One of them, Sunita Singh – a tall, smiling *sardarni* with two little girls – was talking about organising a felucca evening on one of the coming weekends. Felucca evenings were popular in Cairo not only among the Indian community but amongst the Egyptians as well. If you lived anywhere on the banks of the river, you could see the old-fashioned sail boats drift by on sunset evenings, full of revellers getting away from it all on the waters. Nalini had seen them many times from her bay window but had never joined anyone for an evening on a felucca.

'You will come, won't you?' Sunita said to Nalini. 'You'll enjoy it.'

'I would love to,' said Nalini politely, hoping that she didn't sound as unenthusiastic as she was feeling.

'I will call you when we decide on a day and a time. And if you need a ride, someone coming from Zamalek will give you one.'

'Thanks,' said Nalini, and watched the ease with which the young mother-of-two moved between the guests and spread the idea of the felucca ride. There were many takers. Within half an hour, the food, the drinks and the music had all been farmed out among those interested. Only the date and the exact time remained to be fixed.

It was then – about an hour after their arrival – that Nalini heard Vinod Gupta call out loudly.

'I say, where is that Rattan Malhotra? It's almost nine thirty. He was supposed to be here early.'

There was a slight lull in the conversation. No one answered the host's question.

Standing in the middle of a group of women, twirling an empty glass in her hand, Nalini felt herself go all alert, her heart standing still for an unusually long moment before it began to beat again. So he was coming too, was he? She found, suddenly, that she had to move in order to get the unexpectedly static circulation in her legs going again. She also needed another drink. She spotted the bar at the far end of the living room. As she moved towards it, she noted that though he had asked about Rattan Malhotra again, Vinod's repeated question had remained unanswered.

'Nobody seems to know him or his whereabouts,' thought Nalini as she automatically refilled her glass with orange juice and added some ice to it. Wanting something to do urgently, Nalini walked towards the kitchen, and soon found herself standing in the doorway watching Madhu and her maid Safiya frying *puris* in a large *kadahi* filled with hot vegetable oil. Madhu was showing Safiya how to use more effectively the small contraption which flattened small balls of dough into even, round *puris*. While Safiya was slow and clumsy, Madhu was able to use the gadget quickly and efficiently. But Safiya was keen to learn, and wanted to try again so she could increase her speed and make more *puris*. Madhu let her, and for a moment both she and Nalini watched Safiya have better luck with the numbers she could produce.

It was just then that the phone rang in the kitchen. Madhu moved towards it, and Nalini could hear everything quite clearly. The phone call was from Rattan Malhotra. He could not come. He was running a high fever, and would come over some other day.

'Have you seen a doctor?' Nalini heard Madhu ask.

He had not. Neither did he know how high his fever was because he did not have a thermometer. He had just taken a Disprin, and was waiting for it to take effect.

Madhu put down the phone and, wiping her hands on a carelessly slung apron around her waist, walked into the living room in search of her husband. He was standing in the middle of the group of men surrounding Gautam Thapar. The conversation had moved from politics in India to the politics of Egypt. Somebody was telling one of the lesser-known Mubarak jokes. Madhu stood quietly behind her husband for a few seconds. She was waiting for the final punch line and the point at which the whole group would burst into loud guffaws of laughter. It was only when this was over that she drew attention to herself. Vinod turned around immediately, and followed where she led him.

Standing in the doorway of the kitchen and the living room, Nalini saw her say something softly in his ear. Vinod's face showed surprise first, and then concern. From where she stood, Nalini noticed that he had made some sort of a decision. Soon, husband and wife had crossed the room towards the foyer. She saw Vinod say something to the waiter hovering there with a tray of drinks, and picking out a bunch of keys from a peg hanging on the wall, he stepped out of the front door and was gone.

'Vinod has gone to fetch him,' Nalini heard Madhu say from behind her. She turned around and saw that her hostess had entered the kitchen, and was in the process of taking off her apron and washing her hands with soap at the sink.

'Fetch whom?' said Nalini.

'That Rattan Malhotra. You know the new Indian who came into town recently . . . you met him, didn't you? He was there at the Independence Day reception . . .'

'Yes. I know who he is. I have met him,' said Nalini flatly.

'He is ill . . . has a high fever. I don't think he should be alone in his apartment. I am going to spread a fresh sheet on the bed in the guest room. Would you like to give me a hand?'

'Sure,' said Nalini. Draining her glass of the last dregs of orange juice, she put it into the rapidly filling sink of dirty glasses, and followed Madhu out of the kitchen.

The Gupta guest room was at the far end of the apartment – all the way down the hallway. Nalini followed Madhu automatically. Her mind was far away, in some moment of suspended time. She watched Madhu fold up the bedspread in quick, neat movements, lay it down on the back of a sofa chair, move to the cupboard, and from its last shelf at the bottom, take out a set of sheets and a blanket. Nalini helped her spread the sheet, and put a pillowcase on the pillow. She laid out a sheet and a blanket at the foot of the bed, and took a quick look around the room.

'There, that should do,' said Madhu. 'Poor guy! Hope it is only the 'flu. It is much around these days. We couldn't leave him there alone in his apartment. We Indians should help each other, don't you think?'

'Yes, of course,' said Nalini, and marvelled at how quickly the Guptas decided on such things.

When they returned to the kitchen, the pile of *puris* had grown. Safiya seemed pleased with herself. Madhu praised Safiya and, lighting the other two burners on the far side of the *kadahi*, put two pans – one full of curried lamb, and the other full of black lentils – to heat over a low flame.

'We can take a break, I think,' said Madhu, giving a last look at her kitchen before stepping out of it. 'And eat as soon as Vinod returns with Rattan.'

Madhu shepherded Nalini into the sitting room, telling her quietly that there was no need to tell the others about where Vinod had gone or that Rattan was unwell. They would all feel the need to look in on him, and she was sure that Rattan would not be up to this. Nalini agreed, and felt immediately that she was part of a little conspiracy. A small, quiet thrill ran up her entire body. It was so powerful that she took a quiet look around to see if anyone else had noticed. To her relief they had not.

She saw Madhu move from group to group as they stood around talking. Everyone was relaxed and free. Even her own father seemed a different person here. She saw Gautam Thapar's face: the two stiff Scotches-on-the rock had done him a world of good. The strained lines of grief around his eyes had eased, and he seemed much younger. Nalini could not help but compare this party to the stiffer, formal ones at Bharat Bhavan. It would be nice to have one's own circle of free-and-easy friendships, thought Nalini, and wondered when things would change for her.

It was about forty-five minutes later that Madhu beckoned her urgently. 'They must have come,' Nalini told herself, and followed Madhu outside to the landing where the elevator doors opened. Nalini walked up and waited with her. They were hardly there one silent minute before the doors opened.

Vinod emerged, with his arm around Rattan Malhotra.

'I brought him with me,' said Vinod, addressing his wife. 'He was in no state to be left alone.'

'Of course,' said Madhu, calmly removing an overnight bag from Rattan's hands into her own. 'Come along, my dear.'

Rattan allowed himself to be led along, but all the time his eyes were on Nalini. She had said a quiet 'Hi' to him when she saw the surprise on his face, and he had smiled back weakly. He was still in his suit, now crumpled, with its jacket thrown carelessly over his shoulders.

'He could hardly get up to open the door,' Vinod was saying. 'I almost left because he took so long to open it. I thought he wasn't there!'

'I think it's the 'flu ... two people in my office had it recently. I must have caught it from them,' said Rattan apologetically.

By this time they had moved into the apartment, and Rattan had been herded swiftly down the passageway into the guest room. Madhu told Vinod that he should return to the guests, and that after making Rattan comfortable, she would come out and serve dinner. Vinod left Rattan to the two women, and returned to the living room.

Nalini did not know what she should do, and hung around in the doorway. But Madhu had no such qualms. She showed Rattan where the bathroom was, and indicated that he should change into the pyjamas he'd brought with him. Rattan did what he was told, and disappeared into the bathroom. Madhu instructed Nalini to bring one glass of water and another of orange juice for the patient.

Nalini went off immediately to the small bar, and asked the waiter to fill the two glasses. Holding one in each hand, she made her way carefully back down the hallway towards the guest room. On the way, she met Madhu hurrying to the kitchen.

'Rattan is in bed, and I've put a Crocin tablet on the night-stand near him,' she told Nalini. 'Make sure he has it, and see if he needs anything else. I am going to serve dinner. It's very late – almost eleven – and my guests must be really hungry!'

It occurred to Nalini to wonder why it was she who had been asked to do all these things for Rattan Malhotra in his sickness. Did the Guptas know something she did not? What would her father think?

Rattan was in bed, lying quietly with his face turned away to the window.

'You are supposed to take one tablet of Crocin,' said Nalini softly, as she set down the glasses on the night-stand beside the bed.

Rattan did not reply, but turned over on his back. She cast him a quick glance, and saw that he was looking at her with an amused smile. It made Nalini slightly nervous, and she bent over to pick up the Crocin tablet and remove its wrapping. He watched her without saying a word, and took the tablet. He swallowed it quickly, and drained the glass of water.

'Thanks for your concern, Florence Nightingale! First it was smoking, and now it is this . . .'

Nalini looked him in the eyes and saw laughter in them. She took a deep breath and said nothing. A faint blush spread across her face, and Rattan saw that a fine wrinkle of hurt had crossed her forehead. He saw her turn quickly, pick up the glass, and make as if to leave.

'Hey!' said Rattan, quickly putting out a hand to hold hers. 'Please don't go! I'm sorry. I did not mean to tease you! I thought we would have dinner together, here in this room . . . because you will not have lunch with me. You refused the other day, remember?'

Nalini was silent. She watched, as if from a distance, her hand in his, and felt her mouth grow dry, and her legs weaken with feelings she had not known before. She felt that Rattan Malhotra had been holding her hand a long time – only she had not realised it before that moment. She was intensely conscious that her fingers might be cold, and slightly trembling. She stood very still for a few seconds. She did not know what it was in her face that eventually made Rattan let go gently. She felt the heat of his hand withdraw immediately, and a chill shiver passed through her.

He saw the imprint of his fingers on her white wrist fade slowly.

'I am sorry about my comments on your smoking,' said Nalini somewhat formally after an awkward silence. 'I won't do that again.'

'Oh God, I have upset you, haven't I? ... Really, I don't mind at all. In fact, it is good for me that someone says they do not like my smoking. I should never have begun in the first place!'

Feeling somewhat recovered, Nalini wanted to ask why he had done so, but wondered whether this was the right moment to ask. She decided it wasn't, but he seemed to guess what was in her mind.

'I'll tell you some day. Some day soon,' he said, turning his face away from her towards the window.

'Tell me what?' asked Nalini.

Rattan did not reply. She saw that he looked very tired suddenly, and immediately felt contrite. She told him he should rest, and try to sleep a little. Hearing her voice, he turned to look at her as she talked. Her long hair shone a warm henna brown, and the solitary string of small pearls around her throat added just that touch of elegance to the simple style of her pale cream silk *salwar kameez*. Her face was serious and concerned.

Suddenly, he could not bear the thought of her leaving. His mind, even through its haze of fever, thought how difficult it had been all these weeks to find an appropriate excuse to meet her again. Now she was here, a touch away, but at the point of leaving. He had to do something to keep her from going. 'I am hungry,' he said abruptly into the silence that hung between them. His voice sounded so unnaturally loud that Nalini could not help smiling. She looked completely disbelieving, her eyes widening in surprise.

'No, really! I am not joking. I am hungry ... I never had any lunch at work today. I was feeling so lousy. And now I feel sick with hunger ...' he reiterated.

Nalini asked him what he wanted to eat, but Rattan assured her that he only wanted something light – like rice and yogurt. He tried to get her to promise that she would bring her own plate too, and eat it in the guest room with him.

This Nalini would not do.

'Aren't you afraid that I will catch the 'flu from you?' she rebuked jokingly.

But he shook his head.

'That will be a good thing, won't it? Because then I will be able to bring flowers when I come to see you!'

Nalini had nothing to say to this. But she did have some odd feelings of satisfaction as she left immediately after, and walked towards the kitchen.

As it happened, Nalini did eat her dinner that night with Rattan Malhotra. She was one among the two or three others who sat around the bedroom with dinner plates balanced precariously on their laps. After Nalini had gone to organise Rattan's dinner, Vinod had come in with a doctor summoned earlier on the phone. The latter had quickly examined Rattan and suggested a course of antibiotics that were to be given after he had eaten. An hour after the Crocin had taken effect, Rattan's fever started to come down. After laying out the buffet for the guests, Madhu prepared a tray for her patient. She handed it over to a waiter to take to Rattan, calling out to Nalini to make sure that everything was all right.

It was at this time that Gautam Thapar heard Madhu's request to Nalini, and asked her what was happening. Nalini told him briefly how Rattan Malhotra had been taken ill and been brought over, and how Madhu had asked for her help. If Gautam Thapar felt anything was odd about this request he did not show it. He went in briefly to check on Rattan and rejoined the guests. Nalini found herself among the last in the line for the buffet and just as she was wondering where she could find a place for herself, Madhu suggested that they sit with Rattan for a bit. Two other of Vinod's friends were already there, sitting on the edge of Rattan's bed with their plates. Madhu made a place for Nalini on a chair on the far side of the room, and perched herself on the dressing-table stool.

Nalini saw that while the others were enjoying their dinner, Rattan merely picked at his. But neither did she eat much. The conversation flowed easily. But between all the compliments that were being bestowed on Madhu for her cooking, Nalini found herself exchanging glances with Rattan. When Madhu finished eating and made to leave the room, Nalini also stood up to go with her. Rattan almost opened his mouth to request her to stay, but there was something in the look she cast him that prevented him from doing so. In that look he understood that she would feel awkward with only men – whom she did not know very well – in the room. And that, whether he liked it or not, she was an Ambassador's daughter who had already stretched proprieties somewhat. He knew that he would not see her again that evening. He waved her a surreptitious good-bye to which she responded with a slight smile.

He saw her stand up, adjust her *dupatta*, and then her long flowing hair, and a minute later she was gone.

On the way home, Nalini was rather quiet. Gautam Thapar looked at his daughter sitting alongside in the back seat of the chauffeur-driven car and gazing out of her window. The street lights along the corniche all the way to Zamalek from Ma'adi cast successive fleeting shadows across her face.

'That was a fun evening, wasn't it?' he said, in an effort to break the silence.

'Yes, it was,' said Nalini, and remarked pensively on what a nice couple the Guptas were – so helpful and friendly.

Gautam Thapar wondered whether this was a reference to the way they had helped the unwell newcomer to Cairo. For a second he thought he would mention Rattan Malhotra by name, but then decided against it.

'We must thank them for the lovely evening,' he said, and let it go at that.

Nalini did not say anything.

Nalini was restless and fidgety at work all the next day. The office was rather quiet, Gamal being on casual leave in Alexandria. Nalini had come in bleary-eyed and tired from a night of sleepless tossing in which her mind had been on Rattan Malhotra lying ill in the Gupta guest room. She had re-lived a hundred times every moment of that most unexpected evening. As she sat at her desk trying to concentrate on the computer screen in front of her, many odd questions kept passing through her mind. What, for instance, would her father be thinking? Why did Madhu Gupta call upon her for help when so many other women had been present? The Guptas were the only ones, as far as she had observed, who seemed to know Rattan. Could he have said anything about her to them?

She did not think so, for there was really nothing to tell. Just two brief encounters – one at Independence Day, and one in the streets of Downtown. By 11 a.m., however – when Fuad, the office factotum, brought her a cup of over-sweetened tea – she decided she had to do something.

'I have to say thanks any way for the evening,' she told herself at last, and dialled the Gupta residence. Madhu picked up the phone. She recognised Nalini's voice immediately, and graciously accepted her thanks for the evening.

'How is the patient?' asked Nalini somewhat tentatively, at the same time as she tried to make her voice light and careless.

'He is awake, but his fever is high, one hundred and three! I just dosed him with Crocin and penicillin. It will take a day or two. Would you like to speak with him?'

'No, oh no ... I was just ...' said Nalini hurriedly.

But Madhu cut her short. 'Here, talk to him. It will do him good. He's lying here, like a martyr, feeling sorry for himself!'

And before she knew it, she heard Rattan's 'Hello?' in her ear.

'Hello. I mean ... Hi! It's me, Nalini,' she said, stuttering a little. 'How are you feeling?'

'I'm fine. Just fine ... a little high on body temperature, that's all!' said Rattan, a laugh in his voice heavy with a cold.

'I'm sure Madhu and Vinod will take good care of you,' said Nalini carefully, her calm recovered. Her tones had become formal again because she did not know what else to say.

'Everybody is taking good care of me. Cairo has some very nice people in it,' said Rattan. Nalini found herself tongue-tied. Why, of all times now, could she find nothing to say? What must he think of her?

Rattan noticed her silence, but did not allow himself to wonder about it. He asked her quickly where she was calling from. When she told him that she was calling from work, he asked her what she did, and whether she enjoyed her job. Questions of this kind were easy to answer, and in a minute or so the conversation between the two was flowing as naturally as if they had known each other some time.

She told him how she thought herself lucky to have found something to do in Cairo.

'Diplomatic life has so many restrictions on what the family members of a Head of Mission can and cannot do,' explained Nalini. 'But my working as part of the editorial team on the Culture pages of the *Al-Ahram Weekly* does not present "a clash of interests" with anything else.'

'What sort of editing do you do?' asked Rattan.

'Well, many of the articles are written in Arabic first and then translated into English. The translations are often of poor quality. I help straighten them out, often needing to return to the original in Arabic with the help of someone who knows both languages.'

'I did not know that it takes all this to bring out just one issue of the weekly!' said Rattan.

'The editing team is huge, and largely made up of expatriates,' said Nalini. 'I work with three British people – all my age – who have come from England to look for jobs. They trade on being the most authentic users of the Queen's English!'

'I hope the Editor knows enough English to see what is being published each week,' said Rattan.

'I guess he does ... although he does have the support of two or three senior people, all Egyptians, who were schooled in either England or the USA. It is they who make sure that nuances in each article reflect the policies of the newspaper as a whole.'

'Do you write for the paper in your own right also?' asked Rattan.

'Yes, I do. I review books ... new fiction by Arab writers – but all in translation, and other titles too. I have also written some articles.'

'I shall look out for your name every week,' said Rattan.

They went on to talk of other things. Nalini did not realise it then, but Rattan was doing all the asking and she found it easy to tell him what he wanted to know.

They spoke for a good ten minutes.

It was only when the subject of her mother's death came up, at Rattan's instigation, that Nalini found herself choking suddenly into silence. When he noticed her reaction, Rattan could have cursed himself. After a few incomplete sentences, her replies became formal again.

'I am sorry to have gone on talking so much,' she said stiffly. 'You must have a real headache by now ...'

'I'm fine, I assure you,' said Rattan, trying desperately to reassure her. 'I am feeling a lot better, believe me ...'

But Nalini cut him short.

'That can't be true. Madhu told me your fever was a hundred and three. I should stop making you talk, and let you go ...'

'May I telephone you?' said Rattan, cutting sharply through the formalities of her good-bye. He knew that his question sounded abrupt, even rudely demanding. But he felt suddenly desperate to see her again. He had to chance her refusal, and take cues regarding future meetings from whatever she decided.

He waited anxiously for her reply.

There was a longish silence. Nalini felt her stomach muscles tighten for one intense moment. She felt something momentous was about to happen. She said a hurried 'yes', and telling him to look after himself, wished him a polite good-bye.

Lying facing the windows of Vinod Gupta's guest bedroom, Rattan went over his conversation with Nalini Thapar. Though his fever was high, and his head and body ached all over, he could not help feeling good about how the last twenty minutes had gone. 'She felt the need to inquire after me!' he thought wonderingly. He was not so alone in Cairo, after all. The realisation made him feel a little woolly, even light-headed. He told himself that he should sleep a little. It wasn't noon yet, and in the distance he could hear Madhu's voice speaking broken Arabic with Safiya. When she came in next, he would ask her some more details about Nalini Thapar and her father. He wished, for the hundredth time, that he had not said anything about Mrs Thapar, for it had made Nalini unhappy and silent. He wondered how long ago it was that she had died, and how it had happened.

It must be hard for her, young as she was, to run the house in place of her mother.

The thought of absent mothers made Rattan think of his own – and their last conversation. He had been rather rough with her and he felt bad. 'I should call her soon,' he told himself. Tanvi's death had really affected her, and Rattan wondered whether she had returned to her own house yet.

Turning over in bed – away from the bright light flooding in from the windows – Rattan closed his eyes in preparation for a small nap. As he did so, he thought that the next time he talked with Pammi, he would tell her to forget Tanvi, forget that his young wife had chosen to die on him.

For a while Rattan lay still, with his eyes closed. Rags of memory – loose, unconnected, yet strong and vivid – swam into his consciousness through the befuddlement of fever. The figure of Tanvi hanging from the ceiling fan floated before his eyes. He could see clearly the edges of the patch of her spit, wet on her breast. She seemed to sway from side to side as if in slow motion. But her face was, surprisingly, blurred. Soon, she seemed to sway out of sight altogether, covered over in a warm cloud of mist.

His last thought, before he dozed off, was that for once the memory of his dead wife had not covered him over with the sense of weighted dread as it invariably had done in the past.

When Madhu looked in on her patient half an hour later, she found him sleeping deeply.

Panna the Fakir Revisited

While Rattan Malhotra slept deeply in the Gupta guest room, his mother was having a hard time sleeping at all. Pammi had stayed on in London in a rented apartment all these months after she had bade a stony farewell to her son. Noni joined her whenever he could. However, for the most part, she found herself alone. She had some friends in the distant suburbs, and met them a few times, but then gave up: they all wanted to know about Rattan and his young wife's death.

After spending a few dismal days watching TV and reading in the apartment, she decided to go sightseeing, spending the days with groups of anonymous tourists at monuments and cathedrals. Pammi stayed in London for four months, taking care to return to India some time before *Diwali*. It was this important date that determined her departure from London. She had to make sure that its festivities were completely avoided around the precincts of 73 Hauz Khas. The Malhotra household could hardly be seen to be 'celebrating' the festival after the terrible tragedy in their home, and she could not trust the servants to be completely discreet about candles, *mithai* and *patakas*.

Pammi arrived in New Delhi in the last week of October. Noni was somewhere on his travels, and would come in separately, two days later, on a flight from New York. Ram

Singh made sure that Kishore was at the airport to fetch her, and after a smooth transit through customs, Pammi found herself unlocking the doors to her bedroom, with Ram Singh following behind her dutifully carrying her suitcases.

For a couple of days after her arrival, Pammi kept to herself.

But, inevitably, her return to New Delhi did not remain hidden for too long. Soon, the phone began to ring, and her friends of long standing attempted to do what they thought was best: keep her busy socially and help her forget the terrible event. This did not, of course, include card parties. No, those were not at all appropriate so soon after the tragedy. But there was no need, they pointed out, to be alone or remain cut off from the daily flow of things.

But each of the women who visited Pammi found her strangely withdrawn, not speaking much, and certainly not initiating any conversation. As soon as they would arrive, they would be ushered in – in the old style – by Ram Singh, and be made to sit in the sparkling living room. After a few minutes, Pammi would enter, dressed in soft, pastel-coloured saris with old *pashmina* shawls thrown lightly over her shoulders. Everyone noticed that though nothing seemed changed in her appearance, the old air of confident social centrality was gone. Her visitors would feel the awkwardness of the hushed silences of her presence, they would rush into speech, all asking the same questions: how had her trip been? Was London cold? How was Rattan?

But they would not receive much by way of a reply. In fact, within the short period of two weeks, her friends found their all-too-solicitous visits going contrary to what they had expected. Pammi would just sit there, nodding to Ram Singh to bring in the coffee and the perfectly prepared mid-morning tidbits that went with it. These were duly picked at, and then silence would descend. Pammi made it clear that she was not ready for anything like old times yet. They could finish with the formalities quickly, and leave. This was indicated coldly and distantly — by the way she held herself and the expression of disinterested hauteur that marked her face.

They left, wondering, and full of feigned concern.

This no longer worried Pammi. She knew deep inside that she was done with them. She had moved far away, into other realms of experience completely beyond their ken, and where she would have to journey alone.

Any, and all, explanations would be totally beyond their comprehension.

Just before turning in one night, about three weeks after her return from England, Pammi told Ram Singh that she needed to go out of the house the next day, and would he please make sure that Kishore the driver was not sent off anywhere for a household errand?

'I will leave at eight o'clock. Tell Kishore to bring the car around to the back of the house — in the service lane — and let me know immediately he has done so,' said Pammi. 'I don't want to waste any time.'

If Ram Singh found anything odd about this request, he did not let it show.

'Yes, madam, we will go as soon as possible,' he said.

'Thank you, Ram Singh,' said Pammi firmly. 'But I will go alone.'

'But you cannot go so far — and in that area of town — by yourself! You will need an escort,' said Ram Singh, his voice full of proprietary outrage.

'No, there is no need, thank you,' said Pammi, showing no surprise that he seemed to know her destination.

Ignoring him gaping at her in amazement, she moved away towards the staircase that went up to her suite of bedrooms.

* * *

The next day Pammi woke up early, and was showered and ready well before the arrival of Kishore. Ram Singh found her tidying her room already fully dressed in a cream-coloured silk sari and shawl when he went in with her morning cup of tea. When asked about what she would have for breakfast, he was told that she did not want any, and that she was ready to leave as soon as Kishore arrived.

There was no one in the back lane when the car carrying Pammi drove off from behind 73 Hauz Khas. Unlike the road in front of the house, the back lane was a mess. The previous day's rain shower had left puddles of water standing about in a wet slush, and at every fifty yards stood the upturned trash cans from each house in the street. Uncollected garbage littered the lane, and here and there the odd alley cat sniffed at a pile in its search for an edible morsel of food. It was not a happy sight. But for once, Pammi did not notice. In fact, since her return, she had never been to the back of her own house – and had certainly not stepped out into the back lane. Had she done so, she would have noticed that her long absence from the neighbourhood had undone all her efforts at keeping the lane behind her house as clean as possible. It was she who had sent notes to all home-owners on the street requesting that each made sure that their household trash was managed carefully by their servants, and that it was not left outside overnight for alley cats and dogs to get at. She had had some success.

But her absence in the last few months had seen things reverting to the usual, dirty pattern.

On any other day, this would have annoyed Pammi. But today, as Kishore negotiated the wet mud piles on the road in an effort to keep the car he had just cleaned from getting muddied again, Pammi's mind was elsewhere. She was thinking more of her destination, of whom she would be meeting, and whether he would recognise her. This latter thought worried her more than anything else and she clutched tighter the rather large, black handbag that lay on her lap. The bag contained an

old document that she had taken no pleasure in looking at again
after all these years. It was her son's *janam patri*. The very same
that had been the occasion of an unwelcome prediction so many
years ago.

'His own will eat him up. Or very nearly.'

Pammi had taught her face to remain completely impassive
whenever she thought of those words. After Tanvi's death, she
had taken to thinking a lot about them. It had taken only a few
days after the cremation for her to recall the prophecy. In all the
years after Rattan's birth, she had never had occasion to either
recall the visit to Panna the Fakir or to refer to her son's *janam
patri*. She had always thought of herself as a modern woman who
did not believe that these things were important. She had gone
to the old fakir only because her old-fashioned, superstitious
mother-in-law had insisted on it.

But when she had opened her Godrej cupboard (to retrieve
all her expensive jewellery and put it safely in the deposit box
of her bank) just before her hasty departure out of the country
two weeks after Tanvi's cremation, her fingers had encountered
the old *janam patri* wrapped in a piece of red cotton cloth in the
far recesses of the deep dark cavern of the safe. Her fingers had
encountered the bundle's forgotten outlines, making her wonder
for a puzzled moment what it could be that was sharing such
precious space with her gold, diamonds, and other jewels.

The moment she saw it, she had known what it was.
And when she had shaken it open gently and seen all the
writings and diagrams of the constellations of stars supposedly
ascendant at her son's birth, she had recalled the prophecy.
The memory of it had made her feel just a little sick, and
she had to move quickly to the edge of her bed so she could
sit down.

So this was it. His own had 'eaten' him up? Or at least,
very nearly?

It was this sense of a connection between what had been
said so many years ago and what had happened in June that

had consumed Pammi in recent months. The fakir's prophecy haunted her as nothing else had done.

Now that she was back – and somewhat calmer than before – she felt something urging her to visit the fakir once again.

A few days after her return, she made some discreet inquiries. An old man now, Panna the Fakir still lived in his hut on the mound near Majnu ka Tila in Old Delhi. All kinds of people still flocked to him for many things. Pammi wondered whether he would remember her, and the little baby she had carried to him all those years ago. A part of her hoped that he would – for wasn't it always easier to go to somebody you knew rather than to somebody you didn't? However, another part hoped that he wouldn't – for then she would be able to hear what he had to say about her son's future without his knowing about the complicating events of the recent past. However, the more she thought about it, the more she wanted her meeting with the fakir to be only about the future. About what lay in store – and not at all about what had happened.

Pammi did not focus on the journey all the way to Old Delhi that morning. It was only when Kishore turned the car onto the little rough road that led to Majnu ka Tila, that she came to.

There were far more huts than she remembered. Some of them were pukka structures made of bricks and had permanent stone roofs. The narrow road had been paved, and seemed to zigzag crazily towards the hut where Panna the Fakir saw his devotees. Unlike her last visit – the driver had been different then – Kishore had no difficulty negotiating his way right up to the gate of a small picket fence, which encircled shoulder-high bushes of the prickly *keekar* plant. These hid somewhat the hut itself, which as far as Pammi could see, had not changed much.

As she stepped out of the car, Pammi avoided looking at Kishore's face.

He, in a deferential way, asked whether she wanted him to accompany her.

She shook her head. 'Please wait in the car,' she instructed briefly. 'I will not be long.'

As Pammi opened the little gate and made to walk the twenty yards to the doorway of the fakir's hut, she was a little surprised to find that there was no one around. The place seemed deserted at this early hour of the morning. As far as she knew, the major bulk of devotees paid their respects to old Panna in the evening. Now it was barely nine a.m. — but she had expected to see at least a few people awaiting their turn. And since she was not in a happy frame of mind, she would have preferred the anonymity of being one among many seeking the fakir. Her isolation was mortifying — even scary — for it made her feel she had been singled out all too glaringly in her disastrous kismet. As she followed in solitude the narrow path of beaten earth up to the doorway of the hut, she wondered what she would find, and did not relish the idea of walking in upon the fakir unannounced.

But she need not have worried. An old woman, dressed in a faded cotton sari, came out of the doorway of the hut. As she did so, she saw Pammi making her way towards her. Pammi waited until the old woman had disentangled a bucket full of dirty water from the ends of a dirty *chiq* curtain that hung in the doorway, put it down at her bare feet, and then turned to look at her enquiringly.

'I have come to see Panna *maharaj*,' said Pammi in calm tones. 'I sent a message yesterday ...'

'Yes, yes ... I remember now,' said the old woman, peering myopically through square thick-lensed glasses. 'They said you would come early today. I will see if he is ready to receive you. Please wait here.'

Pammi had known that this visit would not be pleasant, but it had to be undertaken. She had done her best to look nondescript: no make-up or lipstick, and her simplest clothes. And yet her difference from the surroundings, she well knew, was stark. She thought of how she would appear to a passer-by:

a well-off woman wearing a good quality silk sari, simple gold studs in her ears, professionally hennaed hair tied up behind her head in a neat French roll, standing barefoot outside the hut of an old fakir in a poor neighbourhood. And cringed inwardly as she waited in dreadful anticipation of whatever lay in store for her. Her husband was far away, and only God knew how her dearly beloved son was doing in Cairo, for they had not spoken in weeks. With Rattan's *janam patri* weighing heavily in her handbag, Pammi wondered how Cairo was treating him; whether he was as tortured still as she was; or whether he had learned to find an inner calm. She wondered whether he had managed to keep his past hidden from his new circle of acquaintances, or whether it had followed him even there, leaving him unable to escape it. Whenever she thought of this, her sense of horror almost killed her. She could not bear to think that he might be more racked and torn all by himself abroad than she was here at home.

Pammi could not have stood outside the fakir's hut more than a few minutes but it seemed as if she had been there an age. The mid-November morning chill crept up her bare feet, and she began to wish she had worn more than an old shawl. The ground was soggy from the previous night's rain, and she could feel her soles grow slowly damp. She was relieved when she heard the slow shuffling of the old woman's feet. They were approaching the doorway of the hut.

'This is it,' she told herself.

Whatever it was, or had to be, she was ready to face it.

By this time, the old woman had moved the old *chiq* curtain to one side, and was making way for Pammi to enter the hut. It took a while for Pammi to get used to the drastic reduction of light inside. Her first impression was one of an immense dinginess that seemed to recede further and further the more she peered into the dark spaces inside the hut. And it was some space, stretching out bare and unadorned, on either side of her. The whole place seemed so different from the last time. She did not, for one thing, remember the interior being so vast. She tried to look around in the gloom, but found that her eyes did not find any outline or shape to focus on.

As her eyes adjusted to the dark gradually, she found that the little light that there was in the hut came from a smoking lamp that stood on the floor, somewhat to her right side. It flickered continuously in the wake of a hidden and mysterious draught that seemed to wind its way around the hut, catching even at the edges of her sari *pallav*, and the fringes of the end of her shawl hanging from her right shoulder. With the draught came the smell – the strong smell of incense – urgent and overpowering, bullying all other smells that lingered so inevitably in the temples of God. The mixture hit Pammi's nostrils with a force that sent her senses reeling. And even as she wondered what that sound was – that *shai shai shai* that hovered suspended in the air above her ears – she saw him emerge suddenly, sitting there cross-legged on the floor behind the lamp.

A dark outline of a figure in Budhha-like repose, awaiting her entry into his domain.

The sight shook Pammi into a complete and utter stillness. The whole atmosphere, and the sheer presence of Panna mahahraj (as the old woman had insisted he be called) made her feel as if she had entered a dark, nether world of life which seemed powerful enough to overtake the lighted one she had so far imagined herself to be living in. There was a weight here that hemmed her in, dwarfing her into feeling that she was a minute speck in the scheme of things, and the more fool she in thinking that all of life was the way she saw it, or went the way she wanted it. If one went along comfortably, it was only because the dark powers allowed one to do so. And when they struck, they would do so silently but inexorably. It only took a minute for something to happen that would change the entire pattern in the kaleidoscope of one's life. And no matter how much you tried or wanted it, you could not re-create the same pattern as in the minute before.

Nobody in the hut spoke. The silence stretched. Pammi felt

deep, wild eyes staring at her even as the *shai shai* rang in her ears. She took a step forward, and bent her head downward in order to see more clearly. It was then that she noticed that the figure squatting in front of her was indeed the Panna maharaj of her last visit. He was now a much older man, whose staring glance was magnified by a set of thick glass lenses set in square-shaped frames. He was looking at her with great concentration. Pammi felt that he was looking right into her heart, and a nervous shiver passed all the way down to her feet.

'Who are you, and why have you come?' said the fakir, in a deep peremptory tone.

'I'm Pammi ... Pammi Malhotra. I have come to you before,' said Pammi, her voice emerging from her throat in a thin cracked squeak.

'And when was that?' asked the fakir.

'Many years ago ... I know you won't remember me. That is why I have brought this. This *janam patri* ... it is of my son ...'

The fakir did not say anything. He waited. As Pammi fumbled in her handbag to take out the rolled parchment in its red cloth covering, she was aware that someone had moved from behind the fakir. A quick glance showed that it was the old lady. Pammi noted subconsciously that with her movement, the *shai shai* noise had stopped. It had come from a small wooden contraption that stood above and somewhat behind the old fakir. It was a wooden stand, much like a clothes-horse of the old days. Between its two poles hung a smooth wire along which swung, from one side to the other, a plume of silver-coloured horsehair. Its lower ends moved to and fro just above the fakir's head.

The fakir peered into the open parchment held out in front of him by the old woman.

'Sit down,' he said in a peremptory voice, waving a regal hand at his visitor.

Pammi sat obediently. There was absolute silence in the

hut. It seemed to go on and on, and she wondered how any place within the city limits of Delhi – so overcrowded by its ten million people, could be so quiet in the middle of the morning. But as the fakir re-read the *janam patri*, no outside sounds penetrated the hut.

Suddenly the fakir spoke. 'Aha, I remember now! So it has happened.'

Pammi was silent, but she found that her head had bent low of its own volition.

'So why have you come?' said the fakir. 'What had to be, has been.'

'For absolution,' said Pammi quietly, her eyes still on the ground.

'What absolution?' said the fakir.

'The weight of it is too heavy,' said Pammi. 'Help me lighten it.'

'Hmm. So you destroyed him, born of your womb,' said the fakir, looking sadly into the distance.

Pammi made as if to speak. No, no, she wanted to say. It isn't he who died. It was his wife, Tanvi ...

But the fakir seemed to know this already. A dismissive nod of his head indicated that she should remain silent. Pammi was only too relieved, and waited for him to speak.

The fakir sat quietly with his eyes closed. He seemed in deep meditation. The old woman carefully refolded Rattan's *janam patri* along its original creases and tied it neatly into its red cloth covering. She came up to Pammi, sitting cross-legged on the floor, and handed it her. Slowly, she walked back to her place behind the fakir and began pulling the string that moved the horse's tail to and fro above the fakir's head.

Once again the flame of incense began to flicker, and the *shai shai* began to fill the room.

'Leave everything. Whatever you had to do, you did. It is time for penance,' said the fakir suddenly, his voice loud in the silence.

'As you say,' said Pammi, her voice a whisper.

'Two things you will have to do. First. Go to the Kartiki temple on the banks of the Yamuna river on the way to Kanpur. Take your partner with you, and perform the rituals the priest there asks of you. Give him my name, and tell him I sent you. As for him, your son, he will be better off without you.

'Second. Remember this: the less that is said and done, the better. Silence is golden, and the world a veil of illusions. Do not try to look through them.'

Pammi did not reply. Her head bent lower, almost touching the floor. As her eyes filled with slow tears, she could feel that a tremendous weight had slipped away from her shoulders. The purpose of her coming had been vindicated. She raised her head slowly, daring finally to look at the old fakir. She found that his eyes were closed, as also were those of the old woman behind him. It seemed to Pammi as if they were no longer aware of her presence, and that she had been dismissed. She closed her own eyes, and let the tears that had collected in them slip silently down her cheeks. She stood up slowly, and silently. Clutching tightly her son's *janam patri* and her handbag in her hands, she bowed as low as she could.

Saying a soft *shukriya*, she backed out of the hut.

Pammi's ride back to 73 Hauz Khas went much the same way as had her journey to the old fakir. Nothing on the road registered in her consciousness, and Kishore (probably sensing his mistress's inner tension) had not asked permission to put on the almost always required cassette of Hindi film music. So oblivious was Pammi of her surroundings that she did not notice that Kishore had quite forgotten that they had exited the house from the back gates. Pammi had assumed that he would repeat the earlier route on the return journey. But she found that, as they neared home, the car was turning into the main road in front of 73 Hauz Khas.

208

It was only when they reached the front gates that Pammi came out of her reverie.

'Why did you not come in through the back?' she asked Kishore, a little of the irritation she felt charging her voice.

'I am sorry, madam, but I forgot,' said Kishore, at first surprised and then genuinely contrite. He had been Rattan's driver, and had felt compassion for the family with whom he had worked briefly, but who had always treated him well. 'Should I turn around the other way? I can, and it won't take a minute,' said Kishore, wanting to make amends.

But Pammi had already seen that the two security guards had recognised the car, and were in the process of opening the gates.

'No, this is fine. The gates are open already,' said Pammi. 'You can drive straight in now.'

If Pammi had used a back-door departure to prevent her comings and goings from becoming the object of speculation by her neighbours, her return by the front gate undid it all. As it happened, she arrived back before one o'clock, just in time to catch Shyam Lal, the postman, delivering the day's mail next door at *Sahayata*. Since it was a Saturday, and the Indira Gandhi Memorial College for Women was closed, it was Maneka Saxena's day to volunteer at *Sahayata*. Maneka had had a busy morning, for it was the day a local doctor and counsellor held court. She had worked hard to see that the rush of women wanting advice got their turn, and a fair share of each expert's time.

She had chosen to step out of the Reception for a surreptitious smoke just at the point that Shyam Lal was parking his bicycle against the wall by the gate. She saw him sorting out a bundle of letters for *Sahayata* and decided she would walk out and meet him. As she did so, she saw Pammi Malhotra's car drive up to the gate next door, pause a while at the gate, and then drive up to the house.

In that pause, Maneka managed to catch a clear glimpse of Pammi.

Maneka did not notice that Pammi looked wan and withdrawn, or that even her face showed that she had lost weight, that she was dressed in a plain silk sari. As far as Maneka was concerned, Pammi Malhotra of 73 Hauz Khas was the wicked mother-in-law who surely had a lot to do with the mysterious death of her daughter-in-law five months earlier.

'So she is back, is she?' Maneka told herself, peering over the gates of 73 Hauz Khas, and watching the car carrying Pammi drive up to the porch. The security guards watched Maneka warily, but did not say anything, rushing rather to close the tall gates, and lock them securely from the inside.

Maneka turned away, wondering whether there was any point in renewing public disapproval of the Malhotras by the old strategies of *dharna* and slogan-shouting outside the house. Maybe they, at *Sahayata*, had given up too soon, and that is why the Malhotras had got away scot-free. For, as she recalled, the public outcry had petered out a few weeks after the knowledge that the Malhotras had left the country. To shout outside an empty house was no use at all.

But now they were back – the lady herself was back – and she could be made to pay for it.

By this time Maneka had come face to face with Shyam Lal, standing there waiting for her to take *Sahayata*'s mail from him.

'When did they return, the neighbours?' asked Maneka.

'Recently,' said Shyam Lal evasively.

'What has she come back for, now that she has killed her daughter-in-law?' said Maneka with a viciousness that surprised Shyam Lal.

'Hush, hush, *behenji*! You should not talk like that! How do you know ... or anyone know ... what happened? We should not pass judgement without knowing all the facts ...' said Shyam Lal.

He stopped, slightly breathless. It was a long and weighty

speech for a postman whose work all these years had entailed a silent delivering of mail to the houses on his beat.

'That is precisely what is wrong with our country,' said Maneka intensely. 'It is we who let things be, and care nothing about the fact that they could so easily happen again. Until things happen to someone in our own family, we do not care at all. People like the Malhotras should be lynched ... and you are telling me that we should forget about it all ...'

'No, no, *behenji*! That is not what I meant at all. We should all be very vigilant ... but what is the use of raking it all up from the past, and shouting and yelling. How will that help anything ...?'

'Well, what else should we do? Can we do?' asked Maneka impatiently. 'This kind of thing has happened so many times before. And what do you people do? Say all the things that you just said, and forget about it all. Everything goes back to just as it was, and nothing changes ...'

Maneka stopped there, mid sentence. She had realised, suddenly, that she could have gone on and on, but it would have made no difference to the old man standing in front of her. He was, as she noticed, looking downwards, and a deferential stoop had come into the upper part of his torso. There was no possibility of discussion here, or any meaningful conversation. Maneka stretched out her hand to take the bundle of letters for *Sahayata*; and, shaking back her rather untidily combed hair turned away.

'Thank you,' she said. 'We'll see you tomorrow.'

'Tomorrow is Sunday,' said Shyam Lal mildly. 'There is no post delivered on Sunday.'

Maneka did not comment, though she gave the old man a withering look at making so obvious a point before walking away.

Shyam Lal knew he had been dismissed. He was relieved, because he really did not want to get into any controversial discussion with Miss Maneka of *Sahayata*. She was too much for him. Too much for any decent man, in fact. He wondered what her life story was. Did she have any children? Did she have a husband? And if she did, how did they put up with her?

Maybe she was a completely different person at home, a *bheegi billi*, who saved all her shouting for *Sahayata*.

The thought of Maneka Saxena's contradictory personas made Shyam Lal chuckle quietly under his breath. He could just see her at home, standing bent behind the gas stove, cooking away until the sweat poured down the sides of her face, and her hair slowly getting damp and wet. Having done all her painful duties, she would save up her anger about her lot for her next day at *Sahayata*, and how she would get at the Malhotras and the world.

The more Shyam Lal thought about it, the more true it seemed to him.

By the time he had pedalled down to the end of the road, Maneka's supposedly split personality had become a reality in his mind.

Afloat in a Felucca

In the days that followed her inquiry about his health, Rattan began to call Nalini on the telephone. The first time was when he returned to his apartment five days after the dinner party at the Guptas. He called Nalini at the office.

As she chatted, Nalini kept one eye on Gamal, hoping all the while that he would not notice her longish conversation. But he was busy holding forth about the latest events in the morning newspapers. While the rest of her colleagues debated whether President Mubarak had a firm hold on the activities of Islamic fundamentalists in his country, Nalini spoke in soft tones with Rattan. He asked her how she had been, whether she had caught the 'flu from being in the same room as him, and whether he needed to bring her flowers in her convalescence. She laughed softly, and told him that she had not been ill at all, and that maybe her antibodies had been strong enough to resist all the infection that he had been trying to pass on to her.

It was his turn to laugh, and tell her quietly that he was back in his own apartment, and he gave her his home phone number saying that she could call him there any time. Nalini scribbled it into her diary, telling herself that this was something she was not going to do. Rattan spoke of having returned to work, and of how he felt a little weak still but was recovering. He also suggested that they should go out to lunch some day soon.

She said a hurried yes to this, and moved on to some other, inconsequential subjects. They said good-bye, and rang off.

Nalini did not call Rattan. He waited a few days, and called her again at work. She was pleasant enough, but Rattan made her feel that she was being a little unfair on him, that she had been somewhat cold, even churlish. She was wondering how she could make amends when, a few days later, they met again.

But, as usual, quite inadvertently.

Sunita Singh called. The picnic dinner in a felucca on the Nile planned at the Guptas' party was on for the next evening – a Saturday. It was to be an informal affair, with everyone bringing in a dish or two. They would meet at the corniche at 7.30 p.m. and then they would move out onto the water. Nalini was pleased and accepted the invitation. Having made sure that someone would come by Bharat Bhavan and give her a lift, she asked about what she could bring by way of a contribution to the dinner.

At first Sunita said that nothing was necessary; that they did not expect those who were not married to cook. But Nalini was adamant. She would bring some *biryani* and some soft drinks; some plates and glasses. Sunita thanked her, and promised to let her know who would fetch her.

Nalini mentioned the felucca trip to her father the next morning as he sat in the study drinking his morning tea and reading the local morning papers.

'Who's organising it?' asked Gautam Thapar casually.

'Sunita Singh and all her friends, I suppose,' said Nalini. 'Will it be all right if I go with them?'

'Yes, *beti*. The only reason why I ask is that, these days, one has to be careful. The situation here is quite bad politically. The militants are plotting against Mubarak's regime. Anything can happen anytime, but one should not panic. A couple of hours on the water should not make much difference. But keep your eyes and ears open, will you?'

'Yes, Papa. Ajay and Minti are going to be angry with me,

because I promised I would take them to see a movie. But I guess we can go on Sunday,' said Nalini.

'No. No movies in a movie theatre for a few days, my dear. They have been receiving bomb threats. We can get one for the video at home,' said Gautam Thapar, and looked up meaningfully at his daughter through his reading glasses.

'Yes, Daddy,' said Nalini, and moved away to look through the pile of newspapers and magazines lying on the floor near his chair. They reminded her that it was still two days to Bag day.

'I wonder if there will be any letters for me this Sunday,' she mused. She was expecting a reply from Maneka Saxena. Nalini's mind went eagerly to the prospect of her friend's impending visit to Cairo. Only a few weeks were left. When would that girl ever finalise her programme and tell her about it?

Not till the very last minute, she was sure.

When Nalini arrived on the corniche with the Singhs, the streetlights were just beginning to come on. Sunita's husband Satnam had parked the car close to the very edge of the busy road, and was hurrying around helping his wife to unload the food and drinks onto the pavement. He wanted to move his car away quickly – to the empty spaces on the other side of the road – in order to park safely. Dressed in jeans and a comfortable pair of flat shoes, Nalini moved quickly to the boot of the car. *Aji* had tied the biryani pot into an old tablecloth, and so it was easy to haul out and place on a stone bench along the corniche. She returned to pick up a cardboard carton full of Coke and Sprite cans, as well as plastic plates, glasses, serviettes and cutlery. The carton was a little heavy, and Nalini knew she would have to use both hands to lift it. She stood still a moment to adjust the strap of her handbag so that it would stay on her shoulder before she lifted the carton out of the boot. She was just beginning to bend over when she heard a firm voice speak softly behind her.

'I'll get that.'

The voice was Rattan's. Nalini recognised it even before she turned around and saw him. She said a low-voiced 'Hello', and moved out of his way as he lifted the crate and walked towards the stone bench where other contributions were being collected.

'I didn't know you were going to be here today,' said Nalini shyly.

'Neither did I,' said Rattan, trying hard not to notice everything about her in too obvious a way. 'I am glad you are, though,' he added quietly. 'It's changed the evening for me.'

Nalini gave him a look, which Rattan chose to interpret as being a mixture of reserve and self-conscious pleasure. He was pleased, but said nothing. He had never seen her in jeans and tucked-in T-shirt before. They made her look younger and carefree, and belied the wary reserve in her eyes. He noted that she wore her hair loose and flowing. Lapis and silver earrings hung long on either side of her face, giving her an air of charming casualness. She wore very little make-up, and the slight nip in the air had added a glow to her cheeks. He saw that his presence had disconcerted her more than hers had him. She would need a few moments, he was sure. And he gave them to her by turning towards Sunita, who was organising everyone's descent of the steps to the water's edge where the feluccas were tethered.

Satnam was looking for the boatman whose felucca they always hired. When he was found, warm greetings were exchanged between the Indian and the Egyptian. Soon Satnam began haggling in broken Arabic over the price for three hours on the water. A cool breeze came by, its gusts rippling the water in shimmering waves. Standing at the edge of the group, Nalini was glad of the warm jacket she had brought along. It would be even cooler on the water. The men had gathered around the boatman, and there was much gesticulation and looking at watches to make sure of the time from when the group could be charged for their evening of pleasure. By now all the food and drinks had been brought down the steps and everyone waited till they knew which felucca they were to go in.

Rattan made his way over to Nalini. She and Rattan were the newcomers, and it seemed natural that they should gravitate towards each other. Or so Nalini told herself.

'Do you know everyone here?' Rattan asked, looking around to make sure that no one heard them.

'Yes, sort of. I've been to their homes, and they have been to ours. But I would not say that we were best friends or anything,' said Nalini carefully. 'But they are all really very nice ... I mean, very friendly, and go out of their way to be welcoming.'

It was a long reply; but Nalini felt it important that Rattan should know her relationship with the other guests. What Nalini was trying to say was that, were she at home, she would not necessarily have chosen to be with this group of people. But there were not many single, young people to choose from within the Indian expatriate community in Cairo and she had to make do with what was available. All these were hardly nice things to say, however, and so she had never said them. But the group – at least so far – had determined her social life in Cairo.

Rattan understood her perfectly. Though he had made some friends at work, and had spent many evenings with Egyptians, and American and British colleagues from the office, everybody tended to do more meaningful socialising with their own kind. It was somewhat easier with the Americans and the British, but with the Egyptians it was, ultimately, the language that came in the way. Rattan had realised that if he did not want to spend long evenings moping around in his apartment alone, he too would have to seek out the Guptas and the Singhs.

There was a shout of 'all aboard' from Satnam. Rattan turned away to help load all the food and drink onto the felucca. The women were helped in first, and then the restless children. The boatman was already at the far end of the boat, and was standing at the helm to make sure that no one upset it too much while climbing in. In a few minutes, everyone was aboard and seated. The boatman gave a loud yell in Arabic, and began untying the ropes that had tethered the boat to rings on the bank. His friends on the shore gave it a few hard pushes to set it moving. In a few minutes, the full felucca was heading outwards on to the open water.

It was inevitable that Rattan found himself seated next to Nalini. He had made sure of it, and Nalini had helped him by being among the last women to climb aboard. He had followed close behind her, carrying a Thermos full of ice cubes in one hand and leaving the other free to help her climb onto the boat's edge. As Nalini steadied herself in front of him, Rattan moved quickly to the centre of the felucca, and set the Thermos of ice down on the floor next to the makeshift table in the centre of the boat. As he returned, he watched Nalini look for a place for herself down the end of one side of the boat. Rattan followed her quickly, and in a few moments had sat down beside her.

Under the cover of conversation and laughter, Rattan whispered quietly to Nalini that she should relax, and enjoy herself. She did not reply, but felt grateful that he understood. It was always awkward for her when she mingled in the Indian community as a single woman unaccompanied by her father. Whoever sat next to her would always be suspect – in her eyes as well as in those of the others – of wanting to ingratiate themselves with the Thapar family. But there was nothing either she or anybody could do about it.

For a few minutes, the conversation was general. There was much discussion about how *Diwali* was to be celebrated. Vinod Gupta, ever the leader, had much to report. The community had decided they were going to organise a gala evening in one of the local hotels. There was an immediate discussion of how funds should be raised. Should they find a few sponsors to underwrite the whole event? Or should each person be charged individually for the evening? Should they invite artists from India to provide entertainment, or should local talent be used? Should the food be vegetarian or non-vegetarian?

This latter subject became the centre of a heated discussion. Some felt that since it was ultimately a religious occasion, the food should be vegetarian. This would also help keep the costs down.

However, Satnam felt that this would make for a very tame evening. 'Why should we be bullied into vegetarianism? Those who don't want to eat meat need not do so. But those of us who do, should at least have an option!'

Nalini and Rattan listened silently to the debate. However, after a while Rattan saw Nalini turn her head away in exasperation. He saw that her attention had diverted to the waters flowing gently by, and to the setting sun streaking the sky in shades of orange and grey. Even now, though it was already November, the days were long enough to have these last rays stay around to mingle with the artificial lights of the corniche. It was a magical moment, which she seemed to be enjoying deep inside her own private self.

Rattan knew better than to disturb her. He let her be, watching her face surreptitiously. A bird flew up from the darkening waters, its dark silhouette streaking the sky. Nalini's eyes followed its flight. Her face tilted upwards, affording him a view of her long neck and the soft cleft at the base of her throat visible above the low round neck of her T-shirt. A thin gold chain with a small medallion pendant hugged it closely. He continued to look at her unobserved and did not speak until he felt her return to the moment around her. The debate on vegetarian food was still going on, and choosing what he thought was an appropriate moment, Rattan asked quietly, 'So what would you prefer?'

'Huh . . . ?' said Nalini, for a moment bewildered.

'They are talking about the food still . . .' Rattan reminded her gently, somewhat amused.

'Oh, the food! . . . I don't really mind, anything,' said Nalini, trying not to reveal her sense of *déjà vu* about the subject. 'This discussion takes place every single time something has to be organised by the Indian community!'

'Really?' said Rattan.

'Yes,' said Nalini. 'If you have lived in as many countries as I have, you would know that expatriate Indians all over the world seem to do things in the same old way.'

'I suppose so,' said Rattan and smiled.

'Is this your first time out of the country?' asked Nalini.

Rattan did not reply, choosing in the pause that followed to look around at their companions in the felucca. He could hear Sunita's voice speak loudly about the question of entertainment for *Diwali*. Somebody said that there was enough talent in town. Why send for more from India? Sunita was a singer, and if needed, her singing could carry the whole evening.

'No, no. I can't sing alone ... There should be someone else with me,' said Sunita attempting modesty.

Nobody was aware that one of the children at the other end of the boat was listening intently. When she spoke her voice was loud and thin and could be heard by everyone in the felucca.

'Why can't Sunita Auntie sing today? I mean "now" ... so we can enjoy the present?'

Everybody laughed. This was deemed a good idea and the preparations for *Diwali* were shelved to a later time. After a few minutes of banter, Sunita decided to sing. She chose a song from a film that had been the rage in the seventies. It was, as was to be expected, a romantic one, and brought forth memories of earlier times in India. Everyone on the felucca was silent, and listening. Night had fallen completely, and a half-moon hung benignly over the river. The waters of the Nile lapped softly along the wooden sides of the old-fashioned boat. As the felucca moved towards the centre of the river, the sounds of the traffic on the corniche receded. Sunita's voice floated over the waves, and intermingling with the tones of her voice was the accompanying humming of those in the boat who knew the song well.

Both Rattan and Nalini were silent.

'Do you know the song?' asked Rattan.

'Not really. I seem to have missed the movie when it first came out, and so missed the song too. But I remember it being played on *Vividh Bharati* at some point during my college years at Delhi University.'

'Well, I don't know it at all. And that, I guess, is also the answer to your earlier question. Like you, I have lived many years outside India in my youth.'

'Really?' said Nalini, smiling inwardly at his cynical mention of his youth as a thing of the past. Rattan did not look much older than in his late twenties.

But his saying that he too had spent long years abroad intrigued her. She proceeded to ask him where he had travelled and lived. He answered in low tones. While Sunita sang her songs, the conversation between Rattan and Nalini revolved around his undergraduate years in the USA, and her life as the daughter of a diplomat who had three-year assignments in different capitals of the world. They were careful to keep their voices low, occasionally giving up speaking in order to appear to be listening. They also made sure that they clapped appreciatively every time a song ended. He told her about how, after working a few years in the Big Apple, he had chosen to return to India. She told him about her advertising job in New Delhi, which she had had to give up on the death of her mother. They agreed that it took a long time to adjust to life upon returning from abroad, and how acutely they felt the cultural gaps in their sense of life in India simply because they had lived long years away from it.

'This is inevitable. It is what always happens when you return after having lived long years away,' said Nalini. 'India waits for no one. It moves along, in its own momentum.'

Rattan nodded in agreement. 'Each person has to make the effort to join its march through history. And, for those who have been away from it, there can be enough to remember it by provided you have garnered enough memories of your experiences in it.'

'In this felucca, everyone here seems to have enough of those,' said Nalini, sighing deeply. 'Only I seem to feel that I could have done with some more!'

Rattan remained silent.

He had some memories he could have done without.

But he could not help looking at Nalini sharply. Had she heard something about him?

Much was told, and shared that enchanted night. But Rattan did not mention either his marriage or the death of Tanvi. Nalini did not notice that, except for his mentioning that he had returned to India two years ago to begin working with his father, Rattan did not (unlike her) say much about his more recent past. What she did notice was that, suddenly, he seemed not to want to talk any more. The gaps in communication between them lengthened, and eventually petered into complete silence. Once or twice she stole a sideways look at his face, but he did not seem keen to alight on any other new topic of conversation. She put it down to the fact that either the children around them had become noisy and restive, and wanted food, or simply that he did not want to talk any more. She felt a little unhappy, telling herself that she should not feel badly if he did not want to tell her as much as she had told him. The thought made her turn her head away from him, and huddle into her jacket with an involuntary sigh.

Remaining silent, she tried to concentrate on what was happening in the felucca. And to ignore Rattan's heavily silent presence by her side.

As for Rattan, his mind was not there in the boat – either with her, or with anyone else in it. It was elsewhere, far away. Rattan sensed Nalini's withdrawal at once, knowing all too clearly that it was he – and his own sudden influx of memories – who had been responsible for it. He felt badly, but could not bring himself to speak. Luckily for him, at that moment, one of the boys mentioned dinner, and a shout went up for food. Sunita had stopped singing some time ago, and asked everybody whether they were ready for dinner.

'Let the children begin,' said Satnam, holding up his half-empty glass of scotch and soda towards the moon. Its brown and diamond shine sparkled enticingly in the night.

'We shall join you soon.'

Nalini knew that the time had come to serve – for each woman present to open up whatever she had brought. Soon everyone was eating.

Nalini saw that Rattan had a full plate, and was obviously enjoying his meal. She noticed that he had taken a large helping of biryani – the biryani that had been cooked in her father's kitchen. She was pleased at first, conjuring up in her mind's eye the picture of a lonely bachelor in a dingy flat, with only stale corn flakes and a couple of withering oranges in his refrigerator. But her second reaction was one of irritation at herself. Irritation for having this great urge – this typical, all-too-banal urge – to make sure that 'the brute' was fed. Why did she have to wonder how Rattan managed life on his own? She was just like all other traditional Indian women whose first instinct was to make sure that, before everything else, 'male hunger' was looked after!

But then, the very thought of 'male hunger' made her blush a bit, and she hurriedly began telling herself that the hunger she had been worrying about only included food and nothing else. The confusion this generated in her mind made her choke, and she burst out into a splutter of coughing.

'Give her some water, will you, Rattan,' said Sunita, ever alert to the needs of the others around her.

Rattan hastily filled a glass with water and handed it to Nalini even as he took her plate, still full of food, away from her. He was all concern, and even took the liberty of thumping her back gently. When she was recovered, Rattan returned her plate to her, and encouraged her to eat. She did, but self-consciously.

Everyone around was eating and talking, but Rattan and Nalini remained silent. Soon, Nalini noticed that Rattan's plate was empty. After a brief pause – in which she seemed to be making some kind of decision – she spoke again.

'Your plate is empty. You must have some more,' she tried to say firmly.

But her voice, as it emerged from her throat, sounded more cracked than firm, and the effect was quite comic. It brought a smile to Rattan's face, coupled with a look of some surprise. What was with her? He peered at her closely, but saw nothing except some feelings of embarrassment that he could not understand. Surely she was not feeling awkward because she had choked on her food? Rattan could find no answer. But when he found that she was determined to serve him a second helping, he did not say no, but acquiesced quietly.

They did not speak much after this. The conversation had turned general, and even somewhat serious. One of the men present had returned from a trip to New Delhi earlier in the week, and had heard rumours that the Ram Janam Bhumi issue was taking a serious turn. The Babri Masjid was in danger of being torn down. There were, as usual, many views on the issue. No one said anything that was clearly anti-Muslim, but Nalini knew that there were some in the felucca who felt that the Congress had gone too far in appeasing the Muslim community merely for the sake of votes.

Nalini did not enter the discussion. She knew better than to do this – whatever she said would, directly or indirectly, be read as echoing the views of her father. And that would never do, since it was the requirement of his job that he be perceived as being discreet, if not entirely neutral.

Soon, somebody brought up the subject of the past, and the sins of history. Nalini was relieved at first, because the discussions become more general. But soon the past itself became problematic.

'Phew, this is a hot one ...' said Rattan, looking around carefully to make sure that no one heard him or her.

'Yes,' said Nalini. 'India and its layered historical past ... pasts actually! How can one just decide which of these should be resurrected into the present? It's a dangerous game, and I do hope that the people in authority at home take it easy.'

Rattan did not say anything for a few moments, but he began to look at Nalini speculatively. 'So you keep up with the politics of our country?' said Rattan.

'Yes, I do. Though I am no expert. But we get the weekly Diplomatic Bag with the newspapers from home, and I do read them. They keep you connected more than CNN or even the BBC.'

'You are lucky. All of us other Indians here have to be dependent on their coverage of news from India. They are the only ones in English,' said Rattan.

'I can lend you some Indian newspapers if you like ... although they are always a week old,' said Nalini whispering softly in his ear.

Rattan thanked her, also keeping his voice low. She said she would try to get the first batch to him on the following Monday. Rattan was pleased, feeling a small sense of satisfaction flow through him. He felt Nalini relax slowly by his side. He could feel her left shoulder touch his without any sense of the self consciousness that had made her keep a discreet distance from him in the earlier part of the evening. As the night moved on, temperatures dropped and the breeze grew colder. Rattan felt Nalini move a little to snuggle closer into her jacket. She spent a few minutes trying to do up the zip in the front, and managed after a few unsuccessful tries.

When she was done, she found that Rattan's arm had moved behind her back, and lay unmoving along the side edge of the felucca. She wondered for a minute about what she would do if she found his hand moving to touch her shoulders. And panicked.

But Rattan knew better than to rush her.

And sure enough, when she was convinced that it would stay there behind her, neither provocative nor demanding, she relaxed. In a few minutes she felt its warmth creep into her gradually, and was glad for it.

The Festival of Lights

Filled with the nostalgia of distance, the Indian expatriate community in Cairo celebrated *Diwali* in a big way in that year of 1992. As the discussions on the felucca party had predicted, the India Association of Greater Cairo formed a special high-powered committee to organise the event. Satnam and Vinod Gupta were part of it. Consisting of seven members in total – of which three were women – they thought of every small thing that would make the evening a success. A swanky banquet hall in a local five-star hotel was rented as the venue; the food catered by one of the two Indian chefs resident in Cairo; and the *diyas* were flown in from New Delhi especially for the evening.

These latter created a problem, for the hotel authorities deemed them a fire hazard, and banned their use. However, after some diplomatic persuasion, the manager of the hotel allowed a token handful to be lighted around the space earmarked for the *rangoli* on one side of the entrance lobby to the banquet hall. Since the hall was on the rooftop of the hotel, this area was just outside the elevators that carried all who came up eighteen floors to the venue. As the Cairene Indians entered the lobby, the *diyas* would greet them; and the flickering shadows of the flames and the brilliant stars visible beyond the huge glass windowpanes could only double that special *Diwali* ambiance of the evening.

All this would, no doubt, make up for the absence of *patakas* and other crackers, completely disallowed in the hotel premises. The music was to be loud and gay, western and Indian, and the food non-vegetarian. The meat-lovers had won out; silencing all objections by pointing out triumphantly that the tariff per person was to be as low as if the meal had been only vegetarian. This had been done by a few of the more well-to-do in the community subsidising the expenses for the evening. The reasonable per-head costs made for fuller attendance, and the organisers hoped for a record number of men, women and children from all walks of life being part of the celebrations.

And so it was that *Diwali* that year became an eagerly awaited festival. Nalini could not help remarking on how every country really celebrated wholeheartedly only once in the year: the Christian world had Christmas; the Islamic world had *Eid* at the end of *Ramadan. Diwali* was a public event only in India, and those Indians who lived abroad did their best to make their celebration as festive as possible so that it could remind them of their times at home.

As she dressed for the evening, Nalini wondered about Rattan. Surely he would be there? This was not a select, small party where only a few chosen ones were invited by a host. This was a community affair where each person was responsible for himself attending. Would Rattan choose to do so?

Anyone watching Nalini Thapar as she arranged the pleats of her magenta-pink silk sari in front of her mirror would have noticed that she was taking pleasure in dressing. Without being fully conscious of it, she had now begun to enjoy the prospect of socialising with her father. Her earlier instinctive reluctance had given way to a sense of anticipation at the possibility of meeting Rattan. He could always be part of any evening of Indian expatriates in Cairo, and this lent excitement to her preparations. By the time she had combed her hair and done her eyes, expectancy had cast a glow to Nalini's face and a spring in her walk.

Ajay and Minti did not notice anything unusual in their

sister. Neither did the hawk-like *Aji*, who, along with Mani Ram, were to accompany them. Only Gautam Thapar noticed the sparkle in Nalini's eyes. Watching his elder daughter speculatively, he noted how party-going did not seem to be problematic any more. He wondered whether this change of mood applied only to community gatherings. What about diplomatic parties where it was known beforehand that the guests would be mainly Egyptians and/or other foreigners? Would she shed her reluctance for them?

As for Rattan, he had heard about the plans for the evening first from Vinod and Madhu, and then from every other Indian he met. He could not help recall Nalini's exasperated views on the menu in the felucca, smiling to himself as he did so. He bought an entrance ticket, and when the Guptas pressured him playfully into buying tickets for the raffle, he bought the whole book of twenty in good spirits. The Thapars would, inevitably, be the chief guests for the evening, and it was a foregone conclusion that he would meet Nalini again.

Rattan took his place strategically near the entrance and waited with a group of people till he caught Nalini's eye shortly after she entered the room. It was better to meet her this way than to wait until the Thapars were seated at their reserved table. Then it would seem far too deliberate, besides being too public a context for him to exchange even a few private words with the daughter of the Ambassador of India. And so it was that, after the members of the *Diwali* committee, Rattan was amongst the first to greet Gautam Thapar and his family.

Unaware of his devising, Nalini greeted Rattan with a shy, yet warm smile. When he held out his hand, she shook it with a firm grasp. But it was a while before she could speak to him. The Thapars were surrounded by others wanting to greet them, and it was only when Gautam Thapar began moving forward towards their table that Nalini hung back a little, and turned to face Rattan walking right behind her.

'Hi!' she said. 'How are you?'

'You look beautiful,' said Rattan, taking a close and appreciative look at her face, glowing unusually pink. A pair of long gold earrings highlighted her eyes, and surrounded her with an air of glamour. A shawl hung stylishly off her right shoulder even as her left one supported the carefully arranged folds of the sari *pallav* hanging down her back, a glitter of dull gold.

'Thanks,' she said. 'You look rather good yourself.'

But her voice had taken on a society manner, as if aware that there were people listening who would be hanging on every word she uttered.

However, Rattan carried on, undaunted.

'So they put it together!'

'They always do, and I'm sure it will be a fun evening,' said Nalini.

Rattan did not reply. He was looking around at the crowds still streaming in, crowding the lobby and the doorway. His face registered an almost disgusted scepticism. Nalini noticed his mouth curl slightly as he turned his face to look at her again.

'Don't expect too much,' said Nalini smiling. 'It's a community function. Everybody is here – and when it is this way, it will be a little crowded and messy. It will be like an Indian wedding . . .'

'I guess so . . .' said Rattan, and was immediately reminded of his own. Keeping a firm hold on memories that came uninvited, he searched for something to say. But found himself suddenly tongue-tied.

But he needn't have worried, for a group of young girls had come up to Nalini and surrounded her. They were calling her 'Nalini *didi*', and complimenting her on her sari and appearance. They did not mean to elbow him out of the way, but Rattan found himself suddenly on the outer edges of the crowd around her. Nalini noticed that this had happened, and over the heads of the chattering girls she spoke out to him.

'I'm glad you came. Maybe we can have dinner together later . . .'

If there was anything else she had tried to say, Rattan did not hear her. He waved a hand in agreement and moved away. Putting a hand into his jacket pocket, he took out a cigarette and lit it, inhaling slowly. On the other side of the circle surrounding Nalini, he saw that Gautam Thapar was talking to a group of others. He too had been pushed aside. Smiling slightly, Rattan walked towards the Guptas. Taking his time to join their conversation, he kept a close watch on Nalini's movements. He saw her join her father after the young girls had moved away, but only briefly, because soon after she become engulfed by a stream of colourfully dressed women who came up to greet her. Although by this time the Thapars had reached their table, they only sat down on their respective chairs when Vinod, master of ceremonies for the evening, got on the dais and asked everyone to settle down so they could begin.

The programme was a long one, with many groups of wives and children singing and dancing. Some of the singing – as for instance by Sunita Singh – was above the ordinary, and such items drew loud applause. But Rattan saw Nalini and her father remain neutral in their appreciation of each piece presented. They clapped and smiled with the same enthusiasm.

Rattan was amazed at their patience, especially Nalini's. He could not imagine how she had schooled herself to be this way evening after evening. As for himself, he felt boredom creep in, making it difficult to wait for dinner, and the prospect of meeting Nalini again. He thought about how glorious she looked. It was the second time that he had seen her in a sari, and the magenta suited her to perfection. She had greeted him warmly – far more warmly than he had expected – and it had made him happy.

But then he thought of her reference to weddings, and immediately Tanvi was there before him. Suddenly the all-too-loud and vivid present fell away, and Rattan was back in 73 Hauz Khas.

Since Tanvi's death, Rattan had become more than normally aware of how relative space and time were in the human consciousness. One could be in one place and yet be miles away in another circumstance, feeling its reality as the more real. Here he was living in Cairo; and yet a word, a gesture, a smell could make him spend half his waking hours in the world of New Delhi, reliving his last moments with the dead Tanvi – with her weight, her wetness, and her wild eyes open in a vacant stare. And the passage between the two worlds was always a long one, leaving him exhausted.

And, there were no witnesses or companions on this journey of his psyche. He carried its burdens alone.

It was Madhu Gupta's peremptory call that brought him back to the present.

'Hey, Rattan? Where were you? Your glass is empty, and so is mine. Could you refill them, please?' she said, exercising in an open and confident way her rights as his protective guardian and mentor.

'Of course,' said Rattan, getting up from his chair and collecting the glasses.

'What happens to you? I've noticed that you are always switching off. What do you keep thinking of? Is there a girl somewhere . . . that you've left behind?'

The others on the table laughed, but sympathetically. Madhu was really being more kind than nosy.

'It's nothing like that at all,' replied Rattan, refusing to be drawn. Soon, the image of the dead Tanvi faded from his mind, and the *Diwali* ambiance gradually took over. Somebody was singing a *Diwali* song on the mike, and the words swung around the banquet hall, drowning out all other thoughts and sounds. The audience was joining in deliriously.

Rattan moved away swiftly, and walked towards the bar.

Meanwhile, Nalini saw that Ajay and Minti had chosen to eat

with their friends and that her father had filled his plate from the buffet and chosen to move to another table. This left Nalini by herself. She quickly decided that she would throw in her lot with the Guptas at the other end of the room, knowing full well that Rattan was part of their group. A helpful waiter added an empty chair to their table, and laid out a cover for her. Rattan saw her intentions quite clearly, and as in the felucca, made sure he was seated next to her. But this was not before she had dispatched him to fetch her shawl and her handbag from the table where she had been originally seated.

All the others undoubtedly saw Rattan's attentions to Nalini but chose to ignore them. They did so, not pointedly but tactfully, and made for the gradual evaporation of Nalini's initial self-consciousness. After half an hour, Nalini had forgotten who she was, and had begun to participate with ease in the conversation.

'We never celebrate *Diwali* like this at home,' said Rattan, addressing himself to Nalini.

'No we don't, do we?' agreed Nalini, looking around. 'This room is full of people, knowing each other only because they have been thrown together by circumstance.'

'When I was a boy, *Diwali* meant being in the streets, and waiting for the dark so we could light *patakas* – all those bombs and *chakras* and *anars* and . . .'

'*Phool jharis*! I used to love those,' said Nalini, interrupting his sentence quite unconsciously. 'I hated bombs and would run inside whenever they were set off.'

'And I loved them the most. Dad used to buy an obscene amount of them when I was a kid,' said Rattan. 'But after I went to the USA, it all stopped.'

'Outside the country, *Diwali* is always a holed-up affair,' said Nalini, regret in her voice. 'But we make the best of it.'

Rattan smiled, commenting briefly that the organisers of the evening would hardly appreciate the Marriott hotel ballroom being described as a 'hole'.

Nalini laughed. Leaning back relaxed in her chair, she was on the point of saying something light-hearted and funny about *Diwali* in the Marriott ballroom when she was pulled into her official role by hearing her name being announced by the master of ceremonies. Miss Nalini Thapar was asked to come up to the podium and give away the prizes for the raffle. Quickly adjusting her sari, and leaving her shawl draped over the back of her chair, she walked up to the dais. A box wrapped in tinsel – containing the counterfoils of all the raffle tickets sold – was held out before her. She was to select the winning numbers against the whole range of prizes offered that evening.

Expectancy was high in the banquet hall, each guest looking carefully at the numbers on their raffle tickets spread out before them on the table. Every time there was a winner, squeals of excitement and triumph rang out in the different corners of the room.

The surprise of the evening lay in the penultimate prize – a fully paid Nile cruise for two aboard one of the Oberoi cruisers – being won by none other than Rattan Malhotra. His friends at the table screamed loudly, drawing more than usual attention to themselves by the noise they made. Vinod and Madhu had stood up, and were thumping Rattan on his back offering their congratulations. Rattan was a little embarrassed by his surprise win, because he had bought the raffle tickets offhandedly, only pretending an interest in the celebrations planned for the evening. And now he had won!

Nalini was embarrassed too, and hoped that no one thought that his win had anything to do with her. It certainly brought them together publicly. As she handed over the vouchers for the cruise to Rattan, he tried to pretend a casualness he did not feel, and she donned her formal persona. But she did take silent credit for the fact that, whether he wanted it or not, he was now indelibly included as a recognisable member of the community.

'Thanks a lot,' said Rattan. 'You brought me luck!'

'You'll have to bring me some too!' said Nalini lightly.

'You could come on the cruise with me,' dared Rattan quickly, his voice low.

Nalini did not reply; but he could see that he had floored her, and a hint of pink had begun to mark her face. But the more he thought about it, the more attractive seemed the prospect of her coming on the cruise with him! It was, indeed, a good idea ...

But one he knew was far from being a real possibility.

By the time Nalini returned to her table, everyone had examined the details of the cruise offer. The Oberoi Hotels had been generous, for it included board, lodging and sightseeing for two people in the trip. Though Nalini could not be sure of this, it seemed to her that all present had already speculated on who his partner would be. But Rattan had not responded to the teasing, smiling good-naturedly at the various suggestions made. His attention was on Nalini, but she was keeping her eye on her father and what he was doing. It was time to leave, and soon she would have to join him, and collect her brother and sister. And *Aji* and Mani Ram.

As the conversation moved to farewells, the Guptas were planning other events and making sure that Nalini would agree to be part of them. For a second Nalini wondered whether this was deliberate. But then somebody pointed out that they should see as much of Cairo as they could, because time was running out. Most of the Indians on the table were on three or four year assignments in Egypt, and were already more than half way through them. There was so much to do and see both inside and outside Cairo. When the Guptas pointed out that this was true for the Thapars as well, Nalini could not help but agree. And so it was that a drive outside the city to an old Coptic monastery was planned, as also a trip to the Muquattam Hills. This was going to be soon, and would include all those present at the table. The Guptas took the lead to organise both trips, and promised to choose a Friday, and inform everybody.

When Nalini agreed, just before moving away from their table, that she would love to join them all, she noted that it was understood by everybody that Rattan Malhotra would come too. As she said her good-byes, she saw that Rattan had lit a cigarette. But she decided that this time she would not remark on it.

'Bye, everybody,' said Nalini, stopping a minute to kiss Madhu on her cheek in farewell.

All Rattan received was a cheerful wave of her hand, and a look that did not say anything at all.

The Indian community had hardly recovered from their *Diwali* celebrations when an unusual visitor to Cairo made them all excited once again. This was the visit of the tall actor from Bollywood. Amitabh Bachchan's visit took Cairo by storm, his Egyptian fans crowding the airport and his hotel way beyond expectation. Everyone knew that the Egyptian authorities allowed only a limited number of Indian films to be imported into the country for screening in theatres and television for fear that the audiences for their own films would suffer. The newspapers even had a cartoon of President Mubarak talking to the great Bachchan to ask when he was leaving! The Thapar household was amazed at his popularity among the locals, and tickled pink at the prospect of having to invite him to a reception in the grounds of Bharat Bhavan. Before they knew it, his hosts had a mega event on their hands, and the whole Embassy staff and resources were requisitioned to organise it. Nalini took the day off from work, helping her father to make sure the arrangements for food and security went off without a problem.

In the middle of preparations, Nalini had occasion to talk to Rattan. He had called her at the office one afternoon when she told him about the reception, and invited him to it.

He, however, was reluctant to accept the invitation.

'I don't really go to Hindi films,' said Rattan, trying not to let his indifference show in his voice.

'Really? Not even one?' asked Nalini, amused.

'Not really. I am no fan of actors ... or actresses for that matter ...' said Rattan by way of explanation.

'Oh do come,' said Nalini. 'You sound pompous and disapproving! Are you, really?'

Rattan had nothing to say to this. How could he tell Nalini that his own life had come to resemble a Bombay film ... a lurid and gory Bombay film, complete with shame, betrayal ... and a dead body?

But Nalini persuaded him to attend the reception. She warned him not to be late, as she did not want him to miss anything.

It was just as well that Rattan arrived early, for had he come even half an hour later, merely getting in through the gates of Bharat Bhavan would have posed a problem. Its lone entrance was swamped with security personnel and members of the Embassy staff making sure that only those who had invitations found their way inside. The road was full of Egyptians – men, women and children – who had got wind of the great man's arrival. They chanted out his popular songs and strained at the rope cordons on either side of the road set up by the harassed policemen. Despite every precaution, there were a few gatecrashers into Bharat Bhavan who had to be thrown out unceremoniously.

The actor was late, coming in just as those waiting had almost given up on his arrival. The tall, magnetic-voiced hero was pleasant enough, allowing Gautam Thapar to introduce him with grace and patience to Egyptian officials from the Department of Culture, and other film producers and directors. Nalini told Rattan that there were some plans of collaboration on an Indo–Egyptian film, in which the hero would be Bachchan and the heroine one of Egypt's many talented actresses.

Rattan tried to look interested, but inside he wondered at the odd variety of things an Indian Ambassador's office and family had to deal with. Later, the actor mingled with everybody, and even signed autographs for some of the guests. Rattan was introduced to him, but apart from shaking hands, did not speak with him at all. But he did watch Nalini maintain – with some grace and unselfconsciousness – an easy flow of conversation with Bachchan. He heard her recount briefly how she often had to claim kinship with him to get out of tricky situations. At this Amitabh Bachchan laughed a little, saying that many all over the world felt that he was one of them anyway. Nalini also laughed, fully aware that only this sort of inconsequential chitchat was possible in such artificially formal contexts. Soon, she moved away, allowing others to also get to meet and talk with this special guest from Bombay.

Nalini spent the last of her free moments with the Guptas, the Singhs, and Rattan. Madhu was pleased about being able to meet the great Bachchan, and pointed out how it would have been far more difficult – even impossible – to meet him in India. There were some advantages in being expatriates abroad – at least you could access visiting dignitaries from India! She continued talking in her own inimitable way and ended by commenting on how life in Cairo had become exciting and eventful.

'Now that the weather has improved we should not let things slacken. I haven't forgotten about our sightseeing trips in and out of Cairo,' said Madhu, her voice full of enthusiasm. 'I hope you will come, Nalini?'

'Yes, of course,' said Nalini, and could not help looking at Rattan.

He was there, standing in the shadows and looking at her through the haze of smoke that was, inevitably, surrounding him.

The Guptas kept their word. The first to get off the ground was the afternoon trip to the Coptic Monastery outside Ma'adi. When Nalini was collected from Bharat Bhavan by the Guptas at about 2.30 p.m. two Fridays later, she found Rattan Malhotra already on the back seat of their car. He had remained inside as Nalini had descended the majestic steps leading out of Bharat

Bhavan's entrance door. As Vinod opened the back door of the car for Nalini, she saw Rattan. He moved her carelessly thrown handbag and jacket more towards the middle of the seat so she could sit comfortably. His presence took Nalini by surprise, because although she had hoped secretly to see him, she did not think he would be among the first she would be talking to. As Vinod negotiated his way along the corniche to the other side of town, Nalini wondered whether they were to pick up anyone else. As if understanding what she might be thinking, Rattan said softly that Rashmi and Rohit Gopal lived in Ma'adi – a new suburb quite popular with the personnel of private enterprises – and would join them on the way.

'We called them just before we left. We go straight to their house first and then on to the monastery,' said Rattan.

Madhu heard him from the passenger seat and explained that, besides the Gopals, there would be another couple who would be joining them.

'They're new here – just like Rattan was a few months ago,' said Madhu.

Their names were Ruchi and Shyam Grover, and Shyam was the area representative for Cadbury's, Egypt. They were also thinking of living in Ma'adi. Nalini remarked that it was kind of the Guptas to make sure that newcomers felt welcome.

'I met both of them at the Gopals' the other night, and Ruchi told me how bored she was in their hotel rooms. So I thought this would be a good way for us all to get out! After all, Vinod and I haven't seen the Coptic Monastery either!'

'Neither have I,' Rattan interjected mildly, knowing full well that Madhu would have something to say.

'You?' said Madhu affectionately. 'You wouldn't see anything at all if it weren't for us. You'd only stay holed up in that flat of yours, and not go anywhere at all, if you had your way . . .'

Rattan did not reply, but met Nalini's eyes as they looked at him speculatively. She noticed that he had not bothered to respond, but had sat smiling quietly in the shadows that flitted in and out of the back seat. Before anyone could say any more, suddenly loud film music flooded into the car. Madhu had inserted her first tape into the cassette deck, and unknown to her, the knob of the tape deck had been left on at high. Her husband protested loudly even as Madhu hastened to lower it to acceptable levels. A small wrangle ensued, the husband accusing the wife of never understanding that music had to be heard at medium — and not loud — volumes. Madhu also made her case, pointing out that it was not she who left the knob on 'high', but the *bawab* who cleaned the car.

Rattan looked at Nalini as the arguments in the front seat went back and forth. She could not help smiling, and quietly lifted her finger and put it to her mouth, indicating that they should keep quiet. Rattan agreed. Both sat in companionable silence until Vinod spoke again.

'Does anyone know the details of the monastery?' he asked.

It was Nalini who replied. She told all in the car what she had read in the many guidebooks that littered her father's study. Fleeing the infamous King Herod, Mother Mary and Baby Jesus were supposed to have sheltered in it for a few days, and subsequently set forth to Assuit in the south of Egypt in a felucca.

'One can still see the original quay to which the boat was tethered, and the same steps used by the holy duo,' said Nalini, trying not to sound like the guidebook she had read.

They listened to her carefully. When she had finished, Vinod pointed out that he had not known that there were any Christians in Egypt, and had been surprised to find that the Egyptian Christians, or Copts as they were more popularly known, counted themselves as amongst the oldest Christians in the world. A serious discussion about the status of minority communities in Egypt ensued; and, inevitably, comparisons between India and Egypt came about. Madhu tried to suggest that India was better at dealing with its minority communities. But Vinod disagreed.

'You were busy making sandwiches while I heard the latest broadcast from CNN. The Babri Masjid issue does not look too good. December is coming closer, and Narasimha Rao does not seem any clearer about what he is going to decide.'

Although Vinod's words seemed addressed mainly to the back seat, it was only his wife who chose to respond. For in the short silence that had followed Vinod's statement, Madhu had understood that neither Rattan nor Nalini were going to join the discussion.

'Rao still has time . . .' she said mildly.

'What time!' said her husband dismissively. 'He'd better decide quickly, or else things will be out of his hands!'

Madhu withdrew, but only because Nalini helped her. She had taken out her guidebook from her handbag, and began reading more about the establishment of Coptic Christianity in Egypt. She pointed out that Islam had come into Egypt almost seven centuries later and ever since then, over a period of time, the Copts had been pushed into a minority status, even needing to seek governmental permission before building a new Church.

This was news for Vinod, and diverted his attention to the subject of the separation of religion and state, and to counting which countries in the world were theocratic states. He could have gone on and on, but nobody in the car responded. Madhu kept silent knowingly; Rattan was made to because Nalini had pressed her hand warningly on his lying unmoving on the seat between them.

Her touch was like electricity through him, and made him turn sideways to face her. She shook her head slightly, suggesting that they avoid the subject altogether. He agreed, making sure that his smiling acquiescence was not visible to Vinod in the rear-view mirror. Both were glad that, at that moment, Madhu changed the cassette, and older Hindi songs replaced the relatively newer ones playing earlier. Vinod seemed to enjoy them – much more than his passengers in the back seat of his car – and was soon singing along in his loud baritone. Nalini wondered what Rattan thought about being subjected to film music from Bollywood even in a car, and could not help smiling. But his face was deadpan, and gave nothing away.

It was a beautiful afternoon. Since the road along the Nile all the way to Ma'adi was not as crowded as it would have been on a weekday, Vinod was able to maintain a fairly high speed. All the windows were down, and the cool November air swept into the car, loosening the hair from Nalini's long plait hanging down her back. It brought a biting pink to her cheeks. Her printed *salwar kameez* boasted of earth tones, and as the wind undid her hair, she tried to control it by covering her head with the rust-coloured *dupatta* that went with the outfit.

The Gopals were waiting impatiently for their arrival. And so were the newly arrived Grovers. Hardly married six months, they had decided to stay as close to the Gopals as possible. But they were yet to find an apartment. Till they did so, they were happy to be moving out of their hotel rooms, and begin sightseeing.

As the *muezzin* called out to the faithful for afternoon prayers over a nearby microphone, the Guptas swung into action. As the longest resident Indians in that group, they took over. Vinod gave instructions to the Gopals to follow them, and soon the two cars wound their way to the outskirts of the city along the Nile. Ultimately they reached the monastery.

Its precincts were more crowded than was suggested from the quiet gates, or the three unassuming, mud-coloured domes that stood huddled together, seemingly touching each other for mutual support. As they walked through the entrance, groups of people – all Copts in their Sunday best – were walking up and down, or sitting on the benches and lawns, enjoying the last rays of the sun. It took the Indians a few minutes to remember that even though it was Friday – the normal weekly holiday in Islamic countries – it was also considered as the Sabbath for the Copts. The second service of the day had just ended; and the evening one would begin at sunset.

They had come at a good time. Or so a young priest informed

them as they wound their way through the crowds. He spoke mainly to Vinod, who was told that if they were keen on seeing the holy parts of the monastery complex, they should do so immediately. Vinod agreed on behalf of the group, and soon the priest had designated one of the young men lounging around with his friends to act as guide. His name was Hani, and he knew enough English to tell them about the association of the spot with Mary, Mother of Christ.

The eight hurried after him. He took them first to the main church, an old building that was in the process of being renovated. An air of musty yet venerable belief hung around the dimly lighted pews, the fraying carpets underfoot adding to the impression. On their way out, they were shown the famous Bible that had been found some decades earlier, preserved and dry in the waters of the river behind the monastery. It was open at a particular page, which Pope Shenoudah, head of the priests of the Coptic Church, had read as a sign of the Egyptian Copts being blessed by Jesus himself.

While the others hurried out after Hani, Nalini hung back a while. She had seen a trough on the counter by the door. It was full of sand, and a tray full of unlit candles lay by its side. Within the trough, a handful of lighted candles stood, their flickering flames casting shadows on the wooden-panelled wall behind the trough. Nalini picked up one of the unlit ones, and holding its wick to one already lighted, waited until hers burst into flame. Then she carefully stood it in the sand, making sure that it would not topple over when she let go. It didn't; and when she was satisfied, she stood still, her eyes closed, and said a prayer.

Standing behind her, Rattan watched her actions quietly. For a moment he thought he would do the same. There was so much absent in his life that he could pray for. But his reasoning, sceptical mind scoffed: did he have to do what others were doing? And, what could he ask of the powers-that-be, anyway? There was nothing that he could thank the Gods for – they had done their worst already.

Bitterly, defiantly, he decided against it.

But Nalini had no such knowledge, or any such qualms. Having said her own prayer, she turned around to Rattan. 'Why don't you light one?'

'I don't really believe in these things . . .' began Rattan apologetically, moving towards the heavily panelled open doorway of the church. He was beginning to feel caught, even imprisoned.

Outside, the bright light and open air beckoned escape.

But Nalini reached out an insistent hand to his, and was gently forcing his fingers to pick up a candle. As he did what he had seen her do, he felt the light touch of her fingers linger on the back of his hand. Her hands were cold, much colder than his were. His candle took a while to light, and Rattan wondered whether this was an ironic comment on the state of his life. He almost laughed aloud in mockery at himself, but refrained, thinking that his companion might take it amiss.

'You don't have to say whether you believe or don't believe . . . there are powers larger than us, aren't there? . . .' said Nalini, still holding his hand as they waited for the flame to steady in the trough of sand. 'In any case, candles are candles . . .'

Rattan did not say anything. As she hurried him out to look for the others, he wondered whether she was laughing at him. He almost said something cutting and mean; something that would shake her out of her smug and neat view of things. But then, he felt her slowly warming hand in his. And in the sudden crush of people in the doorway, he was pushed closer behind her. Feelings of a normal, instinctive chivalry firmed the grasp of his hand around hers even as the free one moved protectively to hold a soft shoulder. His face was close to hers as he escorted her down the steps.

Soon they were outside. There was still an hour for the sun to set, and yet another beautiful Cairene evening awaited them. Always in Cairo, when one faced the waters of the Nile, the world seemed to open out into the ancient, original freshness of when civilisation first began. They stood a moment, their eyes adjusting to the outside light and taking it all in.

They spotted Madhu first, and then the others as they turned the corner of the church. Hani was standing at the bottom of a small staircase that descended along the side of the church wall and led to the level of the water. Madhu, Vinod and the others were gathered in a circle, listening intently to what Hani was saying. Addressing mainly Madhu and Vinod, Hani was making explanations, his hands rising and falling as he gesticulated in typical Egyptian fashion. Throughout their descent, Rattan held on to Nalini's hand, making it awkward for her to move down the narrow staircase. But she sensed that Rattan was not going to let go of it easily, and so pretended there was nothing unusual in his doing so. But when they neared the Guptas and the Gopals, Nalini freed herself firmly. She knew that Madhu at least had noticed, and did not want to give her any opportunity to remark upon it.

Madhu *had* noticed, but knew better than to go anywhere near the subject. She grabbed Vinod's hand and persuaded him to move on to the special spot for which the monastery was famous. Hani was all too ready to oblige, and walking a little quickly positioned himself into leading the way to the point where the holy quay was visible from the banks.

There wasn't much to see. A set of ten steps – roughly hewn out of the banks – had been cemented over crudely. At their end was a quay of about five feet that went into the water. A chain barrier prevented visitors from walking down the steps or the quay.

'They are frail, and will not be able to bear the burden of visitors,' said Hani by way of an apology.

Nalini looked at his face. Young as he was, his mind and heart seemed full of awe at the associations that went with the place. Nalini looked at Rattan, wanting him to see what a believer Hani was. But she found that Rattan was looking at her face, and not Hani's. Later, when she pointed out that Hani seemed a strong believer in the family history of his God, Rattan smiled sceptically.

He also, at the same time, began to look for a cigarette in his pocket.

Both gestures froze the smile on Nalini's face. She turned away, and moved forward towards the Guptas. Rattan did not like this, but he did not stop smoking. He stepped away, a little annoyed at Nalini's disapproval. He needed to smoke! Why did she not seem to understand this?

It was a good half-hour before Rattan was able to find a place for himself at Nalini's side. She had spent all those precious moments making friends with Ruchi Grover, and talking to the Gopals. Now that the Indians had seen everything there was to see, they bade farewell to Hani. Vinod tried to tip him for his services but he would take nothing. The Indians were guests of Egypt and it was his duty, he said, to show them around. As the group neared the gates, Madhu suggested that they have the sandwiches she had brought. Vinod and Rattan went off to the car to fetch them. Soon a bench was found, overlooking the waters of the Nile; and tea and sandwiches shared by all.

The drive back found Nalini and Rattan once again sharing the back seat of the Gupta car. Under the cover of the music from the dashboard, Rattan spoke quietly. 'It'll take me a while, you know.'

'For what?' asked Nalini.

'To completely stop ... smoking, I mean.'

Nalini did not say anything, but looked away.

But when Rattan put his hand out to look for hers, she allowed him to find it. She liked it when she found the warmth of his quickly transformed her cold one.

And when she moved her other hand into his, he warmed them both, even though it meant that she had to lean sideways a little to do so. The only thing they were careful about was that the two in the front seat of the car did not notice anything unusual.

They need not have worried. The Guptas were too worldly-wise to be spoilsports in the very beginnings of so eligible a romance.

PART FOUR

A Dip in the River

Far to the southwest of Delhi – somewhere along the border of Rajasthan and Gujarat, and deep in tribal country – flows a wide and shallow river meandering along in twists and turns on a pebbled bed that has existed unchanging through the centuries. It is a temperamental river, drying out almost completely when the summer equinox makes the length of days and nights as equal as their temperatures, but becoming full-flooded almost immediately after the longest day on 21 June, receiving monsoon waters from catchment streams flowing in from wetter climes.

Earlier, in the height of summer when the water is a trickle, the tribals of the surrounding villages venture into the midst of the riverbed, encroaching on its territory and setting up house. When the breezes of April begin to whisper smouldering messages in each ear, they know that they can be sure of a few months of settled life; and, almost overnight, build their makeshift dwellings out of collected stones and bricks, a small corrugated piece of metal, and wet mud to hold the three together. Small streams meander by, enough for cooking, bathing and washing. The children and the goats play; the thin cattle graze sleepily; the men go off, deep into the interior for the work of the day; the women wash, cook, and tend one – only one – round of cash crops growing quickly on the rich alluvial soil around the huts, their songs carrying far and away on the hot *loo* breezes looking to ripen raw mangoes on trees on the far banks.

Come 21 June when the celebrations are over, the huts are torn down, meagre belongings tied up in bundles, and the whole mini village begins its trek back to life on the banks. Every child, goat, and cow knows that the time has come: the clouds have begun to gather, darkening the skies; the streams have begun to widen; and the waters have begun coming in a rush.

'Move, move,' they seem to say. 'Your time is over. This is our home, our wide and open space. We allowed you, temporarily ... but now, could you please leave?'

'Yes, yes,' say the women. 'We will, we will! But give us time, give us time ... to pack and get our households together!'

A few days later the pebbled bed becomes a river again, swelling mightily, with stomach bulging from extra waters swallowed day in and day out. Standing on the banks, the tribals watch this transformation in awe, praying every morning to its power, and its strange, annual sea change. They pay their obeisance in an old temple, built, they say, in the twelfth century, by a local rajah for his favourite priest who, having done his time in the court, wanted to take *sanyas* from all things worldly. The rajah was loth to see him go, but the priest insisted. He promised to be available whenever the rajah wanted. In order to locate him once and for ever, the rajah suggested that he live in a remote temple where he could pray and meditate as he wished, and yet be found when needed.

The priest thought this a good idea, and thanked the king for his thoughtfulness and regard. The best temple architects were dispatched, the exact spot selected, and the temple built. As requested by the old priest, it was to face the waters of the river, its sides open on three sides to take in the spirit of this most powerful of the four elements. Its back was to be to the mainland, supposedly with no regard to welcoming any living beings that might choose to come and worship.

But, as happens often in India, a wandering tribal discovered the temple and its holy priest, and told the rest of his tribe. Before the priest knew what was happening, the tribe had moved from its last settlement and decided to set up camp around the temple. Soon one hut was joined by another, and another. All the inhabitants were respectful of the priest's desires, and kept their distance. But over the years, the temple and its priest became their point of reference and pilgrimage. Till the day of his death, the priest was unable to become the detached *sanyasi* he had set out to be on leaving the court; and accepted gracefully the new role the Gods seemed to have written for him.

Inevitably, he became an advisor: on mainly spiritual matters, but also on some other, purely personal ones. He had already observed the habits and rituals of the villagers carefully, and accepted them. He also introduced some new ones. He told them the stories of the great epics, and how to celebrate the special occasions laid out in them. He explained to them the importance of the river, and the powers of the Almighty suggested by its different shapes. By the time he came to die, the community around him had learned to chart the four seasons of the year more clearly. When the season of festivals came in the third quarter of every year, they knew what to do. They knew that whatever they did would have to include the mighty river, and soon its waters become integral to their feasting and celebration.

Even today, as becomes the custom continuing from those times, it is not only the huts that glow with *diyas* in the dark night of *Diwali*, the great festival of lights. As that first priest taught, even the river is made to welcome the triumphant Lord Rama home to Ayodhya. Lights bob on its black waters, afloat on small boats made of banana leaves. If you look at that night from above, the whole settlement seems a-twinkle, one of its outer edges defined by an uneven row of lighted pinheads hugging the banks – like fireflies in the dark. You can hear in the distance the muffled sound of ritual chants, floating unseen on the still-warm air. The priest in the temple leads these, and only when he gives the signal do the tribals gather to light fireworks, and burst into song.

But once *Diwali* has come and gone, and when it is flowing sure and confident, the river is sought for certain other, darker ceremonies. On *Kartiki Purnima*, the first full moon night after *Diwali*, a strange event takes place in the shallow waters near its banks. It too is supervised by the priest in the temple. At exactly midnight, when the moon hangs round and silent, he blows sharply on an old conch shell, signalling to all the participants that the time has come for the annual purge. The makeshift curtains from the doorways of each hut are pushed aside one by one, and the men emerge first. After a pause, the women step out, seemingly reluctant. A silent whisper of signs indicates that they should begin to move. At a given point in time mutually understood, the men begin to herd their women towards the dark shade of the *banyan* tree standing guard at the point where the river curves into a rounded U-shape, and from where a narrow path leads straight into the water.

The men are in their *lungis* or loin cloths, and the women are bare from their waists upwards, their oiled breasts glistening in the light of the moon. The eyes of the women shine white with fear, their sharp almond-shapes standing out from the darkness of faces and the even darker outlines of kohl. Their foreheads are smeared with the vermilion of smudged bindis, and their long black hair hang loose and tangled on their shoulders.

Slowly their number grows, and soon the protective cover of the old banyan tree becomes too small to contain all the people below. At first there is silence, broken only by the shuffle of feet and the intoning of the priest's chants. Each man stands close to his woman, the faces of some grim with purpose; those of others somewhat more lascivious. The breeze blows chilly, cooled by the full light of the silver moon. The women shiver, and the men titter.

'Oh God, Destroyer of Evil spirits. Help us rid ourselves

of their power. It will be good for us. It will be good for the village.'

This is intoned over and over by the priest as he walks slowly, swinging his *thali* laid out with the incense-laden flame of an *arti*. As he comes nearer, the men begin to repeat his words after him. At the seventh repetition, the priest blows the conch shell. As the hollow, thin sound wafts high above the ground, the men begin to move towards the water, pulling their women in after them. As each puts their first steps into its cold folds, sharp gasps of sound fill the air. Soon these turn to loud squeals.

And then, when the conch stops blowing, the thrashing and threshing begins. The women are held tightly by their men, and dunked into the water. And beaten mercilessly. Thwack, thwack, and thwack. The water both protects and hurts the men who beat and the women who are beaten. On the bank, the priest intones his prayers, swirling the incense flame round and round in the silvery darkness of the night to chase away the evil spirits. Away from the banks, the men lash at their women in the water. Breasts and hands touch in wild abandon. The women scream, and the men pant with fervour.

The whole exercise lasts about half an hour.

When all the prayers have been said, the priest blows on the conch shell once again to signal the end of the ritual. The men move away – after one last lunge – and begin walking to the shore. The women wait a few minutes, and then begin to run, covering their naked breasts with crossed arms. They come out together, the waters parting at their bidding and letting them go with one big splash. They run up the banks, untouched – but under the laughing eyes of their men. Soon they are gone, swallowed up by their huts. Inside they feel safe, their yearly ordeal over. Soon they change into dry clothes after having rubbed in oil and ointments to soothe their raw beaten flesh.

*　　*　　*

That year, two strangers to the village also participated in the annual ritual. She arrived with a male companion the day before at dusk, having walked the last four miles of her journey from the point of disembarkation from the local country bus. She wore a faded white sari and on her feet were kolhapuri *chappals*. In her hand she carried a small duffel bag containing another set of similar clothes. Her companion was simply dressed in an old pyjama and *kurta*. He was tall, and walked with a firm stride. Occasionally he would attempt to talk to the woman who walked beside him. She would rarely answer. But when she did, it was to say something in sharp, low tones that were so harsh and final that they would shut him up for a while. As they entered the outskirts of the village, she commanded him to find out where the temple was. He did so by asking a passer-by. The latter, seemingly in a hurry, said something briefly, waving an arm towards his right. Even though she was a hundred yards away from the encounter between her companion and the passer-by, the woman set forth as if understanding everything. The man loped after her, showing his irritation.

But she ignored him and walked on, and he could do no better than to follow her.

They saw the temple as they rounded a clump of dusty *neem* trees growing in low clusters along the path that led upwards towards it. They saw its back as it sat, poised on high ground, with a commanding view of the waters. They climbed up the forty-four steps, the woman first, and looked around. In the half-light of evening they, at first, saw no one. This seemed to annoy the woman somewhat. Tugging impatiently at her sari *pallav* that she chose to wrap firmly around her shoulders, the woman looked questioningly at her companion.

He saw her accusatory look, shook his head and shrugged his shoulders. She gave him a withering glance, and moved into the middle archway that led into the open courtyard. Hanging from a central beam was the large temple bell. The woman saw it as she walked in, but hesitated a moment before she raised her arm. She paused a moment, thinking intensely, and then pulled at it. It made a much-too-loud clanging sound which surprised her. She faltered, quite taken aback, and almost fell. Her companion held her gently. She allowed him to help her, but shrugged him off when she found her feet. He did not react but murmured something in low tones. But she shushed him up, indicating that she was hearing something.

She was right, for a shadow emerged from the right. It was the temple priest. She bowed low when he came in front of her, and asked politely if she could speak to him for a few minutes. He accepted her *pranam*, and indicated that they should follow him around the back of the temple. The meeting lasted about ten minutes. The priest inquired who they were and why they had come so far to so hidden a place in the countryside. She explained her circumstances, and what she had come for. He wondered how she had heard of this place. She told him, after a slight hesitation, her whole story.

He heard her out, his face unmoving.

When she asked whether she and her companion could be part of the annual ritual purges the next day, it was the priest's turn to hesitate. Did she really believe in such things? After all, she was a townswoman, smart and modern, and he did not think that she would take all this in the spirit that it was supposed to be.

'This is serious business ...' he told her sternly. 'And the spirit of the mighty river, swollen and majestic at this time of the monsoon, would not take kindly to any scepticism or disbelief.'

The woman hastened to assure him that she believed – that she *really* believed that this was the only thing that could save her, and give her guilty heart some peace.

The priest was silent for some moments.

He then asked one final question. It hit her straight in her heart. It was about her companion, the man who had come with her. She did not answer for a few seconds. When she did, she did not look at him although she knew clearly that he was looking at her. Her answer was firm – even vehement – and her voice choked with tears. This was the last time they would be together, she assured the priest.

She even went so far as to add that she had told him so even before they had left New Delhi.

The priest accepted her explanation and her promises. He proceeded to tell her about the rituals of the next night, and the prayers that they had to say through the whole of the next day by way of preparation. She listened to him carefully, occasionally asking him a question or two. Although she had schooled herself to show nothing of her feelings on her face, occasionally it would grimace in pain.

She only made one last request: that she and her companion be permitted a little privacy in the completion of the rituals the following night. After all, they were not of the village and perhaps its residents would not like outsiders amidst them at a time like this. She also said that she was a little afraid to be part of such a large unknown crowd, with only her companion to protect her.

Could they, therefore, partake of it all some distance away? On the other side of the temple?

The priest thought about it a moment. His face had taken on a stern, admonitory look. He gave no immediate answer to her request. Instead, he pointed out that if they chose to be away from the others, no one would be there to make sure they did everything they were supposed to. This, however, upset the woman so much that she began to sob hysterically. Her companion tried to calm her, but she brushed him off. When she had controlled herself somewhat, she spoke in a tone that was just above a whisper.

'I would not have come all this way – incurring the wrath of all – if I did not intend all this sincerely, and from the depths of my wretched heart!'

The priest did not say anything, but with a wave of his hand, granted her what she wanted. He told them that they could spend that – and the next – night in the temple and that they should prepare to leave on the third day at first light. The woman nodded in relief, wiping her eyes with the ends of her *pallav*. As she did so, she bent low before the priest.

He blessed her and her companion, and retired.

The next night, while the residents of that cluster of villages performed their rituals of purification at the open spot where their ancestors had done so for hundreds of years, a man and a woman performed theirs in secret, barely a mile away. If the priest wondered at what they had done and how they had done it, he did not say.

But inside his heart he knew that the river was there, huge and powerful, and that its spirit would know exactly if any less-than-perfect mortal had tried to hide anything.

The Red Serviettes

It was the bomb blast in Tahrir Square that was responsible for closing the distance between Nalini Thapar and Rattan Malhotra. It happened one weekday afternoon, late in November – sometime between one and one thirty p.m. – and caught everyone by surprise. Those inside the restaurant where it happened never noticed the small package that lay behind a row of small potted plants to the right of the glass entrance. They had streamed in for a quick lunch, immersed in conversation with companions, or brooding on the agendas of meetings planned for the afternoon. The manager – a young Egyptian with an earnest expression – had his attention focused on the relative fullness of each table, and on making sure that a waiter got to each as quickly as possible with the menu card. The fuller his restaurant, the happier he became. It meant that the restaurant was doing well, and more revenue might mean a bigger bonus at the end of the year from the owner.

And so it was that, after the *muezzin*'s noontime call to prayer was over, he never thought once of stepping outside. And thus, did not notice a nondescript parcel wrapped in brown paper tucked away behind a pot of green fern.

He did notice – although somewhat unconsciously – the Indian couple that entered behind a few loud-talking Egyptians laughing at the newest Mubarak joke being told by the last man in the group. They waited in the doorway behind the Egyptian group that stood awhile chattering amongst themselves. He saw the hostess wait politely until the last laugh had died away to ask how many they were.

'We are seven,' the man telling the joke pronounced loudly, as if the number had some great significance. Everyone laughed again, and the hostess smiled too as she indicated that their table would be somewhere deeper inside the restaurant. She led the seven inside to where a table for eight was being laid for lunch.

In the foyer behind them stood Nalini and Rattan, waiting patiently. It was then, as the group moved away, that the manager noticed the Indian arrivals, and stepped forward.

'Just two?' he asked softly, looking appreciatively at Nalini dressed in a *salwar kameez*, in a cool sage green.

'Yes,' said Rattan. 'And could we have somewhere quiet?'

'Would you like to go upstairs?' asked the manager conspiratorially.

'Yes, that would be nice,' said Rattan, ignoring his typically Egyptian interest in them.

He took Nalini by the arm, and followed the manager up the staircase. The latter found them an alcove table along the back wall of the restaurant. There were no windows here, and so no view of the street, or anything else outside. It was a dimly lit table, but it was in a corner, and was perhaps the most quiet in the whole restaurant. The manager waited deferentially until both Rattan and Nalini were seated. Making sure they were comfortable, he signalled to a nearby waiter to come and take their order. He left soon after, and for a few minutes the two were alone at the table.

'So you did agree, finally, to lunch with me,' said Rattan attempting to speak in a light tone. He was always amazed how, in each meeting with Nalini, she always seemed to insist that whatever was between them needed to begin all over again.

'Yes. I guess it was inevitable,' said Nalini, trying hard not to let the ever-quick blush flood her face. 'You were never going to give up asking, were you?'

'No, I was not,' said Rattan. 'And I am glad you understood this. Though why it should have been so difficult for you to agree to a simple lunch I can't imagine.'

'I don't know how to explain . . .' said Nalini, breaking off mid-sentence and looking away into the dim distance.

Her profile became a point of great interest to Rattan. He had not seen it as sharply etched as today. This was because she had tied her long hair into a smart, twisted knot pinned high behind her head. Her demeanour had a severer aspect than any time before, but it also highlighted her long nose and strong chin in a new way. He knew that this lunch invitation seemed to have been a real problem, and wondered whether he had stepped beyond some invisible code of behaviour which he should have known about, but didn't.

As for Nalini, what she had said was true. She did not know how to explain. Or indeed *what* to explain, for the question of her lunching out alone with an expatriate young Indian had not arisen in Cairo before. How would she tell her father about it? And what would she tell? It was not that he would not approve, but he could get some wrong ideas. And she did not really wish to make any explanations, no matter how rudimentary.

All these silent concerns gave her face an anxious look. She had also begun looking furtively around the restaurant to see if there was anyone she knew, or who would recognise her. Rattan understood immediately that she was feeling awkward, and decided it was better to eat. Without waiting for her to finish what she was saying, he turned his attention to the waiter, hovering assiduously around them with the menu card. Rattan handed it to Nalini, and the attention turned to food. They discussed their order for a bit, and, eventually, the waiter left.

For a few moments, silence hung in the air.

Rattan watched her sitting just a few feet from him, and felt her inner shyness come between them. What of the hands they had held on the trip to the Coptic Monastery? Had she forgotten? The green suited her, but it also gave her an air of remote elegance. He knew instinctively that he would have to step carefully, because now, at last, it was he and she alone who would be responsible for how things would work out between them.

Sitting there, waiting for their meal to arrive, Rattan was acutely reminded of his days in the USA where he had 'done' lunches with so many women. But none of those encounters had resembled this one. There was an air of vulnerability about her, and a wrong move would make for complete disaster and take her away from him for ever. After a long time, Rattan felt that life was a challenge, and worth living fully again. He would put Tanvi and his scarred past behind him.

'Why are you so silent today?' asked Nalini eventually. She had been looking speculatively at Rattan and, sensing his wary reserve, was wondering about it.

Around them flowed the hum and chatter of conversations from adjacent tables. However, the one immediately on the left of them was empty. In the few seconds that elapsed before Rattan answered her question, Nalini noticed the smartly folded, red serviettes, standing stylishly in fours, awaiting use on all the tables. She looked around at the simple yet elegant décor of the room, and began wondering absently why the man in front of her was still silent. Slowly she turned her head and began watching his face surreptitiously. Was he contemplating lighting his inevitable cigarette? Was it going to be today that she would have to tell him that she didn't really like his smoking? That she was even allergic to it?

However, that silence was the lull before the storm. The storm of a bomb that exploded exactly five seconds after she had mouthed her question. There was a loud booming sound, followed by the aftershocks of successive smaller ones, and a split second later, Nalini found herself thumped backwards against the wall as her chair gave way under her. She slid to the floor even as the table in front of her tilted, pinning her down under it. Something hit the back of her head, and then seemed to be constricting her chest. She felt the wet of water everywhere as the jug on the table shattered. The table seemed to be weighing down on her more and more heavily, and it took her a few seconds to realise that it was Rattan's weight slumped across it which was pressing her down, squeezing tightly the top half of her breasts so she could hardly breathe.

Nalini could not afterwards recall the exact sequence of events that followed, but she remembered moaning softly. She felt something pull at her shoulders and the front of her shirt, heard the noise of ripping fabric, and fainted.

Then, miraculously it seemed, someone freed her; and she felt the air flow back freely into her lungs. Her head was spinning. She opened her eyes slowly. But then, bright light forced them shut again. When she opened them again, she saw Rattan's face close to her own. He had lifted the table, pushed it aside, and was bending over her. All around were sounds of people shouting and screaming, and the air was full of dust. The still-warm air of a Cairene November flowed all around. The sunlight was dazzling.

'Are you OK?' she heard Rattan ask frantically.

'I think so . . . what about you?' said Nalini, trying to sit up, and feeling self consciously for the tips of her fingers and toes. They seemed whole and unhurt. She looked at Rattan, wanting to make sure for herself that he, too, was not hurt. 'You have blood on your face,' she said in sudden panic. 'Are you hurt?'

'I don't think so,' said Rattan carefully, feeling the side of his face with his left hand. It came away with a little blood.

'My God . . .' said Nalini, almost hysterical. Her hand automatically reached for her *dupatta*, a green chiffon. She held up an edge, and dabbed at his face. Some blood stained it, but not much.

'It's a cut ... a small one, and not very deep,' she said, with relief in her voice.

'What about you?' said Rattan. 'Are you hurt?'

'I don't think so, though my head is smarting a bit,' said Nalini, trying to stand.

Rattan helped her to her feet. His hands moved under her armpits, and she felt his strength lift her up. She searched for her legs, and tried to make sure that they could support her weight. They could, and she straightened to stand upright. She found that her face had come very close to Rattan's chest. She could smell the front of his shirt, and saw immediately a large stain of blood on his tie. She was beginning to say something, but he spoke before she could.

'Are you sure you are OK? ... Because there is more blood on you than on me!' said Rattan.

Nalini saw that his eyes were fixed on her right shoulder.

'What is it?' she asked, looking at his face even as she felt his fingers touch her flesh. She felt him move a part of her *kameez* off her shoulder, and push the strap of her bra to one side.

'There's a gash here, and your *kameez* is torn. I think the edge of the table caught the front, and ripped it,' said Rattan as calmly as he could.

She bent her chin downwards in an effort to look. She saw it then, the gash. It was deep, and ran halfway down her right breast. The top of her bra had been ripped a little, and its edges were stained with blood.

For a minute Nalini panicked, raising her eyes wildly at Rattan's face, close in front of her.

'Hey, it's OK. The cut is quite deep, though,' said Rattan gently. He made a pad out of his handkerchief and in a few seconds he was holding it to the top of her breast.

'We should get you to a doctor.'

'No! No ... I'll be fine really,' said Nalini, raising a hand to take the handkerchief from him, and hold it to her breast herself.

Her gesture was sudden, almost grabbing, and was accompanied by her moving a step backwards away from him. It was only then that she felt a sense of awkwardness at being so exposed. Rattan saw her face blush a deep red even as she stumbled away from him. He saw her clutch at the torn shoulder ends of her *kameez* and cover her shoulder.

Understanding but deliberately ignoring her feelings of embarrassment, he turned her around to face him. The blood on her breast was beginning to ooze through her quivering fingers. Finally – and with firmer fingers – it was he who thought of adjusting the pad of his folded handkerchief neatly on top of the gash, and tucking its four ends inside her torn brassiere. He slid the ends of her *kameez* under the strap on her shoulder, making her neckline a little wider and deeper than before. But once the *dupatta* was around her neck, no one could tell that she had been hurt.

Only then did they look around. Everywhere was noise and confusion. There was a large hole in the middle of the restaurant. Through it you could see the destruction below, on the ground floor. At the bottom of the hole sprawled a few bleeding bodies in the middle of upturned chairs and tables, broken glass and rubble. Sounds of moaning rent the air. There was a mad scramble among the guests and the waiters to get out of it all. Those who could, were moving away through what was once the entrance of the restaurant. The front of the building had been completely blown away, along with part of the roof.

If Rattan and Nalini were still on the first floor, it was because their table had been along the beams that defined a corner of the building. As it happened, theirs – and the empty table next to them – were the only ones that had remained on what was once the first floor.

'We seem to be marooned here ...' said Rattan, holding on to Nalini tightly. 'Along this ledge. The staircase seems fine, though. We should try and go downstairs.'

'No, wait,' said Nalini warningly. Her voice sounded weak,

and all her weight was on him. 'It might be dangerous . . . it might cave in under our weight . . . Let's just wait a bit, and see.'

'You're probably right,' said Rattan, and stopped moving towards it.

But this was also because he had noticed a uniformed waiter sprawled, lifeless, along two steps of the staircase. An upturned tray was lying next to him. It was an unpleasant sight, and he did not want Nalini to see it. There didn't seem to be anyone else on the ledge with them.

He shouted for help.

But nobody heard him on his first attempt. Or the second. There was too much confusion below. There was nothing to do but to wait.

Though the glare of the sun shone bright and warm, Rattan felt Nalini begin to shiver. He put his arms around her, and she could not help but put her head down on his shoulder in response.

'This is beginning to hurt,' she said feebly, and put out her left hand to her breast. The blood was beginning to soak through the folds of the handkerchief, and was staining her *kameez*.

Rattan looked around desperately. On the floor, amidst the debris, were some of the red napkins that had once adorned the tables. He grabbed a few, and took a few moments to fold three together into a neat square. Nalini watched him detachedly. When he put his hand inside her shirt, and removed his handkerchief from under her torn brassiere, she did not move, but watched as if in slow motion, how he replaced the once-white handkerchief with the wad of the red napkins.

'At least now the red stain won't be visible,' said Rattan, attempting a joke.

But he got no reply from Nalini. She only smiled weakly, aware dimly that his hands had felt cool on her flesh, now throbbing hot with pain. The cut on his face was beginning to grow a solid, protecting layer of dried blood along its surface. It gave his face a crooked, rakish appearance. But she did not have the energy to tell him so. Standing completely still, and with eyes half closed, she felt him tuck in the ends of her *kameez* once again under her bra strap with gentle fingers.

'Hey, don't pass out on me, will you! I won't know what to do!' he said softly, shaking her gently. She opened her eyes as if with an effort, and looked at him. The old smile had lit his eyes.

Nalini did not reply, but when he bent his head and put his lips to her forehead, she let him kiss her. His touch was soft and gentle, as if aware that this was hardly the moment. She did not respond, but Rattan felt her surrender completely to him. He could not help holding her closely.

But the embrace squeezed her breast.

'That hurts . . .' she protested, her voice low.

'I'm sorry,' he said, immediately moving away a little, and putting out a hand to stroke her face. Her hair had come undone, and some pins were sticking out dangerously from over her shoulder. He picked them out, and handed them to her. She clutched at them even as he smoothed stray, dusty tendrils away from her face.

Below them, a crowd had gathered, and their shouts could be heard ringing across the square. In the distance, the sound of a fire engine jangled against the wailing sirens of police cars.

And the dust, hanging in the bright glare of the afternoon, settled on their hair.

It was almost an hour before Rattan and Nalini were rescued from the ledge.

Nalini's face was white. 'Take me home, Rattan,' she whispered.

'I will, but after you have seen a doctor,' said Rattan firmly, and led her slowly away.

He told a group of solicitous Egyptians standing in the crowd that he would take Nalini to the doctor himself, and then home. The Egyptians looked dubious, but there were so many others, more seriously wounded, that it would only help if they got out of the way.

In the car, Rattan looked at Nalini leaning back with her eyes closed. Through the transparent fabric of her chiffon *dupatta*, he saw the ends of the red napkins. Was the blood soaking through? He could not tell and knew he had to get her to the hospital quickly. Before disaster struck again. No, he could not let that happen.

Not again. Not again.

This time he had been there, right there, knowing clearly and exactly what had happened, and *how* it had happened. And he was going to make sure that everything was going to be taken care of well in time. As the lights turned green, and the traffic surged forward in typical Cairo fashion, he could not help thinking of a time back at home in New Delhi when he had weathered rush-hour traffic only to find that he had been too late. When the dead Tanvi, hanging from the ceiling fan, came before his eyes, he shook his head to rid the image from his mind.

By this time Nalini had opened her eyes and was watching his face, concerned at his bleak expression. She put out her hand and touched his arm, asking him softly how he was doing.

His face softened as he looked at her. 'We'll be there in a few minutes,' he replied.

Nalini's gash was a deep one, and the doctor recommended stitches under anaesthesia. When she had been wheeled into surgery, Rattan called Gautam Thapar. If he was surprised at where his daughter had been lunching that afternoon, he did not show it. He asked after Rattan but was reassured that a small surgical plaster across his left cheek was all his daughter's companion needed.

Rattan told him all that had happened; but neither could guess which political terrorist group was responsible for so horrendous an act. When Nalini was wheeled out of surgery and left sleeping in a recovery room Rattan was persuaded to go home. Gautam Thapar had brought *Aji* to be in the room with Nalini.

Aji was most suspicious of Rattan, looking him up and down as if he had been responsible for her dear girl being so hurt. Rattan tried to reassure her, but *Aji* was not to be placated. She gave Rattan a few more withering looks, and told him that he was not needed any more, and that he should go home and look after himself.

Rattan was quite amused and, giving one last look at the pale, sleeping form of Nalini, he moved to go.

So much for being alone in Cairo.

He had found a friend, a sweet and lovely friend.

But he had also made an enemy.

Single Parent

The same week in New Delhi, Maneka Saxena was trying to sit down to a somewhat late dinner with her son.

'What's for dinner?' asked Ahmer peevishly, his small face screwed up in his typical mealtime pout.

'Oh, rice and dal ... the usual!' she guessed, her mind elsewhere.

'Why can't we have something interesting?' complained Ahmer, his large eyes plaintive and accusatory.

'They are interesting,' said Maneka trying to sound enthusiastic. She had walked into the kitchen and was in the process of lifting the lids off the *kadahi* and the pressure cooker. Meera the maidservant had left their meal prepared. The rice lay in a separate pot on the side, along with the *rotis* rolled tight in a napkin so that they would remain moist.

'No. They are not,' said Ahmer definitively, his fingers playing absently with a Rubic cube. He moved away from the kitchen and made himself comfortable in one of the easy chairs in the living room.

His mother did not respond, but went about the business of laying dinner.

It was quiet in the small living room, although the sound of Ring Road's heavy traffic hummed steadily in the background. Nondescript inexpensive curtains in a practical navy blue hung in the windows, and on the floor was a large *coir* mat, lifted up and shaken out on the terrace each morning when Meera did the cleaning. A few simple chairs circled a small television, and on one side stood a dining table with four chairs. A wooden sideboard, helpfully built into the wall by the landlord, was cluttered with jars of jams and pickles, and bottles of filtered drinking water.

Along the front edge stood the ketchup bottle and a half-eaten plate of French fries. It was covered over by a faded but clean napkin. The room was dimly lit, the lamp on the small desk on one side of the television being switched on only when Maneka was working.

Maneka's home was in a centrally located *barsati* – that uniquely Indian metropolitan phenomenon in which people lucky enough to be home owners built up every single inch of space that was allowed (by the municipal authorities) above their own roofs, and rented it out to tenants to supplement their incomes. In this way they added to the number of dwellings available for the ever-increasing population of the capital.

Finding one had not been very easy. All landlords were fussy about the bona fides of their *barsati* dwellers. For, when all was said and done, they would undoubtedly attempt to live full lives right 'on top of their heads'. This could easily pose problems. The 'character' of divorced women like Maneka was always suspect in the eyes of prospective landlords, and she had been turned away more than once. Finally she had found a suitable one, but the landlord – a retired army major whose greying moustache dripped suspicion – had given her a long list of rules to be followed. It had ended by an admonition of a personal nature.

'No men visitors allowed, yes?' he had warned heartlessly. 'This is a decent colony. We do not want any hanky panky going on here.'

Tired of Bhasker and the whole of his gender, Maneka had agreed easily, even vehemently. She told the doubting major that she was sick of men, and wanted nothing to do with them. Thus, Maneka had found herself with a place to live that she could call her own. And she was more than lucky, because this *barsati* boasted *three* rooms. Although two of them were rather small, at least now Ahmer and she could have separate rooms to sleep in. And the large roof-top terrace was a boon both in winter and summer.

The successful search for rooms of her own put an end to the endless speculation and discussion that had, inevitably, followed her divorce. Initially there had been some talk of her moving permanently to her mother's house. However, given the fact that Mrs Mahajan lived in a very conservative, middle-class neighbourhood, Maneka had felt it inappropriate that she return there. On the other hand, neither had the older woman really wanted to give up her own home — where she had lived for so many years — and move in with her daughter. This was what many of her colleagues in the school where she taught expected her to do; and Maneka, too, had tried to persuade her. But Mrs Mahajan had not agreed.

When asked why, she would give no coherent reason.

This did not mean she did not have one. But it was one she chose not to tell her daughter; or, indeed, anyone else. In the way she saw the future for herself and her daughter, she felt that her absence from the daily pattern of her daughter's life would give Maneka a better chance of finding someone else — of finding another husband. Now that she was divorced, a second, 'arranged' marriage was out of the question. If a mother moved in with her daughter, theirs would come to appear as a more or less 'complete' household. Maneka was not yet thirty years old. Her mother's presence could scare away any male friends she might, in time, care to make.

And so it was that Maneka began to live in a *barsati* in South Extension. It did not take her long to begin feeling comfortable in it. In fact, she quickly came to see herself as a householder like any other, complete with child and a new ration card.

And viable in the eyes of the world.

As Maneka fussed over her son that late November of 1992, the evening was turning cold. Shivering a little, she walked over to the windows and pulled the curtains. The noise of traffic on nearby Ring Road receded a little. Ahmer had finished his homework, and she had persuaded him into having a quick bath. The packing of his books for the next day at school had taken longer than normal. And, now that it was almost 9.30 p.m., the little boy looked ready for bed.

She had better feed him quickly.

Wiping wet hands with the ends of her faded brown *dupatta*, Maneka walked up to her son still sitting in an easy chair. He watched her approach but pretended he hadn't.

'*Khana* time!' said Maneka, attempting a cheerfulness she did not really feel. But Ahmer was in no mood to respond. Holding him firmly by his shoulders, Maneka led him to the table and sat him down.

'How was school today?' she asked in an effort to get him to talk.

But Ahmer had other things on his mind. 'I want a hamburger,' he whined, thinking of the brightly lit facade of Nirula's not far from the house.

'But you've already had French fries!' said Maneka. 'And Meera made you so many that you could not finish them!'

'She would not agree to make them at first,' complained Ahmer. 'But I *forced* her. I told her to make a whole lot!'

As he said this, he made a triumphant face at his mother.

'You should not have been given them so soon before your dinner. It spoils your appetite,' said Maneka, trying to remain as calm as possible and mentally making a note to instruct Meera *not* to feed Ahmer with fries.

Although she had not scolded him, Ahmer sensed his mother's disapproval. He understood instinctively that there was no use in pursuing the subject of hamburgers. It was late, and he knew that there was no way his mother would agree to a change of plans.

Mother and son finally sat down at the table. Maneka served her son and, making sure that he had everything, then served herself and began to eat.

In the background the announcer on television had already begun reading the 9.30 p.m. newscast. The Babri Masjid issue was getting serious. Maneka wondered idly what action Narasimha Rao, the Prime Minister, would take. From what she could understand, he had not said anything definitely either way. He was taking his usual 'consensus' approach. This made her a little angry because, as far as she could see, there was no point in breaking down a structure already four hundred years old even if it had been the product of religious prejudice. Moreover, Narasimha Rao's supposed tactfulness seemed to amount to indecisiveness. If he went on this way, events would take on their own momentum, and he would find himself no longer in control.

In any case, the whole Babri Masjid problem had raised a number of issues. If the Moghuls had exercised Muslim power so many years ago, did it automatically follow that all the monuments they had constructed should be demolished now in 1992 when India had proclaimed itself as a secular democracy at least forty-five years ago?

As she served herself to a second helping of rice and dal, Maneka went over the acrimonious debates she had heard in the staff room of her college that morning in the tea break. Sitting huddled together eating samosas from the college canteen, some of her friends from other departments had felt strongly and categorically that it was time to destroy the Masjid and reinstate the holy birthplace of the Lord Rama as a temple of worship. The sins of history had to be righted. In support of their stand, they had cited the example of Israel and the Jews who had carved out a whole nation for themselves on the basis of proof from texts as old as the Old Testament.

Others, of the opposite view, had been equally vociferous. India's past was old and long, and so chequered that it could be very dangerous to remember this portion of it rather than that. How could one group justify their choice of what they remembered over that which others had forgotten? Maneka wondered why the so-called 'Hindu majority' were feeling so insecure, and at once came to the conclusion that it was political strategy on the part of the BJP party that was responsible for the revival of the Babri Masjid issue.

Maneka wanted to talk more about this hotly debated subject with someone, but for the moment had to remain silent. She did not have a phone to call anyone; and in front of her sat Ahmer, not yet old enough to be her companion in such discussions.

In any case, this was hardly the moment to think of politics and history. As she looked at Ahmer's plate, she found that he had hardly eaten anything. He was playing around with the rice and dal on his plate. Maneka had not realised how long she had spent with her own thoughts, and that all the while Ahmer had stayed quietly with his. The only difference was that she had also eaten her dinner, but the little boy had not. This made Maneka feel a little guilty – as well as a little angry.

How difficult Ahmer was, and how much it took out of her to communicate with him!

Sitting there trying to persuade her son to eat, all her feelings of resentment against being a single parent rose to the surface: it was so easy for Bhasker to just forget about it all – forget about the fact that he had a son who had to be looked after, spent time with, and coaxed into eating every single mouthful.

She looked at Ahmer, trying to keep her feelings tightly under control. He returned her stare, not really meaning to be deliberately provocative or difficult. But the stare had a negative effect on his mother. She felt anger rise in a powerful wave, tried to keep her face passive and show no emotion. It took her a few seconds to be able to do this, for as she told herself, there was no use getting angry.

It would do no good to either her or him.

Behind them, she heard the sign-off tune of the newscast as it came to an end. It was 10 o'clock. It was better to call it a day, tuck Ahmer under the covers, and then relax for a while before retiring.

After Maneka had put Ahmer to bed, she heaved a long sigh. The day had been long and difficult, particularly at *Sahayata*. The shelter was crowded; and she had had to hold off a particularly irate husband who insisted that he take his runaway wife home. The wife had not wanted to go, and Maneka had told her to remain upstairs out of sight, before things got too heated. The only way the husband would leave the premises was when one of the *chowkidars* had threatened him, and told him to return the next day in a calmer frame of mind.

The day had really tired Maneka. She was ready for her break, ready for her visit to Cairo.

'I should really write that letter to Nalini, or else it will get too late and I will have to call her long distance. And that I cannot afford.'

New Delhi,
17th November 1992

Dearest Nalini,
This is just a short letter to let you know that my travel dates have been finalised. Shall be with you on the 9th of December and will be able to stay till the 9th of January 1993. A whole month! I cannot believe it. Hope these dates are OK with you. I shall most probably come alone, because Mummy has agreed to look after Ahmer for me. I

know it is a long time for us to be apart, but things have been difficult for me after the divorce, and I do need this break.

Life has been very hectic, and very tiring. I was working hard in college so that I could get my teaching done in time. The Principal hummed and hawed, but she agreed finally to let me take two extra weeks off before the Christmas break. I assured her that I would finish teaching all the required classes before leaving. The students couldn't care less. For them it is so many fewer lectures to attend!

Sahayata is busy too. As I wrote in my last letter, our fame is spreading, and now that people know that we have a place where women can stay, they are coming in droves. We are going to need more and more volunteers. Women do want to help, but many leave when they find the intensity of the involvement needed is too much for them. It gets too much for me too sometimes, although this is probably because of the first part of the day, which I have to spend in college teaching. I would really like to work at Sahayata full time, but the money is not enough. There are no Dads around to take care of me, you know! And of course, no husbands!

Our neighbours at Sahayata are a scream. A few days after Diwali, there was a big fight in the servants' quarters next door. Apparently, after killing off the young woman for dowry, the old mother-in-law has gone a little off her head. She has begun going to some crazy fakir in Old Delhi and consults him about her future. Ha! She is also supposed to have taken this mysterious trip out of town to some God-forsaken part of the country ... Gujarat or something ... and returned to be in 'maun vrat'. By this what I mean is that she has given up speaking to anyone. Isn't that funny?

It is even funnier because, a few days after her return, she broke her maun vrat and screamed at all her servants at the kitchen door. There was an argument amongst them, at the end of which she is supposed to have fired her old bearer ... the one with the military moustaches. He is supposed to have protested violently, but she went hysterical and forced him to leave. Which I believe he did. Of course, the master of the house was not around (he never is!); and neither was the son (who never is, either!). I guess, now she is back into her maun vrat.

So, as you can see, Delhi is exciting! Shall tell you more on arrival.

My flight particulars are as follows:

Flight C 230 Egypt Air, arriving Cairo, 9th December at 4.50 p.m. Hope you will be there to meet me.

Looking forward to being with you,

Love,

Maneka.

Folding her letter in three, Maneka slipped it into a long envelope, wrote Nalini's address, and stuck a few stamps on it. She put it prominently on the table near her books – so that she would not forget it on her way to college the next morning. Switching off the lamp, she tiptoed quietly to the adjacent room where Ahmer was sleeping. She peeped in, before turning away towards her own room. Slipping in under a light blanket in her own bed, Maneka breathed a long sigh.

It was still weeks before her holiday in Cairo. She wondered what it would be like, and what Nalini was doing.

How lucky her friend was to be able to travel, and live in foreign lands! Maybe she herself should have thought more before choosing to be a lecturer at the Indian Gandhi Memorial College for Women. Maybe she should not have been so influenced by Bhasker and his left-of-centre views and, like so many other of her contemporaries, should have sat the Civil Service Examinations. Maybe she could have made it to the Foreign Service, and eventually become an Ambassador like Nalini's father. Then Ahmer would have been like Nalini, a Foreign Service child. And maybe ...

At this point Maneka shook her head in exasperation. What did she think she was doing? Building castles that were so far away from her own, real world! In any case, it was far too late now. Moreover, whatever she or anyone else might think or say, there was no doubt that she had a life going for herself here in New Delhi, and she would not change it for anything. She had a permanent, tenured job; she had *Sahayata*; and she had a wide circle of friends. *And* she had Ahmer, her dear difficult little Ahmer.

Thinking of all these positives in her life, Maneka shut her eyes and made as if to sleep.

Sleep she did, deeply and well. She was amused to recall next morning that she had dreamt that she was running in abandon in a wide-open space covered with golden sands. In front of her had loomed the Egyptian Pyramids, and before them sat Queen Cleopatra on a golden throne, bedecked in jewels, and surrounded by the great panoply of power . . . slaves and messengers, court advisors and handmaidens, camels and horses. And there was also a snake – *and* a rolled-up carpet.

The recollection brought a smile to her face. How strange it had been!

But it made her note, ruefully, that though her dream had included an Egyptian queen – looking, she thought, suspiciously like herself – it had not included a Julius Caesar . . . and certainly not a Mark Antony.

Convalescence

The bomb blast in Tahrir Square became the talk of Cairo for months afterwards. The local and international papers were full of it and its consequences for Egyptians, and foreigners everywhere debated Mubarak's hold on Egyptian affairs. Local Foreign Office personnel spoke of it in hushed whispers in their offices, homes, and in the drawing rooms of their diplomatic friends. The terrorists were deemed to be gaining ground, and future random attacks seemed a real possibility. It was also clear that such attacks would put Egypt among those places in the world that had become taboo for tourists and other visitors. And sure enough, barely twenty-four hours after the news had flashed all over the world on CNN, hotels, airlines and tour group managers reported a rash of cancellations. Since the majority among those killed in the restaurant blast were white foreigners, many tourists already in the country chose to cut short their visits and return home.

Not many in the diplomatic community got to know of Nalini's injury. Neither did too many Egyptians or Indians. Because Rattan and Nalini had left the restaurant by themselves after the blast, their names were not reported in the count of those injured. Gautam Thapar was glad, and did not mention it in the officers' meeting he chaired the following Monday morning at the Indian Embassy. As he led the discussion on what precautions the Embassy personnel would have to take, he kept the focus general, pointing out that while everyone would have to keep their eyes and ears open, there was no need to panic: the Indians were not the specific targets of the Egyptian fundamentalists.

However, he did order restricted movement in public places, especially for Embassy families. This meant that women and children would have to stay off the streets and public places for at least a week. Depending on the situation, he would review these orders in the officers' meeting on the following Monday. He suggested that the men use their lunch hour that day to shop for provisions so that their wives would not need to step out. Children were not to walk back from school under any circumstances, and were to stay at home upon return.

While there was no question of Nalini returning to work for some time following the blast, Rattan went to work the next day as if nothing had happened. Since he hadn't been hurt, and no one knew of his lunchtime meeting with Nalini, his involvement in the blast remained unknown. So when, the next day, the others at the office spoke at length about the explosion, nobody noticed that Rattan did not say much. Neither did he choose to tell them. This was not in any way unusual, for although Rattan was deemed friendly enough, his colleagues found him reserved, and somewhat preoccupied whenever they had tried to be friends with him. He was, however, good at his work; and his performance, four months after joining the branch office in Cairo, was considered well above average. In fact, Rattan's boss was now making plans to send him out of the country. It was time to begin a marketing and sales initiative.

In the morning meeting on the day after the blast, Rattan was informed that he was to begin travelling – to other parts of Egypt as well as to neighbouring capitals – to see how sales could be increased. His first trip would be in the next ten days.

Though Rattan had acquiesced publicly to every plan made for him by his boss, in private he felt a complete reluctance. As he walked out from the conference room he felt his heart grow cold. Hadn't he always wanted this? Hadn't he always known before he came to Cairo, that his sales job would involve being always on the move? That travelling would keep his days hectic and his mind occupied, and leave him less time to think and brood about Tanvi and her horrible death? Hadn't he thought that this would be his ultimate salvation?

It was only at the end of the day, as he was driving home that he allowed himself to see that things had changed. Had this come at any other time – at any time even a week before – he would have been pleased. However, now that he had shared the horrible bomb blast with Nalini, the prospect of leaving the city dismayed him. It was not as if he met her every day, or even spoke regularly to her . . . But he had got used to knowing that she was there: in the city, in her father's house, just across the river.

In fact, he had become almost sure that when he stood for a few minutes on his balcony every night, he could see her windows. It was stupid, he knew, to think that he could identify them. But it was a game he played every night, just before going to bed. From where he stood, enjoying the cooling breezes of the night flutter over his face, he could feel her presence. Not near. But not far away either. In this he found a solace he could not quite explain to himself. Travelling would increase that distance. And prevent possibilities. This he did not want at all. Not after what had happened.

Not that he knew clearly *what* had happened. When he asked himself this question, he got no clear answers.

When Rattan went to see Nalini at the hospital the evening after the blast, she was surrounded by Ajay, Minti and *Aji*. The brother and sister said quiet, unsuspecting 'Hellos', but *Aji* was openly hostile, looking him up and down with almost hatred in her eyes. Nalini looked oddly fragile tucked in a light blanket in a large single bed in the small hospital room. She was pale, and her beautiful hair had been pulled back into two schoolgirl plaits framing her face. Her white nightgown came up high along her neck, keeping tightly out of view any dressing or bandages on the gash that he had so carefully tended the day before.

When he walked over to the bed and handed her a bouquet of flowers, she took them from him with downcast eyes, and burying her nose in the sweet-smelling yellow roses, said a soft 'thank you'.

'How do you feel?' he asked, knowing clearly that *Aji* was standing across the bed, and watching him with the eyes of a protective hawk.

'Better than yesterday,' said Nalini, looking up to his face with curiously pleading eyes.

He waited, expecting her to say more. But she didn't, and as Rattan waited, the silence stretched for some minutes in the room. It was broken by *Aji* who moved suddenly, and came up to the bed with a determined stride to take the flowers away from the patient.

'I do not have a vase here,' she said, addressing herself pointedly to Nalini. 'But I will put them in this jug. Minti can arrange them. And you will have to drink water from the bottle here.'

'Thank you, *Aji*.'

As Nalini said this, her face broke into a smile – albeit a strained one – for the first time. She looked at Rattan as she did so, and he smiled in return.

But then *Aji* spoke again.

'And your father is expected any minute,' she said, her voice firm and forbidding as she walked towards the bathroom.

'Yes, I know,' Nalini responded, her smile disappearing even as she tried not to let exasperation creep into her voice.

But Rattan noticed that the old woman's announcement had made Nalini apprehensive.

He waited till *Aji* and Minti had carried the flowers to the bathroom. It was a few minutes before he spoke.

'You are being well looked after, I see,' he said.

'Too well, actually,' she said, smiling a little once more.

'How do you feel?' he asked her again, indicating that his earlier inquiry had been a meaningless, formal one, and to which he had not received an answer.

'Much better. They gave me six stitches yesterday.'

'Do they hurt?' asked Rattan.

'A little,' she said embarrassed, looking away towards the windows.

'Is there anything I can do?' asked Rattan softly, watching the slow pink of her blush stain her cheeks. 'Can I give you some Crocin pills? Same dose as you gave me?'

'I am already eating them. If I eat any more, I'll sleep all the time,' said Nalini with a smile, turning her face so that she could look straight at him.

'And dream of me, perhaps?' he said, his voice low and his face deadpan.

To this she said nothing but gave him a firm, dirty look even as she lifted one finger to her lips asking him to be quiet.

'I'm sorry. How long are you likely to remain here?' asked Rattan, deliberately changing the subject.

'For another two days. Then, if all is well, I can return home,' said Nalini.

By this time *Aji* and Minti had returned with the flowers. Minti had arranged them as well as she could in the water jug, and put it down on the night-stand with a small clatter. *Aji* hung around, deliberately. Nalini indicated to her that she should let them talk.

But even though the old woman moved away reluctantly, Nalini and Rattan could not talk much. So aware was she of the presence of others in the room that she chose to spend the rest of Rattan's visit introducing him to Ajay and Minti. The latter had been watching the two surreptitiously, and Nalini knew that she would have to do some answering after Rattan left. Ajay was the more unconcerned, leaving the comic book he was reading only briefly to make the required small talk with his elder sister's hospital visitor. But Minti continued to look speculatively at her sister.

Soon it was time to leave. Rattan very much wanted to bend over the bed and kiss gently the woman he had held in his arms the day before. But of course, there was no question of doing this, even though he knew from the look on Nalini's face that she too was re-living those moments.

'Thank you for coming to see me. I felt so alone until you did. But could you please not come again . . . I'll explain later . . . What I mean is . . . I will phone you when I return home,' she said quickly, her eyes downcast.

She really looked worried and uneasy.

It took all of Rattan's self control to refrain from touching her. He could feel *Aji*'s disapproving glance bore through him. And there were Ajay and Minti hovering in the background. He gave her one last look, and turned to leave.

'Get well quickly. And I will wait for your call.'

Nalini smiled weakly, and waved her hand in good-bye. He said a quick 'see you' to Minti, who had also been looking at him somewhat appraisingly. He shook hands with Ajay and left.

Old *Aji* stood her ground, watching him carefully as he passed through the door, and out of the room.

The hospital visit left Rattan restless and confused. Not much had been said, and yet the sight of Nalini hurt and in bed, and everything that had passed between them unsaid, increased his sense of being linked inextricably to her. As he walked to his apartment, Rattan wondered whether he was reading too much into the completely unforeseen event in which he and Nalini had been involved. But then hadn't he worked assiduously to keep in touch with her these last few weeks? When he weighed all this in his mind, he felt that the blast, though frightening and ugly, had really worked to move them towards each other in a way that they may never have done, if left to themselves.

It was really odd that everything had happened so . . . because he hadn't, in his wildest dreams, imagined that he would have felt himself linked to another woman so soon after Tanvi's death. Rattan wondered about the workings of Fate . . . the Fate that his countrymen believed in so easily but which he, educated in the so-called Western tradition, had learned to look at askance. But as events had shown, there was no doubt that he was being well and strongly propelled in certain directions by some power he could not quite understand.

'I feel like a small speck of dust in the dark being blown by a high wind without knowing where it is going to settle, if it settles at all.'

In the background he could hear, dimly, the night's call to prayer by the *muezzin*. The last words died away, leaving behind a hollow, cavernous silence. His apartment received him with mute indifference. He looked around. It seemed bare and unhomely. He had rented it furnished from the landlord, and did not care much for the imitation baroque, gold-footed furniture. Gold-leaf lamps and the odd matching vase dotted the room. In the windows hung heavy claret-coloured silk curtains, edged with gold braid and tied back with large, braided bows, also in gold.

He had tried over the last few months to feel at home in the place, but had not succeeded. Gilt-edged sofas and tables made no sense when you were sick at heart, hardly ever there, and when you were, you spent your time in the bedroom sleeping after a hard day, or occasionally watching the last English newscast late at night.

Given this frame of mind, Rattan had never thought of inviting anyone to his home except in the very beginning when the Guptas had come over to see the place. Even then, it was Madhu who had gone in the kitchen to make some tea for the three of them. She had remarked on the contrast between the fancy china and glassware stocked in the china cabinet and the low-quality tea bags and powdered milk with which to make the tea. At that time, Rattan had laughed and said he was still new to the place, and was still in the process of getting organised. That had been at least four months ago.

But it wasn't really that much better now.

As Rattan walked into the kitchen, he knew that there was not much he would find by way of food. With his mind still on the workings of Fate and Nalini, Rattan opened the refrigerator. There was nothing but some eggs, some bread and a packet of cheese slices. He quickly took those out, and in a few absent-minded minutes he had made two dry, unappetizing sandwiches, eaten them, and washed them down with a glass of cold water.

Dumping his plate in the sink, Rattan walked out onto the balcony. His eyes looked out automatically to where they did every night: towards the Indian Ambassador's residence. He knew Nalini was not there, but still his eyes remained fixed on the lights. As he stared at them, the vision before his eyes blurred. The river and the sparkling lights fell away and in their place arose Nalini as he had known her: first, a Nalini standing aloof in a white cotton sari, wiping perspiration away from her face; then a Nalini smartly dressed in sage green, her hair tied in a cool French knot; then a Nalini squashed on the floor, only her head and the upper portion of her slender neck visible over the fallen table; then a Nalini in his arms as he had used his handkerchief to stem the flow of blood from her breast; and then a Nalini in a hospital bed, all hidden away, in a prim white nightgown.

This last image was especially painful, arousing feelings that churned his stomach. He had so wanted to hold her at that moment, to envelop her in his arms, and rid her of that white pinched look that had marked her face, and bring her back to life.

For he didn't — *he absolutely didn't* — want to be too late this time.

Pushing aside firmly the memory of Tanvi resting heavily and dead in his arms, he tried to concentrate on Nalini. It wasn't easy, and the struggle between guilt towards one and responsibility towards the other brought a glaze of tears to his eyes. He brushed them aside impatiently, and cursed the Gods inwardly for putting him through all these things, one after another. Was this some kind of test that had to be passed? What else had been fated for him? How long was it to go on? And what was he supposed to do? How was he supposed to think? To feel?

By God, how was he supposed to *feel*?

Because, rightly or wrongly, he did feel something for her, for this Nalini who seemed always to be thinking about everybody else first, even when she was the one who had been injured, in a bomb blast, in a country that was foreign, and where even those shouting out in the agony of blood, screamed out in a language different from her own.

Lying huddled in the hospital bed, she had seemed so worried, hating her own sense of vulnerability in front of her father, *Aji*, and her younger sister and brother. Her injury would now come in the way of her responsibilities as surrogate mother and lady of the house. And this had brought on an anxiety that seemed unnecessary to Rattan. Was it fair that she be asked to perform the maternal role always, when he (and anyone else too, he was sure) could see clearly that, at a moment like this, it was she who needed 'mothering'?

Rattan wondered what Mrs Thapar had been like, and how she would have responded to her daughter being caught in a terrorist explosion with a man she barely knew.

Rattan could not help but remember Tanvi's mother. She had come over to Hauz Khas the moment she had heard of her daughter's death, but not talked to anyone in the Malhotra household except him. She had even, as he now recalled, stayed away from his mother from the moment of her weeping arrival, choosing to stand close to him all through the hurriedly organised ceremonies of Tanvi's cremation. But through all her grief, she had always hugged him tightly, telling him that he was a good man, and that Tanvi had been lucky to have him.

His own mother, Pammi, in contrast, had been dry-eyed – amazingly dry-eyed. Now that he had begun thinking about mothers and their relationship with their children, Rattan wondered what Pammi was doing, and felt immediately guilty for not having phoned her in days. She had been so much in charge when Tanvi had died, making sure that the whole episode had been over as soon as possible and that the story had stayed out of the press. That was good, because without her, the whole affair would have become a scandal. However, beyond that first intense hug from Pammi when he had called her to the bedroom, she had been all control and rationality.

Hauling himself back from New Delhi into his Cairo apartment with a shudder, Rattan left the balcony and went into the bedroom towards the telephone. He felt, suddenly, an intense need to communicate with home, and to find out what was happening in 73 Hauz Khas. It took a few minutes for the numbers to connect, and when they did, the phone rang. And rang. Nobody picked it up. Rattan clicked off in irritation, and tried again. This time Hari Ram answered. Rattan immediately imagined him having shuffled down the corridor from the kitchen at his usual snail's pace, slowly picking up the phone and saying 'hello, hello', in that loud distant voice intended to speak to someone in outer space.

'Sahib is out of the country, and memsahib is not at home,' he told Rattan. In the brief conversation that followed he was told that Ram Singh was not there either. The memsahib had thrown him out of his job, and he had returned to his village for good. 'The whole thing was a mystery and Ram Singh had become very annoying to the memsahib,' said Hari Ram. When asked where she was, Hari Ram said she had gone to the fakir in Old Delhi to do her *pujas*.

Pujas?

Rattan was astonished, and enquired, 'What *pujas?*' Hari Ram laughed a little nervously, and told Rattan that the memsahib had become very religious lately, and that he should come and see for himself. Rattan assured him that he was planning to visit soon. It was, after all, already four months since he had left Delhi! He then asked Hari Ram about himself and his family in the village, and after requesting the old cook to tell his mother that he had phoned, he rang off.

The conversation left Rattan frustrated and quite surprised. The last time he had phoned, his mother had been reticent and not really in the mood to talk. This *puja* stuff – and fakirs – were new things, and he would have to find out more about them. It was really too bad that she'd not been there because he had wanted to tell her about the bomb blast in Egypt, and that he had not been hurt. He didn't want her to hear about it from anywhere or anyone else.

Now he would have to keep calling until he actually talked to her.

They kept Nalini in the hospital all of five days. On the sixth day she was allowed to return home, with clear instructions that she should rest for two or three days, and only then return to work. Her father requested the hospital authorities not to disclose Nalini's injuries as being the result of the explosion in the restaurant.

On the journey home, Gautam Thapar cast a concerned glance at his daughter. Her face was pinched and pale. It really was dreadful that she had been caught in the blast. Besides worrying him to death, the whole episode had only added to his sense that her coming to Cairo had not done her much good. He was acutely aware of how her life had changed – and not for the better, he was sure – when she had so dutifully stepped into her mother's shoes. Used always to being comfortably in charge, he still had not got used to feeling so helpless and dependent. Like most Indian middle-class males, he had never given a thought to matters such as housekeeping. Ambassadorial assignments meant big houses and elaborate entertaining. All this needed not only a housekeeper but also a supportive companion, especially if you wanted to live an effective and fulfilling diplomatic life.

He had never imagined having to run a home and entertain formally *all* by himself.

He knew that Nalini had instinctively understood this. She had jettisoned her own independence without a moment's hesitation. He was now quite dependent on her presence in the house, and could not imagine how he could do without her.

Was he being selfish in thinking so?

Probably.

'I should be thinking of her setting up her own home ... and not getting buried in mine!' he told himself grimly.

And immediately thought of Rattan Malhotra. The young man had obviously been concerned for Nalini – was there something between them? It was more than possible. He wondered whether this was the right moment to talk about it. 'I am glad you were not alone,' he said finally, deciding that he had to speak.

'Alone?' said Nalini, coming to with a start.

'In the blast,' said Gautam Thapar.

'Yes, I am glad Rattan Malhotra was with me. I so often pass that way alone. Had it happened then, I don't know what I would have done ...' said Nalini.

Gautam noted quietly that his daughter had used Rattan's full name in an effort to render more formal their reference to the young man.

'Have you known this Rattan Malhotra long?' he asked, deliberately referring to him in the same way.

However, Nalini was not fooled. 'Not very,' she said

casually. 'This was the first time I had lunch with him. I only agreed because he was so insistent . . .'

'That's OK,' said Gautam Thapar hurriedly. He did not want Nalini to feel that he disapproved, or that she owed him any explanations. He trusted her. 'I am glad *he* wasn't also hurt,' he continued quickly. 'That would have been quite disastrous. He wouldn't have been able to help you or himself . . . and then anything could have happened . . . And of course, it would have been all over the newspapers. Mischievous journalists could easily speculate that the whole affair was retaliation against Indians because of the Babri Masjid affair . . .'

Nalini was surprised. 'But surely it was nothing like that! It was only chance that took us to that restaurant. We could just as well have chosen another one . . .'

'I think you are right. I personally think that it was local politics that were the cause. But if it came out that the daughter of the Indian Ambassador was one of the victims, then . . . So, I am glad you were not alone.'

'So am I,' said Nalini feelingly, turning away from her father to look out of the window.

It was obvious to her father that she was imagining what might have happened. And certainly recalling with gratitude that Rattan Malhotra had come to her aid. He cast her a surreptitious glance. Though her face was still pale, Gautam was sure she was blushing faintly.

He smiled an inward smile.

Something was surely going on here. He needed to find out more about this young man – and what exactly had brought him to Cairo.

Upon her return to Bharat Bhavan, *Aji* escorted Nalini up to her room and asked her what she would care to eat. Nalini did not reply. In fact, *Aji* found her charge silent and preoccupied. As was usual with her, Nalini had walked straight to her seat in the bay window of her room, and was making herself comfortable on the cushions. She winced a little as she did so, because the whole effort of tucking her feet under her had brought her knees up to her chin, and stretched uncomfortably the stitches in her breast.

While *Aji* moved around the room putting things away, Nalini's mind was on the events of the last week. She had had enough time to think about them in the hospital.

Aji had questioned Nalini closely about Rattan. She was sure that Rattan was after her, and that her innocent and naïve charge should have been more careful. Nalini had protested – the blast had hardly been his doing. Anyway, she was an adult and could go out with whomever she wanted without being foolishly taken in.

But *Aji* was not satisfied.

'You don't know today's men. They are very clever. And your mother is not here to look out for you,' she had said, looking down sternly at the young woman she had helped to raise.

Nalini was not convinced.

'Oh, come on, *Aji*! He is not that bad. He is a decent, respectable chap, with a good job . . .' she said, smiling for the first time.

'Oh, really?' *Aji* said, her voice laden with scepticism. 'He looked very shady to me. I shall ask sahib to find out more about him. We don't know anything about his family, or his background. Who knows, but he might have something to hide!'

'Really, *Aji*, you have too fertile an imagination!' Nalini said, exasperated. 'It's all those Hindi movies you see . . .'

But *Aji* was not to be cowed down or shut up. She began a long monologue on the perfidiousness of the world in general and of men in particular. Nalini knew that once started *Aji* could go on and on. But there was a way to stop her.

'You know what?' she said, cutting right through her diatribe. 'I *will* have some of that *keema matar* you mentioned.

And, maybe we can have some yellow dal to go with it?'

If Nalini had brought up the subject of food only to distract the attention of her beloved *Aji*, she succeeded. Immediately diverted, *Aji* took one look at the clock on the wall, and noted in dismay that it was approaching noon. If she did not go downstairs to see what that idiot of a Mani Ram was doing, nobody would get any lunch!

Nalini smiled at her retreating back, and settled down more comfortably in her bay window. The Nile reflected the sky in a deep winter blue, and it seemed to her that it was intent on welcoming her back from her week-long exile in the hospital. Across, on the far bank, she could see the traffic flow slowly against the grain of the water. Its hum floated in and out of the open doors of Bharat Bhavan, and mingled easily with the hum of bees and other insects buzzing among the hollyhocks that had just begun flowering under her window.

Nalini had hardly been alone fifteen minutes when she heard the noon time call to prayer.

'*Allahu Akbar; Allahu Akbar; Allahu Akbar ...*'

The *muezzin*'s voice was soothing, and suggested the regular ordering of the passage of the days. It was amazing how something that had initially seemed an annoying disturbance had come to be accepted as a normal and familiar part of the waking day. It was a good idea to leave whatever you were doing and think of the Almighty just for a few moments. You didn't really need to lay out a rug, or wash your hands and feet. Or, indeed, to kneel down and say the specific prayers required by the Koran.

To focus on things unworldly periodically throughout the day was, really, not so bad after all. It reminded you that there were always things more powerful around you, and whose bidding had to be acquiesced to whether one liked it or not.

At least this is what Nalini told herself that afternoon as she heard the voice of the *muezzin* die away. If she had felt her life reaching a dead end in these last few weeks, it was certainly not the case now. Now everything was up in the air. Rattan had entered her life, and she did not know what to make of it. Was it right for her to feel that something special had happened between them? It could, after all, have been only a response to the moment – that moment of extreme feelings when a gut-wrenching fear had given way to relief at being alive and relatively unhurt.

And if she had felt this way, couldn't he have also?

And there was, of course, the question of the phone call. As Nalini reminded herself repeatedly, she had promised to call Rattan a week ago. She hadn't, yet. But then, she had said she would call *only* when she returned from hospital. She would give it a day or two, and then phone him.

Nalini sat quietly in her bay window for another quarter of an hour, and then got up to check the mail. Her father had put two letters on her desk. One from her grandmother was rather short, and told her that Maneka had sought her help in choosing two saris for Nalini. She had enjoyed her trip to the sari store with Maneka, and had subsequently also made up a small parcel of sundry things – like Lipton's Green Label tea, two kilos of Moong dal, 250 grams of *moti elaichi* and some *supari*. She had also instructed Maneka to buy some fresh *adrak* the day before leaving, and hoped that it would survive till she landed in Cairo. Nalini was touched, and knew very well that there would also be unspoken, surprise gifts for her, Ajay and Minti. And probably *Aji* too.

The other letter – Maneka's – was, as usual, seemingly written in a hurry. Nalini was aware of a high level of fatigue, even stress, being suffered by her friend. The divorce had hit her hard, and Nalini could not help feeling that, as time passed, she was feeling more and more alone. Maybe she and Ahmer should have lived with Mrs Mahajan. Maybe the latter's so-called 'long term' view of her daughter's future had not taken into account the sheer loneliness of Maneka's existence.

'Perhaps I should have advised her to live with her mother,' thought Nalini.

All this had happened almost two years ago. How things had changed since then! Her friend – once the envy of all those without boyfriends and facing the prospect of dull arranged marriages – had now become a single parent fending for herself. And Nalini had returned to live in her father's house. Her life in New Delhi was over. Her mother was dead and she was in Cairo where the Nile flowed past her window.

Putting away Maneka's letter in its heavily stamped envelope, Nalini got up from her seat in the bay window. She was stiff, and the cushioned seat under her was dented in a round compressed hollow. And yet, as she adjusted the dressing at her breast, she could not help but be secretly thankful that, by the grace of the Almighty and in contrast to Maneka's, her world was still complete and protected. She looked at the squashed cushions in her bay window in suddenly lightened spirits. Was all this gloominess really necessary? Hadn't she sat around much too long? Even the cushions were protesting!

Collecting her mail in both hands, she stretched warily, and walked away from the window. She looked around. Here she was in Egypt – privileged to live in one of the world's oldest civilisations; and on the banks of one of the world's most famous rivers. Her mother was dead – but her father wasn't. He was there, thank God, trying always to make sure that the family was well provided for in a caring and loving environment. There was no way she could go back to those halcyon days of the past; but neither did her mother's death have any power to continue hurting her.

She was glad to be in Bharat Bhavan. At least she had a lovely home to live in; and at least she hadn't been alone in the blast. Rattan had been with her.

Life was not so bad after all.

* * *

Nalini returned to work the day after her second outpatient visit to the hospital when they made sure that all the stitches had healed, and that there was no possibility of infection. Her colleagues gave her a warm welcome. Gamal Shukri shouted out her arrival in tones loud enough for everyone to hear. When asked what had been wrong with her, Nalini told them, with a straight face, that she had had a bout of pneumonia.

'No wonder you look so pale!' said Gamal. 'Now, what can we do to get that colour back in your face?'

Nalini ignored the implications of his rhetorical question, and for once was happy that his inevitable teasing had not made her blush. She did not respond immediately; instead she looked at him rather speculatively for a few seconds and said that she would think about it and let him know in a few days. The others in the room burst into laughter, and it was a while before everyone sobered up and got down to work. In the quiet moments that followed, Nalini felt – for the first time since her arrival – a sense of belonging in Cairo. She had finally made a circle of colleagues who missed her when she was absent. She couldn't see them as close friends just yet; but she felt she was getting there.

The thought of friends made her immediately think of Rattan. He was a friend – maybe a little more than a friend? This uncertainty, and the sense of awkwardness at being physically exposed before him, weighed heavily with her and she still hadn't phoned him. It was almost two weeks since they'd last met, and now that she was so close to his office and home, she felt his waiting more acutely.

It was really not fair to him, she told herself; and by lunchtime had decided that she was going to try anyway.

But, instead of Rattan it was his Egyptian secretary who answered and, in her lisping, accented English informed Nalini that he was out of town. He had been away five days and would be returning late that night. Nalini did not know what more to say – so complete was her disappointment. It was with an effort, and after an unnaturally long pause, that she said she would be much obliged if he were told that a Nalini Thapar had called, and that she would try calling him at the same time the next day.

The rest of the day and night were hard for Nalini. She was preoccupied all evening, and was very relieved that her father was to be out for dinner. Ajay and Minti were in the middle of exam preparations, for there were only three weeks left before the Christmas break, and they needed her to be around. She spent an hour or so until dinner time making sure that they were at their desks, after which they all sat down to eat.

Dinner was a simple affair that evening, and by ten o'clock everyone had turned in. Nalini tried, not very successfully, to read. As she switched off the lamp by her bedside an hour later, all she could say to herself was that it served her right to have put off phoning Rattan as long as she had.

And more than ever before she was convinced that Life had its own way of getting even.

Commitment

Rattan phoned Nalini about half an hour after she got to work the next morning and his call caught her by surprise. Rattan said quietly that he wanted to see her as soon as possible. He could make himself free by about four in the afternoon. Could she get away? Nalini said yes — she would tell Gamal that she had something urgent to do.

Rattan suggested meeting in a restaurant. But Nalini's father had ordered that all Indian Embassy personnel should avoid public places. In any case, she did not think she could face a restaurant again so soon after the blast. Rattan proposed his apartment, and after a brief pause, Nalini agreed.

Thus it was that, just before five o'clock that evening, Nalini Thapar found herself standing outside Rattan Malhotra's apartment door on the ninth floor of a high-rise building in Downtown, Cairo. She stood behind him in silence, feeling quite sure that if her father saw what she was doing, he would surely disapprove — as much (if not more) as *Aji*, and with more power than her old maidservant to stop her. As she saw Rattan open the door and switch on a light, she felt intensely that there was something right about all that was happening, all that she was doing. Rattan had always known where she lived, but how could she ever know where he lived until she saw it for herself?

There was a brief, awkward silence as they passed into the

foyer of the apartment. Rattan put down his briefcase just inside the door of the living room and loosened his tie. He took off his jacket and hung it over one of the dining chairs.

'Come,' he said. 'I have something to show you.' Rattan took her by the arm and walked her through his bedroom. Nalini had a quick vision of a neatly made bed, and a desk full of papers in a somewhat bare room. As soon as he had unbolted the white French doors, they went through them onto the balcony.

'This is my favourite place in the whole apartment,' said Rattan, as they stood looking out over the Nile's sunset waters. It was a pretty sight, and being early December, the breeze was cool.

'I have a bay window in my bedroom,' said Nalini. 'I sit there a lot too.'

'Do you look this way?' asked Rattan looking at her.

'Sometimes,' said Nalini, avoiding his eyes.

'I look your way all the time,' said Rattan. 'But I can't decide whether it is better to do this in the daytime, when I can see the buildings a little more clearly, or at night, when I try to imagine which twinkling light belongs to your room.'

Nalini did not know how to reply to this.

Rattan's thoughts were racing: 'I need to talk to her. I should tell her about Tanvi ... about my marriage ... and her death. I should do it soon ... today maybe. Before she hears of it from someone else ...'

He looked around and waited a little. Nalini's face was turned away from him. As her eyes turned unseeing onto the vista in front of them, his mind and heart were full of apprehension, even confusion.

Should he or shouldn't he? Wasn't this as good a moment as any to begin to tell her what she ought to know about him?

But, though he tried as hard as he could, he could not bring himself to begin saying anything about himself. Surely the great 'story' of his past would spoil the time, the moment, the evening?

It was the first opportunity really, that he had had Nalini to himself. Completely to himself.

Ultimately, his pleasure in her presence won the day. He would find another moment — another occasion — to tell her all.

Even as his conscience began to chide him for being a coward, he tried to concentrate on not letting his face show what he was thinking. And succeeded. It was getting dark — the early creeping darkness of a winter evening — and the gathering shadows hid his face. Man and woman stood together, watching the sun set and the lights of Cairo's fairyland come on, one by one. In the beginning, they talked of this and that, and other inconsequential things, Rattan only in monosyllables. Just as Nalini was beginning to wonder what was wrong, Rattan spoke — his voice low and sober. 'That was a close shave the other day.'

'Yes, it was,' said Nalini. 'I have never been more afraid. The only other time was when my mother died ... Fear is awful. It is the one emotion that makes one feel acutely each human being's essential loneliness in the universe ... And I hate being alone!'

Rattan felt her shudder beside him. Her last sentence had been said in a rush — as if she had just confessed something she never had before.

He did not say anything.

'I don't want to think about it,' she said speaking again, and shaking her head from side to side to reiterate her point.

'Don't think about it, then! Thank God it's over,' said Rattan, looking at her with a hidden sympathy. 'But I am glad I was with you when it happened.'

'I'm glad too ... That we were together, I mean,' said Nalini hurriedly. Rattan's voice had taken on a warmth that was both welcome and embarrassing. 'Supposing I had been with someone else ... or completely alone?'

'He would have helped you too, I suppose,' said Rattan. Though he had been quick to reply, deep inside him he did not like the prospect of her being with another man and he helping her.

Nalini understood the implication of his words.

'I wasn't thinking of another man!' said Nalini, outrage in her voice. 'I was thinking that one could have been alone and anywhere — at work, at home, in a car, sightseeing, crossing a road ... or just buying vegetables ...'

'I know what you meant ...' said Rattan, cutting her short. 'I was only teasing you. But, I am *really* glad we were together, you and I.'

Nalini gave him a withering look, and turned her head to look out at the darkening sky. However, a small smile played around her mouth. The view from the balcony was breathtaking. She turned instinctively towards Bharat Bhavan, trying to distinguish the lighted windows of her father's house. Sometimes she thought she could place them exactly; at others she was not so sure.

'When did your mother die?' asked Rattan suddenly.

Nalini looked at him sharply. It was a deliberately straight and blunt question, and Rattan met her gaze squarely. She did not reply for a few seconds.

'Two years ago ... she had cancer. It was discovered too late.'

'What kind of cancer?' asked Rattan.

'Leukaemia.'

'Where did she die? I mean ... in which country were you then?'

'I was in New Delhi. The rest were in Copenhagen ... When I reached her, it was too late.'

'That is too bad,' said Rattan.

'Yes. I could not do anything for her ... Maybe that's why I don't really like to talk about it.'

Immediately, Rattan put his hand comfortingly on hers resting on the parapet of the balcony. He felt her stiffen, but even though she glanced quickly at him, she did not remove her hand from under his. The lingering sadness in her voice hung in the air, making him forget temporarily his own bereavement.

But Nature seemed bent on not responding to their mood. A pink and orange dusk streaked the sky. It found its reflections in the waters below, and picked out the glowing tones in the fine skin of Nalini's face. Her hair, in a long plait today, hung over the same breast that had been hurt in the bomb explosion. He could see it rise and fall as she breathed. Loose, curling tendrils teased her ears and the sides of her face. Rattan felt her swallow quietly once or twice. He was not sure about this, but he also thought he saw a hint of tears glaze her eyes. He gave her a few minutes, thinking he would speak of other things when she was recovered.

But she spoke before him. And it was about something completely different. 'Do you know how important balconies have been in the life of Egyptian women?'

'Balconies?' asked Rattan, taken by surprise.

'Yes, balconies. This one, on which we are standing, is an open one. But not too many decades ago – when houses did not rise more than three or four storeys – balconies were covered over with elaborate wooden latticework known as *mashrabia*. While the men sat and talked in tea shops in streets and alleys, the women looked at the world from balconies above them – through the holes in the *mashrabia*. In this way they could see, but not be seen. It's another form of the *purdah* system.'

'Really? Now Egyptian women can be seen everywhere, moving around freely,' said Rattan. 'And I don't see much *mashrabia* around.'

'You can still see lots of it in the older parts of the city, where houses dating back to the earlier parts of the century still stand. I can show you some in Khan-El-Khalili and other areas around the Al-Azhar mosque. In fact, most mosques have some areas cordoned off by *mashrabia* – for women to pray in private.'

'I would love to go on a walking tour of Old Cairo with you. You seem to know so much about everything ... and

I don't get out enough,' said Rattan. His voice had become heavy and brooding. 'Of course, work keeps me busy ... and travelling. But I should make more of an effort to see Cairo.'

Nalini looked at him. Her hand was still under his, and as he said these last words, his had clenched a little before moving away as if involuntarily. Nalini almost said that she *had* noticed that he was not visible much in local gatherings; but something in his face had a prohibiting effect. She remained silent.

Meanwhile, Rattan was cringing inwardly about not being honest with Nalini as to why he didn't socialise much. He should ... he had to ... tell her about Tanvi ... and quickly.

But he found it so hard to do so.

Here she was, for the first time really alone with him in his apartment ... so close to him ... and without any audience, or a public context to determine her persona. It had been such hard work to get her to come. She seemed easy and comfortable – for the first time unselfconscious and free. He could not *now* talk of Tanvi.

Later maybe. But not now.

Nalini responded instinctively to the sudden anxiety in Rattan. She saw his hands pick up the packet of cigarettes – and the lighter – lying on the broad ledge of the balcony, and fidget with them suggestively. She knew he wanted to light up, but was not doing so because of her.

'Do you have any brothers or sisters?' asked Nalini, thinking to begin anew their conversation together.

'No, I am alone. I had an older sister, who died before I was born.'

Nalini waited for him to say more. He did not. She tried to imagine him, a single child, at home. Had he been spoilt and difficult? And moody, maybe? She was going to ask about this jokingly, and lighten the mood. But just then the bulbs on the corniche below sparkled into life, pushing out of sight the now darkened sky, and leaving no room for the sparkle of stars. In a few moments it grew colder and windier. Nalini gave a slight shiver. Rattan put his arm around her protectively.

'You shouldn't get cold. You have just come out of hospital. I didn't ask how you feel?'

'I'm fine, really. Just a little wobbly in the legs.'

'We should move inside, and sit down ... I'm sorry! I seem to have forgotten how to be a good host!' said Rattan, escorting her through the French doors.

He offered to make tea, and Nalini said she would help him. Rattan's kitchen was spacious. On one side was a barely used expensive cooking range, a work counter, and a sink for washing dishes. On the other were the refrigerator and the oven. The white cabinets over the counters had red doorknobs. There were some dishes — a cereal bowl, a couple of plates, some glasses and cutlery — lying washed in the dish drainer. There were also two saucepans with handles, lying washed and upturned, on the other side of the sink.

For the rest, the kitchen was bare.

As she stood in front of the refrigerator, she remembered her speculations about Rattan's kitchen a few weeks ago, on the evening of the felucca party. The gleaming door handle of the Westinghouse refrigerator sparkled invitingly. Suddenly she had this urge to hold it, and open the door to see for herself what it actually contained. The less-than-edible foodstuffs of an Indian bachelor's home that had made her choke over her dinner that night! What had they been? Stale cereal and dried-up oranges?

She tried to remember, and a broad smile passed across her face.

'May I look inside your refrigerator?' she asked, turning around to look at Rattan, the smile still shining from her face.

She looked so tall, even beautiful, that Rattan caught his breath. She was dressed in a printed silk *salwar kameez* in deep blue, with a chiffon *dupatta* to match. In her ears were the same blue lapis earrings she had worn on the evening of the felucca picnic. A double strand of lapis beads circled the base of her throat – and below that he couldn't see anything. The neck of her *kameez* was high. That, and the plait hanging over it, hid completely the hurt on her breast.

Neither of them knew who moved first, but at an unspoken signal they found themselves moving closer to each other. Madly; desperately; hungrily. As Nalini felt Rattan's arms go around her, she knew that Rattan was going to kiss her. And she also knew that this time it was not going to be the quiet gentle touch on the forehead she had experienced earlier. She resisted him a little bit in the beginning, but that was because she felt that things were moving too fast, and that she couldn't quite register or savour everything that was happening.

But when he bent his head and put his mouth to hers, she knew that she was ready, and wanted him to kiss her just as much as she wanted to kiss him. His lips were gentle at first, feather-light, and questioning, seeking reassurance. But then, when he sensed her response, a hungry desperate passion took over. Her lips parted automatically, and she could feel his tongue part her teeth, and move insistently inside her mouth. Her eyes closed as she allowed his tongue to reach past hers, deep into her throat. She tried to respond in kind but couldn't, and moaned softly. Immediately he released her, lifting his mouth away from hers. She felt herself freed. As she took a deep, surfacing breath, the air rushed into her lungs.

But soon Rattan pulled her close again, his hands moving insistently across her back so he could feel the warmth of her skin under the silk of her *kameez*. When she protested that he shouldn't squeeze her so tight because she still hurt, he immediately moved away a little, and holding her shoulders with both hands, looked at her with a dark intensity in his eyes.

'Are you going to kiss me, too?'

'But I just did . . .' protested Nalini.

'No, that was me who did . . . now will *you*, please? So I am sure that you also want to . . . kiss me, I mean?'

She did, as best she knew. And he loved her for it.

PART FIVE

Snowflakes in Garhwal

North of Delhi, in a small hill village in Garhwal, the end of November brings snow. Not too much just yet, but enough to augur more in the two coming months. The village children welcome the flurries, running out of huts and semi-bricked dwellings and into the swirling flakes as they descend silently to the ground. Their fair faces red and their noses wet, they run around playing catch until their mothers call them inside for the noontime meal. The next day, when the sun comes out yellow and bright – and quite belying the raw coldness of the morning – the inhabitants breathe a sigh of relief. At least the wet ground will begin to dry, and all outdoor work become easier.

On the morning after the first flurries hit the village that year of 1992, the sun came out nice and bright. It shone off the melting waters, wetting the hillsides and the spikes and cones of the *deodar* trees everywhere around. The person happiest to see it was a man who had returned two days earlier from the dusty and warmer city of New Delhi. Garhwal was cold, much colder than where he had come from. And he did not like it. He growled this aloud to his wife Parvati, who heard him in silence.

Short, fair, and somewhat round-faced, Parvati was sitting on her haunches at the kitchen-end of the small, semi-pukka hut, trying to coax the fire in the grate to burn a fuller flame. She wanted her dal to cook well in time for lunch. She was blowing into the grate with a long, heavy, metal *phukni* in an effort to make the flame burn hotter and brighter. But she was not being very successful. The high wind outside blew gusts of air backwards into the chimney, resulting in the small room being filled with smoke. It was getting into her eyes and making them water. It was also making her nose run.

She did not dream of complaining. This was the way of life every morning. It only got worse than normal when the wind was high.

But it was annoying greatly the man in the room.

'Can't you stop all this?' the man said loudly, coughing in irritation. He was a big-built handsome male, given to twirling a typical army moustache in a truly macho fashion. 'How is one supposed to sit in here with all this smoke around?'

The question, as the wife well knew, was a rhetorical one. She put down the *phukni* and stood up. Adjusting her *dupatta* over her head, she walked towards a *charpai* standing against the back of the hut.

'Shall I put this outside for you? The sun is nice and bright . . .' she said suggestively, with her back to the man. Her voice was low, unruffled.

He did not reply. But when she returned inside after laying out the *charpai*, he got up and made as if to go outside. But before doing so, he walked over to a peg on the wall, where a small shaving mirror hung. He took it off the peg, and walked over to the doorway. Lifting aside the curtain with one hand, he held the mirror up to his face with the other, and peered at it. After a little while he moved a little bit so that the curtain rested on his shoulders. Using his free hand he smoothed it over his face. It was a gesture of unconscious yet complete vanity. He spent a few seconds looking at himself, but did not seem to like what he saw.

Parvati noted his dissatisfaction with much concern. It did not augur well for the next few days.

She was a little relieved when he hung the mirror back

on the peg, and, wrapping himself in an old blanket, stepped outside.

Parvati returned to her fire. Her face was grim. She had not yet recovered from the absolute shock of the sudden return of her husband. In the past, every return home had usually been preceded by a letter announcing the date of his arrival. Part of her preparations included letting her friends and relatives know of his impending return. It also gave her time to spring-clean a bit, as well as cook and put by those few extra things her husband liked to eat.

But this time, his return had caught her unawares. She had been sitting outside in the sun late one afternoon cleaning rice, when one of the children had come running to tell her that her husband had been seen at the bus stand two hills below, and that he had asked for Dukhia's cart to pull his luggage up to their hut.

Luggage? she had asked herself in wonder. What luggage? Usually he visited only with a duffel bag full of a few clothes and gifts. Had he come all set for a permanent stay this time? For a few seconds she had just sat there, wondering, her fingers poised mid-air and still clutching three small black stones picked out from the unclean rice. With a long sigh she had allowed them to descend quietly in resignation by her side.

Life would surely change now. It would no longer be the same. Her mind spelt out the thought in slow repetition. It was a good thing, wasn't it? To have her husband back? Because, by God, she had seen difficult days waiting for his money orders. Her mind quickly re-lived the time when the naughty Munni had touched a live, electric wire by mistake and almost got electrocuted; the time when Ishwar, their five-year-old imp, had run straight into barbed wire and lacerated his knee; the time when old Trilok, the *bania*, had screamed at her in front of everyone because she had had no money to pay for basic rations . . .

She shuddered slightly, and shook her head. It was no

use thinking now ... about the past. About all those things. Whenever she had cried about the absence of her husband, her neighbours had calmed her down by telling her that she was not alone among the wives – there were many others like her whose husbands had left them to look for work in the huge cities in the plains. They would all return one day, slowly but surely. And return for good, when they had earned enough.

Now hers had returned. And come to stay, it seemed.

Now everything would be different.

And, what would he do here? How long would it be before he grew restless, and longed to return? For she knew, from other returning men in the village, that those who had tasted life in the big cities could never take to life in the village again. There was no work here – other than tilling the ground, tending the sheep and the goats, and the selling of the milk and the eggs. All this she was doing by herself, anyway. And yet they had needed his income from the city ...

By the time her mind had dealt with these things, Parvati's hands had already collected the rice. She had put the cleaned portion in a shining, stainless-steel container; and the rest back into the gunny bag. She would finish it another day. It would be better to go inside the hut and wait for him there.

She had proceeded, somewhat self-consciously (for who was looking?) to the mirror on the peg, and looked at herself. A short, quick glance, after which she had picked up a comb from a niche in the wall, quickly combed her hair, and plaited it. She had barely finished when she heard a commotion outside the hut.

Her husband had arrived.

As Parvati waved the smoke away from her face, she still did not know what the immediate future held for her. It was a week today since his arrival, and as she had predicted, her husband was already fed up. As Parvati cut up potatoes for *sabzi*, and kneaded the dough for chapatis, she came to the conclusion that he seemed, for some unknown reasons, to have been *forced* to return to the village in a way he never had been earlier. It was this — and not the cold and wet — that was making him so irritable and unhappy.

She had tried to question him the previous night about what had happened. But he told her meanly to shut her mouth and go to sleep. She had tried to, keeping still as a mouse as she heard him snoring next to her. But she had not slept a wink, wondering all the while why he had not wanted to touch her even once in all these seven days.

And the snow flurries had not helped. They had forced him to stay indoors, and complain incessantly about the weather, and about the difficulties of living in a hut whose roof was too low to allow him to stand tall and upright. New Delhi was so much warmer. And this sleeping on the floor — and all the smoke — was getting him down.

'I will have to do something about it.'

Lifting the lid of the pot on the fire with the ends of her *dupatta*, Parvati could see that her dal was almost ready. It seemed to have cooked faster, now that he was outside. And she could not thank God enough for sending the sun out that morning. Now at least he could sit outside on the charpoy, and leave her in peace.

Parvati watched the bitterness in her husband fester for many days before the event that changed the face of things. It was the coming of the postman who made it to their village twice, sometimes three times a week. One day — about three weeks after the arrival of her husband — he came to the door of their hut. He needed a signature. Soon, it went around the village that her husband had received a money order. It was for a large sum of money. Someone whispered it had been for no less than two thousand rupees! And that — as the few lines scribbled on the back had made clear — this much would come for him every month.

Every month.

Two thousand rupees was a lot. The village was impressed. Parvati's friends came in to congratulate her. She made tea for them, as was the custom, but from her face they could not tell whether she was happy at the news. In fact, the more the village celebrated the sudden wealth of her husband, the more her heart filled with dread.

And sure enough, she was not surprised when she found that, despite the bounty he had received, her husband's anger and bitterness did not decrease even by an inch. And neither could she do anything when she found that most of the money was being spent at the local liquor shop. By the end of the month, it was quite a common sight to see Parvati emerge from her hut at noon when the sun was at its height, prepare a *charpai* in the most protected corner just outside the hut, and her husband spend the rest of his day lying there, getting over his hangovers.

Cafeteria Confusions

After those tentative yet passionate kisses exchanged in the apartment in Kasr El-Nil, Nalini could not help wanting to meet Rattan every day. Rattan also longed to see her. Given the constraints of Nalini's life, the most appropriate time to meet was early evening. While Nalini's hours in the *Al-Ahram Weekly* were more flexible, Rattan's workload was heavier, and even included frequent tours which took him out of the country for stretches as long as a week, even ten days.

Nevertheless, every day that he was in town, Rattan would try his best to meet Nalini at her office before she left for the day. Sometimes they would meet in the foyer of the building and walk out to a nearby tea shop. At other times they would sit in her car a while, exchange a kiss or two, and then Nalini would begin talking of needing to return home. Rattan would see her off, go back to his office to put in another couple of hours' work, and return even later to his empty and uninviting apartment.

Once they chose to go to the Gezira Club in nearby Zamalek, deciding to walk around the soft track especially built for the purpose. While they enjoyed the walk in the evening's beautiful sunset moods, Nalini immediately became self-conscious. The Gezira Club was the haunt of Ambassadors, and other diplomatic personnel, both Indian and foreign. She did not want to be seen by them, and have her father inadvertently hear that his daughter had been seen with an eligible man.

Needless to say, this state of affairs was hardly satisfactory, especially for Rattan. Besides the frustrations of being close enough to Nalini, and yet as far away from her as if she were on another planet, such secrecy was completely unacceptable to Rattan. He did not think that he and Nalini were doing anything wrong, and was becoming impatient with the subterfuge. Soon after her visit to his apartment, Rattan asked Nalini whether she felt the need to talk in comfort and privacy. Nalini agreed. But whenever Rattan suggested they meet for lunch or dinner, she would prevaricate, even refuse.

'I haven't told anyone at home yet.'

'Why don't you do so?' Rattan would ask, trying to keep the exasperation out of his voice.

'I should. I will ... really. Soon.'

As for repeating her visit to his apartment, he didn't dare suggest it again.

In fact, Rattan was as angry with himself as with Nalini. He longed to tell her that he had come to love her. But first she needed to know about Tanvi and no moment seemed right to begin telling her. Then again, Rattan thought he should wait a little. He was sure of his love for Nalini, but until he knew she cared as much for him, what was the need to burden her with the unnecessary secrets of his past? Maybe she simply needed more time.

Whenever he recalled their evening together in his apartment he could not help but wonder at Nalini. She still had a long way to go to rid herself of traditional inhibitions. Were other Indian middle-class women like her? Though she had responded to his kisses genuinely, she had withdrawn immediately after, quite overpowered by their kissing, her face flushing a deep pink, and her mouth shaking tremulously. It was he who had made tea, and watched her drink it in small, burning mouthfuls that had brought tears to her eyes. Though they had moved to sit together on the sofa in the living room, he had not tried to kiss her again. She had barely drunk half the mug, when she said that she had to go. He had helped her with her things, and walked her down to her car. But he had hugged her gently in the dimly lit foyer, feeling immensely protective towards her, as she had lain her head trustingly on his shoulder. He had smelt the shampoo in her hair, and the slight whiff of perfume mingled with the natural fragrance of her body.

Though he had wanted many things, he had not dared to ask for them. It wouldn't do to rush her. He would, for the time being, take it easy, and concentrate on enjoying every moment he could have with her.

Rattan almost got talking to Nalini about Tanvi the day they drove up to the Citadel. Situated atop a small hill on one side of the city, the Citadel consisted of an old fort-like structure, complete with prison and mosque, which had been built hundreds of years ago. Rattan had never been to it. Sunset was hardly an appropriate time to be sightseeing inside. But the drive itself was a treat, and the view of the city from on top of the hill unique. After making a brief tour of the mosque – about to be closed to the public for the day – Rattan and Nalini found a quiet spot outside the fortress walls hidden somewhat behind a low mound of rock and stones. Dressed in trousers and sweater, and with her hair flowing, Nalini seemed like any other modern Egyptian girl who had eschewed wearing the *hijab*, or hair covering. They made her more anonymous than when she wore *salwar kameez*. She seemed more relaxed today than ever before, even volunteering to hold his hand. They found a large stone, and sat looking at the panoramic vista of the city below them.

'Have you been here before?' asked Rattan. 'You seem to know your way around.'

'I remember coming very soon after our arrival in Cairo,' said Nalini. 'An Egyptian couple from the Foreign Office brought us up here for a drive. But everything was so strange and new then, that it was hard to take it all in *and* remember it clearly. This is what always happens with the things you see within the first few months of a new posting.'

'I still have not seen the Pyramids,' said Rattan, his face deadpan.

As he knew she would, Nalini expressed shock.

'You've seen other things, but you haven't seen the Pyramids?'

'No, I haven't. But you know that I never go sightseeing unless I am taken!' said Rattan, slightly tongue in cheek.

Nalini gave him a look. But as Rattan hoped, she did volunteer to take him, and they wrangled amiably about which weekend to go. Nalini had a few scented *elaichis* in her handbag. She rooted around for the little silver box, and offered Rattan some.

'These are the Muquattam Hills,' began Nalini, chewing her *elaichi*. 'There is a large cannon somewhere here, which sounds loudly across the city every evening in the month of Ramadan to signal the end of fasting.'

'Wish it would sound now . . . at this very minute, and break our fast too!' said Rattan, putting his arm around Nalini, and turning her around to face him.

'What fast?' said Nalini.

She did not receive a reply because Rattan had pulled her towards him, and was kissing her, all gentlemanly caution and memories of a dead wife vanishing in the presence of flesh and blood. Nalini kissed him too, and passionately. But when she found that one of his hands had moved away from her shoulders and was beginning to caress her neck, and was moving alarmingly close to her breast, she moved away, inhaling sharply in shock.

'Don't,' she pleaded. 'Please . . .'

Rattan withdrew immediately. Still holding her close, he

looked at her face. Her eyes asked for everything and yet seemed afraid to give of herself. Rattan understood her reluctance as arising from a deep-seated fear of experience and felt instinctively that it would not be right to force her.

Was this not the right time to tell her exactly what she had come to mean to him?

'I do love you, you know,' he said softly. 'And someday ... soon ... I hope you will be able to say the same to me.'

Rattan had not expected to make such a declaration of love and was quite surprised at himself. The words lingered meaningfully in the open air.

Nalini did not know how to answer.

'This is Egypt, you know. It is conservative. People may be watching. The fundamentalists ... they may object ... even lynch us,' said Nalini at last, exaggerating desperately in her awkwardness.

'But there is no one here,' said Rattan. 'I checked already.'

'You checked already? You are a smart one ... And what if there is another bomb?'

'I'll know what more to do this time,' said Rattan boldly.

'You did enough,' said Nalini, the memories of the disaster cooling immediately the hot blood that had begun coursing through her veins.

'It brought us together,' said Rattan. 'And for that I am grateful.'

By this time Nalini had stood up, and was dusting the seat of her trousers. Rattan got up too, taking her hand in his insistently. Her hair flew in the breeze, her lips were almost bare, and as they walked together, he wanted to stop and kiss away the last vestiges of her lipstick. But she was not looking his way, and he knew that all was over for the evening.

For the first time Rattan understood what it would have meant to fall in love with a conservatively brought-up girl in India. It had been different with Tanvi. He had been her husband, and all the cues, traditionally, had been his. And yet, there too there had been inhibitions . . .

Memories of Tanvi rushed in, unbidden. Rattan wanted Nalini, but the more he wanted her, the more he knew they really had to talk and that he must insist on it.

'Can we meet tomorrow, early?' said Rattan suddenly, as they reached the car, an unexpected urgency in his voice.

'Early?' said Nalini, turning to face him.

'Around four? And we will go to my apartment,' said Rattan firmly. He had put both his hands around her face, making sure that she was looking into his.

Nalini's eyes widened in surprise.

'Yes, in my apartment. I know you have been avoiding going there. But we need to talk. And we can't do it like this.'

Nalini remained silent and turned her face away to avoid his eyes. But Rattan was adamant. 'I'll pick you up when I can get away. Where shall we meet?'

'I'll call you sometime before lunch,' said Nalini, her voice low and serious.

So it was decided, finally.

As Rattan revved the engine of Nalini's Beetle, and drove out of the Citadel's car park, he knew he had twenty-four hours in which to rehearse for his new love the story of his life.

When Nalini arrived in the office the next day, there was an air of suppressed excitement in the small room shared by the editors working on the Culture pages. She was a few minutes late, and the others were huddled together, talking in small whispers.

As soon as she walked in, Gamal welcomed her with impatient fondness. 'Come on, Nalini, hurry up! We have been waiting for you. It is Nayyara's birthday, remember?'

Nalini had not forgotten. Plans to celebrate it had been discussed in secret all week. It was finally decided that everybody would meet for lunch in the roof-top cafeteria. They would end the meal with a cake and a gift. Gamal Shukri was organising it all.

By the time Nayyara arrived, all was arranged and the cake ordered. Greetings and hugs followed for the next ten minutes, while everyone greeted the birthday girl.

'You Egyptians are as sentimental as us Indians,' said Nalini when things had quietened down.

'When is your birthday?' asked Gamal immediately.

But Nalini was not to be drawn. Gamal tried his best to get her to tell them, but she didn't. Gamal told everyone that he would find out, and let them know soon enough.

At two o'clock, Nayyara was called away to the Editor's office as planned. All the others quickly made their way to the cafeteria upstairs, ordered the food, and settled themselves around a large table. When they spied Nayyara being escorted by the chief editor, a loud shout went up.

In the preparations for the surprise luncheon, Nalini was not able to phone Rattan until way past one p.m. and by this time both he and his secretary had gone out for lunch. Nalini immediately regretted not phoning earlier. Now she would have to come downstairs in the middle of the party to try again.

Rattan was faintly annoyed to find no message waiting for him upon his return from a corporate luncheon with his boss and other officers from the Egyptian Department of Commerce and Industry. The afternoon was busy, and the phone rang incessantly; but he finally got to call Nalini. He was told by a male voice that 'the Culture Pages' were in the Pyramid Cafeteria upstairs, that 'there was a birthday party, or something . . .' Rattan thanked him, and rang off. It was already way past three p.m. He would try once more in half an hour.

When Rattan did so, he still did not find Nalini. He decided impatiently that repeating phone calls to her was wasting his time. He would go to the *Al-Ahram Weekly* anyway, and look for Nalini in the cafeteria.

*   *   *

The entrance to the Pyramid Cafeteria was a little hard to find, hidden as it was behind a false trellis partition covered over with a trailing plant whose leaves were full of dust, and seemed withering in response to a change of seasons. But the noise of diners was loud enough to suggest where it was.

One table, in the far distance and along the windows, was more than over-crowded. There was a cake in the middle of it, someone was lighting the candles, and the others talking in anticipation. Somebody started singing 'Happy Birthday' in a loud baritone. The others joined in. Immediately, there was a lull in the conversation on the other tables, all heads turning around to see what was going on. The birthday girl stood up to blow out the candles, and everyone clapped. Soon they began talking again.

Rattan suddenly saw Nalini, her blue *salwar kameez* almost totally hidden under a long V-necked wool sweater coat. She had worn her *chunni* like a scarf around her neck. Her hair hung down her back in its usual rich folds. She was standing by a tall, laughing Egyptian who had one arm around her, and with the other was putting a piece of birthday cake in her mouth.

'One more, one more,' shouted the others around the table, amidst loud applause.

Acknowledging defeat, Nalini opened her mouth again, and swallowed another mouthful. The clapping increased and then subsided. Everyone sat down again. Rattan saw that the Egyptian was sitting close to Nalini, and saying something to her which the others could not hear. He saw she did not respond; but a smile still hovered around her mouth.

Instinctively, Rattan decided he should not reveal himself. Hurriedly pulling up a chair, he sat himself down at the nearest empty table. And, without being seen, watched Nalini with her colleagues from 'the Culture Pages' of the *Weekly*.

In twenty minutes it would be five o'clock. Rattan wondered whether Nalini would really be able to get away. Did her work colleagues know about him? Since she was always so concerned with secrecy, Rattan thought it better to play safe, and keep himself out of sight.

Rattan's decision, however, had strange consequences. The more he sat there incognito, the more he did not like what he saw. The Egyptian had monopolised Nalini, and she was giving him all her attention. While the others watched the birthday girl open and appreciate her gift, Nalini and the man had their heads together, oblivious of what was happening. Once he saw the man put his hand on hers, casually. But Nalini removed hers, equally casually. The action irritated Rattan. It was obvious that this man was interested. And she, his Nalini, did not seem to mind at all.

It was just as well that the party broke up soon after. Everyone stood up and moved towards the exit. Nalini was one of the first to stand, all the time looking anxiously at her watch. As she picked up her bag and shawl, the tall Egyptian said something in her ear. Nalini laughed a cool, natural laugh, but shook her head.

'No, Gamal, not today. I have to be somewhere. And I am late already.'

'Who are you going to meet?' asked the man, following her closely as she walked towards the exit.

'Oh, Gamal. Really? Must you know everything?' said Nalini, the exasperation in her voice loud enough for Rattan to hear.

'Yes, my dear. I would like to know everything about you! And I make no bones about it,' said Gamal.

'Not today, Gamal. Not today. I shall tell you tomorrow. Today I am in a hurry,' said Nalini walking faster.

It was at this point that Rattan decided to reveal himself. He stood up quickly and stepped right into her path. 'Hi! Were you looking for me?' asked Rattan slyly.

Nalini stopped right there, her mouth a round O in shock. 'My God, you frightened me! What are you doing here?'

'Looking for you,' said Rattan, his face deadpan.

'I have tried to call you all morning ...' began Nalini. But Rattan had taken her hand, suggesting indirectly that she introduced the two men.

'Oh, this is Gamal. He works ... we work together, on the Culture Pages,' said Nalini hurriedly. 'And this is Rattan. Rattan Malhotra.'

They shook hands, sizing up each other warily. Nalini put an end to the awkward silence that hung in the air. 'Should we go, Rattan?' she asked tentatively, forcing a smile.

'Yes, we are late already,' said Rattan. He had not meant to sound difficult, but his voice revealed a haughty annoyance.

'I'll see you tomorrow,' said Nalini, looking straight at Gamal.

'We must work on the article about new archaeological findings in Alexandria for the next issue. It has to go in this time,' said Gamal, his voice rigid with warning.

'We'll finish it, I promise. Tomorrow,' said Nalini, her voice placatory.

'We'd better,' said Gamal his voice stiff and peremptory. With a small formal bow of farewell to Rattan, he turned on his heel and walked away.

Rattan – who still had Nalini's hand in his – held on to it firmly.

On the drive to Rattan's apartment, there was silence in the car. Nalini thought of a hundred ways to break it, but could find nothing appropriate to say. She could not tell what was bothering Rattan. It was true that much time had been wasted by messy phone calls that hadn't achieved anything. But she did not think that Rattan should be so upset about it.

Moreover, there was no sin in attending a colleague's birthday celebrations in a roof-top cafeteria!

But Nalini didn't say this aloud, for in some unclear sort of way, Rattan had made her feel a little guilty. Of what exactly, she did not know. Suddenly restless at the all-too-palpable tension in the car, Nalini sought something to do. She took a comb from her handbag, and began combing her hair. In a few seconds she had pinned it up in her usual knot. All through her combing she kept looking sideways at Rattan's face. It remained grim.

It was just as well that the drive to his apartment was a short one. Rattan's mind was skirting a hundred ideas, all in quick succession. The more he tried to tell himself that today he would talk about Tanvi, the more a tall Egyptian man intruded to dominate his imagination. All the way up in the elevator he tried to get his thoughts to focus, but found it hard to do so. He did not even think of Nalini's possible objections when he lit a cigarette, and drew on it in quick short puffs. They calmed him, but only somewhat. He did not look Nalini's way at all. He might as well have been alone in the elevator car, his face half hidden in the smoke surrounding his head.

He went straight into the kitchen and opened a bottle of scotch.

'What will you have to drink?' he asked Nalini.

She was looking at Rattan carefully. His hair had been tousled by the strong breezes over the river, and his cheeks were darkly shadowed by the beginnings of blue-black stubble. A dark frown marked his forehead, making his eyebrows curve in an angry, almost sinister shape. He was dressed in a formal suit and white shirt, coordinated with a classy navy tie. A heavy corporate air hung about him. It seemed as if he had come hurriedly out of some important business meeting. 'He looks older today,' Nalini thought to herself, and wondered whether these late-afternoon meetings were becoming hard for him. But she did not know how to say this. And felt guilty.

'I'll have some tea, I can make it myself.'

Rattan gave her a look, and stubbing out his cigarette in a plate, put some water on to boil.

'I'm sorry, but I don't have anything to eat,' he said roughly, moving towards the refrigerator to take out a tray of ice cubes for his drink.

'That's fine,' said Nalini quickly. 'I don't want anything. I just ate.'

'Yes. A whole lot of cake, as far as I saw,' said Rattan. His voice deliberately displayed no emotion.

But Nalini's face did. Her eyebrows rose in reflex, her eyes widened, and her lips parted in a comprehending smile. So it was the cake that had been bothering him!

'Yes, I was force-fed a lot of it. Much more than I wanted,' said Nalini with a straight face. 'But one should be sporting, don't you think?'

Rattan gave her a look, but did not say anything. The silence grew.

'Well? Don't you think so? It was Nayyara's birthday after all!' said Nalini, mischievously.

There was no reply.

They carried their drinks to the living room and made themselves comfortable on the sofa. Rattan had already drunk half his scotch in big gulps on the way. He sat, slouched and brooding, twirling the glass moodily in both hands.

'What is the matter?' asked Nalini.

Rattan did not reply.

'Now that we are here, we should relax, shouldn't we?' she said again, her voice carefully light.

She put down her cup, and stood up. Stepping carefully over his outstretched legs, she came to stand before him. Bending over slowly, her hands moved towards the knot of his tie.

'To begin with, you can take this off,' she said gaily.

'I have to return to work,' said Rattan warily, watching her face close to his.

'You can retie it if necessary,' she retorted, holding it aloft triumphantly in her hand. But though Rattan had allowed her to do as she pleased with his tie, he did not allow her to move away. Before she realised what was happening, he had pulled her down on his lap. And stared at her for a few seconds.

'Who was that man?'

'Which man?' said Nalini, taken aback.

'The man who fed you the cake,' said Rattan finally, as patiently as if to a small, uncomprehending child.

'Oh him! That was Gamal. We work together. He's always trying it on. But no one takes him seriously.'

'But he takes *you* very seriously,' said Rattan soberly.

'Well, I don't ... if that's what you are worried about,' said Nalini.

Rattan remained silent. Nalini looked at his face, so close to hers. His eyes were narrowed slightly as they stared at her, and his jaw was clenched as if in possession of some strong emotion. A vein pulsed visibly through the dark curling hairs at the base of his throat. She could smell faintly the mixture of cigarette smoke and designer cologne he always wore whenever he met her. The effect was quite overpowering.

'What is it?' said Nalini. 'You're not thinking that he and I ...'

But Rattan did not let her finish. He put his hand roughly behind her neck, pulling her towards him as he did so. When he kissed her, it was more gently than she had expected. She kissed him back fervently; but though she felt his body tense in urgent response, she also sensed that he was holding himself back.

'What is it, my dear?' asked Nalini, quite perplexed.

Rattan stared deep into her eyes. This was the moment – the opening he had been waiting for. He had something grave to tell, and she was asking him to tell it. He tried to think of Tanvi, his dead Tanvi. This Nalini, sitting on his lap in all her breathing, all-woman reality, had to know about her. *Had* to know about her. Had to know about her ...

But at that moment, Nalini moved on his lap. Her hands began caressing the back of his head and the long column of his throat. When she began to kiss him again, he could not help kissing her back, strong and hard. He could feel her right breast press against his chest. He wanted to hold the other one, and feel its dome-like shape in his palm. Sensing instinctively that the time was right with this otherwise touch-me-not woman, he did so, slowly and gently. His touch was like lightning, making Nalini inhale sharply even as her eyes closed in reflex to savour one sense at a time. But she did not really object. She merely put her own hand over his, even as her lips disengaged from his to take a few more deep breaths. Both hands felt a heart underneath, beating faster than usual.

Tanvi and her memory disappeared without trace.

'I want to see if your gash has healed,' Rattan said, at length, his hands holding Nalini's shoulders. He was trying to read in her face and eyes all that she was thinking and feeling.

She was standing in front of him now, a slight frown in the middle of her forehead. His statement was really a request, a seeking of permission for them to venture further together. As she understood this, her confusion grew. As it was, she had stood up in reflex a few seconds earlier. She had *had* to disengage from his hold in his lap because, suddenly, she had begun to feel below her a length, hard and unyielding – something that hadn't been there earlier but had begun pressing against her in urgent summons. Despite herself, her own nerve ends had heightened in response in ways not ever known or felt earlier. The experience had left her quite overcome and had resulted in her quickly moving his hand away from her breast. As she had moved away, Rattan had followed suit, turning his face away from her and taking off his jacket. He had thrown it carelessly on the sofa and, calming his own ardour somewhat, had come up to her from behind. Slowly, he had turned her around to face him. As his eyes searched her face, he waited for her reply.

A slow blush coloured Nalini's face and neck a deep, hot pink. She had only a few hazy seconds to decide. Should she accede to his request, or firmly turn away and put an end to everything? It was not done she knew, as a conservatively brought-up girl, to be here, allowing a man's hands to caress her before she was married. But she was no longer a child, no shy unknowing teenager! Wasn't she a grown woman who had a right to look for her own happiness? A right to put aside the past dull years of duty and propriety?

In the present were her overheightened senses and a pulsating heart. They signalled that she was being held by a man, ardent and loving, and in whose arms her every nerve end came acutely alive. If he wanted to make love to her, she too wanted the touch of his hands on her body; she too wanted to explore his male one – so close to hers and yet so different from her own.

She looked at Rattan, her eyes full of love and desire and yet pleading for a return of her faith in him.

'Oh Nalini! I love you so!' whispered Rattan, his voice a little hoarse with emotion. 'Don't be afraid ...'

So he had understood immediately. Lifting a hand, Nalini put her fingers against his mouth to prevent him from saying anything more.

'I'm not. Really ...' she whispered, wanting to say more but not knowing how to say it.

However, she had, without realising it, swayed closer to Rattan. His hands lifted away from her shoulders, and moved, as if in slow motion, towards her. They were gentle as they cupped her breasts. Her eyes closed involuntarily as she gave in to all the varied sensations his touch aroused.

'Oh God, how I love you! And it took me so long to accept it!' she said, at last, her eyes still closed.

Rattan kissed her again, slowly leading her out of the living room into his bedroom. He sat her down on the bed. Kneeling down on the floor in front of her, he looked up at her face, not believing that she was actually there, as he had dreamed. He passed his hands over her face – his fingers moving slowly over her forehead, eyes, nose and mouth – to convince himself of her living presence, and that all that was happening was really true. Slowly he picked out all the pins from her hair, watching in fascination the rich, red-brown strands uncurl over her shoulders, and allowed his hands to feel through its thick and sensuous texture.

When he lifted her *kameez* over her head, she did not stop him. Her breasts were rounded and full. Over the top of the right cup of her brassiere he could see clearly one edge of the gash he had tended a few weeks ago. He touched it once or twice with light fingers before bending over to caress it with his lips. He kissed her forehead, eyes and mouth again – slowly at first, and then with a growing passion.

Suddenly, he disengaged; and leaning closer, he passed his hands under her armpits to undo her bra across her back. As he did so, his face touched her body once again. She could feel his lips bite her ear and his rough cheek scrape the side of her neck through her hair. The clasp of her bra took a few seconds to undo. Moving backwards a little, Rattan's fingers slowly removed the lacy straps from off her shoulders. As he put the bra aside, Nalini heard him inhale sharply. As she put her hands around the face so close to both her breasts, Rattan's eyes were on the scar on the right one, now revealed in its full length. It had healed pink and cleanly, but the skin over it was still tender. He kissed it along its length, until his mouth reached the brown aureole of its erect nipple.

He hesitated only a second before he took it inside his mouth.

As he helped her stand somewhat later, Rattan was quite overcome. So was Nalini, as she stood half dressed and suddenly shy in front of the man she had come to love. Dressed only in her blue silk *salwar*, she looked tall and sensuous, and immensely desirable – like a woman straight out of the legendary *Arabian Nights*.

'Did anyone ever tell you how beautiful you are?' he said, his voice deep and grating. But there was a wicked look in his eye.

'Of course not!' said Nalini quickly, revealing that one essential fact about herself without meaning too. When his hands moved towards her narrow waist, she did not stop them. They brushed past her navel, just about visible in the centre of her flat stomach. Slowly he undid the drawstring of her *salwar*. In those tense, electric moments, both stood still as the blue silk fell in bunched folds at Nalini's feet. Her panties followed soon after. Rattan watched her step out of both and, pushing back the covers, helped her to bed. As he brought the blankets to her chin, he kissed her forehead. Quickly he moved away to remove his shirt and trousers.

Soon they were together in bed. Nalini received Rattan's warm body with her own quivering one. As he settled down beside her, he sensed her nervousness and tried to lighten the mood.

'You know, I have one too,' he said mysteriously.

'Have what?' whispered Nalini, shivering a little. It was chilly in the room.

Sitting upright beside her, Rattan turned around to show her his own scar – the mark that had been on his right shoulder since birth. Nalini sat up too, leaning over his shoulder to get a better view.

'May I touch it?' she asked, looking into his eyes so close to hers.

'Yes, of course,' said Rattan.

Her touch was soft, feather-light.

'It's quite large – almost the whole width of your shoulder!' said Nalini in awe. 'Does it hurt?'

'No ... not really,' said Rattan, firmly pushing away intruding memories of its misbehaviour during bad nights in the recent past. As he spoke, he stroked Nalini's face. He could feel her breasts press against his bare chest.

'I don't think about it much,' he said, as he slowly laid her head on the pillow behind them. 'My mother always said I should not bother about it. But my grandmother said it was a "sign" that singled me out!'

' "Singled you out" for what?' asked Nalini. She was peering up at Rattan's face as he lay over her.

Rattan did not know how to answer this. Fate *had* 'singled' him out. It had devastated his life, banishing him from home and hearth. It had destroyed his wife and their happiness together.

But wasn't that some time ago? Tanvi was still a memory that haunted his dreams and drove him almost to madness. But beneath him was Nalini, her hair spreading rich brown against the white pillowcase; her body alive, cool-warm and giving – and waiting for him. He was quiet for a moment.

It was a moment in which, unknown to Nalini, all the past – and the recent present – were remembered. And forgotten.

'For loving you,' he said at last in reply, and bent his head – first to kiss her lips, and then to move lower to the scar on her breast.

Two Friends in Cairo

As Nalini Thapar saw Maneka Saxena emerge through the Arrivals door at Cairo's International airport a few days later, feelings of warm affection coursed through her heart. It felt wonderful to be meeting someone she had shared so much with, and who would often know what you were going to say even before you completed your sentence. However, as Nalini greeted her old friend, her excitement cooled a little. Dressed in faded jeans and in a sweater that had seen better days, Maneka looked tired, and surprisingly older than when Nalini had seen her last. Her shoulder-length hair, always thick and somewhat unmanageable, had been tied up carelessly in a ponytail held together by a red ruffle that sparkled in bright contrast with the drab clothes. On her shoulder was slung a duffel bag, heavy with odds and ends, giving her walk a burdened, slightly lop-sided air. At Nalini's warm 'I'm so glad you are here!' Maneka, looking at her well-dressed friend, only said soberly, 'I'm so glad I was able to get away.'

On the long drive back into town, they talked without pause, cutting into each other's sentences in an effort to catch up with everything as quickly as possible. The first subject was Ahmer. It had taken all Maneka's mother's powers of maternal persuasion to allow her to leave without him. Mrs Mahajan had agreed to look after her grandson. She shut up her home and moved into Maneka's apartment. Meera, the maid, would be there as usual.

Maneka had felt a little guilty for taking such a long vacation, but her mother had persuaded her, saying that if she were spending so much money, she should make her trip worthwhile. Her colleagues at the Indira Gandhi Memorial College for Women felt the same, and so did her friends at *Sahayata*. And to be honest, she had felt the need to get away and take her first long break after her divorce. The Thapars were generous people, and she felt that a holiday in their more than luxurious home would afford her a welcome change from her tired life.

Many other subjects of conversation followed each other in quick succession. Yes, Nalini said she had begun to like Cairo, now that she had been here more than a year. No, you could not see the Pyramids on the long drive back from the airport to Zamalek. They were on the other side of town. Yes, she had a job — a small job — as junior editor in the *Al-Ahram Weekly* newspaper. Yes, 'Ahram' meant 'pyramid' in Arabic. Yes, it was a weekly issued every Thursday; and yes, it was in English.

'Of course it is in English, silly,' said Nalini squeezing her friend's hand affectionately. 'How could I work for it otherwise? I don't know any Arabic!'

'Oh yes. There's Arabic to think about ... Give me a few hours, will you? I will soon get the picture!' said Maneka with some effort.

'You look exhausted,' said Nalini, all concern.

'Well, it was so hectic getting away. I kept worrying about whether Ahmer would be all right. I hardly slept at all.'

'Well, now you are here,' said Nalini. 'You can relax, and forget about everything for a month.'

'That's just what I need.'

There was a pause in the conversation. Maneka was watching the buildings of Heliopolis that lined either side of the road. They passed the Indian temple, designed by a Belgian architect for an eccentric European count who had lived in Cairo in the earlier years of the century. A monumental temple right in the heart of the city of a thousand mosques? Maneka was delighted. It was not used any more, but was regarded as one of Cairo's antique structures. Nalini had never stopped to see it. Both women decided that they would put it prominently on their list of must-see buildings in Cairo before Maneka returned.

The sight of the temple reminded Nalini about India.

'So what else is new?' she asked.

'New? Well ... the latest on everybody's mind is the demolition of the Babri Masjid,' said Maneka.

'Yes I heard on CNN that they had torn it down, and then of course we read the details in the Embassy dispatch,' said Nalini. 'Are they now going to build a temple to mark the birthplace of Lord Rama on that very spot?'

'It's caused a lot of heartache among the Muslims,' said Maneka. 'So I don't think they will be able to begin any kind of construction yet. The whole affair was quite unnecessary. The past should be left to remain in the past ... but I guess when it can have political advantages, people choose to resurrect it.'

'The Indian community has been talking about the whole issue here too. But you know how it is. News from India trickles in slowly. We have to rely on CNN and the BBC to hear about things,' said Nalini. 'The issue has divided people. The staunch Hindu types think the same way as the Hindu hardliners at home, and feel the demolition was justified and long overdue. But others are more laid back, and feel we should look forwards and not backwards. Everybody knows their history – no doubt about that – but you can't spend your time supposedly righting its wrongs.'

'I know what you mean. We have discussed the issue threadbare in college,' said Maneka. 'But since the demolition took place two days before I was leaving, I could have done without the whole episode because it became another cause of tension. As you know, in our beloved country, you never can tell what the consequences of such events will be ... in the streets, and otherwise. But you remember Malti Duggal? She was kind enough to deposit me in the airport.'

'That was nice of her. How is she?'

The conversation then turned to their other mutual friends. Only once did Maneka interrupt her narrative about New Delhi — and that was to exclaim loudly in admiration when she first saw the Nile.

'So this is that world-famous river,' she said in some awe. She watched it in silence for some minutes as the driver negotiated heavy afternoon traffic through the narrow lanes of one of the numerous bridges over the Nile. It flowed by and under, unconcerned. On the far bank a small boat bobbed up and down, tied close to the edge of the water. A woman was standing at one end of it, trying to fold a net together.

'Is that a fishing net?' asked Maneka.

'Yes. Even women fish here, and then grill the catch on a rickety stove, right in the middle of the boat,' said Nalini.

Maneka was fascinated, and by the time they reached the island suburb of Zamalek, she had forgotten some of the travails of her departure. Nalini was glad to see her friend relax.

When they entered the gates of Bharat Bhavan, it was past six o'clock. The evening had turned chilly. Ajay and Minti were pleased to see Maneka *didi*, giving her warm hugs of welcome. *Aji* also hugged Maneka, but not before she had looked her up and down, taken in her faded blue jeans and ill-fitting sweater, and commented on the fact that she looked so much thinner. Maneka returned her hug, and all the while heard the older woman say, in tones of affectionate scolding, that women had to look after themselves because no one was going to come down from heaven to do so. Nalini and Maneka exchanged glances, and smiled.

Aji and her homilies!

'You may be tired of them,' said Maneka to Nalini. 'But I

enjoy hearing what she has to say. She is wiser than you and I will ever be.'

The rest of the evening was spent unpacking and settling down. Maneka was shown her room, with its own bathroom. She was impressed, and told Ajay and Minti that she intended to have a good time enjoying all the amenities of their father's house. She used the last phrase rather often, and Nalini could not help noticing that she was included as living 'in their father's house'. She remembered how the phrase had come between her and Rattan, and smiled at the memory.

So much had happened since then.

She looked at Maneka as she stepped in from exploring the Nile-facing balcony. While she had been busy admiring the view, Nalini had, inevitably, looked Rattan's way and was wondering when she would be able to tell the most exciting news about herself to her friend.

In fact, she was a little surprised that Maneka had *not* noticed any change in her.

This had worried Nalini: surely everybody who knew her well would be able to tell that she was in love, that she was part of some man's life, and he part of hers? But on that first day after – when she found that her heart was singing, and when she wanted everybody to sing with her and see the world in all the beautiful hues she had never noticed before – nobody had. Neither her father; nor Ajay, nor Minti. And certainly not *Aji*.

And no one at work.

They had all gone along as usual, busy in their daily patterns of living. She had so wanted them to stop: to understand where she had been, and be part of her happiness! But as she had looked longer at all those who had a bearing on her life, she had realised that none of them was really ready to be told. In any case, what *could* be told? She needed to get to know Rattan better. She hardly knew anything about him or his family. She knew they lived in New Delhi, but that was about it. Though she felt a little guilty about keeping so big a secret from her beloved and protective father (a father who had her best interests at heart), she soon accepted the fact that it was better this way – better that she and Rattan savoured their secret in private for the time being.

There was time enough to tell.

And now her friend was here, an old friend whom she had seen through *her* life's highs and lows. A friend whom she knew better than Rattan. Would she be able to tell her? Or indeed, should she tell her? What had happened was so personal and private, something so completely special between Rattan and herself that to discuss it with a third person would amount to a betrayal. It would be a hard thing to do.

Maybe she would not do it all.

As it happened, the rest of the evening provided no opportunity for heart-to-hearts. Gautam Thapar came in from work, and settled down for the evening with his children and their friend. The conversation was more about New Delhi rather than life in Cairo. The demolition of the Masjid was much discussed. Maneka gave her version of events, repeating in some detail the polarisation of views from her college. Gautam Thapar then asked about Narasimha Rao.

The mention of the Prime Minister's name made Maneka quite angry.

'He is so wishy-washy . . . he could have stopped the whole affair if he had wanted to, whatever he may say now, after it is all over.'

Gautam Thapar was quite amused at Maneka's heated views, and did not comment much. But Maneka wanted to know what he thought of the whole affair.

'When you deal with history, you have to be careful,' he said, hedging a little. Maneka was not satisfied.

'Oh, Uncle Thapar! You are being too much of a diplomat! What do you really feel?'

But Gautam Thapar was not to be drawn. He merely

joked and prevaricated, saying repeatedly that walls had ears, and that they were, after all, in a Muslim country, and must be careful. This was a sobering thought, and Maneka asked immediately whether there had been any repercussions in Egypt. The Ambassador of India looked at the two young women sitting in front of him, and smiled. One was his daughter who knew what was going on almost as well as he did. The other was her friend, young, intelligent and curious, who wanted to know all, but was in Cairo for a holiday. To spell it out would have been repetition for one, and a holiday-damper for the other.

But something had to be said.

'We all have to be a little careful ... there have been some bomb blasts in the last months, and the episode in Ayodhya will have some repercussions in Muslim countries all over the world. I'm afraid India does not look very good at the moment. But hopefully, it will pass. People will forget ... For us here, in Egypt, we hope that Egyptians will.'

Nalini asked about moving about in the city. Would there be any places they could not go? Gautam Thapar said that, until the coming weekend, they could walk around *only* in Zamalek, and not go further afield, except perhaps to take Maneka to the offices of the *Al-Ahram Weekly*. He would review the situation on the following Monday.

'What of the Nile Cruise? We are booked to leave just after Christmas, remember. I hope we will be able to go ...?' asked Nalini, somewhat anxious.

'I hope so too. But that is almost two weeks away. We shall see about that when the time comes ...' said Gautam Thapar, getting up from the dining table where they had lingered after dinner.

Later, the two friends sat together for a chat in Nalini's bay window, looking out onto the Nile. The night had become cold, and there was no question of opening the windows. Nalini's 'fairyland' and its sparkling reflections in the water left Maneka awestruck.

'I write all my letters to you sitting here,' said Nalini. 'And also sit here and read all those that I receive.'

Maneka said that every time she wrote to Nalini from now on, she would picture her friend sitting in her bay window.

Nalini asked about Bhasker, and whether all the legalities involving the divorce were finally over.

Maneka sighed deeply. 'Yes, they are over. Supposedly. Ahmer goes to his house every other weekend. But you know how Bhasker is. Half the time he's not in town ... which suits me fine, because really I want Ahmer to stay with me. But when that ex-husband of mine is there, and it is his weekend to have Ahmer, he behaves as if he, and only he, is the responsible parent. And that they – father and son – have some kind of bond that is more special – and superior – to the one I have with him.'

'Superior?' asked Nalini in some surprise. 'What does that mean?'

At this Maneka got really angry, and told Nalini that she was sorry but she was a real innocent, and did not even begin to understand the complications of a bitter divorce. She began to explain, with feigned patience, that it was not merely a question of custody – she was very happy to have Ahmer mainly with her. But that *did* leave Bhasker free and unencumbered. *She*, on the other hand, had to think of *all* his needs *every* single hour of the day. *And* night! All men were the same – complete bastards, out for frequent selfish sex and good housekeeping. Nothing else mattered to them. She herself was more than glad to be done with them.

Maneka's tones were harsh, and hit Nalini like a whiplash. How things had changed!

She could not help but recall with a sense of panicking sadness how, only a few years ago, when Bhasker and Maneka had fallen in love, all the girls in the class had been so envious. The two had seemed so well matched and compatible, and all set to conquer the world. They had been regarded as 'so lucky' to have escaped the whole institution of the arranged marriage. Not for them awkward and humiliating drawing room encounters (in which girls – with bowed heads – brought out tea served on heavy trays for prospective grooms and their accompanying families) after which both were supposed to say 'yes' they had liked each other. Maneka and Bhasker had decided everything for themselves as thinking and knowing adults who could make 'adult' choices. And be responsible for them.

While all these memories flashed past her, Nalini's face continued to have a hurt look about it. Her friend's words had been cruel; a lashing out that had been completely insensitive to her lack of experience. Nalini told herself that perhaps Maneka had not meant to be so deliberate and unthinking; that it was her sense of hurt that had been responsible for her being so carried away. Moreover, there was one other important fact that had emerged from Maneka's tirade. All that she had said was quite true. She, Nalini, did *not* know the exact nuance of such things.

But then, how was she supposed to know when she was at the other end of things: she had only just found a man she liked and had fallen in love with. But of course, this was not the moment to point this out. Loving and mating were always a precarious business.

Maneka's words put a damper on Nalini's deeper feelings, making her recoil. Though she was not aware of it at the time, a decision unconsciously crystallised in her mind: if she ever got around to telling Maneka about the love in her life, she would be very careful about what she said. In fact, she began to wonder if she had been wise to ask Rattan to join Maneka and herself on the Nile cruise. If Maneka was so bitter about love and men, how would she feel – and behave – upon seeing her and Rattan in love, and together? Moreover, no doubt Maneka had her reasons to be as bitter as she was, but was there any need to burden the fledgling relationship between herself and Rattan with her friend's particular brand of animosity and cynicism?

Nalini quickly thought through different possibilities. She even thought seriously about trying to tell Rattan to cancel his trip. But then, she thought better of it. Rattan was not in the country. Even if she could get hold of him, what would she say? That her friend was difficult and might cause trouble? And would he, just because of her vague fears, stay away? Surely not!

In fact, if she knew him at all, not only would he make it a point to come but he would also laugh at her!

And she did want to see him again, so very much.

Finally, Nalini decided that though the meeting between Maneka and Rattan was inevitable, she would do everything to spare him Maneka's views on men.

Maneka, meanwhile, was regretting her outburst. She hadn't meant to go on so. But she had, and ended up shouting at her friend as if she had been responsible for her miserable situation.

But then, Nalini was a sympathetic listener, and had always both elicited and respected confidences. All through college, she had always been the sensible one, who came up with the clearest interpretations of a situation. Everybody in college had told her things, and asked for her opinion.

'I am sorry . . .' said Maneka.

'You must be tired . . .' said Nalini. Both spoke together, stopping each other mid-sentence. It was Nalini who continued speaking. 'The rest tomorrow,' she said firmly. 'Time for bed.'

'Yes, I guess so,' said Maneka, suddenly feeling exhausted. Nothing good would come out of anything she said now. It had been a long day for her. She needed to sleep. She got up slowly, allowing Nalini to lead her to the guest room. The covers of one of the twin beds had been folded down, and the cream-coloured sheets looked inviting. In fact, the whole room, lighted softly by a single bedside lamp, looked cosy. Nalini went up to the windows and closed the small gap *Aji* had left in the curtains. The outside, with its night view of the Nile, receded.

'I'm so glad to be here,' Maneka said softly.

'I'm glad you came,' said Nalini and left the room.

✳ ✳ ✳

Nalini spent the next few days showing Cairo to her friend. Maneka marvelled at all the shops standing so close to each other, much like they did on Janpath. But unlike in New Delhi, those here included the surprising cheek-by-jowl juxtaposition of a butcher's shop with one selling flowers. Flowers and flesh? They hardly went together, and Nalini told Maneka that, in the beginning, she had been just as stunned at the matter-of-factness of some aspects of Cairene life. They went in and out of small, stylish boutiques, but spent the longest time in the shops selling antiques and handicrafts.

Their favourite was named Mamluke. Maneka knew immediately what she wanted to spend her foreign exchange on. But Nalini stopped her buying anything that day, saying she should first visit the great Egyptian souk, Khan-El-Khalili, before she began spending her money. Mamluke and its collection would still be there afterwards. Maneka agreed, though reluctantly. In the afternoon, they sat around on the lawn, savouring the warm afternoon sunshine, holding hot mugs of coffee to ward off the slight chill in the breeze flowing over the waters of the Nile.

Maneka felt the tensions of the last few days flow out of her, slowly relaxing her body and mind. As she looked around at the date palms and the annual flowers growing gaily in neat beds along the side wall, she could hardly believe she was just sitting there, with nothing to do or worry about for the next few days. By five o'clock Nalini suggested they walk out again, on the other side of Bharat Bhavan where two sisters named Souad and Meharab, daughters of an old rich family, had turned the road-level floors of their father's apartment building into a small art gallery where they allowed new, young artists to display their work.

Nalini and Maneka walked up and down, viewing the canvases on the walls.

One of the sisters, Meharab, was sitting there, behind the signature book. Nalini introduced Maneka as a friend visiting from India, and Meharab told them about the artist. He was struggling to make a name for himself and was hoping to sell some of his work. Were they interested in buying any of the canvases? Nalini said a hurried 'no thank you', and moved away to see the remaining frames on the far side of the room.

'I can identify with the artist clearly. He must be living in some small place on the other side of town, trying his best to earn a living. Like me,' said Maneka as they walked around.

Nalini was silent for a few minutes.

'Like all of us,' she said, daring Maneka to say something different. 'My father doesn't *own* Bharat Bhavan, you know. We just live there because that is the house he is given as Ambassador of India. We never forget what the reality of our life is. He – and all of us with him – go home to a middle-class life in India. And I still live in his house.'

'You are lucky, my dear,' whispered Maneka with feeling. 'Life alone and independent is a hard, lonely thing. I hope you never have to face it.'

'I will have to, some day soon. I had begun to, remember? But because of Mummy's death, I am here in Cairo,' said Nalini quietly.

Maneka felt a little contrite. The last thing she wanted was to appear in any way envious of her friend's situation. Nalini had always been very generous and giving, but there was an air about her that suggested that she had been spared life's harder edges. In contrast, her own father's death so early in her childhood had exposed Maneka and her mother to tougher choices. This was difficult to explain to Nalini, because she in no way saw herself as rich or well off. In fact, Nalini always saw herself as part of the struggling middle class, never quite understanding that no one around saw her life as a 'struggle'. She had always had the great safety net of a viable Indian family around her. Its provider was a strong, loving, and well-known father whose protection was unconditional, and would remain so as long as she needed it. Mrs Thapar's death had shaken the family, and her death was keenly felt as a loss, but it had not affected the foundations of family life in Bharat Bhavan.

It was on Saturday afternoon – when Gautam Thapar had retired to take his mandatory once-a-week afternoon nap and Ajay and Minti had gone off to visit some schoolfriends – that Nalini and Maneka found some extended private time together. Both began talking about New Delhi. Nalini was deeply interested in Maneka's life because it reminded her of what it might have been for her had she stayed on in New Delhi. And what it might be like when she chose to return. Though her teaching life was the most necessary for her survival, Maneka's mind was full of Ahmer and her activities in *Sahayata*. Teaching was something she did every day because she had to. Her other, more meaningful, activities were built around it.

Sahayata had become quite established in Hauz Khas. All its teething troubles were over, and now that the number of its volunteers had increased, its activities had widened to include all-day counselling, and medical and legal help. The newest project was the establishment of a phone-based help line, manned by volunteers for eight hours during the day to begin with. Its justification was that many women could be helped before things got so bad that they had to leave their homes. There were also some indications that the phone help line might find a wider network of users: men and women, young and old, in need of anonymous support as they tried to survive in the ever-growing metropolis of Delhi. The hitch so far lay with the government-run agency that was supposed to sanction at least six extra lines for *Sahayata*. Maneka had been the one to suggest the idea, and was doing her best to get it going.

Nalini told Maneka that the British Deputy Chief of Mission's wife, a woman named Vivian Manners, had set up the same sort of thing in Cairo recently. It was called 'Befrienders', and Vivian had worked hard to co-opt many members of the diplomatic community to volunteer time on the English-speaking lines. Maneka was immediately interested.

'Maybe you could get a few tips on how they work,' said Nalini.

'Yes,' said Maneka. 'I would also like to see what kind of training they give to the volunteers.'

Nalini said she would arrange a visit to Vivian within the coming week. It would be something to do, for her father had not yet given them leave to go sightseeing in the city. News from India was not good. The few days that had passed after the demolition of the Babri Masjid had been followed by violence in Bombay and Delhi and some other cities. In Bombay, Muslims had gone on the rampage in revenge for the desecration of the Masjid. There were retaliations, and many had been killed. The news trickled into Cairo, once again through the prompt coverage of CNN and the BBC. Muslim Cairo was offended, and Gautam Thapar warned that everyone should remain at home. Nalini was upset, regretting that Maneka had come at such a time. But Gautam Thapar said that things would calm down, and that they should have some patience.

In the following week, Gautam Thapar permitted Nalini and Maneka to make short specific trips into town. These did not include long walks, either through Downtown or through historic sites in the old city. But Nalini was allowed to take Maneka to her office and meet her colleagues. Gamal was hospitality itself, asking Fuad, the office factotum, to bring out all that he had in the pantry to lay before the guest from India. Maneka was touched, and immediately agreed to Gamal's suggestion that they go out to lunch one day soon.

It was a whole week before Gautam Thapar allowed them to drive to the other side of town to see the Pyramids. An Embassy car with a chauffeur was arranged, and the two women set off shortly after lunch.

'Don't hang around too long at each site,' Gautam Thapar said, a little apologetically. 'You should try to be back within two hours.'

Nalini agreed, but could not help saying that this would be a squeeze because it would, at that time in the afternoon, take at least forty to fifty minutes to get there. This is precisely what happened. The Pyramids road was crowded, and Maneka commented that everybody looked happy and gay, and that the street scene was much the same as in India, reminding her of Bombay. The high-rise buildings made the streets below them seem like alleys.

When they turned off the road and came to the quieter area surrounding the Pyramids, Maneka was amazed by the open space that stretched out before them. Each pyramid was surrounded by a stone walkway. Maneka was especially impatient to get to the base of the biggest one – the great edifice built by King Cheops to mark the site of his burial chamber. As the two women walked up to it, Maneka commented in surprise on how huge the whole structure was.

'That is the reaction most people have when I bring them here,' said Nalini.

Most visitors' perceptions of the Great Pyramids of Egypt were from photographs, and these showed the three pyramids together, probably photographed from some distance. In real life, they stood well apart, each towering towards the sky in a majesty of solid stone that was breathtaking. Nalini heard Maneka gasp in awe as she stood at the base, touching the first row of huge stones, titling her head upwards to catch a glimpse of the tip of the pyramid. It was hard to do so.

'Can we climb up?' asked Maneka.

'Yes, you can, a little of the way from the outside. And then you can climb the passage inside the burial chamber, right to the very top,' said Nalini, watching the excitement on her friend's face. Maneka wanted to do both. Nalini joined her on the climb to the huge hole in the stones where you could move inside the pyramid, but declined climbing the narrow chute that allowed access to the top.

'I've done it once. It's a little too claustrophobic for me,' said Nalini. 'I'll stay here.'

Nalini waited, trying to look casual and relaxed but all the while alert to the scene around her. As usual, there were quite a few people everywhere. But there were not too many Western tourists. Although Nalini was not by nature of a nervous disposition, she was glad of the chauffeur standing by, at a discreet distance. At one point, when he felt a group of boys had come too close, he yelled out something sharp and admonishing in Arabic, and they moved away, laughing loudly. Nalini was glad she was in jeans and not *salwar kameez*, which would have made her Indian identity all too obvious. On the other hand, Nalini was convinced that they could not have heard about the demolition of a mosque in India.

But then, of course, you could never tell, and there was always the threat of local fundamentalists. Nalini wished that Maneka would hurry down and would not want to climb up the two smaller pyramids. But Maneka was enthralled, and in no mood to forgo the great Egyptian experience she had come so far to enjoy. By the time they reached the opening of the next pyramid, Nalini did not have the heart to stop her friend, and chose once again to wait outside. This time her wait was not so long; and the last one was even shorter. Once the three were done, the two women got into the car and began to wind down the road behind the Pyramids towards the great stone statue of the Sphinx below. Maneka asked Nalini about the great period of Egyptian history when the Sphinx and the Pyramids had been constructed. Nalini looked in her guidebook to make sure they got the facts right. They admired the great figure of half-man half-lion carved in stone, and wondered what the sculptor had tried to say. Like others before them, they could come to no conclusions. Only Nalini remarked, feelingly, that she was glad she lived on the other side of the huge city where she could not feel its gaze. If you lived any nearer, you would always be aware of that mysterious head keeping an eye on you, like a great municipal watchdog!

Heart to Heart

It was in short quick trips that Nalini got Maneka to sightsee in Cairo. Their trip to the souk was memorable, although it was hard work for Nalini to drag Maneka quickly through all the alleys and by-lanes of Khan-El-Khalili. Every time they returned from one destination, Gautam Thapar would heave a secret sigh of relief. The bomb blast – and Nalini's miraculous escape – had frightened him. Although the subject was not talked about in the house, everyone had it on their minds all the time even though the instructions were that it would be business as usual.

This is why Maneka did not get to know about her friend's almost disastrous involvement in Cairo's political life till she was well into the second week of her stay. She heard of it only because of a telephone call for Nalini one evening. The security guard who manned the phone came in to say that a sahib was on the line, and would like to speak to Nalini.

As Nalini got up to leave the room, her father cast her a quick, inquiring glance that was not lost on Maneka.

When Nalini returned, she did not say who had called. Her father's face had a question on it, but after a brief pause, he chose not to ask it. Maneka – savouring the first sip of white wine from her glass – told herself that she must ask Nalini later who the caller had been. Nobody spoke for a while. Gautam Thapar broke the silence by beginning to talk about the latest news from India. He told them briefly about how things seemed to have calmed down in Bombay and other places in Maharashtra which had seen riots after the demolition of the Masjid.

Nalini, however, had her mind on the situation at hand.

'What is happening here in town?' she asked with a frown on her brow. 'We will be able to cruise down the Nile, won't we?'

Gautam Thapar was silent for a few moments. He looked at the apprehensive faces of the two women in front of him. He had made some inquiries, and was happy to find that the last ten days had passed off relatively peacefully in Egypt. It was hard to refuse permission for the excursion. His reply was a cautious one. He pointed out that it was still a few days to Christmas, and since they did not have to travel till two days after, they need not decide anything firmly until then. In the meanwhile, he would go ahead and confirm their reservations on the cruise boat.

Nalini thought that this was as good an arrangement as could be made under the circumstances, and went on to describe the route the boat would take, sailing all the way down to Aswan from the great historic city of Luxor.

'We fly from Cairo to Luxor on a local shuttle flight, and reach there some time before four o'clock in the afternoon. Most of the tourist boats begin receiving guests after then. It takes about three hours for everyone to check in. They then serve dinner, and begin their journey southwards around nine o'clock,' explained Nalini.

By the time dinner was served that evening, Maneka had learned more about life in Cairo than she had read about in books. And she had read many, hunting them out in shops and libraries in New Delhi before coming. The Thapars confirmed her impression that Cairo itself contained relatively few historical sites belonging to Pharaonic times as compared to those dotting the banks of the Nile south of Cairo. Cairo had the Pyramids and the Sphinx, and the whole complex of ancient structures built around them. Everything else belonging to the early kingdoms in Egyptian history was to be found southwards on either side of the Nile. All cruising boats docked alongside each of these sites, and made sure their guests got to see all of them, accompanied by well-informed guides.

There was, of course, the huge collection of Pharaonic artefacts to be found in the great Egyptian museum in Cairo itself. It was situated at the head of Tahrir Square, not far from Nalini's office. When Nalini found that Maneka was getting impatient about being able to see the great sites along the Nile, she gently reminded her that they still had the great museum to go to in Cairo itself, and that they could see its various collections slowly and carefully over the next few days. It was a place that needed more than one visit, especially if you wanted to do justice to the four great periods of Egyptian history.

Dinner was somewhat late that evening. It was almost eleven o'clock when everyone retired to their respective bedrooms. All the way upstairs, Maneka thanked Nalini for having invited her and said how relaxed she had begun to feel, especially in the last few days.

'New Delhi and its problems seem so far away,' said Maneka gratefully. 'I'm luxuriating in the distance that separates me from them.'

As the two friends sat together in their nightgowns before turning in that night, Maneka could not wait to ask Nalini about her telephone call.

Nalini was sitting at the edge of Maneka's bed with a nail file in her hand. At Maneka's question, she stopped filing for a second and looked up directly at her friend without replying. She looked down again immediately, and began filing once more. There was silence in the room.

'Well? Who was it?' asked Maneka, suddenly more curious than she had been earlier. She turned her head on one side, like a small, eager bird on the look-out for a worm, and looked at Nalini piercingly.

'That was just a friend. He works for Bechtal. We met him a few months ago,' said Nalini, without raising her eyes.

'Who's we?' said Maneka astutely.

'Dad and myself. Who else did you think I meant?' said Nalini, attempting a red herring.

'And he calls *you*?' asked Maneka, with a laugh in her voice.

'OK, OK. So you've guessed right. He's a friend. A good friend,' said Nalini. 'And ... and ... he called to tell me that he is going to be out of town for the next few days. That's all!'

'"That's all"? ... So, that's *all* there is to it, is it?' said Maneka outraged. 'Come on, Nalini! This is not fair. I've told you everything. And you ...'

Nalini looked at her friend speculatively, a half-smile playing around her unpainted mouth.

'I guess this is it. The time has come ...' she said, seeming to speak more to herself, and leaving her sentence tantalisingly unfinished.

'Time for what?' asked Maneka, all curious and excited.

'I was going to tell you soon enough ... I met him a few months ago. Yes, I like him ... I like him a lot, actually. And I'm going to get you to meet him. Soon. But you don't have to mention it to anyone because it's a little secret at the moment ...'

'Do you mean your father doesn't know ...?' asked Maneka in some surprise.

'Oh, he knows that we know each other,' said Nalini. 'But he doesn't know how serious it is ...'

'Serious? Now come on, Nalini. You have to tell me all.'

Nalini looked at her friend, sitting up all alert in her quilt and gazing at her in excited anticipation. The time had come, she could see, that she would have to tell her friend everything. Settling herself under the blanket at the foot of Maneka's bed, Nalini told her friend how she had met Rattan, and how, over a period of time, they had been drawn to each other.

But throughout her narrative, she kept her references to him vague – deliberately omitting his name and a description of his person. This happened quite instinctively, for somewhere deep inside she was being protective about herself and Rattan, and the all-too-precious yet undefined connections they had shared together. The memory and hurt of Maneka's outburst was still vivid, and Nalini could not help thinking that her friend's convictions and her all-knowingness were too red-hot for what she and Rattan were trying to forge together. Too much exposure to such heat could so easily destroy what had only just begun.

Thus, though Nalini kept talking without cease, her narration focused more on the description of the different events and fortuitous meetings that had thrown her and Rattan together. Maneka was all ears, and Nalini could see that her friend was happy for her. The bomb blast episode came as a shock, and Rattan's gentle and protective behaviour earned him many points in Maneka's eyes. She was also, however, a little scandalised as she tried to imagine how her proper and elegant friend had dealt with being so vulnerable and exposed before a man she had only just got to know.

'Weren't you terribly embarrassed?' asked Maneka.

'I was more afraid than embarrassed,' said Nalini soberly. 'When I look back on the whole episode, I'm grateful that I was not alone. He knew what to do and acted so quickly and efficiently that we managed to get away incognito, and our names were not in the count of the dead and the injured.'

'And now, you love him, don't you?' asked Maneka bluntly.

Nalini took a few moments before she replied. In those moments she asked herself the same question. Since that fateful day when she and Rattan had made love, Nalini had often asked herself why she did not feel guilty for violating the unspoken promise that was expected of all Indian daughters to remain virgins until they were married. She had no clear answers. Maybe it was because she was already twenty-six – clearly past the supposed dividing line of twenty-five before which all decent girls should have been married – and was older and more responsible for herself. Maybe it was because she was a little tired of being surrogate mother and hostess. Maybe it was just because – yes, just because – she liked Rattan Malhotra, and loving him that evening had seemed the most natural thing to do.

'I do, I think,' she said, answering at last Maneka's question.

'And have you . . . ?'

'Yes, I have. All the way,' said Nalini quickly, deliberately preventing her friend from completing her question.

'Good for you,' said Maneka after only the briefest of pauses, her enthusiastic tone belying the look of shocked amazement that swept over her face. Nalini saw it at once, and knew that whether Maneka admitted it or not, she had surprised her friend. It was a strange feeling – this sense of complete assurance about the rightness of what she had done. And she was grateful that Maneka had not hummed and hawed about the unconventionality of it all.

She and Rattan had not met even once after that decisive evening, for he had left the country soon after. She had not realised that he was to travel out of the country the very next day on a long marketing trip for the next two weeks. When she had lamented the fact that they would not be able to see each other for so long, Rattan had smiled briefly and, putting his arm around her, had said that it was just as well.

'We need a little time to think about what has happened,' he had said reflectively, as they left the apartment and walked to her car. They found the corniche full of people going about their daily evening business. Their presence, and the normality of their behaviour, had made her feel sharply the contrast with her own heightened experiences in the last two hours. She had been so sure that everyone could tell from her face what had happened, and for a few seconds felt keenly the enormity of what she had done.

'You will think about me, won't you?' Rattan had said as he helped her into the driver's seat.

His voice had been somewhat grim, and Nalini remembered being slightly surprised.

'Of course I will. I'll be thinking of you all the time ... and waiting for your return,' she had said shyly.

At this he had shut her door and, putting his hand through the open window, caressed her face gently.

'Don't ever stop waiting for me,' he had said quietly. 'No matter what happens.'

Nalini re-lived all this as she sat before her friend that night in December. But not all the details of that earth-shaking evening were told. The memory of Maneka's anger and cynicism had made her wary. What she had shared with Rattan was too precious to be endangered by the contemptuous derisiveness of her friend. Maneka tried her best to get her to tell her everything, but Nalini was reticent. 'He was wonderful,' was all she would say, and nothing would get her to reveal more.

'So what's his name? When can I meet him?' asked Maneka.

'Soon enough,' said Nalini. 'Daddy does not know this, but he will join us at Luxor and be on the cruise with us.'

Sons and Mothers

One of the things that Rattan did on his travels to the Middle East just before Christmas that December of 1992 was to detour to New Delhi. He had not planned this, but the days that had followed the extraordinary evening spent with Nalini in his apartment had left him confused. He still could not believe that Nalini had responded to him so intensely. Every time he thought about the moments they had shared, he could not forget that he had known her for a mere four months, and that their actual meetings had been few. This was surprising enough, but what made it all so complicated and precarious was the fact that he had *not* been able to tell her about the most important fact of his recent past.

This truth gnawed at him all twenty-four hours of the day. The more he thought about it the more he came to realise that, as time passed, it would get more and more difficult to do so. He imagined a series of different scenarios in which he would sit Nalini down in front of him and begin to tell her about his marriage to Tanvi and her sudden, shocking death. The moment Nalini's intently listening face appeared, his mind would go blank, and the sense of a stumbling tongue winding around inadequate words would make his mouth go dry and bitter. This was so often an actual physical sensation that Rattan had taken to carrying small plastic bottles of water in his briefcase so that he could rinse his mouth repeatedly.

Besides being beautiful and intelligent *and* the daughter of an Ambassador, Nalini was nothing if not honest. She had this way of looking straight at you with a glance that went right through the pretences of social behaviour. Despite the pressures of the formal, diplomatic social scene, Nalini had managed not to lose that straightforward approach to all she met.

He had begun to wonder whether this got her into trouble of any kind. Everyone he had known socially so far had deemed such directness as old fashioned in the decade of the nineties. But, Rattan knew, it was precisely this quality in Nalini that had attracted him. It had also, initially at least, infuriated him: it was so easy for her to walk the world proclaiming silently that she was honest because she had nothing to hide. This was, after all, the way *he* had been till lately. But, as he saw clearly, he could not for that reason justify being dishonest with her. She deserved to know all before she made her commitments. He knew that she had slowly, and in her own measured way, dropped her reserve of the world and come to care for him.

And he hadn't told her.

Also troublesome was the fact their affair had happened so soon after Tanvi's death. What, for instance, would Tanvi's parents think of so quick a change of heart and loyalties? In the little time that he had known the Madans, they had always been kind and loving, giving him pride of place in their lives. He was their one and only son-in-law, and they had given him unconditional love and acceptance. Though it was true that most parents of women in India inevitably and traditionally behaved so with the husbands of their daughters, Rattan did not think it right to take their affections for granted.

And then, there were his mother and father to think of. How would they respond? Even though they were far away, Rattan thought they might disapprove. In fact, Rattan could not help worrying that his mother and father had been behaving rather oddly lately. The last three times he had called home, no one had been there. His father was out of the country and his mother was not available. The new second servant had not known much, and when Hari Ram, the old cook, had been summoned to the phone (at the third phone call), all he could tell Rattan was that the memsahib had not been doing too well lately, and had taken to staying two to three days at a time at the *ashram* of Panna the Fakir.

Panna the Fakir? Again? It had taken Rattan a few minutes of questioning to realise who the old cook was referring to, and between a crackly, uneven phone line and the old cook's general reticence, it was some time before Rattan understood who exactly he meant. His first reaction was one of irritation. What was his mother doing getting involved at this late stage in life with phoney god men? He had this vision of his mother getting slowly mesmerised by some middle-aged, unrealistically black-haired, bare-bodied fake who would get her to believe in strange ideas.

Rattan did not want this for his mother. Or for his father, for that matter. He had long known that the relationship between his parents was not ideal: it was one based, like so many marriages in his parents' circle, on a workable distance. His father was expanding the business, and all of his mother's complaints about his absence had never really stopped him from doing what he wanted to do. He knew his mother had not liked it. But Rattan had attempted to calm her down and tell her that she could hardly object to his working hard for even he himself had been all ready to go and settle down into an active business life with his father.

However, Pammi's absence from home, and the news of her choosing suddenly to spend days and nights in an *ashram* on the north side of Delhi worried Rattan. He was just wondering whether it was time to make a trip home when he received a phone call from his father. Noni was calling from London, and after a few brief minutes of business conversation, Noni told Rattan that maybe he should think about flying into New Delhi.

'Your mother needs to see you, I think,' Noni said casually even as Rattan tried to decode the sub-text of his father's words.

'Is anything the matter?'

'No, not really,' said his father. 'She seems to be missing you ... it was quite a shock for her too, you know. For all of us actually ...'

Rattan silently calculated whether he would be able to make it to Delhi and back before 27 December, the date of the cruise down the Nile with Nalini.

'I can be there a couple of days before Christmas Day, and return to Cairo on the twenty-sixth ...' said Rattan at last.

'Excellent,' said Noni, with unusual warmth in his voice. 'Let us know the day and time, and I will try to be there too. We can have a family reunion.'

'That will be nice,' said Rattan, and wondered whether it would also be a good time to tell his parents about Nalini.

So it was that Rattan decided to tag on a trip to New Delhi at the end of his two-week tour in the Middle East. He told Nalini about it during their brief telephone conversation.

'I hope you'll still be able to make it to the Nile cruise,' said Nalini anxiously. This was all that she could think about.

Rattan reassured her, and went on to tease Nalini about the clandestine nature of their meetings. But as Nalini pleaded conscientiously about merely needing a little time before she was ready to make it all public, Rattan was well aware that it was he who needed to sort himself out before he could make his involvement with Nalini known to everyone.

The first thing he did when he put the receiver back on its cradle was to look for the bottle of water lying in his briefcase and drink from it deeply. It tasted tepid and stale, and did not do much to wash away the worried taste that had begun to dry up his mouth as soon as he had begun his teasing.

*   *   *

Rattan flew into New Delhi late in the night of 20 December. The driver had come to receive him, but when the car drew up in front of 73 Hauz Khas, he found his parents' home dark and uninviting. In contrast, all the lights were on next door, their glare lighting up the driveway even of Rattan's home. As he got out of the car, a loud thin scream floated over the silence of the night, to be followed immediately by the sounds of altercation until they were shushed up by a woman's firm voice. Rattan looked questioningly at the driver, busy taking out his bags from the boot of the car.

'What is happening next door so late at night?'

'Oh, nothing really. The usual. Some woman must have come into the shelter and has begun her wailing. This *Sahayata* is a real nuisance. They should not allow such homes to exist in residential neighbourhoods.'

Rattan did not say anything to this. The mention of *Sahayata* had aroused old memories, and not pleasant ones. So he was home again. Standing in the unlighted porch waiting for Hari Ram to open the door, Rattan measured the distance between the horror of his last few days in New Delhi and the relative amnesia of his life in Cairo. Squashing firmly the vision of the women from next door screaming abuse at him and his family, he stood silently in the dark and hoped that the next five days would be peaceful. When he finally opened the door, Hari Ram looked sleepy and somewhat dazed. When asked where his mother was, Hari Ram informed him that she was not at home. In fact she hadn't been home for the last three days.

As Rattan climbed up to the second floor, the deep, unliving silence in the house was palpable. Although the bed had been made up for him, his room smelt dank and musty. The curtains were pulled tightly across the windows, and since it was already December, there was no question of switching on the air-conditioners to freshen the room. It was inevitable that the memory of Tanvi hovered in the room as oppressively as her weight had when he had disentangled her from the ceiling fan. Rattan had dreaded this revisiting, but had known that there was nothing he could do about it. He had put it off long enough, God knew, but now he would have to deal with it.

He tried to push his mind on to other things, but failed. He tried to think of Nalini, and immediately felt mean and conscience-stricken. For when he began to bring her face before his mind, it was quickly blurred over by that of Tanvi. His wife's small piquant face, with its close-cropped hair and sharp nose, superimposed itself solidly on Nalini's long brown hair and patrician features. It was just as well for him that, tired as he was from all his travels both literal and emotional, he fell asleep quickly.

The next day dawned bright and sunny. At the breakfast table Rattan spoke in some detail with Hari Ram. It was hard work, because the old cook did not, as was his wont, volunteer any extra information about anything that Rattan asked him. Rattan could not help recalling that had Ram Singh been here, everything would have been different. He wondered aloud why his mother had sacked him, but got no response. When pressed, Hari Ram only said: 'Everyone has their length of time cut out for them. He had finished his in this house.'

Rattan looked speculatively at him for a few minutes. It was a philosophic reply if ever there was one. But it was so typically Hari Ram to say such things that Rattan, though curious about what the words meant, did not bother to pursue the matter. He chose instead to focus on what he had really come for: to find his mother and talk to her.

But Pammi was at Panna the Fakir's *ashram*. In fact, that is where she had been for the last three days. Hari Ram had also given the same information to Noni sahib, calling from abroad.

'The sahib is coming tomorrow. He knows you are to be here. I sent the driver to the *ashram* to tell the memsahib yesterday that *both* of you were coming. The driver said he gave her the information ...

I thought she would return with him. But she did not.'

By the time Hari Ram had finished articulating these many sentences, he was somewhat breathless and uncomfortable. His voice had gradually sunk lower and lower, descending at the end almost to a whisper. Rattan felt sorry for him, and decided immediately that the best course would be for him to search her out, and bring her back himself. He checked whether the driver had come for the day, and shortly after breakfast, set forth.

As the car turned the corner off Ring Road and wound its way along the *keekar* trees towards Panna the Fakir's *ashram*, Rattan's hand involuntarily went towards the birthmark on his right shoulder. He had seen it that morning in the shower, and had been reminded of Tanvi who had not liked it, and had said so. And Nalini? She had traced it with long delicate fingers, her touch feather-light and unfearful. She had, in fact, kissed it gently more than once, her lips lingering on its dark outlines a while and then moving away to caress his neck and mouth.

The sight of the brightly lit scar that morning – and all the memories associated with it – had not done well for the equilibrium of his morning. He was glad, therefore, that the *ashram* fence was now visible, and in a minute Kishore would be looking for a place to park the car. Rattan's eyes swept over the place. The *ashram* complex was unpaved but clean, the loose dirt revealing the lines left behind by a hand-held broom. There was only one building on the right-hand side of the space, approached by a small, deeply trodden path. As he walked up, Rattan wondered where, in the bare drab spaces of this place, his mother was hiding.

'What does she find here?' he wondered in irritation, and for the first time allowed himself to feel hurt at her complete lack of pleasure and attention at his return home. Hadn't he, after all, let everyone know of his coming?

There did not seem to be anyone about. He saw a greying, almost torn curtain flapping at the doorway. But when he moved it aside he saw that the door behind it was shut. He tried to push it open, but it was bolted down, and would not budge.

He stepped back a little, wondering what to do next. Suddenly, a small puppy turned the corner of the building and, barking loudly, ran up to him, his tail wagging in greeting. Rattan instinctively bent down and began to pet him. When he looked up, he saw that a young woman, with long oiled hair and dressed in a faded drab *salwar kameez*, had also come around the corner. She was standing there, watching them both.

'I have come for my mother, Mrs Malhotra. Do you know where I could find her?' asked Rattan.

'She must be part of the group of devotees sitting and listening. What is her name?'

'Her name is Pammi. Pammi Malhotra.'

The young woman's face looked blank. 'Nivedita *behenji*'s *katha* is on. Why don't you come and see for yourself.'

Saying this, she beckoned to Rattan. The puppy followed them both yelping a little, his tail wagging furiously.

It took Rattan a good few minutes before he could spot his mother amongst the motley crowd of women seated cross-legged on the ground. Their backs were towards him, and from where he stood, almost all seemed dressed in dull, over-washed saris, their heads covered and bowed low. An aisle of sorts had been left free in the middle should anyone present wish to approach the dais. No one spoke except the speaker, and she was sitting at the far end, on a slightly raised platform, covered with a red and blue striped *durrie*.

Rattan did not know it then, but she was the same old lady with the myopic eyes under square glass frames who had led Pammi inside to meet with Panna the Fakir a few months earlier.

Rattan tried to catch her words even as his eyes roved over the group of the fifty-odd women listening to her. It took him a few seconds to understand her Hindi since it was of a very high, almost literary quality. Given that she was small in build and hardly visible above the heads of the listening women, her voice had a sharp, clear ring to it – of someone used to being heard by the back benches of a classroom. As he lowered himself to sit discreetly at the rear of the gathering, Rattan still hadn't spotted his mother.

As his eyes continued his search, his mind registered that the *katha* that morning was devoted to the story of Ahalya, the Cursed One. She had been accused by her husband of having impure connections with a man outside her home. In fury, her husband had cursed her into silence, and she had been turned into a completely unspeaking statue of stone. It was Lord Rama who, struck by the beauty and innocence of the woman embodied in the stone figure, had accepted her story of complete innocence and freed her. Her husband had also been asked to forgive her, and it was only then that she had been able to return to normal life.

'Sometimes, when things unwanted happen and you can't do much about them, the best plan is to keep silent. At this time *maun* is all.'

These were the last words of the Nivedita *behenji*'s *katha* that morning.

What finally helped Rattan identify his mother amongst all those similarly stooping, sari-covered backs was the sound of a small sob – quickly hushed – that emanated from the front two or three rows just as the *katha* drew to a close. As the last words of the old woman petered into silence, one stooping back moved a little, as if in an involuntary shiver. Rattan saw the raised arm of a woman pulling a sari *pallav* tightly around her back and head. Having accomplished this in a determined manner, it then began delving around in a dark handbag in search of a handkerchief. Rattan suddenly caught a glimpse of the woman's face. It was only a glimpse, but he knew immediately that it was his mother.

There was nothing that Rattan could do except wait for Pammi to turn around and spot him.

She didn't do so until the young lady who had escorted Rattan told her that someone was there to meet her.

It was then that Rattan saw his mother turn her head around, slowly, very slowly. When she finally walked up to him, Rattan saw that his mother looked rather strange, quite unwell in fact. She had lost weight, and her face was gaunt and haggard. Dark circles ringed her eyes deeply. There was a look of a wild dementia about the eyes themselves.

But her mouth was pursed tightly, and bespoke determination and control.

Rattan was so shocked at this drastic transformation in the woman he had known and loved all his life that he could not speak. Mother and son looked at each other in utter silence even as they hugged each other. The son towered over his mother, and Rattan was amazed to discover that Pammi reached only just above his chest and well below his chin. He did not remember her so short. Had she shrunk? As he hugged her tightly one last time, he could feel her tremble a little. He held both her shoulders, and pushed her a little away from him.

'Whatever is the matter? What have you done to yourself?' asked Rattan finally, for he had, in the beginning, not known what to say. 'Let's go from here. Let's go home. We can't talk here,' said Rattan firmly, and began ushering her towards the gate around the building.

But she caught his arm and pulled at it. Without saying anything she indicated that she did not want to go home, and that they could sit awhile on the stone bench under the *keekar* bush near the gate.

Rattan protested vehemently, but Pammi was adamant. She still did not say anything, but led her son to where she wanted him to sit. Rattan allowed himself to be led; and soon mother and son were sitting side by side, attempting conversation. It was merely an attempt, because Rattan found it hard work to get his mother to talk. It took him a few moments to notice that their dialogue was not really dialogue at all: he asked all the questions, and she replied either by shaking her head, or uttering monosyllables.

'What is the matter with you?' asked Rattan, a worried annoyance clearly marking his voice.

But Pammi did not reply. Her gaze had focused itself on some point in the distance in front of her, and seemed deliberately to avoid Rattan's face. He tried again to ask her some more questions. However, she remained either silent or noncommittal in her gestures.

'Let's go home, shall we?' said Rattan, telling himself to remain calm since this was getting them nowhere. 'Papa will be coming in from London this evening, and we can all have dinner together as a family.'

This seemed to upset Pammi considerably, and Rattan felt her stiffen. She still did not say anything. But when Rattan made as if to leave, she refused to stand, and gently pushed aside Rattan's hand from under her elbow. He had been trying to help her up, but she wanted to remain sitting. Rattan let go, and stood standing above her a minute, watching her face. It was impassive. But her eyes still looked wild, and her mouth was pursed tighter than before.

'Come on, Ma, Let's go. It is getting late ...' said Rattan. But she still did not reply.

'Aren't you coming home?' asked Rattan, surprise in his voice. It had dawned on him, suddenly, that maybe she did not want to come home at all.

She shook her head slowly. And when Rattan repeated his question, she replied in the same way – shaking her head slowly from side to side.

'How long do you intend to stay here?' asked Rattan in exasperation.

'A few days. A week. A month. Maybe for ever ...' she replied, in a low cracked voice.

At this Rattan grew quite angry. His handsome eyes squinted down at her in the glare of the morning sun. What was she thinking of? These *ashrams* and fakirs were no place for her!

'But I have come only to see you. And I am here only for three days ...' said Rattan, obvious hurt in his voice.

At this Pammi turned her head and looked straight at her son. Her face had taken on a softer look, and her eyes had grown moist. She reached a hand and tried to touch him. But it could only reach just above his waist. Rattan caught her hand and pulled her to her feet.

'Let's go, Ma ...' he said, as persuasively as he could.

But she was adamant. 'You go, *beta*, and spend time with your father. I am better off here. But I am glad to see you ... You look well, and thank the Almighty for it.'

Rattan stood there nonplussed. Her words emerged from deep within her, and seemed to have been articulated with an effort. His eyes searched her face in concern. She did not seem well at all. Maybe she needed to see a doctor.

But the moment he mentioned the word, she got agitated and immediately made as if to move away from him.

'No doctors, *no* doctors ... no one can help. I am not ill, you know.'

Her lips continued to move after she had finished speaking, but so incoherent were her words that Rattan could barely hear what she was saying. He tried to get her to speak again, but she would not. He tried to persuade her that he needed her to be in 73 Hauz Khas. She only glanced at him wearily for a minute before looking away again.

Rattan realised that it would do neither of them any good to push for her return home at that moment. He would talk to his father when he came in that evening, and they would, together, decide on what was best for her. He looked around. The *ashram* seemed quiet and peaceful. It was almost mid-day, and the sun lent a warm glow to the simple ambiance of the place. In the distance he could see that some of the white-clad women who had gathered for the *katha* were now congregating at one edge of the compound in the far distance. They seemed to be moving towards a sort of outhouse in the distance.

'Are there only women here?' asked Rattan.

His mother nodded.

'How long have you been here?'

'Don't worry about me. I am safe here. I have food and shelter. I'll come home soon.'

This was the first clearly coherent sentence that Pammi spoke that day. And, after this, she refused to speak any other. Rattan tried once again to get her to talk about her plans, but she refused to be drawn. She just hugged him tightly, and when he moved away to look at her searchingly, she caressed his head with her right hand in the traditional way. Rattan automatically bent low to receive her blessings – for blessings they were, though sad ones.

And, no matter what he felt about the context in which he was receiving them, he knew that a mother's blessings could only come with the best of wishes for him.

When he hugged her tightly in thankfulness, there was a painful lump in his throat even as moisture glazed his eyes.

It was with a heavy heart that Rattan walked away towards the gate and beckoned to Kishore, waiting in the car, to drive him away.

'Will the memsahib not return home too?' asked Kishore, as he closed the door behind his passenger.

'No, she wants to stay a few more days,' said Rattan, his voice firm and prohibiting all further queries.

There was silence in the car. Rattan's mind was full of a hundred questions. What had happened to his mother? Why had his father not told him about all this *ashram* living? For the first time, Rattan was filled with anger at his father. His mother had always complained that Noni was completely self-absorbed and neglectful of her. But he had never taken her accusations seriously. 'He is only a workaholic' he had always told his mother, and chided her against stopping men from doing what they had to do. Noni was, after all, a successful business man – one of the more successful ones in New Delhi – and you could hardly expect him to stay home just because his wife wanted him to.

Of course, his mother always complained about his father's absences. But then so did many of his mother's friends. That was the talk among all the women of Delhi's high families. Their husbands were always following the path of newer and newer contracts, and would go wherever they existed. The money involved was huge, and it was, after all, from these huge sums that the women got their housekeeping money to run elaborate households – and pin money to buy clothes and jewellery.

But, as Rattan firmly reminded himself, had any of the women in his parents' circle come to be like his mother? Someone – something – must have been responsible. It must be the death of Tanvi. They must keep talking to her about it. And if he knew anything about women at all, he knew that not all of them could have been sympathetic. Maybe his parents too should have moved out of the country, and changed their place of residence. Many others in New Delhi – wishing to escape India's heat and dust, bad roads, power cuts and corruption – wanted to become Non-Resident Indians. More than any of these, his parents had a better reason to wish to leave. In fact, a change of address would do them both a lot of good ...

Just as it had done him.

By this time Kishore had turned into Hauz Khas, the long drive down Ring Road being completed in a blur of tumultuous thoughts. As the car stood outside the gates of 73 Hauz Khas waiting for the *chowkidar* to open the gates, Rattan instinctively looked towards the house next door. The women of *Sahayata*. They all seemed indoors today, for the front of the house was quiet. Rattan was relieved. He could do without his arrivals and his departures being scrutinised.

The thought of constant scrutiny again brought his mother to mind.

No wonder. Maybe that was why! The *ashram* of Panna the Fakir was exactly the change of address his mother needed. At least there she could escape the scrutiny of vicious neighbours.

'When did the memsahib go to Panna the Fakir's?' Rattan asked Kishore.

'About a week ago, I think,' replied Kishore in a flat voice.

'Has she been going often?'

'She keeps going, comes back for a few days, and then goes again,' said Kishore.

Rattan's mind was full of many more questions. But he refrained from asking them of the chauffeur.

Inside the house, a strange, eerie silence hung over everything. Rattan tried to tell himself that he should be used to silent homes since he lived all by himself in Cairo. But that was exile – and this was home. The unsuccessful trip to the *ashram* had disappointed Rattan, and left him depressed. How was he to spend the rest of the day? Deliberately, he knocked everything out of his mind by taking a nap after a light lunch. Waking up late in the evening, he asked Hari Ram to cook his favourite things for a late dinner. He ate the latter in silence and began waiting for his father.

All through his waking moments, he could not do away with the memories of Tanvi. He half expected her to turn up in the room, through this, that, or another of the doors in the house. She didn't of course. And neither did he run into anything belonging to her, either in the cupboards of their bedroom, or in the bathroom – or anywhere else. In fact, there was nothing, not even an old lipstick or photograph, lying around to remind him that she had ever lived in those rooms with him.

Rattan went downstairs to meet his father on his return from the airport. Both hugged tightly. Rattan could see that his father looked older, even though it was only four months since they had met last. Noni found his son looking well, but somewhat serious and pensive. Both did not say what they felt though, and the two men decided that they would share an after-dinner nightcap of cognac before turning in. They decided to meet in the master bedroom suite in half an hour – giving Noni enough time to shower, and get into his pyjamas.

It was strange to be only males in the house. Rattan tried to remember if there had been any time in the past when it had been like this – and couldn't. His mother (and grandmother in the early years) had *always* been around, her strong personality everywhere present even if she had to be out of the house for a couple of days. All instructions would be left with the servants regarding food and cleanliness, linen and trays, turned-down beds and tea with lemon in the mornings. When the new second servant shuffled in with the bottle of cognac, the glasses were all wrong, and the cloth on the tray crushed and grubby. It was then that Rattan became acutely aware of the dull and slovenly air around the house. Everything was where it ought to be, but everything was also slightly askew – as if managed by people who did not see why it should have been there in the first place. Nobody seemed to have cared to see whether the house was aired every day. The tightly shut doors and windows – originally designed for ubiquitous air-conditioning – had kept the natural light out – and spiders and insects in.

Cleaning in India – and in Cairo, as Rattan had discovered – had to be a daily thing, or else a tropical natural life was likely to take over. And while he was subconsciously accepting of his own apartment in Cairo to be less than stylish or even lived in, he found it disturbing to see that his parental home in New Delhi had degenerated into an uncared-for building, manned only by servants.

Rattan watched his father complain about the glasses in a

louder than usual tone. Noni looked tired. His greying – and thinning – hair was somewhat tousled – an unusual sight, since Rattan always remembered his father as well dressed, even dapper in his ways. Today he had seemed nonchalant, even careless about his clothes and appearance.

'Our family is in a bad way,' Rattan told himself and was wondering whether it was wise to say this aloud when he heard loud sounds of shouting through the open doorway. One voice rang out louder than any of the others.

Rattan stood up immediately, and moved onto the landing to investigate. As he peered over the banisters, he could see Hari Ram, the cook, and Kishore, the driver. The new second servant had, by this time, run down the staircase and also joined the shouting group below.

It took Rattan a few seconds to decipher who was in the middle of the fracas. Was not the loudest shouting voice that of Ram Singh, the old bearer of the family? As far as Rattan could remember, he had been dismissed by his mother a few months ago, and had supposedly returned to his village in the Garhwal hills. But what was he doing here? Shouting in their house so late at night?

'I am back. I am back where I belong. Where I have a right ... And no one ... do you hear, *no one* ... should even think of throwing me out.'

Ram Singh's voice was as loud as it was slurred, and it became clear to Rattan that the old family servant was quite drunk. He was hardly able to stand, and his raised arms flailed wildly, thrusting away at Hari Ram and Kishore who were trying to hold him upright as well as restrain him. As they tried to move him away towards the kitchen door, Rattan noted that Ram Singh had lost weight. His face looked hollow and gaunt, his clothes were crumpled and dirty, as though they had been worn continuously for days.

'Where has he come from?' asked Rattan.

'I have come from nowhere. I was always ... *always* here,'

said Ram Singh quickly, slurring over his words in a loud voice as if to make sure that he replied to Rattan's question before anyone else could. Rattan could not help smiling. So he did hear and understand clearly all that was going on!

But still, wasn't the man a little mad! And, whatever was he saying? Rattan shook his head in exasperation. 'Take him away. I suppose we can't throw him out. Why don't you put him to sleep tonight? We can see what he wants in the morning.'

But Ram Singh, even in his obvious inebriation, understood Rattan. 'You will never know what I want, my dear. *Bechara beta!* The great *beta* of the house, hunh! You do not know anything. You will *never* know anything.'

'Shh, shh. *Chup raho,*' said Hari Ram, his voice surprisingly strong and urgent. The cook had put his arm firmly around his old colleague, and was pushing him determinedly towards the passage to the pantry.

'Please go upstairs, sahib. I will deal with him. He does not want anything except to be put to bed. And I will make sure that he does that. He has probably come for money. We can give him some and send him off. That we will do in the morning . . .'

Hari Ram's voice trailed off down the corridor. He had sounded breathless and harassed with the strain of both holding up, *and* pushing, Ram Singh into the kitchen. It was just as well that Kishore had been there to help, because he would not have been able to do it alone. A few more stumbling steps by the odd trio, and they were out of sight.

Rattan was surprised that Ram Singh did not say anything further. But what he did not know was that Hari Ram had nodded to Kishore to hold Ram Singh more firmly while he himself had, deliberately and strongly, clamped his hand on Ram Singh's mouth.

And kept it there until they made it safely – and silently – to the servants' quarters at the back of the house.

PART SIX

From the Floors of Memory

While Rattan spent most of his visit to India at the *ashram* trying to get his mother to talk, Nalini and Maneka looked forward eagerly to their cruise down Egypt's famous river. In the days that followed their heart-to-heart chat, the two women had done as much cautious sightseeing as talking about the love in Nalini's life. Even while inspecting closely any one of Egypt's many historical sites or artefacts, Maneka could not help reverting to Nalini's relationship with Rattan. A Pharaonic queen in love, an ambiguous hieroglyph, patterns in ancient jewellery, a mischievous male guide's conjectures, a deep cut-out of a handsome young man in a chariot, a papyrus depicting feasting and celebration, a bandaged mummy – anything – would set Maneka off with her questions and speculations.

At first Nalini was a little embarrassed by her friend's constant references to Rattan. But as the long three weeks of his absence inched by, Nalini herself began to feel the need to talk about him. As the days dragged on, all that had happened with Rattan seemed to recede into some long-distant time, and doubts began to beset her. She recalled that they had met mainly amidst groups of other people, and hardly ever in private. In the few times that they had been alone together, major events had taken over, leaving no time for questions or free-flowing exchanges of any kind. Yes, even their lovemaking had been an event, as huge and overwhelming as the bomb blast they had been fated to share together.

How much did she know about Rattan? About his family? His antecedents? The warnings of *Aji* came to mind. Whenever any mention of Nalini's getting married came up, the old woman had always intoned that the 'background' of people was crucial. Any scepticism regarding the importance of 'backgrounds', or the impossibility of getting to know anything meaningful about them, was dismissed peremptorily by the older woman: it was her job as an old well-wisher of the Thapar children to look out for them. Fondly yet repeatedly, Nalini was deemed young, inexperienced and completely unknowing of the ways of the world.

Such conclusions always reduced Nalini to an impatient silence. What could one say in the face of an old woman's obvious concern? However, when Rattan now seemed to have been gone an age, *Aji*'s beliefs surfaced unbidden, and try as she could Nalini had to admit that she really did not know anything about Rattan and his 'background'.

Moreover, neither did others from amongst their community in Cairo know much about Rattan.

It began to worry her. However, she did not speak of her anxieties to her friend. But about ten days after Rattan's departure, she called Madhu Gupta and told her that Maneka, a dear friend, was visiting from India and she would like them all to meet.

Nalini thought that perhaps this meeting would give her the opportunity to find out if anything more was known about Rattan.

But the task did not prove as easy as she had thought. Madhu's daughter had the 'flu and so she refused Nalini's luncheon invitation. During the course of the telephone conversation, Madhu let drop that she had not heard anything from the mysterious Rattan Malhotra lately. In fact, she had not seen much of him. Nalini wanted to tell her that he was travelling, but the garrulous Madhu continued her own monologue. A long description of her sick daughter ensued; she hoped that she would recover before their Christmas holiday trip. Nalini could only get in a few words edgeways — completely inconsequential comments about the winter holiday being a good time to be travelling in Egypt.

'The weather is so good these days that many people plan to be out of town,' said Nalini quickly. 'I do hope, though, that they will all be back for the New Year's Eve community bash. Otherwise it will be a dull affair.'

'I hope you will be back from the Nile cruise too,' said Madhu who had been told about it earlier.

'Yes, we shall be back on the thirty-first, sometime after lunch. We should be able to make it later that night,' said Nalini.

And after saying good-bye, Nalini clicked off.

The cruise and the New Year's Eve festivities became the subject of conversation between Maneka and Nalini for the rest of the afternoon. Maneka thrilled at the idea of so hectic an itinerary. Her life in New Delhi was challenging, even satisfying. But there was no glamour in it. She could not remember a single time, in the last seven or eight years, when she had danced on New Year's Eve. They eagerly discussed the details of what the local Indian community had planned for the evening, and Rattan, his antecedents and his whereabouts, were completely forgotten.

Nalini and Maneka flew into Luxor shortly after four p.m. on 27 December 1992. When they landed, the two women barely had time to look around, for brightly painted coaches stood waiting to ferry the whole planeload of tourists to their respective cruise boats tethered on the banks of the Nile.

The drive from the airport in the coach, through a sparse landscape, lasted about forty minutes. As they neared the banks of the Nile, they came into the town of Luxor. Its main street was full of people walking about in colourful clothes. The arrival of the coaches was a daily sight, and many of the town's simple folk stood around to watch the intrusions of strange people from all over the world into their ancient city. Uniformed young men, with *Shaharyar* embroidered on their coats, stood by ready to receive them and their baggage. About fifty yards behind the junction was the bank of the Nile, with a rough pathway running parallel to the water. Dressed in jeans, Nalini and Maneka hoisted their hand baggage and began walking towards the *Shaharyar* as it stood swaying softly in the waters. Painted gaily in red and navy blue, it stood out bright and spectacular against the drab landscape.

Maneka could not prevent a shiver of excitement from running through her.

'What a change! From *Sahayata* to the *Shaharyar* on the Nile!' she said, trying to control the quiver in her voice. 'I feel like a schoolgirl on a field trip.'

Nalini smiled at her friend. She felt much the same herself – for it would not be long before she met Rattan again. Had he come already? Was he on board? As she looked ahead, she found they had already reached the sloping gangplank that covered the distance from the shore to the edge of the boat. Seeing this, both women hung back a little, allowing the porter with their baggage to precede them. Their uniformed host held out a helpful hand, and soon both women had walked down the plank into the boat's reception area. A pretty Egyptian woman, with a large smile on her face, sat behind the counter.

'Welcome to the *Shaharyar!*' she said, holding out a hand for their reservations. The whole area had been decorated in shades of a dull turquoise and green. The concrete columns and copper urns designed to imitate those of the Pharaonic era made the place look like a small but ancient Egyptian anteroom. Two tall potted palms, in the far corners, added to the elegance of the place.

'Both of you share a cabin, yes? The porter will lead you to it,' said the receptionist, adding something in fast-paced Arabic to the porter standing behind with the baggage.

The two women thanked her warmly, and followed the porter down a narrow carpeted corridor lined with a series of numbered doors. Their cabin was neither large nor small. It would probably seem smaller once the sofas on either side were opened out at night to make beds. At the far end was a wide window reaching all the way to the floor of the cabin. It afforded a good view of the Nile through its shiny clean glass panes. The two easy chairs under it seemed comfortable, and on top of the glass-topped table between them was a small basket filled with local fruit. The whole room was well lit and cosy — certainly cosy enough to spend four nights and five days in.

After the porter had gone, Maneka sat down on one of the sofas and looked at her watch. It was well after five p.m.

'So we made it, after all. The way your father sometimes spoke about the terrorists of Egypt, I never thought we would,' said Maneka, lifting her hands to her hair, and passing it roughly through the inevitable red ruffle so that it would hold together.

Nalini had walked into the small bathroom, and was rinsing her face with warm water. She came out rubbing her face with a towel.

'Yes. I'm glad we are here,' she said, somewhat self-consciously.

Maneka looked up, smiling teasingly at her friend.

'And now, I suppose, you will go and look for him!'

'You suppose correctly,' said Nalini, her voice a little muffled by the towel on her face.

'And I shall take a nap,' said Maneka, with studied fatigue. 'I suppose they will give us dinner later?'

'That will be in the dining room at seven thirty,' said Nalini. She was standing before a schedule of events, framed elegantly in glass, and hanging discreetly behind the bathroom door.

'We don't sail until ten — or even later — at night. Well after dinner is over, and the "entertainment" planned for the guests by the crew is under way,' said Nalini.

'I suppose that gives enough time for people with hectic schedules to actually catch the boat,' said Maneka.

'Yes ... I wonder if he managed to catch a shuttle flight from Cairo to Luxor. He was not on our flight, so maybe he caught a later one.'

Nalini looked a little apprehensive. Maneka thought it best not to say any more. She took off her shoes and, adjusting one of the cushions under her head, turned over on one of the sofas and shut her eyes.

Nalini opened her small suitcase and unpacked some of her clothes. She decided to change out of her jeans into a pair of dark tailored trousers with a matching flowing top. She took out a pair of comfortable, flat walking shoes and a black shawl. December could become cold in the evenings. She brushed her hair, freeing it of all its tangles and put it up in her usual knot high at the back of her head. A dash of dusky brown lipstick and she was ready.

She had to go and see if Rattan had arrived.

It took a few minutes for Nalini to retrace her steps through the corridors of the two decks, and find her way to the Reception. The young Egyptian woman was still there, somewhat busier than before, for the foyer was crowded with guests and suitcases, and uniformed personnel escorting their charges. The Oberoi management did things in style, and it made Nalini feel proud that an Indian company had established such a name for itself in the hospitality business in a foreign land.

It was a few minutes before she got her turn at the counter. The young lady behind it was all smiles, and quickly looked into the computer to see if a Rattan Malhotra had checked in.

'Yes, he has checked in. And he was asking about you ... and your friend. Nalini Thapar and Maneka Saxena?'

'That's us,' said Nalini, barely able to hide the relief in her voice. 'Which is his cabin?'

'His cabin is a floor above yours. The number is three-o-four. Would you like to speak to him? I can get him for you on the intercom, if you like.'

'No . . . no, thanks. It would be fun to surprise him . . .' said Nalini hurriedly.

Nalini's knocking on the door of 304 was softly polite, even tentative. There was no reply. Nalini tried not to think that maybe the receptionist had been mistaken about Rattan's arrival. Maybe Rattan had forgotten her, not valued her or all that she had given him . . . and she would die rather than hang around waiting on him.

But even as disappointment and hurt washed all over her, she decided to knock again. This time her knock was louder, more definite in its desperation. And it was heard. The door was opened immediately by Rattan himself with a towel in his hand, in the process of wiping Luxor's sands from his face. His hair was wet and uncombed, and drops of water hung around the lower parts of his face and neck.

Nalini was so relieved to see him that she could not say anything for a few seconds. He dropped the towel, and stretched out his arms towards her. In one step she had entered his cabin and was in his embrace.

'You've come . . .' she said with wonder and relief in her voice.

And she knew then, that nothing had changed between them.

'So you still have your birthmark,' said Nalini, later, using her forefinger to trace its outlines in a gentle movement. Its dark edges stood out sharply against his wheat-coloured skin.

Rattan did not reply. They were lying side by side, naked

and spent, squeezed together on the narrow sofa. Rattan was lying on his side; behind him, along the wall, was Nalini.

'It seems to have gone darker since I saw it last,' she said mischievously, and dug her nail into its outer ridges more deeply than she ever had done before.

'You only saw it once,' said Rattan, wincing a little. 'And you remember clearly its exact colour?'

'Yes I do, I think,' said Nalini, teasingly. 'It is darker, though. What have you been doing to it these last few weeks that you have been away?'

Rattan did not reply, a frown of sorts lining his forehead. His hand had begun reaching out to a packet of cigarettes lying on the floor. Once he had them in his hands, he turned on his back and lay there looking at the ceiling. Nalini sensed that he had not particularly liked her question, or indeed her attempts at humour, and thought immediately of changing the subject.

'No cigarettes, please,' she said, raising herself on an elbow to peer into his face. Her hair had come undone, and its long brown strands spread themselves out all over him. She readjusted her position so that she could lift an arm and reach out to hold his hand and prevent him from lighting up. 'We in India – and in the Third World generally – smoke too much. There's a conspiracy among multi-national tobacco companies to market smoking aggressively outside the West, and make a fool of coloured people – and that means people like you – who do not know any better,' said Nalini, deliberately pompous and preachy in her tone, and with a wicked smile hovering around her mouth.

Rattan listened to her solemnly, looking at her all the while through narrowed eyes. Her mock seriousness was quite comic, for it made her purse her lips like the pernickety schoolmarm of legend. They were beautiful lips, fine and chiselled, and their puckering in disapproval was a distortion that did not go well with her beautiful hair, and the bare lobes of her breasts hanging over, yet barely touching, his body. The combination of all these factors had their own consequences, and for a while there was only movement in the cabin. And some silence.

When they finally got talking seriously, it was much later. Nalini was already dressed, and Rattan was in the process of buttoning a fresh shirt in front of the long mirror attached to the wall. Nalini asked how his trip to India had fared, and whether he had stopped anywhere on the way to Cairo. The questions brought a seriousness to Rattan's face. He looked at Nalini intently for a few seconds, which she did not see, for she was busy picking up her hairpins that had scattered everywhere. Rattan turned away from the mirror.

'We need to talk,' he said brusquely. 'We do really need to talk,' repeated Rattan, as if she didn't understand him. But Nalini did not notice. Standing beside him, and looking at his face in the mirror, she began combing her long hair.

'Yes, we can sightsee, cruise, and talk ... and make love too, maybe ... once in a while?' said Nalini, her face deadpan; but her voice was provocative and mischievous.

Rattan, however, did not respond. Instead he turned, and holding her by the shoulders, moved her around with strong hands to face him. His grip was more than firm, even somewhat rough, and there was something deep and ominous about the look on his face.

'What is it?' said Nalini apprehensively.

Rattan did not reply. Nalini waited a few seconds, and then shrugged his hands off a little impatiently. She gave her hair a couple of final brushes, and putting her comb down, started to tie it all back in the knot she usually favoured.

She knew that Rattan still had his unspeaking gaze on her. It made her feel uncomfortable, even slightly annoyed. But she decided she would not give way to these feelings.

'Are you one of those moody kind of guys who are warm and loving one minute, and go off into the sulks the next?' said Nalini, speaking coolly out of a mouth full of her hairpins.

At this, Rattan laughed, and the hardened edge to the

feelings that had been generated in the room dissipated at once. He watched her complete her toilet in silence, and then kissed her long and deep.

'I do love you, you know,' said Nalini, her voice husky.

'So do I. More than I should, probably ...' Rattan did not allow himself to complete his sentence.

Nalini waited for him to say more. But he didn't. She knew at once that he *had* had more to say, but had chosen not to say it. She wondered why, and what was on his mind. But she let the moment pass.

'I should get back to my cabin and see if Maneka is awake. It's almost time for dinner.'

'Yes, it is past seven o'clock,' said Rattan.

'We can meet in the dining room. I shall introduce you to my friend, and then we can *all* talk,' said Nalini.

'Yes, we can all talk,' replied Rattan seriously. 'But we must get some time by ourselves too?'

'Of course ...' said Nalini, noting the warning in his voice and giving him an exasperated look.

She, too, could have said more, but didn't.

When Nalini opened Room 203 with her key, Maneka was in the bathroom. Her suitcase was lying open on one of the sofas, and its contents were half spilling out of it. Nalini winced at the sight, and knocked at the bathroom door. Maneka replied immediately that she was changing for the evening. She came out in a few minutes.

'So, he's on board?' she asked, a laugh in her voice.

'Yes, he is,' said Nalini, but her tone was serious. She saw Maneka look at her searchingly for a few seconds.

'But why aren't you happy about it?' asked Maneka, concern in her voice.

'I am happy, my dear,' said Nalini, deliberately putting on a broad smile. 'Can't you see?'

'Yes, I can,' said Maneka, pretending to be convinced for the moment. 'When do I meet him?'

'He'll be waiting for us in the restaurant upstairs,' said Nalini. 'We should hurry, or we won't get any dinner.'

Once in the restaurant Nalini quickly spotted Rattan. He had chosen a table by the large windows, the glass throwing off glowing reflections in the subtle lighting of the rather large room. The tables were for four, set in individual alcoves divided by wooden partitions. The linen was in complementary shades of blue, and the cream-coloured walls had murals depicting scenes from Pharaonic times. These were painted in shades of royal blue, carnelian, turquoise and gold. The atmosphere was nothing if not exotic. Personally Nalini thought it was a bit overdone, but the other guests, mainly Europeans and Americans, thought it wonderful. As they wove their way through the tables in the crowded restaurant, they overheard exclamations of appreciation everywhere. It was everyone's first night on the boat, and the first of many meals in its restaurant. This was to be 'home' for five days.

Rattan had seen the two women as soon as they entered, and stood up to greet them. His eyes were on Nalini, her grace and poise. He felt a little bad about having been so abrupt earlier in the cabin, and regretted spoiling such a perfect reunion. He was indeed lucky to be loved by her, he told himself, and felt the urgency of telling Nalini about himself and Tanvi.

Maneka had followed Nalini to the table and sat opposite them. She waited until Rattan sat down, and then began speaking in a deliberately cheerful tone. 'Hi! I'm Maneka. Maneka Saxena. I'm sure Nalini has told you all about me. I hope you don't mind my presence here, but as you know, this cruise would not have been possible if it were not for me! So you will have to put up with my being the proverbial *"kebab mein haddi"*.'

Rattan smiled at this blunt statement and put out a hand in

friendship. Maneka shook it with a firm palm. At that moment a waiter arrived. The women ordered white wine, and Rattan a bottle of beer. Nalini found herself suddenly with nothing to say. It was left to Maneka to begin speaking again.

'So we meet at last. I have heard a lot about you . . .' she said, fidgeting with her hair which was, as usual, hanging somewhat wildly down both sides of her face.

'I hope it was all good . . .' said Rattan, amused at the contrast between Nalini and her friend. The one was tall, well groomed, soft spoken; the other casual, gruff voiced and blunt. Her loudly flowered shirt was slightly crushed, and one of its buttons was missing. Through her collar, open at the throat, Rattan could see that she had used large quantities of talcum powder after her shower.

She did not respond to Rattan's statement, but all the while – and even as her head was bent slightly forward – her eyes were fixed unselfconsciously on Rattan.

'I've been thinking . . . you look very familiar. Have we met? You are from New Delhi, aren't you?' asked Maneka, suddenly looking at him piercingly.

Rattan could not help but return her glance. As he held it, suddenly a truth dawned. As they stared at each other, his mind and subconscious were also, quite involuntarily, resurrecting a memory in which women in white saris, wild hair and red bindis, were yelling at him in accusation and hatred.

It was hardly relevant who recognised whom first, but it was Maneka who spoke.

'I know who you are! My God, I remember . . . and remember clearly. You are the son from next door in Hauz Khas. You are Rattan *Malhotra* . . . and you killed your wife . . . you *all* killed that poor girl, Tanvi.'

Maneka's tone was harsh and loud. As she spoke she had gradually begun leaning forward, both hands clenching the edge of the table. As her face neared the other two sitting opposite her, its expression changed completely. Her eyes narrowed in hate and accusation, and her lips pursed together in damning judgement.

But when she raised her right hand to point an accusatory finger at Rattan, it brushed against her wine glass which fell over, tipping its contents across the narrow table.

Rattan and Nalini stood up instinctively to avoid the liquid, and Nalini automatically picked up a serviette to stem the flow of wine creeping across the table. But her mind went slowly numb, and a cold, stone-like feeling began to wind its way into her stomach. Had she heard right? What was Maneka saying? Wife? Killed? . . . Killed his wife? She looked at Rattan's face. It had turned white . . . as if some ghost had cast its own pale shadow on him. His mouth was clenched tight and his eyes were staring into her own, wide with misery.

Nalini realised that they were getting a lot of attention from other diners. She looked at Maneka, only momentarily prevented from continuing her accusations by the presence of the waiter who had come to help them. As soon as he moved away to fetch another cloth, she began to speak again, her voice loud in outrage.

'My God! You shameless man . . .'

'Will you shut up, and stop shouting?' hissed Nalini, glancing surreptitiously around even as she swallowed to moisten a chalky mouth and a dry throat. She caught Maneka's eye, and willed her to sit down. But Maneka ignored her, deliberately turning away to look at Rattan. It seemed that she was again going to point an accusatory finger at Rattan. Nalini quickly leaned over and held her hand down. By this time the waiter arrived again. It took him a few minutes to remove the cloth, and replace Maneka's spilt wine. In his presence all three were forced to remain silent.

And in that silence, Maneka's hatred for all men, so much in abeyance in her vacation, shone out of her eyes; Rattan knew that his past had risen up from the shadows to haunt his present; and as for Nalini — she did not know what to think. Or feel.

All she sensed was a deep, doom-like dread that something terrible had been disclosed.

And that yet another of Life's crucial examinations had begun for her.

Adrift on the Nile

Maneka's outburst ruined not only the evening but also the rest of the cruise. Maneka was prepared to go on with her accusations, but barely had the waiter replaced the wine than the diners heard a loud horn blowing in the distance. The restaurant simmered into silence, all present straining their ears to hear where the sound was coming from. In a minute the captain appeared, followed by a young man holding a horn. At a signal from the captain, he began to blow it, and it was only when the sound had died away that the captain spoke.

'Welcome aboard the *Shaharyar*! We are about to set sail. We are eighty-three passengers on board today, and I hope that every one of you enjoys this cruise down Egypt's famous river. We have arranged many treats for you, and shall let you know about them by and by. For now, the buffet is ready. Please serve yourselves and keep a watch on the windows. You may see some strange things! In the meantime, a welcome glass of champagne for everyone is with our compliments!'

The captain's words of welcome were uttered in a strong Egyptian accent and a gruff yet loud tone. They were heard clearly by everybody. As they died away, the diners clapped and then resumed their conversation even as the waiters went around the restaurant with trays full of flutes filled with champagne. The waiter serving Rattan, Nalini and Maneka was particularly efficient: they were amongst the first to be served.

'Enjoy!' he said bowing in the typically Egyptian way, and moved to the next table.

He had hardly moved out of earshot when Maneka spoke. 'Enjoy? My foot,' she said derisively, making it clear that nothing was going to deter her any more. 'You did kill her, didn't you?' she said, addressing herself to Rattan.

'I did *not*,' said Rattan coldly, his voice low in warning. 'And I wish you would not speak as if you know everything. In any case, I do not need to make any explanations to you.'

'Well, I hope you may have made some to Nalini, and *she* knows everything,' said Maneka sarcastically. 'I know as much as I want – or need – to know. It was you and your mother together who killed poor Tanvi. You wanted more dowry, didn't you?' Her voice rose a little, and her tone became vicious.

Rattan was about to say something sharp and cutting, but Nalini put out her hand and covered his mouth. Rattan looked at her, and found that hurt eyes were pleading for his silence.

'Please don't say any more,' she said. 'We can talk about this later. Let's not make a scene here, please.'

'You, my dear, are a naïve fool,' said Maneka to Nalini in a voice that dripped a condescending exasperation. 'You are in love with a murderer, and you don't want to make a scene? Isn't that just like you, Nalini? Always the formality of the moment must prevail, no matter how contrary the absolute fact is!'

'Well, I don't see how discussing it *here* will help,' said Nalini, her eyes lowered but her voice firm. 'We do need to talk, but I don't think this is the place, or the time.'

As she said this last sentence, she looked at Rattan. A controlled, white-hot anguish enveloped her face. A muscle twitched at the corner of her mouth, and her eyes were glazed with unshed tears. Rattan reached out to hold her hand, but she moved it away deliberately.

There was a deadening silence for a few seconds. Maneka

seemed as if she would speak again. But Nalini pre-empted her. 'No, Maneka. Not now. I think we should go to the buffet and serve ourselves some dinner,' she said firmly, and stood up.

Since Nalini was in the inner seat of the alcove, Rattan had no choice but to stand also, and make way for her. Leaving Maneka to fend for herself, he tried to follow her. But she walked on uncaring. When he reached the buffet queue, he found that four or five people had found a place immediately after her and he could do nothing about the separation. He was sure that she had done this deliberately, and felt her rejection acutely. He saw that Nalini skirted all the large chafing dishes full of food. By the time she had reached the last of them, only some rice and a little salad were on her plate. She quickly headed back towards their table.

In the few minutes she had by herself, Nalini tried to control her feelings. Tanvi? Rattan and Tanvi? Why was the name familiar? Finally it came to her: Tanvi was the girl whom she had read about, written about, and thought about so many times these last few months. Tanvi and Rattan? And *Rattan*? And *he* had killed her? He who had been so gentle, and loving, and all concern through all the times that they had ... that they had ...

It could not be true! It could not be true!

The trip to the buffet table had cooled Maneka, but only a little. Though she realised that this was not the moment to make accusations, she found it hard to keep silent. The more she looked at Nalini and Rattan sitting opposite her, the more agitated she became. The two did not seem interested in conversation, and were only pretending to eat. Their determined silence seemed to go on and on until she could bear it no longer.

She ate a few mouthfuls of food automatically, her thoughts concentrating on the inherent falsehood of men and the innate unfairness of patriarchal systems prevalent in Indian society. All her feminist beliefs, so much the source and justification for her life in New Delhi, came to the fore. Suddenly, she picked up her glass of champagne and took a large swig. It made her choke a little, and she coughed and spluttered for a few seconds.

But she began to speak as soon as her throat had cleared. Her eyes were focused mainly on Rattan. A burning sneer, like a hot cunning flame, crossed her face. 'My God! How can you just sit there in silence and eat as if nothing has happened? It is men like you – and your mothers – who are the biggest evil force in society. A woman is a commodity for you! She must not only be a slave in a man's home, but also pay to be one. From the highest to the lowest, it is always dowry when a young woman dies. One would imagine that seventy-three Hauz Khas would be enough for you – you, the only son, who will probably inherit everything from your father. And you killed that poor innocent! That Tanvi, who was not taught to fend for herself but exist in waiting – convent-educated and a BA – for the cruel pleasures of a young man like you. Couldn't you have stayed on in the USA and lived with those American girls who would have known how to give you *only* as much as you gave them . . . ?'

By the time she had hissed out all this, Maneka was quite breathless. Her face was red, and her eyes gleamed with a suppressed, visceral hatred. In front of her, Rattan's face had grown grimmer and grimmer, the words 'dowry' and 'slave' enraging him particularly. He knew that Maneka was encouraged by his silence and he longed to shut her up. He could do it, he knew. Maneka could have no proof against him.

But just then, he felt Nalini's hand squeeze his in supplication.

Usually slow to anger, Rattan looked at Nalini with a fierce, angry intensity that seemed to transform him. He was beginning to frighten her a little; but she still felt that all arguments and explanations should be deferred.

'Please, Rattan . . . *Don't*,' said Nalini, her eyes luminous in their anxiety. 'I can't bear it.'

Rattan saw the pain in her face, and knew that he had no choice but to do as she wanted. It took much effort. He glared at Maneka with unspoken rage for a few seconds before he controlled himself. He wondered why Nalini had not stopped her friend from speaking out, and was, instead, preventing him from responding.

Was she enjoying hearing all this?

Or was it that she felt she had a right to ask *him*? A right which had overtaken that of a best friend?

The three hostile diners were forced to stay at their table because of the 'entertainment' arranged by the crew. The presentation ended with a set of instructions regarding sightseeing the next day. First were introductions: all guests had to stand and tell everyone their names, and the country they came from. All were then divided into convenient groups and introduced to their tour guide. Each guest was handed an itinerary for their next day's trip to their first archaeological site. All were to assemble for breakfast in the same restaurant by 7.30 the next morning.

'Thank you, ladies and gentlemen! Everything is in order,' said the young man in charge of the 'entertainment'. He beamed happily at everyone, waiting patiently for the clapping and conversation to die down.

'We now invite you to climb out onto the upper deck and see the stars,' he continued with a flourish. 'On the banks will be all of Egypt, asleep. And soon you shall be asleep also, cruising quietly up the Nile. Remember . . . we have to get going early tomorrow. And begin our tour! It's all organised for you! Good night!'

Everything was, indeed, all 'organised' — and all the way up the Nile. But Nalini and Rattan could not help but feel that they were adrift on it.

* * *

Nalini had barely opened the door of their cabin upon return when Maneka began. 'How could you go and fall in love with a person like Rattan Malhotra ...?' she asked in exasperation.

She was all prepared to go on, but Nalini interrupted her in a firm, steely voice. 'He didn't exactly tell me, you know ... that he had killed his wife,' said Nalini with bitter sarcasm.

This made Maneka more angry. So, she had guessed right: he hadn't told Nalini about Tanvi! Told her nothing at all. 'Did you never talk about anything?' she asked.

Nalini did not reply. Outside the windows it was dark, except where the lights on the deck of the *Shaharyar* had lit up the dark waters on either side of the cruiser. Beyond, on the far banks, the faint silver glow of the waning moon lit up the outlines of tall palm trees and low brick houses, neatly edging the waters. But all this Nalini noticed with only a small part of her mind. The rest of it had gone blank – in a sort of dead confusion.

Rattan, a killer? It was not possible. It was just *not* possible.

'Didn't you ever talk about anything?' Maneka repeated, her voice sharply piercing.

'Oh God! I cannot believe it! I cannot believe it's true.'

Still facing the window, Nalini's stiff back had gone suddenly limp, her shoulders sagging even as she covered her face with both hands. As her mind struggled to remember what Rattan had said, the hollow churning in her stomach increased.

He had not *denied* Maneka's accusations in the restaurant. Or, had he?

What had he actually said? That she *didn't* die? Or, that *he* hadn't killed her? Or? ... Or?

She felt weak and moved to her bed.

At once Maneka was by her side. She put her arms around her friend, and held her close. Nalini allowed herself to be held, and even put her head on Maneka's shoulder.

'He can't be ... He was so gentle and loving ...' said Nalini, her eyes wild but her voice low and wondering.

'Of course he would be gentle and loving! How do you think that he would've got you to fall in love with him if he hadn't been?'

Nalini had no reply to this. It was excruciating to hear of another Rattan – the callous, calculating Rattan – which Maneka had seen so easily.

'Don't,' said Nalini, her voice almost pleading. 'I *don't* want to know. I don't want to know anything.'

'But you *have* to know, Nalini,' said Maneka, her voice rising in exasperation. 'You can't hide away from the facts!'

'I suppose not ...' said Nalini, at last.

'You have to listen to me,' said Maneka, a passionate urgency in her voice. 'You have to ... for your own sake!'

Maneka had not forgotten a single detail surrounding Tanvi's death. Beginning with her own encounter with the new bride outside 73 Hauz Khas on that fatal day, she recounted all that had happened that evening. Tanvi had been found dead, hanging from the ceiling, with a pink *chunni* tied around her neck. The Malhotras had passed it off as a 'suicide', and had been in a hurry to have her cremated. Her parents had been overwrought, especially her mother, Mrs Madan. It was *her* ravings that had aroused suspicion, although when questioned closely afterwards, she had denied everything.

'It was all hushed up, remember? I wrote you all this in my letters, and you even rummaged through old issues of newspapers and found a brief mention somewhere at the bottom of an inside page or something ...?'

'Yes, I remember ...' said Nalini dully, her voice low and beaten.

'We reported it to the Crime against Women Cell in the Delhi Police. They were convinced that it was not suicide, but they could find no proof. In any case, the Malhotras are influential in New Delhi. They prevented detailed investigations. In fact, they *all* left the country immediately afterwards. All of them, even the son ... I mean Rattan.'

'Yes, that must have been when he came to Cairo,' said Nalini. 'And we met on the fifteenth of August ... in the Embassy.'

'Well ... ?' said Maneka. 'And you still believe him?'

Nalini did not reply but got up, in one sudden movement, and walked into the bathroom, closing the door behind her. There, in front of the bright lights, she stared at herself and at the dreadful turn the circumstances had taken. A black, eclipsing shadow had passed over her sun, casting her trusting world into a complete darkness. There were, on the one hand, the 'facts' as Maneka had recounted them; on the other were her own feelings – her own instinctive knowledge of Rattan's love for her. It was true that men were – or at least could be – rogues and manipulators who took advantage of believing women whenever they could. She had been taught this all through her growing years. She had also been told about being wary of appearances: often men were not what they seemed, and that the smoother they were the more sceptical and knowing women had to be.

Yes, she knew all this, she knew all this ... But did all these things apply to the Rattan she had known? Did they?

There were no answers. The tears, held back with so much effort and control, broke free and flowed down Nalini's face. She gave them rein, her sobs heaving heavily in her breast. At first she was thankful that she was alone and could cry without inhibition. But then, the realisation of how alone she *really* was came to her with the force of a high wind, pushing her to some different element of isolated existence. Even her mother's death had not been this way. Then there had been other family members with whom she could share the shock of her death, and mourn her passing.

But this time she was well and truly by herself. And

only Maneka — and Rattan himself — could know the situation.

Maneka, Rattan — and herself. What an odd triangle that was! So complete was her disillusionment that for a few seconds she was completely lost to the world outside — to Maneka beyond the door, to the *Shaharyar* moving smoothly through the Nile, and to Rattan on the deck above, living through his own private hell.

Eventually, her sobs lessened.

Here they were on this cruise, this odd threesome, and there was no possibility of fleeing for any one of them. The thought made her laugh a little hysterically. This cruise, so looked forward to these last few weeks, had turned into a prison sentence — an inevitable confinement from which there was no release. Nalini could not help but think longingly of Bharat Bhavan. Once inside its gates, the world and its unwanted people could so easily be kept out. But here — for the next few days at least — all three would have to meet repeatedly. Be together, eat together — *and* even tour together.

The prospect was stifling, and she longed for some fresh air.

She opened the door of the bathroom and walked towards the cabin door.

'I'm going up to the top deck for a while. I'll be back soon. Why don't you turn in? I have my key, and I won't make a noise or disturb you,' she announced quietly.

The air was cool across her face and shoulders. As she pushed her arms through the sleeves of her jacket, she could feel the chill of the night breeze drawing away the mottled red of her face and eyes. For a moment she focused on her surroundings: on the faint hum of the engines in the distance, moving the *Shaharyar* smoothly towards Aswan in the south; the floorboards of the deck below her feet; the unlit waters below the hull of the *Shaharyar*; and the dark distances of the night sky looming over the Nile. It was a mysterious and awesome sight.

But inevitably Nalini's thoughts moved quickly to Rattan and Maneka's revelations. Why had he not told her anything? *Why*? Was he a clever, vicious playboy given to making young inexperienced women fall in love with him just for the fun of it? Or was he the proverbial die-hard villain? Or just a coward – afraid to tell what he had done? She had been really fooled, hadn't she? ... Fooled into making the very mistakes that all her life she had been warned about? Her mind raced over all the times she had been with Rattan, looking for signs of his perfidy. She could not find any, and marvelled at how good a dissembler he must be, never to have done anything to make her suspicious. In fact, she had never doubted anything when she had been with him.

Rattan had always been kindness itself ...

The memories of all of their moments together were powerful. Though she had been told that Rattan was no less than a murderer, she knew that it was still Rattan she wanted – and *now* as she had then. She wished that he was near her, that she was in his arms – and that he was taking care of all that she was thinking and feeling.

She should have been more surprised to feel, suddenly, Rattan's strong hands grip her shoulders, and turn her gently around to face him. But she wasn't really, just intensely relieved that he had felt the need to seek her out and find her. His touch stilled her turbulent heart.

Why had he come?

To see how she was suffering? And make her suffer a little more?

This is what her head told her. But her heart told her no: maybe he had come just to be with her, and to explain. For surely he owed it to her! There was something powerful and compulsive between them, something that anchored them together, and would continue to do so whatever direction future events might take.

Nalini sighed deeply, and slowly her mind surrendered to

her deepest needs. She moved into his arms. Man and woman stood silently, unmoving, her hair in his face and the wool of his jacket rough against her cheeks.

'I *didn't* kill her, you know,' he said softly, a compelling note of calm in his voice. 'You have to believe me ... you *have* to.'

Nalini flinched. She could not have responded at that moment even if she had wanted to. She wished so much that all could be as before: that she could continue with her secret of loving him and he loving her.

But it wasn't going to be like that. There had been someone else – a dead wife. A *murdered* wife. And he hadn't told her.

'She did die, though, didn't she?' said Nalini into his shoulder.

'Yes, she did. Three months after we were married. But I *didn't* kill her,' said Rattan desperately. He pushed her away a little, and was looking straight into her face.

But her eyes still avoided his.

'Look at me, Nalini, please. You *have* to, while I tell the truth! I was going to tell you, soon – I've been trying to find the right moment. But Maneka beat me to it.'

Nalini heard him in silence. Rattan saw acutely the torment in her eyes, tried to reach out to her again across the distance she had deliberately put between them. But she moved away even further, out of his reach, still silent.

The moment Rattan had wanted so much to avoid had arrived. It had given no warnings, nor allowed any time for preparations. It had come with an apocalyptic bang and seemed poised to destroy everything. Near panic gripped him, and the old, only too familiar feeling of weightlessness and utter inconsequence washed over him. Just as he had begun believing in life's second chances, the past had caught up with him, tossing him around its dark waters like flotsam on a current.

He willed himself to remain calm. He could not allow Nalini to let go of him, because his new life depended on her love for him. He couldn't bear a single moment more of her believing him to be a murderer. He would have to do something – anything – to convince her.

Taking a deep breath, Rattan began to talk. It was hard, for he did not exactly know where to begin. But soon the narrative of his life with Tanvi tumbled out: that dreadful day and the absolute shock of finding Tanvi hanging from the fan in their bedroom, his efforts to revive her, the initial inability to believe that she was really dead, and the sheer horror of all that happened afterwards.

'Outsiders think we killed her; my mother thinks it was suicide ... but I, for the life of me, cannot understand why anyone should have murdered her, or that she wanted to kill herself,' said Rattan, his voice cracked and broken. 'We had had no quarrel ... in fact we had just made love that morning ...'

As he said this, he turned away, walking unseeing to the broad end of the deck. But Nalini did not move. Rattan was a dark figure hunched over the railings. The distance between them seemed to grow further and further, measuring itself over the black unseen waters stretching away towards the dimly visible banks of the river on either side. Nalini felt that they were standing on the earth of two different planets hurtling away from each other because their orbits had been fated to cross only briefly. Soon they would be far away, invisible and unreachable to each other.

And that would be the end.

In a moment of decision, Nalini crossed the deck quietly, and put her hand on his. She tried to look into his face, but sensed immediately that he was elsewhere – in a place where she had not been, nor could go even if she wanted it. All suffering is ultimately solitary business. She had thought it had been herself who was the deceived, and he the deceiver. But now, looking at his ravaged face and deep misery, the question of deceptions seemed a trite, small thing. The realisation dazed her, leaving her with very little to say. And so she stood there, still as a mouse, not daring even to move.

The moment of impasse was put to an end by the bellboy who had been watching them through the glass panes of the door that led to the deck. He had thought twice or thrice about telling them that it was late, but he had, in the truly Egyptian way, been sympathetic to the tension between them. 'Lovers from India,' he told himself, and had made himself comfortable on a stool just near the door. He must have dozed a little, which was just as well, for it had given Rattan and Nalini time enough to climb over – and descend from – the first mountainous hurdle between them. When he sleepily opened the door and coughed gently, both knew that it was time to leave the deck and both also knew that their destination would be Rattan's cabin.

Meanwhile, downstairs, Maneka could not believe that Nalini had walked out on her. Feelings of hurt and rejection flooded through her. She had stood waiting for Nalini to emerge from the bathroom, ready with a strategy about what her friend should do next. But Nalini had chosen to do everything by herself and gone away.

What was she to do next?

Shaking her head briefly, she began pacing the small cabin, her feelings of hurt gradually giving way to anger. The Malhotras – she was still quite sure – were guilty. They had closed off all investigations and made sure that, after the first brief report in the newspaper, none other had appeared. And they had *looked* so guilty, all of them – although she had to admit that Rattan had seemed more stunned than anything.

What a coincidence that he should choose to hide away in Cairo – and that Nalini should fall in love with him! And that she should remain smitten and, at least so far, be quite unable to see another side of him.

Rattan and Nalini – at least visually they made a good pair. They both came from good family stock, and in different circumstances, would have been well suited to each other. She thought suddenly of her host in Egypt, Gautam Thapar. She was sure that he would have approved.

Where had Nalini gone? Had she gone upstairs to think and calm herself? Or had she gone looking for Rattan Malhotra?

Quickly picking up her shawl, Maneka moved towards the door of the cabin.

'One never knows ... she could be in need of some help,' she told herself silently. Of what kind, she wasn't clear.

Maneka found her way to the top deck quite easily.

Despite the darkness of the night, she spotted Nalini and Rattan immediately. They were standing side by side – but not touching each other – at the far end of the *Shaharyar*'s top deck, hunched over the rails. Rattan's back had a stooping look about it; Nalini stood a little more upright, her back covered with her loose hair fluttering in the night breeze. Rattan was talking and, although her head was turned away from him, Nalini seemed to be listening carefully. Occasionally, when the breeze blew her way, Maneka could hear indistinguishable words flow past her ears.

It was a strange sight – suggesting estrangement and intimacy, both at the same time. An immediate pang of envy – mixed also with a strong sense of *déjà vu* – passed through Maneka. Here was a twosome who had no place for a third, no matter how protective or well meaning.

Perhaps by recognising Rattan Malhotra she had already done her bit by her friend.

All she could do was hope that Rattan would be telling Nalini the truth, and that her friend would remain rational and sane, and not get taken in by any red-herring tales aimed at hiding the real facts about Tanvi's death.

She would leave them alone for now.

Maneka turned away as quietly as she had come and returned to the cabin. Sleep came to her soon enough, but not before she had understood that now she would be really alone – more alone than her friend Nalini would ever be.

✳   ✳   ✳

After Nalini left him, Rattan hardly slept. When he did, it was fitfully, his sleep disturbed by bad dreams.

At dawn, Rattan lay exhausted, unable to sleep further. He had told Nalini everything, but he still did not know whether she believed in his innocence. The recollection of her doubting eyes filled him with dread.

He sat up quickly, reaching for the inevitable packet of cigarettes. As the smoke blew around his face, the only thing he could almost be certain about was that, by the time she had left his cabin, Nalini seemed to have exonerated the Malhotra family from being in any way dissatisfied with Tanvi's dowry. A straightforward revelation of their family's assets as contrasted with those of the Madans had, he hoped, made clear to Nalini that there was nothing that Tanvi's retired civil servant parents could give their daughter which the Malhotras could not have bought ten times over. It had seemed strangely crude to reiterate this to Nalini. And, to be fair to her, she too had balked at hearing him say these things. But Maneka's loud accusations had made him furious. They had been degrading and insulting not only to his parents but to himself, an educated and sane man who took the partnership of marriage as a serious business between equals.

He had made all this clear to Nalini. But there had been other questions that he had not been able to answer. If Tanvi had killed herself, why had she done so? If she had not, then who was responsible for her death? There were no answers still. Everyone was mystified. He told Nalini the impasse he and his family had been living through all these months. The same unanswered questions had fundamentally altered each of its members: he – Rattan – she could see for herself; his father had greyed, become gaunt of face, taken to excessive drinking and to working harder than ever; and his mother – his mother had become ill, really ill and yet allowed no doctor near her. She had become abnormal – almost demented, he thought – in her almost complete self-imposed silence.

His mother, in fact, was the person he was most concerned about. He had told Nalini briefly about his recent trip home, and how his mother had refused to talk, or to come home to be with him and his father.

Nalini had listened to him, all attention. She asked a few questions, mainly regarding the circumstances surrounding Tanvi's death. Rattan told her the fateful day's events, that Pammi Malhotra and the servants had been at home, the day being spent playing cards and entertaining her friends to a late lunch. Tanvi, in fact, had been with her mother, returning only in time to be briefly introduced to her mother-in-law's friends before they left. That is all he knew, for it was he who had discovered Tanvi — his mother having gone to Old Delhi to pay a visit to old Mrs Malhotra, his grandmother, after her friends had left.

Nalini found herself — without consciously meaning to — comparing what Maneka had told her with Rattan's version of events. While her friend's words had been full of accusations for mother and son, Rattan's had emphasised his own absence from the scene and the innocence of his mother. If there was anything in common between the two versions, it was the fact that Mrs Malhotra had been in the house.

'I guess your mother would know the most. She was there the whole day, wasn't she?' asked Nalini.

'I suppose so,' said Rattan, trying visibly to recollect the details. 'But whenever I have tried to ask her, she refuses to talk about the evening, and moves away into her little *mandir* room. These days she hardly replies to any questions. In fact, she hardly talks at all.'

Nalini heard his explanations with careful concentration. Her mind was trying furiously to piece into some coherence the sequence of events, as she had understood them. But she was having a hard time coming to any clear conclusions. The effort gave her face a distant, sceptical look that was mirrored in her silence.

Her face and her silence had unnerved Rattan. He wondered what was in her mind. But all his efforts to get Nalini to speak had failed.

But she had lifted her right hand and stroked his face. 'I must go,' she'd said, closing her eyes with a sigh. 'You too should get some sleep. We have a long way to go.'

He had moved away reluctantly, the faint smell of her perfume receding.

But the prospect of her leaving had brought on such a cold, hollow feeling of hysteria that he had immediately caught her hand and pulled her back.

'Don't leave like this . . .' he had said pleadingly.

But she had not responded to his kiss.

Rattan sighed deeply. Outside, the new-morning sun shone brightly. Rattan told himself there was hope still.

At least she had not recoiled from his touch.

The Tombs of the Dead

When they met at breakfast later that morning, the strain between the three Indian travellers was all too apparent. Rattan entered the restaurant first, and like the night before, it was left to him to choose a table.

He wondered what the two women would decide. Would they join him for breakfast? Or would they make their rejection of him and his presence on the cruise evident by sitting elsewhere? He knew what Maneka would want, and smiled wryly at being so clearly and unabashedly damned by her. He was not so sure that Nalini had done the same. He hoped not. But would she be able to withstand her strong friend's persuasions, and at least give him a chance? Perhaps this breakfast was a test — a test that would indicate how the rest of the cruise would go.

Keeping his eyes on the doorway, he was relieved to see that Nalini entered first. He could see her eyes searching the tables, looking out for him; then she came straight towards where he was sitting. Dressed in a pair of beige slacks and a simple red jumper, she wore her hair loose, held back with a red ruffle. She was winding her way around the tables with a grace and fluidity all her own. But there was no smile on her face as she accepted the courtesy of his pulling out her chair for her. An attentive waiter did the same for Maneka. As Rattan had known, the latter's face had a steely look, her eyes glaring at him as if daring him to challenge her conclusions.

Rattan decided to ignore her. It pained him to see dark circles under Nalini's eyes and a careworn look about her mouth. Whenever he felt he could, he appraised her face and eyes, looking for unintended or deliberate meanings in her every word, gesture and glance. But Nalini was unmoving, keeping her face carefully blank. She did not eat very much either, merely refilling her cup thrice with strong black coffee. Breakfast passed silently, the three of them studying the hand-out given to each passenger spelling out the day's programme.

The *Shaharyar*, as they discovered, had sailed only about twenty miles up the Nile during the night, and had docked near one of the main sites containing the ruins dating back to Pharaonic times. Chief of these was the Karnak temple, and the Valleys of the Kings and Queens. Each traveller was informed by the cheerful captain that they would be out for the day, returning only in time for a late dinner. Lunch had already been arranged in a restaurant near the Karnak temple. Coaches were ready for them, and the guides attached to each group were waiting in the Reception.

That morning, there was a newcomer to the group of eight to which the three Indians were assigned. This was a young American named David Winters who was about thirty years old, with a freckled face, warm brown eyes and hair. The cruise was part of his job, which entailed travelling the world in search of interesting destinations for bonus holidays for overworked business executives needing short, relaxing, get-away vacations.

Unlike the other four in the group – a middle-aged German couple who knew little English, and two older Englishmen from Bath who seemed to be travelling together, David Winters was by himself. He had not been seen for dinner the night before because he had arrived late – just before the *Shaharyar* had set sail. With his earnest expression and forthright gaze, he weighed each of his companions-to-be. He quickly came to the conclusion that, if he left the Indians out of his count, sightseeing for him would have to be a lone affair: the Germans were busy with each other and their guidebooks; and the Englishmen (probably a gay couple) hung out together, and did not seem interested in conversing with anyone.

By the time the groups were ready to board the coaches, the strain in the relationship between Nalini, Rattan and Maneka was all too apparent. Maneka glared at Rattan whenever she caught his eye. Nalini looked away whenever she saw this happen, a tight expression around pursed lips.

When Maneka had woken up that morning, she had found Nalini lying awake on her sofa bed, staring at the ceiling. Maneka – almost for the first time in her life – had not known what to say. Nalini had a hard shuttered look about her face that made it clear that any conversation about Rattan would find no response.

'We are to meet Rattan for breakfast at seven thirty,' Nalini had said in low, clipped tones. 'Let's not be late, shall we?'

'Nalini . . .' Maneka had begun saying.

But Nalini had not let her complete her sentence.

'Let's enjoy the cruise . . . and the sightseeing . . . that's what we came for, didn't we? Let's just forget Rattan for the time being,' she had said firmly.

Thus, though Nalini sat next to Rattan, she kept her eyes glued to the guidebooks she had brought with her from Cairo. Maneka did the same, but would often – deliberately it seemed to Rattan – engage Nalini in conversation in a hard, resolute voice whose aim seemed solely to exclude him. Since she was sitting in a seat behind him and Nalini, this usually entailed her tapping Nalini repeatedly on her shoulder to draw her attention to what she was saying. Rattan kept his eyes in front of him, and watched Nalini forced to turn around to respond to her determined friend.

Maneka's efforts were also watched by David Winters who

happened to be sitting in the window seat next to Maneka. Though all eight in the group had introduced themselves to each other before boarding the coach, they had not had many interactions yet. David kept his eyes before him for most of the time; but he could not help noticing that the rather pensive woman sitting in the aisle seat in front of him was palling of Maneka's attentions. In front of him also sat Rattan, still and quiet, and whose exact relationship with the two women he could not as yet gauge. Keeping his observations to himself, he concentrated on the view from the windows of the coach and what the driver was describing over the intercom.

Rattan sensed David Winter's silent observation of the drama, and was quite embarrassed. He had noticed each one of Maneka's efforts to monopolise Nalini, and the latter's subdued and unenthusiastic responses. He knew that Maneka was really getting at him, and using Nalini to do so. Her continuing provocation put Rattan's teeth on edge. He wanted to stop her – to tell her to give up her pestering and let Nalini be. However, keeping in mind their surroundings – and Nalini's possible objections to the inevitable scene his words would create – he did not say anything.

As he sat gazing with unseeing eyes at the passing landscape he could not help being glad that Nalini had chosen to sit with him – glad for the warmth of her shoulders, and the line of her thigh touching his on the narrow seat. And yet, despite all her closeness he knew that she was planets away. He had always known that the moment in which Nalini learned the truth would be formidable, but never could he have imagined such circumstances.

When they disembarked at the Valley of the Kings Nalini walked on a little ahead, with Maneka making haste to catch up with her. When the group began walking over the rubble and stones towards the mouths of the various burial chambers hidden deep under ledges of the ochre mountain-side, Rattan stayed away from the two women, walking at a little distance behind them. He saw Maneka try to make conversation with Nalini, but noted that the latter was not very responsive. Soon the tour began. Nalini listened patiently to the young Egyptian guide rambling on with his details, but Rattan could tell that her mind was not on them. Maneka, on the other hand, was quite taken up with everything – with the history and the exotic details so evident in the decorations and hieroglyphs on the sarcophagi. She asked the guide many questions, engaging him in long dialogues that made the others in the group somewhat restive and impatient.

The more she did so, the more Nalini hung back, lingering deliberately to scrutinise the deeply etched hieroglyphs decorating the walls and telling their own tales. Some of these, as Nalini found when she measured them, were as deep as two inches. She wondered absently how long it had taken stone carvers to scoop and chisel them out of the hard stone. But soon her interest in all that was around gave way to her own preoccupations. More interested in the detailed explanations of things, Maneka had moved on ahead. After a while, Nalini's place as companion was taken by David Winters who proved himself to be as curious as Maneka. At the third tomb of the Kings, the two had exchanged names and details, compared their guidebooks, and asked other information of each other relevant to the trip.

Rattan was grateful for his presence, as now Nalini and he were thrown together. By noon, Nalini had, with secret relief, accepted the inevitable; and, without making it too obvious, began to stay close to Rattan. The paths between the tombs were rough going, and Nalini trod them carefully. Rattan walked near at hand, his gaze more often on her than on the wonders on the walls. He saw her get hot under the noonday sun, and remove her jacket. He saw her hair gradually come loose from her red ruffle and circle her ears in a way that, weeks ago, had sent his senses reeling on the streets of Cairo. He saw her growing impatience with its thickness as it hung heavily down her back. He wanted to suggest that she tie it up, that she would be more comfortable that way, and that maybe he could help her do it . . . but of course he did not.

He knew the exact moment when she changed her mind. It was just before descending into a tomb that she decided to put out a hand and lift her hair clinging to the sweat on her neck. It was an impatient gesture, suggesting that she had had enough. She let the length of it go suddenly; and, after taking out some hairpins from her handbag, she asked Rattan to hold it for her until she had pinned all its strands in her favourite knot.

Nalini's fingers doing up her hair were, for her, movements ordinary and routine. Rattan had also seen them before. But that day, the now familiar gestures of her hands and body made for a moment of truth. As he looked at her head bent over her breast, her hair in her hands and her pins in her mouth, he felt a strange constriction tighten his chest and stomach. He could not lose her now – or ever – for he could not live without her.

If this was a moment of insight, it only made him close his eyes and turn his face away from her in anguish and incomprehension. More and more questions arose, like spectres from nowhere, hanging before his mind, insisting on answers. If he had come to love Nalini, where did that leave Tanvi? He had loved her too, hadn't he? Yes, he had – warmly and responsibly. And would have continued to do so through their life together. But could it not also be that his love for Tanvi had been a learned emotion? A set of acquired feelings, cultivated deliberately because he had accepted someone else's choice – his mother's choice – about whom he should love?

Was this love that he had come to feel for Nalini truer than what he had felt for Tanvi?

Once again, there were no clear answers. Full of confusion and remorse, Rattan wished fiercely that his past had been completely different, and that no blackening tales had been written on it. But more than anything he wished that he could have met Nalini earlier, before everything important had begun and ended. Now here she was, this woman who had become his life, his very reason for existing, the goal and purpose of his future. He could not bear the thought of being so close to her if he could not kiss her neck, her mouth, even touch her, as many times and whenever he needed to. What would he have to do to bring her back to him? How long would it take? Would it ever happen?

When she turned around for her jacket, Nalini could not see Rattan. He wasn't behind her as she had expected him to be. Nor was he anywhere near by. For a second she panicked. Had he deserted her and gone away, repelled by her cold presence? Maybe he had had enough — of her and her disapproving friend. Maybe everything was finished between them. She looked around, quietly frantic.

She saw him suddenly, some distance away from the others, sitting with his back to her on a tall rock, her jacket and handbag in his lap. She walked up to him, making as little noise as possible. She stood there, sensing that his attention was far away. She could see the back of his neck and head, strong and straight, his mind working, she was quite sure, on the tragic facts revealed yesterday.

'You should have told me, you know ... then it would have been different,' said Nalini softly in his ear, and continued without pausing, 'can I have my handbag and jacket, please?'

She saw him stiffen, the back of his neck flushing mutinously.

'I should have, and I'm sorry ... Will you never forgive me?' he said, without turning around.

'I have to believe you first, don't I?' said Nalini.

And walked away.

But when she saw that he was still sitting there, she retraced her steps, took his hand in hers and pulled him up to follow her.

'Come on, let's go. Or we'll be left behind.'

*　　*　　*

The group had reached the mouth of the burial chamber of King Tutankhamen. The guide was announcing dramatically that a team of archaeologists was at work in its depths, and that they would be finished with it shortly. It would be open to visitors soon. Everyone – especially Maneka and David – were all vocal in their regret at having missed this wonder of all wonders.

Rattan and Nalini stayed silent. The tombs were fascinating, but also morbid reminders of the futility of human desire to be remembered by posterity. While the others seemed to take the gloomy suggestiveness of the sarcophagi in their stride, Rattan and Nalini could not help but read them as a comment on the great voids in their own lives. By the time they had reached the Valley of the Queens, Nalini, particularly, felt a dark mantle of depression shroud her. For each tomb, the guide had a sad tale to tell. The queens of the great Pharaohs were unhappy beings: only in their graves had their lives taken on any meaning. Nalini thought of Tanvi. What meaning had her life taken after her death? And what meaning did it bring to her own, now that she had given her heart to Rattan who was said to have killed Tanvi?

When it was time to return to their coach, Nalini was relieved. She had had enough. So had Rattan, but more for Nalini's sake than his own.

In fact, they sat quietly, in their respective seats in the coach, listening to David and Maneka discuss the relative importance of women in Pharaonic times. Maneka went on and on about the queens who were famous, and proved her point triumphantly when they disembarked at the great tomb of Queen Hatshepsut. There was no doubt that she had wielded great power in her time. She had a tomb as great as any Pharaoh. It was mammoth-sized, the great steps leading up to it spreading horizontally at least three hundred yards each way, and the whole edifice silhouetted dramatically against the steeply ascending stark, yellow mountains of the Egyptian desert immediately behind it. While Maneka felt herself take on power-by-proxy of the dead queen, Nalini could only feel acutely the lack of her own queenliness. She smiled wryly.

Lunch was welcome, giving the tourists a chance to get off their feet and return to the living world. It was served in a small restaurant just outside the great Temple of Karnak, and the rest of the afternoon and evening was to be spent amongst the great columns of the temple. The day was to end at dusk, with a Sound and Light show dramatising the *raison d'être* of the temple.

David Winters completed the foursome at the Indian table for lunch. After all the time they had spent together that morning, it was inevitable that Maneka should invite him to share their meal. When she asked Nalini and Rattan whether they had any objection, they hastily said he was welcome, the unison of their voices suggesting an eagerness that was quite comic. But this only David noticed: Maneka was already in the process of sitting down, and making herself comfortable. Her face and her attention were elsewhere – on the temple they were to see, and on its long, detailed history.

So keen was Maneka to exchange notes on the subject with David Winters that she seemed, momentarily, to forget her great enemy sitting opposite. Rattan knew instinctively that it wasn't exactly an armistice on her part. It was more a question of her being carried away by the moment. The exotic sites around them and an attentive white male – who seemed to take everything she said with seriousness – were factors that demanded heartfelt responses. This left her two other companions free to deal with their emotions, and each other. Occasionally she would remember Nalini, giving her a warning look or two, and then continue to talk with David.

Later, it was inevitable that Rattan and Nalini should walk through the wonders of Karnak together. The grandiose columns, the giant figures of the King and his courtiers, the row of stone lions perfectly carved, the great spread of the whole complex, and the architectural perfection of the dimensions were remarkable to behold. For the first time that day, Rattan took out his camera, and began to take pictures. At first he photographed parts of the temple itself, not daring to ask Nalini to pose before one of the columns. But after he had clicked more than a dozen, she came up to him, and gently took the camera from his hands.

'Stand here, and I'll click you. Photographs without human beings are really quite boring afterwards,' she said matter-of-factly.

Rattan looked at her in some surprise.

'You cannot imagine how many boxes are piled with unseeable photographs of monuments our family has visited all over the world,' said Nalini. Her tone was neutral, as if stating that she knew more about all this than he did.

Rattan agreed without saying a word. But when she had taken a few of him, he took the camera from her, and made it evident that it was her turn. They were in front of the great obelisk, standing away from the main structure of the temple itself. All around lay the dismembered ruins of stone torsos and faces, the eyes staring blindly at the red hues of the late afternoon sky. Standing against the obelisk, her hair now loose and flowing again and the red of her jumper contrasting heavily with the ochre column behind her shoulders, Nalini looked so living a creature, so full of warmth, that it made Rattan long to reach out and hold her in his arms.

But, of course, he did no such thing. He took several more pictures of Nalini, and even got her to smile once or twice, allowing him to hope that, for a few moments at least, she believed that he was innocent of Tanvi's death.

The Light and Sound Show at the temple was spectacular. As the words, sounds, and light effects began to re-create Pharaonic times, Nalini's imagination surrendered to the presentation and Rattan felt her relax. When she shivered slightly, he put his arm around her. She did not seem to mind.

This made Rattan happy for the second time that day.

* * *

The next three days of the cruise passed in more or less in the same way. The *Shaharyar* would sail towards Aswan at night, dock at their next destination before dawn, and have its guests spend the day sightseeing on the banks. Maneka and David Winters spent most of their time together, making Nalini and Rattan wonder silently whether Maneka would confide to the American her suspicions about Rattan. But since David's attitude towards Rattan and Nalini did not change, they concluded that she had not.

There was the possibility of David's travelling to India in the near future. By the last day of the cruise, David was almost persuaded. Maneka promised to be his guide and mentor should he come to New Delhi. She would scout around for obliging travel agents that would help him put together a travel package for visitors to India.

Nalini spent almost all of each night in Rattan's cabin. They were nights spent in a deliberate silence, the need of which was understood instinctively by both of them. Rattan would make love to her gently or passionately, following his instincts about what he thought she would care for. His sole purpose was to make her happy, and to convey his love to her. At first she would not respond, lying there quietly on the sheets – like a martyr – surrendering the soft contours of her body to him. This unnerved Rattan a little but he did not show it. He took his cues from her – responding tentatively to her initially silent acquiescence and more aggressively to her later moments of intense desire. He wondered what was in her mind, why she had given up her inhibitions so completely, and why she had decided – by spending each night with him – to incur Maneka's wrath.

But he knew better than to ask her.

That Maneka objected, Rattan knew only too well. She had made her disapproval apparent the day after their trip to the Temple of Karnak by telling Rattan that he was taking advantage of Nalini. He had shut her up, telling her that she should

stay out of anything that had to do with him and Nalini. Maneka
had threatened to make a scene, but Rattan had reminded her
tersely that she should make sure of how Nalini would react
before she did any such thing. This had stopped Maneka in
her tracks.

That evening, when they returned to their cabin to freshen
up before dinner, Maneka warned Nalini in no uncertain terms
that she was being foolhardy, even rash, about continuing her
relationship with Rattan. She repeated this again and again, once
even raising her voice so loudly that Nalini was sure it could be
heard outside the door of their cabin.

This made her angry, and in a low, hard voice she had
told Maneka to stop at once. 'I know what I am doing,' she
said firmly, moving away into the bathroom and speaking to
Maneka over her shoulder. 'What happens afterwards – when
we return to Cairo – I don't know . . . But for now, I *do* know
what I am doing.'

Maneka was, once again, silenced. This annoyed her, and
she could not help complaining about how that 'bastard'
Rattan had not only come between them, but would also
bring Nalini to ruin. Nalini smiled briefly. 'You sound
like a nun in a nunnery, or else "the world's wife" in a
Victorian novel.'

'Well, you were very nun-like not too long ago, remember?'
Maneka could not help reminding her friend.

Nalini did not have anything to say to this, though
inside she knew that Maneka had not been wrong. But she
could not say that her lovemaking with Rattan had become
necessary. She had rather wondered at this necessity herself,
trying to define what exactly had made it so inevitable in
the first place. There was no clear answer. Were her nights
in Rattan's cabin in the *Shaharyar* merely a way of escape
from Maneka? Of being in wishful denial about her friend's
revelations? Or were they an opportunity to get to know more
about Rattan?

Perhaps it was just she herself, clutching desperately at a time when she could give free, unthinking rein to her love for him *and* all the desire that went with it. There would be plenty of time afterwards, she knew, to decide whether a more permanent relationship with Rattan was at all conceivable. Somewhere, at the back of her mind, a voice told her that its cessation could become a possibility – a more than real possibility. The thought always filled Nalini with a knot of dread which lay heavy in her heart.

But the thought of severing herself from Rattan was even worse, and left her shuddering in terror. Then she would be well and truly bereft – be completely dispossessed of all that life with him had come to mean.

And so it was that, for the first time in her life, Nalini willed herself not to think, not to make any plans, but allow herself to drift with each day, in a state of unthinking but passionate blankness, uncaring of the future. Rattan and she were momentarily alone together, and that was enough for her those four days on the *Shaharyar*.

On the last of the nights in Rattan's cabin, Nalini was more than responsive. In fact, there was a desperate edge to her caresses. For the first time, Rattan found himself lying beneath her, looking into her face framed by her long brown hair. He saw the faint line of stitches on her right breast hanging close to his face. He kissed it passionately, biting on her nipples in turn with a force that made her wince in pain and erotic pleasure. As they reached orgasm together, he saw her close her eyes just a few seconds before he closed his.

'Oh God! I love you so,' he heard her say under her breath.

'What did you say?' said Rattan, unbelieving. 'Say it again, please . . . ?'

But she only sat up and looked at him – and then let her

head burrow in his neck silently, her mouth near the birthmark on his shoulder. As she did so, Rattan felt her teeth dig into it with a vengeance that made him shout out in pain, and push her head away from his shoulder.

'Ouch! That hurt ...' he began. But stopped when he saw that her deep unhappy eyes, full of tears, were fixed on his skin, and her fingers were moving over the raw teeth-marks she had left behind.

Rattan looked at her face in silence, the skin on his smarting shoulder acutely aware of her touch.

'You do know, don't you, that I will never let you go away from me?' he said finally in her ear, his voice filtering softly through her warm hair. His hands moved it aside, and lifted her head up so that she could look at him. 'I know you are going to try — others are going to try — to separate yourself from me. But I will never allow it.'

Nalini allowed her head to be raised, but kept her eyes closed. Large tears slowly rolled down her cheeks. She could feel the gentle touch of Rattan's hands, at first holding her face, and then wiping the wet of her tears away from her cheeks. She knew he was looking at her — in search of faith and reassurance?

Probably.

But her own mind was full of other things — of the fact that this was the end: the end of instinct, and of holding the world and its cruelties at bay. Never again, as far as she could imagine, would it ever be the same again. She could hear the engines of the *Shaharyar* vibrate beneath her. It was moving into Aswan, and would be docking before dawn. There would be the last sightseeing trip to the great dam — and then it would be time to leave, to separate, and to disconnect.

She opened her eyes, but she did not say what was in her mind. Rattan thought it best not to ask her. He knew that these moments were singularly precious, and he spent them looking at her, his hands moving downwards to hold her breasts in his palms.

The Aftermath

There were merely ten days left of Maneka's holiday in Egypt after she and Nalini returned to Cairo. They were spent in recovering from the cruise, and shopping. Nalini took Maneka twice to the Khan-El-Khalili, where she bought gifts for Ahmer, her mother, and her friends at *Sahayata*. The colours and gaiety of the famous Egyptian souk were welcome – they helped greatly in taking away the stressful edge to the remainder of Maneka's stay in Cairo. In the second trip, Gamal Shukri, who had been requested by Nalini to show them some lesser-known streets of the old bazaar, accompanied them.

What the two women enjoyed most was his guided tour through the Bayn El-Qasrayn, or the *Palace Walk* made world famous by the Egyptian Nobel Laureate Naguib Mahfouz in his well-known fictional trilogy of the same name. Nalini had read the books, but had never ventured into the location. Gamal walked them through the famous alleys, pointing out the buildings and other landmarks. Lingering in the innumerable nooks and corners of the old bazaar, Maneka and Nalini were fascinated by how little everything had changed in the half-century that had passed since the novels had first been published.

Maneka immediately thought of comparing the Khan-El-Khalili with the gullies of Chandni Chowk in Old Delhi. A big discussion ensued. Ever the flirt and tease, Gamal provoked Maneka into making long explanations of the location and history of the Indian bazaar. Nalini was amused, but also watchful for her friend. But she need not have worried. As she had warned Gamal earlier, Maneka was quite capable of dealing with the Egyptian brand of badinage while enjoying the light-hearted sparring with Gamal. Rattan and his misdeeds were temporarily forgotten. Maneka seemed happy and gay, soaking in the ambiance of the unique souk, and storing away memories to take back to India.

Nalini deliberately kept the pace of activity hectic in Maneka's last few days in Cairo, but she missed Rattan's presence. Neither called each other, both understanding instinctively that anything further would have to wait for Maneka's departure.

But Nalini wondered what would happen next. She debated about taking her father into her confidence. Gautam Thapar had welcomed the girls warmly on their return but Nalini had to acknowledge how good she had become at hiding her true feelings. Though her heart was in turmoil, even her dearly beloved father could not gauge her true state of mind. He was too far away from the revelations of the cruise — so far away that Nalini instinctively felt that no good would come out of asking his advice.

Rattan had left Aswan on an earlier flight. Nalini had parted from him coolly, replying only evasively when he tried to arrange a meeting upon their return to Cairo. She had been immensely relieved at his departure, for her mind had already returned to Bharat Bhavan in Cairo long before their leaving Aswan. The contexts and compulsions of the real world had begun to cast their weight on her. The moment Rattan had gone, the old subterfuges easily fell into place and his presence on the cruise remained concealed from everyone at home.

Though Maneka had understood that she would have to

keep her opinions and concerns to herself while in the presence of Nalini's family at Bharat Bhavan, she took the first private opportunity available to advise Nalini again. Maneka re-listed emphatically all the 'facts' that she had pointed out before, and began ticking them off her fingers slowly in warning.

Nalini listened without moving. She was standing silently at the edge of the cushions lining the seat in her bay window and looking out at the Nile. Maneka could have shaken her.

But before she could say any more, Nalini spoke. 'I do not think he killed her, you know,' she said. Her voice was low. 'The thing to do is to find out why Tanvi killed herself.'

This made Maneka as angry as she had been many times earlier. But Nalini cut her short, saying she had heard it all before. She informed Maneka firmly that she had decided to give Rattan the benefit of the doubt. At the same time, however, she would begin making her own investigations regarding Tanvi's death.

'And how do you propose to do this sitting here in Cairo?' asked Maneka.

'You shall help me, please,' said Nalini, her voice as even-tempered as her friend's had been impatient and sarcastic. 'I will be in Delhi sometime at the end of April or beginning of May. Till then, you will have to do me some favours.'

For the next half-hour Nalini spoke with determination, and by the time they turned in for the night, she had told Maneka what she intended to do. Maneka was sceptical, believing firmly that nothing new would come out of reopening the case.

But Nalini was adamant.

By the time Maneka left, a course of action was planned between the two women. Its first act would be performed by Maneka, the second by Nalini, and the third, she hoped, by Rattan himself.

Once back in New Delhi, Maneka could not help but think about Nalini and Rattan. After the initial shock of hearing of Tanvi's connection to Rattan, Nalini had been ready to hear his side of the story and give him the benefit of the doubt. Though disbelieving and disapproving of this, Maneka had – albeit reluctantly – noted her friend's faith in him. In her last few days in Cairo, she had also begun to allow the same shadow of credit to creep into her conclusions about the man. This had happened insidiously and without Rattan's presence. Neither had she and Nalini talked about him much. But Maneka's opinion of Rattan could not help being influenced by Nalini's belief that he'd been absent from the house at the time of Tanvi's death. She did not have proof of his alibis just yet. But until she found them, she would not judge him guilty. Maneka could not quarrel with this. And after a while, she began allowing her own prejudiced judgement about him to change slightly. Maybe – just maybe – Rattan had really been innocent.

But now that she was back in New Delhi, her old suspicious conclusions about the man resurfaced. Consequently, her letter to Nalini, written some days after her return, only reiterated her hostility to him and the Malhotra family.

I still think you are naïve, and much too ready to take things at face value. What the Malhotras did with Tanvi is being done by a lot of families in New Delhi. Only the other day, I intervened in one such case in my own neighbourhood. It was too late of course, but at least we got together to heap community disapproval on the family. The parents of the dead girl live in Meerut, and only got to know about the death of their daughter after they could do nothing. It is the same everywhere, and the whole thing makes me so sick.

I tried to meet Rattan's father, Noni Malhotra, as we had decided. It took me a good ten days to get hold of him. His servants were trying to keep his comings and goings secret from me. But the old postman told me about his return into town. When I finally got to meet him, he looked me up and down as if I was a worm from somewhere, was very rude, and did not answer any of my questions. I tried to tell him that I had met his son in Cairo, but he did not seem very interested. Instead, he got mad at me, and began shouting that Sahayata had become a nuisance next door to his home, and that he would have it closed down. I did not mention you, because, of course, he does not know about you. Mrs Malhotra was nowhere to be seen. I am still trying to meet her. Apparently, she does not stay much in 73 Hauz Khas. The postman tells me she has taken to staying in an ashram somewhere. I will have to search her out.

All this will take a little while. Maybe it should wait until you come into town yourself. Because whenever I try, nobody seems to want to tell me anything . . .

Sitting in her bay window on a Monday evening, and reading through Maneka's letter two weeks later, Nalini found herself feeling perplexed not only with her friend, but also with herself. The more she thought about what she had planned, the more restless and unhappy she became. She got up and began walking up and down.

That is how Minti found her when she entered her older sister's room. 'May I see the photographs of your Nile cruise with Maneka *didi*?' asked Minti, just finished with her homework for the evening.

Nalini had hidden away any photo that included Rattan; but the rest she handed over to her sister.

Standing over her sister's bent head, she saw Minti shuffle the photographs, pointing out this and asking questions about that. While the young schoolgirl *oohed* and *aahed* over the scenes in each glossy, Nalini thought of all those absent others that had tried to capture other, more precious, moments she had shared with Rattan.

And there were other memories too . . . those not contained in any two-dimensional snapshots. They were printed indelibly in her mind, and deep in the gut of her senses.

'Perhaps I have been unfair to myself . . . and more than fair to Rattan when I allowed, even sought out Rattan in those dark nights on the *Shaharyar*,' thought Nalini, moving away from her sister, and looking blindly into the darkening night outside.

Maneka had warned her, and warned her repeatedly. And she had not listened. She had been well and truly carried away. How unwise she had been! For now her heart would always be held ransom by him and his unforgettable caresses. It would be so much harder now, to make cold and dispassionate decisions ...

Nalini kept thinking about her situation after Minti left her room, and much after the household at Bharat Bhavan had turned in for the night. She hardly slept, tossing this way and that in her bed as she heard, wide eyed, all the night sounds ticking in the huge house. Her mind zigzagged its way non-stop through all the dark cul de sacs of her situation. She thought of her days on the cruise, of the things she had been forced to discover, and how she had dealt with them. She thought about Maneka's letter. Her friend had not had much success with her inquiries in New Delhi. This began to worry her. Later, it occurred to Nalini that maybe Maneka was, ultimately, a reluctant interlocutor.

Was she also temperamentally unsuited to the task? Perhaps.

With the dawn, Nalini was clear about one thing. Maneka was absolutely the *wrong* person to be involved with Rattan and his past. How stupid of herself not to have realised this in the very beginning! And to think she had actually planned to involve Maneka as both sleuth and mediator!

Nalini would telephone and tell her — as tactfully as she could — to let things be for the time being. She would try calling that very day, and mentally began calculating the time difference between Cairo and New Delhi so that she could catch Maneka at *Sahayata* that afternoon.

Outside the window, the Nile flowed past; but Nalini did not thrill at its early morning loveliness. Today it seemed just a dirty old river, flowing tiredly towards its annihilation, full of the carelessly discarded trash of the sixteen million and more human beings living on its banks, indelibly staining its beauty.

*   *   *

Nalini finally got through to Maneka after four tries only the next day, and had a long conversation with her. Maneka was full of news and details, recounting to Nalini all that she had been doing since she had returned from Cairo. These included a visit to Nalini's grandmother to deliver the gifts that Nalini had sent for her.

'*Naanima* is not doing too well,' said Maneka. 'She is confined to bed, and seemed very weak.'

Nalini was all concern, and wanted to know what the doctor had diagnosed, but Maneka did not know.

'I didn't really ask her,' said Maneka. 'I was there for so short a while. But she asked all about you, and Ajay and Minti. I did not say anything about Rattan . . .'

'Good,' said Nalini firmly.

Maneka began to talk again. Bhasker had gone on a three-month trip out of the country. Maneka speculated on how ironic it would be if her ex-husband had finally landed a job for himself. She was also full of the impending visit of David Winters, who had decided to explore India as part of his work. Maneka seemed quite excited at the prospect, and began to consult Nalini about what she should do to make his stay a memorable one. Nalini tried her best to advise her, but her mind was more on the real reason for her call.

It was only when they had been speaking a good ten minutes that Nalini was able to tell her friend that she should refrain from trying to meet anybody regarding Rattan.

'Just find out the location of the *ashram* where Mrs Malhotra goes, and the residential address of Mrs Madan, Tanvi's mother. The rest I will deal with when I come into Delhi in early May, when Ajay and Minti's school is closed for the holidays.'

'Have you met Rattan again?' asked Maneka, her voice belligerent over the airwaves.

'Not really,' said Nalini briefly, making it quite clear that she was not prepared to speak any further – or even listen to any of Maneka's already known conclusions – on the subject. The long-distance conversation ended shortly after, and Nalini took refuge in her preoccupations.

Nalini *had* met Rattan a few times. When they met on the Republic Day celebrations in that January of 1993, it seemed to Nalini that life for her had come full circle. As in the previous August, the Indian community had gathered on the lawns of the Chancery to sing the National Anthem and unfurl the Indian tricolour. Dressed formally in a printed silk sari and a shawl, her hair tied up behind her head, Nalini had stood with her father and the other officials of the Embassy in the receiving line and had shaken hands with Rattan.

Rattan could see from her face that Nalini had been under strain. When his turn came, he merely greeted her and her father with a formal bow, and had made as if to move on. But Gautam Thapar – after casting a quick glance at his daughter – had stopped him for a few minutes, asked about his welfare and exchanged pleasantries. After exchanging a few witty remarks, Rattan had walked away quickly, and gone looking for Vinod and Madhu Gupta.

Rattan and Nalini had caught up with each other later – after the tea and snacks had been served, and everyone was clustering together in the sun to feel warm in the slight breeze blowing onto the lawns from across the river. It was Rattan who had gone up to Nalini as soon as he saw that she was, for the moment, alone. He had taken a cup of steaming tea in his hands, and without saying anything, had handed it to her. If she was a little surprised, she had not shown it. She had sipped it silently, looking around surreptitiously to see if they could be heard by anyone. But Rattan had known better than to begin anything controversial in so public a place.

'When can we meet again?' he implored.

Nalini had been silent for a few minutes.

'Maybe we shouldn't . . . meet,' she had said finally. 'I mean, maybe we should take a break from each other, and be sure of what we feel . . .'

'I am sure of what I feel,' Rattan had said, cutting her short. 'I am ready to do whatever you want me to do . . . you only have to tell me.'

'It is *I* who have to do what I have to do,' said Nalini. 'Not you . . .'

'Yes . . . I suppose so,' said Rattan, his voice sombre.

'Let's not begin again . . .' Nalini had said quietly. Her face immediately showed her distress. A nerve flickered nervously down the middle of her forehead. 'I'll call you . . . soon,' she said, making as if to move away.

'No, I will call you . . . and you must not refuse to come to the phone,' said Rattan quickly, desperation in his voice.

'OK,' said Nalini. 'But try the office first, please, before you try Bharat Bhavan.'

Rattan barely had time to agree to what she said, because a posse of ladies had begun to walk up to Nalini, their silk saris and pashmina shawls fluttering in the breeze. He saw that Madhu Gupta was one of them, and was looking at him and Nalini speculatively. Rattan had not wanted to face her or anyone else either. By the time Nalini had turned around to greet them, he had quickly moved away, leaving the Chancery through the gates immediately after, without stopping to talk to anyone.

As she watched him leave, Nalini realised that all her efforts at keeping a cold, rational distance from him had come to naught. She still ached for him, and it had taken all her self-control not to reach out and touch him, or to tell the world that he was hers, and she his.

Nalini and Rattan met three times that February of 1993, but on each occasion they spent time with each other only in public places. Much as Rattan tried to have her visit him in his apartment, Nalini would not agree.

Since her phone call to Maneka, she had, subconsciously, begun to see the period between February and May as an interim dedicated to waiting. There were things she had to do, people she had to meet — and they all were far away in New Delhi. Till the Thapar family's trip home in the summer, she could do nothing about them. She did not tell all this to Rattan, for it would have seemed that she was being unnecessarily unfair and judgemental about him. But neither did she want not to see him. Each time they parted, each would go home restive with longing. Their meetings were interspersed with marketing tours outside Cairo for him, and wearisome parties both inside and outside Bharat Bhavan for her.

So it would have continued, until Fate intervened. One day, in the middle of March, the inmates of Bharat Bhavan received a phone call from New Delhi. *Naanima* had been taken ill with a heart attack, and then a stroke. She was in a coma. The doctors had advised that all those who wanted to be with her should come quickly. Closer to her than any other of the old lady's grandchildren, Nalini wanted to go at once. Gautam Thapar looked at his daughter speculatively for a few minutes.

'You had better go, my dear. I know you will not be able to rest in peace if you don't.'

'What will you do with Ajay and Minti? . . . And what about you, and the house?' said Nalini, all concern.

'We will miss you a lot, but we will manage. *Aji* and Mani Ram are there. They will cope . . . You have trained them well.'

Nalini felt torn; but her father, guessing more than Nalini knew, encouraged her to leave immediately. His daughter was looking a little peaky lately, and a trip back to New Delhi might do her some good.

Once the decision for her departure had been taken, Nalini found herself becoming immensely calm. It was the calm that precedes a period of hectic, potentially life-changing activity. So quickly were the arrangements made for her flight to India, that Nalini barely had time to tell Rattan that she was leaving. He was so busy at meetings that it took four or five frantic tries to get through to him on the phone, and their conversation was over in three minutes. She did most of the talking: she was leaving that very night, and no, it would be impossible for them to meet. No, she did not know when she would return, but she would stay in touch.

It was only after she rang off that Rattan realised that she had given him no address or phone number in New Delhi. If he wanted them, he would have to ask her father. And that he did not want to do at all.

A Truth Told

Naanima passed away five days after Nalini's arrival in New Delhi. Those five days Nalini spent mainly in the hospital, sharing shift duties in *Naanima*'s room with her mother's two sisters, and a cousin. They were difficult days, physically and emotionally draining for all around, and particularly hard for Nalini, since, after her own mother's death, it had been *Naanima* who had provided the most comfort and solace. She had always been a matriarchal figure, powerful in the strength she gave to all members of her family, especially its women. There was nothing *Naanima* could not advise you about, and her calm in the face of adversity was a quality Nalini always tried to emulate. In her death, Nalini mourned her mother all over again, and there was nothing her tearful aunts could say to her that would give her consolation.

The next week was spent in completing all the rituals of *Naanima*'s cremation, and other ceremonies. Her house in Patel Nagar was full of relatives, paying their final respects to the universally loved woman. Nalini helped her aunts in making everyone comfortable, even as arrangements were made for the scattering of her ashes at Haridwar, and her last *havan* in the local temple went smoothly. Throughout all this, Nalini could not help thinking how proud her mother would have been of her. Mrs Thapar had always been concerned about how her children would learn the customs, considering they had lived abroad for most of their lives. Now that Nalini had been present for two deaths within two years of each other, she had become well acquainted with all that was required to deal with them.

But her mother was not there to see this.

The day after *Naanima*'s death, Gautam Thapar called from Cairo.

'How are you, my dear?' he asked Nalini.

'I'm fine,' she replied quietly.

There was silence for a few seconds. Gautam Thapar was trying to gauge how upset and affected his daughter was at the death of her grandmother. He guessed that she was quite in control of herself.

'Shall I fly out to you?' he asked, his voice deep with concern.

'Well, the cremation is over. Only the *chautha* ceremonies remain, and they will take place on the fourth day after the death. I asked Meena *Mausi* about you coming yesterday. She did not think it was necessary . . .'

'Can I speak to her, please?' asked Gautam Thapar.

Nalini called for her aunt who reiterated that there was really no need for him to go to so much expense and fly over.

'Nalini is already here, she can represent you and the family. In any case, I don't think you should leave Ajay and Minti alone. You know how it is . . . a trip to India can easily last ten days and more.'

They chatted a little more and then Nalini went back to speaking with her father. She asked about Ajay and Minti, who'd been quite shocked at their grandmother's death. Though neither of them had broken down, they had become a little quieter in their activities.

If Nalini was a little disappointed about her father's not coming to India, she did not show it. The *chautha* ceremony took place as planned and there were many friends and relatives present at the memorial service. It was then that she missed his presence because everyone asked about him, some even wondering at his absence. However, as the days passed, she began to feel that it was just as well. She had told him that she would like to stay on in New Delhi for a few more days, and return to Cairo only in the last week of March, even early April. He had been indulgent, telling her that she could stay as long as she wanted, but that she should be careful about not letting herself get too depressed by the atmosphere in her grandmother's house. Nalini had reassured him, feeling a little guilty about her feelings of relief at his absence, and for *not* telling him about the real reasons for wanting to stay on. Now she could do what she had to do single mindedly and without having to make explanations to any one.

Two days after the *chautha*, Nalini told her aunts that she would like to stay with her friend Maneka Saxena for a few days. Nalini quickly packed a few clothes in a small overnight bag, making sure that they included a few ordinary cotton *salwar kameezes*. Two sweaters and a shawl completed her packing and, hailing a three-wheeler later that afternoon, she wound her way towards the *barsati* where Maneka lived.

Her arrival coincided with Ahmer's return from school, and Maneka's from her college an hour later. The two friends met as in old times, quite forgetful of the strains and tensions that had entered their relationship in their last days together in Cairo. Maneka showed Nalini to Ahmer's room where a bed had been laid out for their guest from Cairo. Maneka was a little apologetic about not being able to give Nalini a room to herself. But Nalini cut her short.

Nalini and Maneka returned to talking of Rattan later, after dinner was done and Ahmer had been tucked in for the night. Nalini sat on Maneka's bed and began the subject herself. Maneka was a little cautious in her replies, feeling instinctively that the days of lecturing Nalini on the wisdom of a relationship with Rattan were over. She did not tell Nalini that her instructions to leave things be had hurt her a little. Nalini sensed her friend's withdrawal and felt badly, but there was nothing she could do about it. She asked whether Maneka had had any success with finding Tanvi's parents' home.

'I've always had the Madans' address,' said Maneka quietly. 'It's Pammi Malhotra's *ashram* that I can't locate.'

This last piece of information brought some of the old outrage back into Maneka's voice. Nalini hid a smile, saying quickly that she would go to 73 Hauz Khas herself and see if she could get it.

'Maybe you should go by yourself to both places,' said Maneka after a pause. She believed that Nalini would have more success on her own. 'They associate me with the women of *Sahayata*, and will think that I have come to make trouble. You, my dear, are not going for that purpose.'

'No, at least, I hope not . . .' said Nalini, her voice serious. 'I am going to find out the truth . . .'

'"What is Truth?" said Jesting Pilate . . .' quoted Maneka, her voice tinged with irony. Shrugging her shoulders, she did not wait for Nalini's reply. 'But I guess, you have to do what you have to do.'

There was silence for some moments.

'You *know* I have to do these things,' said Nalini quietly. Her eyes did not meet Maneka's.

On the next afternoon, Nalini accompanied Maneka to *Sahayata*. After all she had heard, she wanted to see it for herself – see how old friends and acquaintances from college had set up a sorely needed institution from scratch, and actually got it going successfully.

Nalini also wanted to see 73 Hauz Khas, and to meet Rattan's mother.

As they paid off the scooter wallah in front of the gates of *Sahayata*, Nalini looked around. Numbers 73 and 74 Hauz

Khas were as adjacent as Maneka had described them: their driveways separated by a five-foot-high brick wall over which it must have been easy to see — especially from the upper floors of both houses — what was going on in each compound. Now a tall, black wrought-iron fencing (erected after Tanvi's death) hung over and a dense, dark green foliage of some rather wild, unfriendly creeper blocked the view from the ground floor. Since there had been no rain yet, the dust of the end of March coated the leaves and ledges all around. Though the sun was beaming warmer, the *gulmohur* trees lining the road on either side still had their branches bare. And the lawns of both houses had brown, uncared-for and under-nourished patches.

New Delhi seemed preparing for the coming of summer. But Nalini's first impression was that the inmates of both houses were not doing much to survive it. For those in 74 Hauz Khas, other more life-saving subjects occupied their attention: lawns were hardly important in the context of rescuing women's lives from potential destruction. All the money *Sahayata* managed to collect every month was used to pay for electricity and water, kitchen budgets, and legal and medical expenses incurred on behalf of their clients. At the time of Nalini's visit, there were nine women sheltering in *Sahayata*. And each was in a bad way. She got talking to some of them. Their stories were more or less similar. The younger ones had run away from hateful husbands and bullying in-laws; older women had run away from uncaring children. Their stories were heart-rending: when their situations had become life-threatening, they had run away to — or been rescued by — *Sahayata*.

Nalini felt anger rise in her. She understood completely from where her friend had got her hatred of the injustices of patriarchy — and of men in general. It was understandable and justified, and for just those few minutes Maneka's suspicions about Rattan and his family coursed through her own heart. Maneka had overriding evidence that such things happened, and happened frequently. She herself had none. The starkness of the contrast shook her completely, making her need, suddenly, to sit down on one of the old wooden benches that lined the foyer-reception of *Sahayata*. Maneka was inside somewhere, and Nalini was glad of her absence, for it gave her solitary time to know what to think. It was hard to do so. Rattan was far away; but the scene of his (supposed?) crime was right next door.

How would she *now* do what she had come all the way from Cairo to discover?

As she looked around blankly, it suddenly occurred to her that maybe the others in *Sahayata* thought her yet another of its inmates – as much in search of shelter as the other women. The thought made her smile a little. Everyone needed shelter from the essential loneliness of existence. Some found it at once, and easily. Others had to look for it – and repeatedly. For the first time in her life, she felt that she herself was in need of it.

Maybe Rattan had needed to look for it too? And, he *had* a right to that second try, didn't he?

It took Nalini a few minutes to find her feet, and to dredge from the depths of her mind the sustaining quality of her experiences with Rattan. She *had* to remember those – to re-live them in her mind in all their nuance and intensity. And while she did so, she found that she had stood up without knowing it, and was walking down the driveway towards the gate.

Smiling absently at the *chowkidar*, she waited until he had opened the gates. As she stepped out onto the road, she turned her face towards 73 Hauz Khas. Its high gates were shut; and in the sentry box – standing slightly askew outside the gate – dozed a security guard.

'*Bhaiya?*' Nalini called out tentatively. The guard did not hear her.

'*Suniye, bhaiya?*' she said loudly. He heard her, and she watched him stir.

'*Hamme Mrs Malhotra se milna hai,*' said Nalini politely.

At once the guard was all alert. '*Ghar me koi nahi hai,*' he said sharply.

'*Mr ya Mrs Malhotra ... inmay se ek to hoga?*' said Nalini firmly. '*Bahut zaroori kaam hai.*'

The guard gave her a piercing look, his head cocked to one side as if making some kind of assessment. He was a little irritated, both at Nalini and his own situation. Though he had been told to give this answer to all who asked for the owners, he had also got into trouble once or twice for refusing entry to friends and relatives of the Malhotra family. Was this chit of a girl, dressed in a shabby, unstylish *salwar kameez,* a desirable or an unwanted visitor? He could not tell. But he decided to play safe. He opened the gates a little, and yelled out to someone inside.

Nalini caught a quick glimpse of a once gracious house, now in need of a coat of paint. Its windows were shuttered, and the lawn unkempt. Expensive plants in fancy pots – palms and crotons – needed watering. And at the far end of the driveway, just in front of the garage shutters, sat a group of men – servants of the house? playing cards. A couple of used tea mugs lay around, as also did bottles of water, and a steel tumbler or two. One of the men was sleeping, his feet sprawled out towards the gates, and his head resting on a bit of rolled red fabric serving as a pillow. The others were speaking in loud, raucous tones. As the game ended, the winner yelled loudly, and threw down the cards in his hands in a loud gesture of triumph.

Standing at the far end, outside the half-shut gates, Nalini took in the scene.

So this was Rattan's home; the place where he had grown and come of age; left for the USA; returned; married; and lived and celebrated life with Tanvi. Somewhere, deep inside, would have been their bedroom – only too shockingly transformed into the scene of the crime. And now, in this March of 1993, nobody seemed home. Only servants lived there; and in the name of being caretakers, had taken over. She heard the security guard shout

out to a Hari Ram. She saw the latter rise slowly from outside
the edges of the card-playing circle, and walk up towards her.
He spoke briefly, and in low tones.

'*Koi nahi hai ghar mein. Sab bahar gaye hain,*' he said, his
voice low.

'*Mujhe memsahib se milna tha,*' repeated Nalini.

But he said the same thing again.

'*Sahib kahan hain?*' asked Nalini, not yet ready to give up.

'*Desh se bahar hain,*' said Hari Ram.

He gave her one last, conservative look through his spectacles
and turned away. Nalini could tell that he had done with her.
She accepted her dismissal and turned away herself. She had
no reason to disbelieve him. If Mrs Malhotra had been home,
none of the servants would have dared sit around in the
driveway in such casual fashion. She would have to look for
her elsewhere. Maneka was right. It was going to be hard to
meet the Malhotras.

In the meantime, she had another important trip to make.
But she hadn't given up on the Malhotras yet. She *would* find a
way to locate at least one of Rattan's parents.

Even though Nalini had come to dread her visit to Vasant
Vihar, she undertook a rough ride in yet another three-wheeler
to the Madan home two days later. And this too in the teeth
of opposition. It was the day of *Holi*, and Maneka advised her
to wait a day or two before venturing on the roads: everyone
would throw colour on her, and there was also the possibility
of running into hooliganism by unruly teams of young men, out
on a lark. However, Nalini was adamant. She decided that the
only concession she would make to Maneka's dire warnings was
to wait until the afternoon before setting forth. Tradition had
it that colour-throwing would stop by lunchtime. She and her
friends from the university hostel had risked a similar trip into
South Delhi once, and had met no trouble at all.

She tried to put herself in the Madans' place. She tried to imagine what would persuade a respectable middle-aged couple to let a strange young woman into their house, and speak frankly about the tragic death of their only daughter. She decided to be as open as possible, and do her best to respond suitably to the kind of welcome — if any — she received.

As the three-wheeler went up the long Africa Avenue towards outer Ring Road, Nalini looked around. There were signs of colour on the ground. Here and there walked the last few groups of the morning's revellers. Pushing herself as far back as she could into the rear of the rickshaw seat, Nalini tried to be as invisible as possible. A pair of nondescript dark glasses, and a drab shawl wrapped around her shoulders and the lower part of her face, helped to meld her into its darker interior. She noticed that the driver's clothes were spattered a dark green, and he had red marks discolouring his forehead and cheeks. Near her feet, on the floor of the rickshaw, were the remains of purple powder, slowly blowing away as the rickshaw began to move.

So *Holika* had been burnt, and the event celebrated. As they turned into Poorvi Marg, Nalini told the driver of the auto rickshaw where she needed to go.

A few turns down bumpy roads, and Nalini found herself in front of Tanvi's maiden home. B 1/53 said the number on the gate. Below it was printed 'M.V. Madan'. For a minute Nalini debated whether she should ask the rickshaw man to wait for her — maybe nobody was home, and she would have to return. She looked towards the house. It was the only single-storeyed structure between higher ones on either side. Its gate was tightly shut, and the wall along its front face was high enough to hide the windows and doors of the house. Somewhat daunted by the unwelcoming exterior of the house, Nalini took a deep breath. Behind her stood the waiting rickshaw. She decided immediately that she could do without an audience. She paid off the driver; and, taking off her dark glasses, unlatched the gate. Without looking around she walked briskly up to the main door along the side of the house, and rang the bell.

It was a few minutes before she heard some movement inside. It was opened finally – a small crack – by a woman about fifty years old. Her small, thin face peered at Nalini around the edge of the brown wood.

'Yes?' she said. 'What do you want?'

'I wanted to meet a Mrs Madan ... or Mr Madan. Are you Mrs Madan?' asked Nalini, her voice softly tentative.

'Yes, I am Mrs Madan,' said the woman, opening the door a little wider. She spoke again only after she had looked down the driveway behind Nalini to see if she was alone. 'And you are ...?'

'You do not know me, but I am Nalini Thapar. I have just come from Cairo. I need to talk to you ... about something very important ...'

'About what?' asked Mrs Madan, immediately suspicious. Nalini wondered if the mention of Cairo had alerted her.

'I am a friend of Rattan Malhotra, your son-in-law ...' said Nalini.

'I am sorry, but I do not have anything to say about him ...' said Mrs Madan abruptly, stepping back and making as if to shut the door on Nalini.

'Please, Mrs Madan,' said Nalini, immediately putting out a hand to hold the door open. 'I have to ask you a few things ... I mean to marry Rattan Malhotra, and I want to know about him and Tanvi ... Please! You *have* to help me ...'

Her voice was desperate. Mrs Madan stared at her, her eyes rounded in apprehension. 'My husband is not at home now, and I don't know whether ... who are you, anyway?' said Mrs Madan, hints of hysteria in her quavering voice.

Nalini began to speak, trying consciously to make her voice calm and persuasive. She told the older woman reassuringly that she had nothing to fear from her. She was the daughter of an Indian Foreign Service Officer who was currently posted as India's Ambassador to Egypt. She lived with her father in Cairo. If Mrs Madan did not believe her, she was ready to show her red, diplomatic passport to prove her identity. As she said this, Nalini made as if to open her handbag and take it out.

At this, Mrs Madan looked embarrassed, and indicated that it wasn't necessary. Nalini began talking. With a few sentences serving as a preamble, she announced that she had met Rattan Malhotra a few months ago, and had come to care for him.

Mrs Madan heard her without saying a word, curiosity writ large over her face. Nalini wondered what she should say – or do – next. Both women stared frankly at each other. The older woman was looking Nalini up and down – taking in her earnest face, her wind-blown hair, her printed cotton *salwar kameez*, and her feet shod in kolhapuri *chappals*. In turn, Nalini could not help noticing the slightly faded, crushed cotton sari, the straggly hair, the stress lines and harassed expression of the woman in front of her.

For a while nobody spoke.

'You do know, don't you, that after Tanvi's death, Rattan found a job in Egypt and has been living there for the last few months?' asked Nalini, holding on to the door more tightly than she knew. She had understood instinctively that Mrs Madan would need some prodding.

'Yes, I had heard something like that . . . so he told you about Tanvi, did he?' said Mrs Madan slowly, an immense sadness in her voice.

'Yes, he did,' said Nalini firmly. 'But I need to talk to you about some other things . . .'

Mrs Madan was silent. She stood a while, at first looking contemplatively at the young woman standing steadfastly before her; and then gazing over her shoulder to some vision beyond.

Nalini was sure that she was thinking of her dead daughter, and felt badly about resurrecting all those images and truths which she must have been trying so hard to forget. But she put such considerations aside firmly – she had to do what she had to do. Squashing all qualms, she stood there waiting for Mrs Madan to make up her mind.

Mrs Madan did not move or speak. Neither did she look towards her unwanted visitor. Nalini watched her taut face anxiously. The silence grew.

'I could come back tomorrow, if you so wish ...' said Nalini at last, her heart softening, and going out to the bereaved mother.

Again, Mrs Madan did not speak. But her eyes focused piercingly on Nalini.

Nalini tried to guess what was making Mrs Madan hesitate. 'He loved Tanvi, you know ...' she said quietly.

Immediately, Mrs Madan began to cry. Deep sobs racked her body even as her hands found the ends of her sari *pallav* to wipe her eyes. Nalini found that it was she who was holding the door open to the Madan home. She waited quietly for a few minutes, sharing the woman's grief.

'Come in, please. I guess he has a right to make another life for himself ...' said Mrs Madan finally, her words choking between her sobs. Slowly she moved away from the door into the house.

Nalini shut the door softly behind her and followed the older woman to the living room. Putting her handbag down on the floor, she tried to sit as still as possible till Mrs Madan was ready to talk.

It was a while before she did. She began by asking Nalini where and how she had met Rattan, what he was doing, and how he had taken to the death of Tanvi. Nalini told her that he had been devastated, and had only recently begun to feel sane about things. As Nalini heard herself say all this, she realised that her conversation with Tanvi's mother would contain some falsehoods – even some imaginary constructions – about the way Rattan had felt and behaved after he had fled New Delhi. There was no point in doing otherwise. If Mrs Madan had any reservations about her son-in-law, Nalini hoped she would express them. In fact, Nalini quite banked on this — how else would she know how Tanvi's parents felt about Rattan and his behaviour towards their daughter?

'He was a good boy . . . He did *really* care for her. Only that afternoon Tanvi had told me how devotedly attached and gentle he had always been with her.'

'Did they ever quarrel about anything?' asked Nalini.

'No, never. At least, not as far as she told me,' said Mrs Madan.

There was a pause. Nalini let the bereaved mother remain silent in her memories.

'Do you know what she looked like?' asked Mrs Madan.

'Who?' asked Nalini, confused for a minute.

'My daughter, Tanvi.'

Nalini replied in the negative. At this, Mrs Madan got up from the sofa and walked across to a bookshelf lined with a series of photographs in old frames. One of these was relatively new, and outlined the face of a young woman dressed as a bride. She handed it over to Nalini.

Immediately, Nalini felt an extraordinary surge of strange associations with the girl in the framed photograph. The bond tugged at her as a deep sensation in the pit of her stomach. Nalini looked at the girl's small, piquant face, the ends of her shoulder-length hair curling cutely around her ears, and visible below the ends of the golden fringe of the *odhni* covering her head. Her nose was set at a perky angle, and her expression was wide-eyed. There was a certain innocence in the half-smile that played around her mouth. She looked happy and carefree. Nalini felt she had known her intimately, and would continue to do so, for her presence would always remain a shadow hanging over her and Rattan. It would link her with him always in many indefinable ways.

So deep was Nalini in her contemplation of the girl in the photograph that for a minute she forgot where she was. So this was Rattan's Tanvi! She imagined her with him — by his side, in his arms, sharing his bed. What exactly had they shared? A lot probably – and then he had killed her? The thought seemed an impossibility. She noticed vaguely that Mrs Madan had gone to a low cupboard on the far wall, and had taken out another photograph in a frame. Slowly she handed it to Nalini. This one was of Tanvi and Rattan – bride and groom – taken from up close. Both looked radiant, although Rattan had less of a smile on his face than Tanvi.

Did that make him a potential murderer?

'What happened that day?' asked Nalini.

Mrs Madan told Nalini about how her daughter had come in, about noon, to have lunch with her. Tanvi had decided not to join her mother-in-law and her friends for the cards they played regularly at each other's homes once a week. Since it had been Mrs Malhotra's turn that week, she had decided to stay out of the way, and visit her mother. Mother and daughter had talked. And eaten. And talked some more. Tanvi had told her about her impressions of the home she had moved to.

'She was a little in awe of her mother-in-law, but was full of love for her husband,' said Mrs Madan.

'And then?' prodded Nalini.

At this, Mrs Madan began crying again, and it was a while before she spoke. Nalini felt helpless, dark dread heavy in her heart. Was this the moment when she would learn the truth? She watched carefully as the mother pulled herself together. In a low soft voice Mrs Madan described how her daughter had left Vasant Vihar at about 4.30 p.m. She had headed straight to the tailor's to pick up some clothes for herself and her mother-in-law. She had reached home to catch the tail end of the card party. After the guests had all left, there was still time before Rattan returned home – time before she began dressing for dinner. She had decided to hand over her mother-in-law's newly stitched blouses to her. She had gone down the stairs to the floor below, and opened the door to her mother-in-law's room. And . . .

'And . . . ?' asked Nalini, with bated breath.

But Mrs Madan did not speak. As the words jammed in her throat, her eyes filled with tears. But this time they were tears of anger and outrage.

'She should have locked her door,' the weeping woman said at last, completely overwrought. 'That was her mistake. If *only* she had locked her door . . .'

'Who had not locked her door?' asked Nalini.

'Her mother-in-law! That Pammi Malhotra! If she had only made sure that she had locked it, then my Tanvi would not have seen what she did!'

By this time Mrs Madan was really agitated. Unable to contain herself, she got up swiftly from the sofa. Sobbing hysterically, she walked away. Nalini followed. What *did* Tanvi see? She had to know.

'Please . . . Auntie! You have to tell me. You have to . . . my life depends on it!'

Mrs Madan nodded. 'Yes, yes. I suppose you have to know . . . if you want to marry him.'

'Yes I do. So you have to tell me . . . Please?' said Nalini desperately.

It was through the muffling folds of the faded pink sari that Mrs Madan spoke again. 'Tanvi saw Pammi Malhotra – her mother-in-law – and Ram Singh, the old bearer of the family . . .' she said at last, unable to finish her sentence.

Nalini heard Mrs Madan in stunned silence while the exact implications of Mrs Madan's disclosure sank in. Nalini tensed in horror. She tried to imagine what it must have been like for Tanvi to be standing in the doorway of her mother-in-law's bedroom and seeing what she had.

Had Rattan known all this? Had he?

And instinctively she knew that he had not.

It was a while before the weeping woman could answer with any coherence Nalini's further questions. When her sobs quietened, Mrs Madan turned around. Her eyes were red and her mouth quivering. When she was a little calmer, Nalini spoke again. '*How* did you get to know all this?'

'On the phone, my dear ...' said Mrs Madan. 'Tanvi rushed back to her room and called me ... she was telling me everything ... and then they got to her. They must have snatched the phone from her, because suddenly it disconnected ... They must have killed her then ... because they knew she knew.'

'Are you sure of this?' asked Nalini, her throat dry with shock.

'Of course I am not sure! I was not there! Who can ever be sure ... nobody else was there! Only the mother and the servant ... and Tanvi. You expect me to believe that my daughter committed suicide?' sobbed Mrs Madan, her grief now coloured with a wild anger.

Nalini was silent. By this time she had put her arms around Mrs Madan and was holding her tightly. Mrs Madan babbled on, speaking of how there was no proof of anything, and if they had insisted on an investigation, everyone's name would have been in the mud.

'But I don't know whether I did the right thing. I don't know. I don't know at all! Now everyone thinks my daughter was mad, or retarded, or lacking in dowry, or unhinged, or depressed, or whatever ... and therefore committed suicide. She was no such thing. She was innocent. She was innocent ...'

As she led the incoherent mother back to the living-room sofa, an immense calm descended on Nalini. Her instincts had been proved right. She had got the answers she'd been looking for. When Tanvi died, Rattan had *not* been in the house. He had not been involved – he was not guilty.

The knowledge made her feel weak with relief. Her mission had been successful.

Unnoticed by Mrs Madan, tears filled Nalini's eyes. Obviously, Tanvi's death could not have been a suicide. She had been killed. It was important to find out who had killed her. But not crucially so, for now she knew it had not been Rattan. She had been proven right about him.

And that was all that mattered.

By the time Nalini left, Mrs Madan had collected herself but did not speak much more apart from asking a few questions about Rattan. How and where had Nalini met him? Nalini had answered as briefly as she could, and not volunteered any extra information. She assured Mrs Madan that she was grateful for all that she'd told her, for it had rid her mind of any suspicion that Rattan was involved in Tanvi's death.

When Nalini returned to South Extension, Maneka was in the kitchen preparing to feed Ahmer. After an exciting day playing *Holi* with his neighbourhood pals, he was ready to go to bed. By the time the two friends could talk, it was late. Nalini told Maneka briefly that Mrs Madan had confirmed that Rattan had not been in the house, and was quite certain that he had not been responsible for Tanvi's death. Nalini was now preparing herself to find Pammi Malhotra and hear her story. Maneka warned that this task would be harder than her meeting with Mrs Madan. Nalini agreed, but was quite clear that she would not give up her quest.

As Nalini got into bed, she was surprised that Maneka had not guessed that there must have been more to Tanvi's death than Rattan's absence. She also wondered why she herself had not told Maneka the whole horrific story. Maybe it was because Maneka had openly indicated a lack of interest in her messy affairs. Nalini regretted the growing distance between herself and her old friend.

But she thought it was just as well. The fewer people who knew about the truth of that horrendous event, the better it would be for her future with Rattan.

The Meeting

Once he knew that Nalini Thapar was no longer in Cairo, Rattan
grew uneasy and restless, always carrying a heavy, cold stone of
dread deep in his heart. The more he thought about her, the
more it amazed him how this tall, slim woman had become the
centre of his life, his reason for being. And he had hurt her. Once
or twice he chided himself for feeling so – many men were so
casual about the women they met and had made love to, and
they would have called him a fool. Couldn't he begin doing the
same? The thought made him smile bitterly. Why was he trying –
even fleetingly – to clutch at such slender and ridiculous straws?
Nalini was not made for secret liaisons. And neither had he ever
looked at her in those terms.

And this, despite all the hidden meetings and other subterfuges inherent in their relationship.

As he struggled to believe that Nalini would give him a
chance, and hold on to their love, Rattan tried to throw himself
into his work, staying long hours in the office, and returning
home as late as he could. However, just as he was about to
go firm on a hectic marketing itinerary, it occurred to him that
should Nalini call, she would find him missing. The thought
was an unpleasant one, so Rattan curtailed his plans somewhat,
taking short trips away from Cairo even as he waited for some
form of communication from New Delhi. His loner existence in

Cairo became more and more enhanced, and the community did not see him for days together. Only Madhu Gupta missed him, calling him every few days to see how he was doing. She invited him for dinner, but after going the first time, Rattan refused all subsequent invitations. The easy and loving camaraderie of the Gupta home and hearth was too painful to bear.

Once he went out with the gang for another round of sightseeing. As before, it was organised by the Guptas. But it was a trip taken under duress and gave him no pleasure. The historical or the unique had no meaning if survival in the present was in question. Without Nalini as companion, it was impossible even to focus on the sights and artefacts at hand let alone wonder at the glory of the human achievements of the past. Nefertiti and Cleopatra may have been great queens, and been remembered for great deeds. But since his mind was full of regrets, he had no time for them. In fact, his mind had become an unforgiving place, allowing no peace for his errors and his even weaker excuses. It was his own fault. Why had he not told her? He should have ... he should have ...

Rattan was just beginning to despair when he got a call from Nalini in New Delhi.

She had stepped out of Maneka's home in the afternoon with the excuse that she would collect Ahmer from his school bus stop. Her timing was right, for it was almost midnight in Cairo. Rattan had just got in after a long day at work, and was lying in bed reading.

When he heard her voice, he could not, at first, believe that it was Nalini. This was the call he'd waited for these last few weeks, and had almost given up on. Nalini sounded calm and collected – even warm. For once, her silences seemed to disappear. She continued to talk even when he himself was finding it hard to speak. She told him about *Naanima*'s death, and the formalities that had followed it. Delhi was getting warmer. They had celebrated *Holi*. She had been staying with Maneka these last few days, and was having a good time getting to know Maneka's son, Ahmer. Rattan listened to all the details of her life in Delhi, relishing the fact that she was talking as if they were good, old friends and taking pleasure that for the first time, after so many disastrous meetings, she was speaking of normal, everyday things as if nothing had happened.

It was only when she spoke about a 'special request' that Rattan immediately became alert. 'I wanted to meet your mother. Pammi Malhotra . . . isn't that her name?' said Nalini.

'Yes,' said Rattan warily.

'Where can I find her? I went to your house . . . but they would not let me in, or tell me whether she was there at all.'

'Did you go with Maneka?' asked Rattan immediately. 'Because if you did, they would never let you in, or even answer your questions.'

'No, I went alone,' said Nalini. 'In fact, it was she who suggested that I go without her . . . I did, but they still would not tell me.'

Rattan wondered why she was eager to meet his mother.

'Why don't you wait . . . I mean, till we are there together, then maybe I could introduce you to her?'

But Nalini made light of this suggestion, saying that she would like to introduce herself on this visit, and then go again as many times later as he wanted. Rattan wondered why Nalini seemed so keen. In fact, he found her request quite out of character. The Nalini he had known was reserved, and capable of a formality and correctness that could be deemed unfashionable. What was she thinking, wanting to meet his mother without him?

Was she checking him out? Was she going to find out things – about his marriage, Tanvi, and her death?

'She is not too well,' said Rattan, hesitantly.

'That's OK, I don't mind! It's just that now that I am here I thought I would take the opportunity,' said Nalini. She kept her voice casual in her effort not to sound too desperate about her desire to meet Pammi Malhotra as soon as possible.

Rattan did not reply. He was concerned whether his mother would even talk to Nalini if he told her where she could be found. She had been so reticent even with him – her son – a few weeks earlier. How would she agree to meet a stranger? He wanted to say all this, but did not know how.

But Nalini did not wait for him to say more. 'Please, Rattan? I would like to do this, you know. It would help me greatly,' said Nalini soberly.

'She is probably at Panna the Fakir's. This is an *ashram* she has taken to visiting regularly,' said Rattan reluctantly. He told her where it was. 'How will you go all that way to Old Delhi? It is quite a distance from Maneka's house.'

'I know my way around Delhi! I went to university in Old Delhi, remember?' said Nalini, some of her old light-heartedness returning in her voice.

'I guess so . . . a good time to look for her would be sometime around noon.'

'Oh?' said Nalini. 'Thanks for telling me.'

Nalini was pleased. She had the information she wanted. She went on to speak of this and that – asking Rattan about his work and his travel plans. She made no mention of what she had discovered, or how they had parted. Rattan was so floored, that he forgot temporarily his recent status of being the guilty deceiver in her eyes. He wanted so much to speak of their feelings for each other now that the distance of oceans and continents lay between them. But he did no such thing. He joined in with the conversation, glad to hear her voice, and that she had called him.

So thrilled was Nalini with her success that it did not occur to her that Rattan might have been surprised at her request. Her mind was full of her own plans. The path of inquiry she was following had a twin purpose – to know the truth about Tanvi's death for herself; and to make sure that Rattan was vindicated in the eyes of the world if she could prove that he was not guilty. If she was to continue to love Rattan, and trust in him, she must know what his mother had to say. This was crucial. Whether Mrs Malhotra would choose to reveal anything was a moot question. In view of what Mrs Madan had told her, she probably wouldn't say anything at all. Nonetheless, Nalini felt she had to meet her –

to see for herself a woman who had – perhaps inadvertently? – put her own son's life on the line. Surely she would say something – anything – to absolve her son when faced with the girl that he had now come to love? She thought over the possibility of Pammi Malhotra refusing to meet her, or even talk to her. What would she do then? She could find no answer to this.

Nalini reached the *ashram* shortly before noon two days later, having taken her overnight bag with her in the scooter rickshaw. She had told Maneka that she was returning to her grandmother's house even as she had called her aunts (still staying on in Patel Nagar), to say that she had extended her stay in her friend's house. All this involved a lot of subterfuge on Nalini's part, but she wanted to avoid a whole host of questions to which she did not, as yet, have any answers. Not everyone, however well meaning, needed to know about the long-drawn-out process of her falling in love with Rattan. Nalini knew that if she and Rattan married, there would be many eyebrows raised and questions asked. She would deal with them all when the time came.

Though she had her things with her, Nalini did not know where she would be spending the night. Abstractedly watching the rickshaw driver negotiate the heavy traffic down Ring Road, she was surprised at herself. Had her father known what she was up to, he would have been shocked and disapproving. So too would all her aunts and relatives. Even she herself would never have dared be so uncertain about her night lodgings a few weeks earlier. But her meeting with Mrs Madan had been earth-shaking, hurtling her out, once and for all, from the protected cocoons of her childhood, and an unusually extended adolescence. Illicit passion did happen outside the movies, and not all the people involved were culprits or victims.

Nalini had no trouble finding the *ashram*, or in locating Pammi Malhotra. She was led at once to the rear of the *ashram* compound. Along its back wall were a row of single rooms, bare of furniture except for two beds per room. In one of these rooms sat Pammi Malhotra. A white towel was wound, turban-like, around her head. As Nalini approached, she bent over in an effort to dry her hair, wet from a recent washing. Dressed in a white cotton sari and blouse, she looked like any other middle-class, middle-aged housewife.

She did not, at first, look at Nalini, who stood for a minute gazing around, and then sat down on the empty *charpai* on the other side of the room. Even though it was the middle of April, the air was cool inside the windowless, bare room. Pammi went about her business as if she were alone. She shook out her towel, and moving outside the door, put it out to dry on a clean patch on the grass. She went to a small wooden shelf nailed roughly onto the wall, and picked up her comb. She sat at the edge of her *charpai*, laid out with a mattress and a clean white sheet, and began combing her hair. Her tall, still erect figure, and rather large haggard face had an air of a deliberately grave surrender about it. Her eyes did not connect with anyone or anything around her. She seemed intent on her own thoughts, and on the silent words that hovered around her mouth.

At first Nalini thought she was at prayer, and kept as quiet as she could. But as the afternoon wore on, she came to the conclusion that Pammi Malhotra probably thought that she was another guest of the *ashram*, needing to stay for a few days. Looking at the closed eyes and silently moving lips, Nalini also felt that this was no special prayer time – that Rattan's mother would go on this way all day if she did not draw attention to herself.

Not knowing how to, Nalini waited almost an hour more before she chose to speak. She spoke softly, introducing herself as Nalini Thapar who had come all the way from Cairo, Egypt. She said this deliberately, hoping that the mention of Cairo would find – just as it had with Mrs Madan – some kind of response in Pammi. It did not. Pammi smiled vaguely, putting out a hand as if to welcome her to the room and did not say anything.

There was silence for some minutes.

Nalini tried again. 'I know your son, Rattan,' said Nalini, her voice slightly louder – and firmer – than before.

Pammi Malhotra still did not respond, but she seemed to have heard, for Nalini felt that the older woman had suddenly stilled all her body movements, waiting for more to be said. In her turn, Nalini also waited ... and waited, until she realised that *both* were waiting for each other. Nalini was nonplussed, and began to wonder desperately what she should do next. Or even say next. This meeting was going to be so much harder than the one with Mrs Madan. The latter's tears she had been able to deal with. But this deep, uncommunicative silence was a different thing altogether.

And Pammi Malhotra continued to remain silent. Nalini watched her pick up the pillow from her *charpai*, and from under the rough sheet on the bed take out a small mat. This she proceeded to put on the ground between the *charpai*s. After she had smoothed out all the edges with the deliberate, slow movements of her fingers, she sat herself down, cross-legged and buddha-like. As she settled into a comfortable position, she closed her eyes. Soon, her lips began to move with small thin movements. By this time she was quite close to Nalini, sitting on the adjacent *charpai*. Nalini noticed the lean, gaunt profile of high cheek bones and a small narrow mouth, a long nose (that must have looked attractive in a fuller, healthier face), the dark circles under her eyes. Her neck was scraggy – obviously the result of a drastic and sudden reduction in weight – with deep folds of skin overlapping each other in an ugly way. But she seemed oblivious of all these.

A few moments later, her body took on a god-like stillness.

But the expression on her face told another tale. There was no calm there – the moving muscles and twitching mouth had their own troubled story to tell.

Was this woman responsible for the death of Tanvi? Could this ascetic-like figure be capable of the kind of prohibited desire that Mrs Madan had described?

It did not seem possible.

Nalini sat around for a while. The afternoon was on the verge of ending. The slanting rays of a slowly diminishing sun filtered through the doorway, silhouetting the woman sitting on the mat in seeming repose. How long she should wait so, Nalini had no way of knowing, but then a small, shrill bell rang in the distance. Since Pammi had not moved or responded, Nalini wondered whether she had heard it, but a few minutes later Pammi moved a little, and then slowly opened her eyes to focus immediately on the space through the open doorway.

It was only when she stood up that she looked towards Nalini, and gave her an infinitesimal half-smile. But having done so, she immediately turned her face away.

Then Pammi spoke. 'You love Rattan?' she asked, her voice parched and dry.

Nalini did not reply.

'I am sorry . . . I have not spoken in a long time. So maybe I do not sound very clear . . . but do you love Rattan?' said Pammi, clearing her throat as she spoke.

'Yes, I do, very much . . . I met him in Cairo a few months ago, and got to know about . . .' said Nalini, halting as suddenly as she had hurried into speech.

'About Tanvi, isn't it?' asked Pammi, her voice full of a preternatural calm.

'Yes . . .' said Nalini, unable to say more. The aura of Pammi's presence was overwhelming, even frightening. She sounded like a ghost, speaking from the caves of the dead.

'Do you believe him guilty of her death?' asked Pammi. Her voice was low and flat.

'No, I do not . . .' said Nalini trying to sound definitive. But her voice emerged shrill and squeaky. 'But I do not know that as a fact . . .' continued Nalini bravely.

'That is correct. You do *not* know that as a fact,' said Pammi. Her voice was thoughtful, and full of speculation.

There was silence for a while. In the distance could be heard hushed whispers of women talking, and the sound of slippered feet walking the grounds. Nalini remembered the bell, and wondered whether it had signalled the beginning of some activity. It seemed so because she saw that Pammi Malhotra was slowly putting on her slippers. At the same time, she had cast Nalini a penetrating glance that seemed to pierce deep into her soul.

'Will you come with me, please?' said Pammi.

'My name is Nalini,' said Nalini helpfully.

'Yes I know. Nalini Thapar ... I have been waiting for you to come.'

Nalini was amazed. She could not understand what Pammi Malhotra meant by that statement.

'Yes, I have been waiting for you all these months. Now I think all will be under control ... I mean, for Rattan,' said Pammi, as if in reply to something Nalini had said.

Nalini was even more mystified. She did not know what Pammi meant – although it seemed that the older woman felt she was understanding it all. By this time Pammi had begun walking on ahead, and Nalini had to scramble into her slippers so that she could follow her. The two women walked across the open spaces of the *ashram* grounds. They were bare of any attempts at beautification. The grass had dried in most places, and the ground was criss-crossed with paths trodden out by the weight of walking feet. Only one odd tree, growing a hundred years, stood in the middle, lending its shade to one or two women sitting under it. Its trunk was surrounded by a round platform about three feet high, which made a natural podium for anyone who might wish to speak out to a gathering of people.

Pammi skirted the tree in her loping, light-footed walk. She was really quite a tall woman, and walked with a natural elegance that seemed out of place in her surroundings. Nalini thought of 73 Hauz Khas, its statuesque proportions contrasting sharply with the modest 74 Hauz Khas, home of *Sahayata*. The *ashram* made for an even starker contrast. Nalini looked around at the other inmates. They were all women – but a motley lot. Those who crossed their path had uniformly blank faces, and seemed to exist together but in isolation, for other than a slight nod of recognition, no greetings of any sort were exchanged.

Nalini hurried to stay abreast with Pammi, for she was walking swiftly. Around them, the shadows of dusk were giving way to oncoming darkness. The birds were twittering loudly, and the night crickets were beginning to make up the chorus. Somewhere in the distance a buffalo mooed loudly. A bell clanged. A faint smell of incense, heavy and venerable, hung in the air. Nalini followed her leader. What other surprises lay in store for her if she finally got to marry Rattan? Was this the 'Destiny' people talked about so much? So far, Nalini had made her choices carefully, and always faced the consequences bravely. Now everything was out of her hands – out of her control.

For the first time in her life, Nalini was full of fear. Pammi had taken her by the hand and was guiding her along. Where was she taking her? Were they going to meet some *sadhu* or soothsayer? Was she to be part of some strange ceremony or observance? She hoped not; for she was no believer in *jadus* or mantras, and had no desire to be part of any rituals that her rational heart could not understand.

The two women passed through the beaded curtain, the dark passageway, and the deep, cavernous, high-ceilinged huge room that was the abode of Panna the Fakir. Nalini felt the brighter lights of the outer world fade away before the darkness of the dim interior, and for a few minutes she could not see. She could only feel herself being pulled along by Pammi towards a dim source of light at the far end of the hall. She walked blindly, looking instinctively downwards and using her feet to feel the terrain before she put forward her next step. Her head lifted from the ground only when she felt Pammi had slowed a little, and she was in danger of walking straight into her guide's back.

It was then – as her eyes lifted – that she encountered the larger-than-life vision of Panna the Fakir. He was sitting on a high platform, an almost godlike figure considering how close his seat was to the ceiling of the hall. Around his head floated white snake-like trails of foggy incense. They were the only things moving in the room, and seemed to hold heavily in their entrails all the air in the chamber. A few smoking *diyas* lit the place, although afterwards Nalini felt sure that there must have been a few electric bulbs placed strategically behind – and beyond – to ensure the effect of the fakir's dark and majestic presence. He seemed dressed in a *dhoti* of red. His torso was bare, and across his right shoulder was a saffron cloth. It came down to his waist, and seemed to flow parallel to the brahmanical holy string down the same side. His hair, tied in a top-knot, was white, as also was his long and flowing beard that covered the length of his chest.

Standing many feet below – and at a distance of about four metres from the platform – Nalini could feel a prickle of apprehension run up her spine. Pammi tightened her hold on her hand as they came to a standstill. Both women gazed at the absolutely still figure of the fakir who seemed bathed in a fiery glow. Only the flames were missing. So taken up was Nalini by the power of the scene in front of her that she half expected a real conflagration to billow out from either side of the immobile fakir.

Pammi stood beside her, silent and still. As her vision cleared, Nalini ventured to look around. The hall was quite bare, but capable of taking in at least a hundred people as audience to the fakir. What Pammi was waiting for, Nalini did not know.

And then, suddenly, he spoke.

'So you have come,' said Panna the Fakir, his voice rasping through the orange yellow light. It bounced in echoes along the black walls of the hall.

'Yes, Maharaj,' said Pammi folding her hands in a deep bow. To do this, she had to release Nalini's hand. Feeling immediately that her moorings had been cut loose from her, the frightened young woman took a step backwards involuntarily. Pammi's clutch had been her anchor in this strange and dark place. With it gone, she felt adrift far out in a flaming sea. In the confusion, she quite forgot that she ought also to have offered her *pranam* to the old seer. At a complete loss, she stood there, insecurely, and waited.

The fakir spoke again. 'Is she the one? The one we have waited for?' he asked, his voice even louder than before, and booming across the room.

The voice startled Nalini. She looked around nervously.

'Do not be frightened, young woman,' said the fakir emphatically. 'She has met him?'

'Yes, Maharaj,' said Pammi.

'Good. Come here, young girl. Do you know this woman's son?'

'Yes, Maharaj,' said Nalini, her voice a hushed whisper.

'Will you care for him always?' the old seer asked again, his voice loud and peremptory.

'Yes, Maharaj,' said Nalini, but her voice was firmer than before.

'Good. So the evil *graha* is over,' he said, addressing neither of the women in particular. 'Tell her the truth, please.'

There was a pause. Nobody moved. Nalini waited. It dawned on her slowly that this last sentence had been addressed to her companion.

Pammi stood as still as before, neither moving nor speaking. Her eyes had closed, and her lips had begun moving again. Nalini could feel the fakir's eyes boring through both of them. And she could feel the weight of his stare.

The silence in the hall was thick and stifling.

At last, Pammi moved. She turned her face towards Nalini, and with her head hanging downwards, moved her mouth close to one side of Nalini's face. Nalini heard her at first fumble for words. And then she spoke, her whispering voice loud in Nalini's ears.

'She was killed by me, and Ram Singh. Rattan is innocent.'

But even before Pammi Malhotra had completed the last

words of her sentence, Nalini had moved, her hand moving swiftly to cover the older woman's mouth.

But what had to be said, had been said. And heard.

'Shh, shh. There is no need to say any more,' Nalini said softly, her arms going around Pammi. Pammi stood stiffly, allowing herself to be held. Nalini understood her reserve immediately, and slowly released her.

The fakir sat there, a strong overpowering witness. But his eyes were closed. The two women waited. Was this the end? Nalini hoped so, temporarily quelling the dark joy of her discovery deep in her heart. She wanted to dance in open spaces, to celebrate. Now she knew one thing for certain: that her faith in Rattan had been vindicated. So much for Maneka, and the real world! Both would be around them in the future, and would have to be dealt with. But she had her own piece of truth that the world did not know of.

Neither did Maneka.

Could they not go now? Go to where they could breathe freely – and deeply? Would they have to wait for the fakir's permission to leave?

But he took a while to give it.

'*Sukhi raho, beti,*' he said, addressing Nalini, his eyes still closed. 'Now the boy will be fine. She has freed him of the hold of evil . . . But you must bring him to me within the year.'

'*Ji, zaroor.* As quickly as possible,' said Nalini swallowing quickly, and bowing her head in obeisance. His eerily sombre words had forced her to return to the immediate present.

Beside her, Pammi remained silent. And waited. Slowly, Panna the Fakir raised his right hand. Its palm was open, and bent over them.

Was he blessing them? Or was he imparting absolution?

They left soon after, backing out of the place with heads bowed. As they moved, Panna the Fakir seemed to recede into the depths of darkness. And just before they exited into the long narrow passageway leading to the beaded curtain, his aura had become a reddish glow, shining out of the black distance. Nalini took one last look, and moved beyond his presence.

Outside, night had fallen. But even then Nalini could see more than she had been able to inside Panna the Fakir's abode. Where had she been with Pammi Malhotra? Had that been a vision or a waking dream? She shook her head slightly to free her mind of what she had been through. Familiar objects of the world of the *ashram* slowly took shape, making her feel real again. There was the old tree, surrounded by its platform. In the distance, loomed the residential quarters lit by a weak bulb inside each open doorway. Women walked by, their female forms as familiar as her own.

How good it felt to have one's feet on terra firma!

By her side walked Pammi, her back stiff and erect. But her gait was subdued. It was a living reminder to Nalini that blood had been spilt, and its retribution had demanded that she be part of it — that she be a companion to the guilty one's journey to realms other than the rational. Walking silently alongside the older woman all the way to her room Nalini willed herself to sober down. Squashing firmly her singing heart, she told herself that she should not overdo her sense of victory. There *had* been a young girl who had died before her time, and in the vindication of her own intuitive belief in Rattan's innocence, Tanvi could not be forgotten. Instinctively Nalini thought of Maneka. Dear old Maneka! The world would always be difficult for women — although not always in the way thought, or predicted. And, both Maneka and *Sahayata* had been responsible for her discovering the truth about Rattan and the death of Tanvi.

Were it not for them, Tanvi's death would have remained unsolved, and Rattan always stand falsely accused in the eyes of the world. Now at least one person apart from the guilty knew the truth.

In the Shadow of the Pyramids

In Cairo, Rattan waited impatiently for Nalini's return. After that one call, she had not phoned again. Though busy at work, his mind kept returning to her and all she had chosen to speak about. Why did she want to know where his mother was? Why could she not wait till *he* was with her in New Delhi? Had she, in fact, managed to find her? And, had their meeting been successful? 'Successful' was a strange word to use in the context. But Rattan could not help feeling uneasy about the encounter. He wondered how Pammi would react to a strange young woman claiming to know her only son. How would she respond to Nalini? Would she at least give her a decent welcome and a patient hearing? He so desperately wanted his family to create a good impression. However, since he himself had found Pammi's behaviour distant and strange, he had his doubts. Pammi's reaction could only have been negative.

The thought made him squirm, and it took a lot of concentration to stop agonising about it. Some things were out of your own control, and there was nothing you could do. But it was time he made another trip to India. It was already more than three months since he had last seen Pammi. Soon it would be May, and the coming of summer. He should get to New Delhi before the hot *loo* winds made his trip unnecessarily difficult.

*   *   *

Nalini's thoughts were in tumult. Her desire to announce Rattan's innocence to Maneka — and then to the rest of the world — had long given way to a calmer, more considered understanding of the matter. To proclaim Rattan's innocence was also to invite the next question — who, then, had killed Tanvi? Nalini was in no way prepared to answer this question, and others that would inevitably follow. The death of a young girl would always need to be explained, vindicated, and probably even avenged. But if Tanvi's own family had maintained silence, who was she — Nalini Thapar — to reveal the truth?

Also, she was in love with the dead woman's husband. How would publicising the truth help them both?

Moreover, Nalini knew that Tanvi's death — however horrendous — had not been premeditated. As both Mrs Madan and Pammi Malhotra had vouchsafed, Tanvi had inadvertently walked in on Pammi and Ram Singh in bed together. Horrified, she'd run back to her room. The guilty pair had followed, and found her on the phone to her mother. Her death had occurred in the scuffle that ensued. Although both Pammi and Ram Singh had tried to wrest the phone away from Tanvi's ear, it had been Ram Singh's rough handling that had been responsible for the cracking of her neck. In the hysteria that followed, it had been his suggestion that they should make it look like suicide, and the dead Tanvi be suspended from the ceiling. Shaking from head to foot and almost hysterical, Pammi had agreed, her teeth chattering a 'yes, yes' as Ram Singh had made his suggestions. She had not contributed much to the proceedings, even though the business of getting the pink *chunni* tied around Tanvi's neck *and* around the fan had been a difficult business.

But she *had* done her share of helping Ram Singh to complete the task.

What the police or any court of law would have to say about the nature of Pammi's responsibility, Nalini had no way of knowing. Maybe Pammi would be declared legally 'guilty'; maybe she would not. But Pammi had been both sanely present and actively involved. She *had* picked up the dressing-table stool and put it on the covers, adjusting it so it was placed directly under the ceiling fan; she *had* stood on the bed, holding on to the inert form of Tanvi so that Ram Singh, standing on *another* chair, could tie the knot of the *chunni* around the fan. And she *had* stood there and watched Ram Singh kick the dressing-table stool off the bed so that it looked as if the desperate-to-die Tanvi had kicked it aside. She *had* stood there, and watched the girl hang even as Ram Singh had made sure there were no tell-tale signs or any evidence that could implicate them. And she *had* made sure that he picked up the chair (used by him to stand on the bedclothes) and took it away, out of the room.

All these details Pammi had told Nalini at the *ashram*. It had taken Pammi a long time to begin talking.

As the minutes had ticked past, Nalini had felt Pammi's eyes upon her, coming to their own conclusions. Pammi's mind was at battle with itself. She had not wanted to talk further; yet there were questions to which Nalini needed answers.

She had spoken finally.

'How is Rattan?' she had asked, in a louder than natural voice, like that of the newly deaf.

Nalini had told Pammi that her son was doing well, but felt guilty and inadequate after the death of Tanvi. She had also said that she was going to marry her son even though he had not yet asked her to do so. At this Pammi had raised her eyes from the ground and smiled a crooked smile.

At last Pammi had begun to talk. She had made Nalini promise that what she was going to hear would remain confidential between them. If her son was to marry again, his wife-to-be should know the whole truth.

'All I can do, is to clean his slate of the death of Tanvi. None of all that happened was his fault ... and *you* need to know this.'

Having said this somewhat emphatically, Pammi had gone on to narrate the exact circumstances of that fateful evening. Her voice had remained calm throughout, and she had ended by saying that Rattan had not been present at all, entering the house only three hours later.

'But does Rattan know what happened?' Nalini had asked.

Pammi Malhotra shook her head in silence. 'No. He does not.'

Relief had flooded Nalini's heart. 'Thank you for telling me.'

'Thank *you* for trusting in Rattan . . . And you do understand that I will never speak of this again,' Pammi had said soberly.

'You will never need to,' Nalini had replied, looking at her with guarded sympathy, but with an unsaid promise in her voice.

Pammi had not spoken after this; and Nalini had understood that there was no need for more conversation. The hour was late, and the *ashram* silent. Both women had prepared for sleep. Later on, Nalini felt a cotton blanket being laid carefully over her. She had wanted to protest that it was April and she was not cold. But she had felt the gentleness of Pammi's concern for her well-being, and had been touched. Through hidden eyes, blurred by tears, Nalini had seen and accepted Pammi's considerations for her.

Lying still on her bed in the dark, Nalini thought about all that she had discovered and experienced. There were still so many questions. She would, for instance, have liked to know more about Pammi's marriage with Noni Malhotra. What circumstances of desire had prompted a woman like Pammi to become so dangerously caught up with a servant in her own house? She wanted to know whether her husband and son knew of this. It did not seem so – in which case, how had she kept it so well hidden from them? And from everyone else in the house?

Why had Mrs Madan and her husband decided not to pursue investigations regarding the mysterious death of their daughter? Did they really think this silence was the best way out in the circumstances? Did they not feel any desire for revenge — or justice? Had they kept silent because they genuinely thought Rattan to be innocent, and wanted not to destroy his future? Did they love him *so* much?

All these questions also made Nalini realise her complete ignorance of the law. Couldn't she herself be accused of concealing the truth from the authorities?

Nalini lay awake till late. She decided, ultimately, that it was not her place to either ask anything more or tell anything to anyone. She was merely an unwitting outsider to the Malhotra family saga, but one who seemed inadvertently to have become its custodian. It was a burdensome thought, and its weight allowed her to fall asleep — only fitfully — just before dawn.

Nalini left the *ashram* at eight o'clock the next morning, with no more said. She had waited for Pammi to give her a clue about what she should do next. None was forthcoming, and Nalini made ready to leave. But just as she was stepping out of the door, Pammi came up to Nalini and slowly removed a thin gold chain from around her own neck. When she had disentangled it from her hair and sari, she put it around Nalini's. A small 'Om' pendant dangled from it, and was soon lost in the folds of her *chunni*.

Nalini was quite overwhelmed. It was a completely traditional gesture, and took Nalini by surprise. Was this Pammi's way of conveying an acceptance of her place in Rattan's life? Was this a sort of blessing? For the first time Nalini allowed herself to hug the older woman. It was a tight, unspeaking embrace. There was also something final about it. Though both women were overwrought, both remained in tight control, the hint of tears glazing each set of eyes ignored deliberately by the other. When she finally walked out through the doorway into the bright light of a new day, all Nalini could see for a few minutes was a tall gaunt woman with quivering lips and a crushed white sari, raising a hand in silent farewell.

It was in such a state of mind that Nalini hailed an auto rickshaw and returned to Patel Nagar. This was the best. Her aunts would think she was returning from Maneka's, and ask her no questions. Nalini was thankful for the long drive. In the chaos of traffic she could disentangle the truths she had discovered from the conflicting emotions they had engendered. By the time she had paid off the rickshaw driver, she had collected herself, and could put on a calm front before the aunts who were around, sorting out the legalities of the dead woman's estate. That evening a lawyer arrived, and the living room became full of legal details.

'So much to be sorted out when a life ends,' thought Nalini.

Her own life had hardly begun. And yet, there was much to be sorted out there too!

In the few days that remained of her trip to India, the one thought that gnawed at Nalini was how — and how much — she would tell Rattan. The fact that fate had singled her out to be the great revealer of the Malhotra family secrets made her shudder. Would she be the one to tell Rattan about his mother and Ram Singh? Would she be the one to tell him exactly how Tanvi had died? She hoped not; yet she saw that it could become inevitable. She imagined different ways of doing so, but found each scenario unsatisfactory. Rattan knew only the tip of the iceberg of the whole affair.

But why would he suspect that his own mother had something to hide? The thought made Nalini feel badly for Rattan — and for herself who knew the whole tawdry story. Nalini smiled ruefully. What else did she expect? She had actively sought this knowledge, and would now have to live with its consequences.

* * *

Nalini called Rattan the day she returned to Cairo. Her heart lifted as she heard the pleasure of welcome in his voice. For the first time she felt that she too could express her own gladness, and did so, telling him frankly that she had missed him. In her own mind she celebrated the fact that now she did not need to be afraid of her father, her own larger family, Rattan's past, or the truth. It lent confidence, even a sense of gaiety, to her voice. Rattan asked anxiously how soon they could meet and Nalini took pity on him, and suggested they meet on the following Sunday afternoon.

'I wish to go riding by the Pyramids of Giza,' she said, a grave mischief in her voice. 'I have much to tell you, and I don't want anyone to hear. We will ride far away, behind the Pyramids, and into the open desert. Even the Sphinx won't be able to hear us there!'

Rattan accepted, unable to keep the surprise out of his voice. How could she get out of Bharat Bhavan on a weekend afternoon? She had never agreed to any such thing before! Wouldn't the family want to know where she was going? But Nalini said coolly that she would tell them.

Tell them that she was going riding with Rattan Malhotra, and would be back after dinner.

Nalini's ride into the desert with Rattan that Sunday afternoon was the stuff of romance. Not much of a rider, Nalini had, nevertheless, suggested the outing for purposes of her own. She had never been out behind the shadows of the great Pyramids of Giza, and in her current state of mind, wanted to get away from the confines of inner-city living which characterised life in both New Delhi and Cairo. Ideally, she needed a long holiday with Rattan, away from the scrambling reality of the present, away from family, relatives, friends and all the circle of acquaintances that inevitably hemmed her in most of the time. But, given the circumstances, an afternoon where she and

Rattan could talk, undisturbed and in the open, was all that was possible now.

The April day was warm without being hot, and the late afternoon sun shone on the yellow sands, its glare slowly receding. Two friendly Egyptians led their horses along, away from the Pyramids and into the wide untouched open spaces on the plateau of Giza. There was no one else around. After riding for about two hours, the party stopped for a rest in the shadows of a large dune. As the Egyptians and their horses settled down, Rattan and Nalini walked around the dune, out of sight. Finding a hidden niche in the sands, they made themselves comfortable.

Much was talked about and told initially in those enchanted moments. But as the orange sun set, Nalini felt acutely the weight of the graver side of her relationship with Rattan. Though he had asked many questions about her stay in New Delhi, and about her meeting with his mother, none of them were about Tanvi. Nalini was cautious with her replies, watching his face carefully to see if there was anything he knew about how Tanvi died. But there was nothing in his questions that tallied with the facts she had discovered.

Rattan's silence about Tanvi – his obvious reluctance even to mention her – began to trouble Nalini. Surely such silent indifference amounted to a kind of hard-hearted and forgetful callousness? There *had*, after all, been a woman named Tanvi. A woman like herself who had loved and trusted innocently, *and* met with a horrible and unfair end. Was nothing – not even a ratifying memory – owed her by the one she had committed herself to?

And what was she, Nalini Thapar, a reluctant custodian of the secret of the unfortunate bride's death, to do next? Was she also – like society – to go ahead and forget her?

These questions bothered Nalini greatly. Man and woman lay side by side, the still-warm sands beneath them, watching the night fall and envelop them. Nalini felt Rattan relax, but found that she herself was getting restless and uneasy. Suddenly she sat up and bent over Rattan. She tried to look straight into his face, but in the growing dark she could not see it clearly. As her fingers traced the eyebrows, nose and the outlines of Rattan's mouth, she could feel his desire for her grow. She felt him move, turning her over roughly so that he was on top of her. She felt his mouth find hers, and returned his kiss. But when he tried to hold her closer, she resisted, and made as if to move away from him.

'What is the matter?' asked Rattan in surprise.

'Nothing, really,' said Nalini.

There was silence between them. Rattan searched for something to say, but in his perplexity, could not. He moved away to lie by her side, his body stretching against hers in proprietary proximity.

It was she who spoke again first. Her voice seemed to come from a distance, and its echoes whispered across the sands. 'You know, I hated it when my mother died. Death is final. It ends everything, altering the known and familiar equilibrium in relationships,' said Nalini 'Those who leave are never forgotten, their memory always making for a dull ache in the heart. And those who are left behind find themselves playing new, only dimly understood roles . . . and not necessarily enjoying them.'

Rattan remained silent.

'I really don't care very much for being hostess and house-keeper in my father's home,' said Nalini. Her calm tones belied the force of her words.

Rattan did not think he was expected to reply. But after a long pause he spoke. 'It was the right thing to do. And necessary . . . for a while at least . . . It softened the consequences of your mother's death for Ajay and Minti, and your father too,' he said softly, careful to hide his surprise at the angry vehemence lingering under the surface of her words.

When the silence between them stretched even further, he

spoke again. This time his tones were carefully mild. 'And, you do a good job. *And*, it made it possible for us to meet ...'

Still, Nalini did not reply. Just as Rattan was beginning to wonder why she had not acknowledged his teasingly blatant, unsubtle compliment, she spoke again. 'Do you ever think of Tanvi?' asked Nalini.

Her question knifed the darkness between them.

Rattan froze into a stillness; and Nalini felt him do so. He seemed, suddenly, to have shrivelled away and was no longer touching her. The distance seemed to enhance the creeping chill of the evening.

He sat up carefully, his movements slow and deliberate, buying time. She sat up too, dusting the sands away from her tumbled hair. He knew she was waiting. 'Yes, I do ... and all the time. And especially when you will never let me forget her,' said Rattan, a dull deep-seated bitterness in his reply.

Nalini remained silent, knowing that despite the hurt it had caused, it was a question that had to be asked.

'I am sorry if this upsets you,' said Nalini. 'But we cannot forget Tanvi, ever.'

'Who says I have forgotten her? You don't know the half of it! If only I *could* forget, and completely ... Why do you do this? Do you take pleasure in reminding me?'

Nalini did not reply, but felt Rattan's unstated anguish flow in waves around her. How could she tell him that she knew things he did not? And that she too had begun carrying the weight of her own secret crosses? What was she supposed to do with the burden of the knowledge she had sought and gained so recklessly? Would she have to carry it around through the walkways of life, silently alone?

Probably.

As Nalini saw Rattan stand and walk away from her, she understood that there was no point in persisting – no point at all. This would happen every time Tanvi was mentioned. Maybe later, much later – when the uncertainties inherent in their own relationship had lessened and he was sure of her and she of him – they would be able to talk of Tanvi. Or maybe, they would not talk of her at all. Maybe she would just remain a young woman in a photograph adorning some shelf, cupboard or album in her mother's home. And maybe on the hidden, unspoken mantelpiece of their minds – hers and Rattan's.

She looked around. The desert was dark and silent. She saw the first few stars emerge in the darkened sky. Behind her and the man she had come to love were the ancient pyramids. And the Sphinx. The ever-watchful, immortal Sphinx who knew all, but did not tell – a spirit disconnected from the material universe around. As it saw them sitting there – she and Rattan – so must its cool, inscrutable eyes have seen others over the centuries, seeking the privacy of distance from the ancient yet pulsating metropolis crowding behind them. It knew that, in a few quickly tumbling decades, both she and the man beside her on the sands would go down into the dust of history – their smallness and stupidity all intact.

And completely forgotten.

Nalini had a sense of being reduced to a mere speck of humanity, only by chance made to live in this summer of 1993, but repeating the secret history of other loving and hurting mortals before her. There had always been great lovers and great sinners; and even greater sinners in love. This was true in Cairo and New Delhi, and surely everywhere else where men and women sought each other in the great mating dance. What, in the great expanses of time and space, did it matter whether Rattan knew what his mother had done? It was already almost a year since Tanvi's death. Her parents had already chosen to forget and, in time, forgive; and those responsible for her death were already punished to live in their own private hells.

That left only her and Rattan, together in the desert. And a chance to be taken for happiness in a life together.

*   *   *

The ride back was a silent affair. It was dinner at the Mena House hotel that improved matters somewhat. They chose a window table and gazed at the illuminated silhouettes of the Pyramids. Food and fine white wine lightened the mood between the two tense lovers.

By the time Rattan dropped Nalini home, much of their old relationship had been restored. Their farewell kiss outside the gates of Bharat Bhavan was long and passionate, arousing needs that left them impatient and dissatisfied about such mundane cultural imperatives as the necessity to sleep in separate beds and separate homes. But since it was Nalini's first sanctioned night out with Rattan – and it was already past midnight – they gave in to them.

Nalini told her father about her decision to marry Rattan a few days after he formally asked her. The so-called 'question' had become a joke between them, because it was Nalini who pointed out that whatever else existed between them, he had not really asked her to marry him. Rattan's face had quickly broken into a smile. Immediately bending down on one knee, he had asked her, with mock formality, whether she would agree to be his wife. She had laughed and with many kisses agreed.

When Gautam Thapar heard about his daughter's decision, he was relieved, and after Nalini assured him of her feelings for Rattan, further discussion ranged around when and where they thought the wedding would take place. Nalini hedged her answers, saying that it was much too early to decide anything. Rattan was to visit New Delhi in the coming weeks, and would tell his parents about his decision. Only after this could Gautam Thapar meet Rattan's parents, and further plans be made.

Gautam Thapar remained quiet, thinking to himself that he had better move quickly, for he did not particularly like these continuing pre-marital meetings between his daughter and

Rattan Malhotra. But he did not say this to Nalini. He heard patiently all the details that Nalini chose to tell, and remained noncommittal. When she said, casually, that Rattan had been married before, and that his wife had died early, he still did not say anything. But in his mind he was alarmed and decided to investigate.

He would get someone in New Delhi to check on this immediately.

Nalini was not deceived. She knew that the wheels of convention – and no doubt her father's protectiveness – would begin moving soon.

She was ready, though. But for the moment, she would let things be as her father wanted them.

Rattan left for New Delhi three weeks after their sojourn under the stars in the Egyptian desert. The eight days that he was away were ones of great anxiety for Nalini. Nothing at the *Al-Ahram Weekly* was challenging enough, and things at Bharat Bhavan seemed the same as ever. There was a delegation of officials in town, and Gautam Thapar had to entertain them at the residence. To the dinner that was prepared for them, Gautam Thapar invited other Egyptian officials and their wives. Nalini tried hard to be interested in the progress of the bi-lateral talks between the two countries, but found it hard to do so. Her mind was on Rattan, and her own future with him. But at least the responsibility and supervision required to make the evening a success called for some concentrated attention. For this Nalini was glad – it took her mind off her worries for the time being at least. Menus, groceries, seating plans and protocol were issues far removed from love, unpalatable discoveries and second chances. But their sheer repetitiveness and mundane quality was sobering. It made her go around the formal areas of Bharat Bhavan like an automaton, ticking off items from an already memorised check-list of things to do. *Aji* and Mani Ram did what they had to do, and Nalini looked for the finer details to make sure that nothing was forgotten.

The evening was a success, and so were the talks. Egypt and India decided to collaborate on some joint ventures which both sides promised to sign in the next round of talks to be held in New Delhi, three months later. In the next few days Gautam Thapar spoke repeatedly of impending visits to New Delhi, and chafed that three months could easily become much longer, knowing well the delays inherent in the Foreign Offices of both the Egyptian and Indian governments.

Nalini knew there were other reasons as well for his impatience but did not comment on them. She even remained silent when she heard him make long-distance calls to the desk officers in charge of West Asian countries in the Ministry of External Affairs in New Delhi in search of an earlier trip back to India. Nalini wished him success: the quicker things came out in the open, the closer she would be to beginning her own life with Rattan.

The Sunday following the party saw Nalini receive a letter from Maneka in the Diplomatic Bag on her return from work. As Nalini turned the envelope in her hand, she saw that it was a long one – as long as those she had been used to receiving earlier. She was pleased, and relieved. Whatever the contents – which still remained to be read – Maneka had obviously found it as necessary to communicate with her as in earlier times.

Carrying it to her bay window, Nalini sat down to read.

5th May, 1993
Flat no 4, 4th floor
273 South Extension
New Delhi – 110051

My dear Nuns,

Have not heard from you since you left, and thought I would spend a few minutes writing to you as in old times. I have found time to write because teaching finished a few weeks ago. I was so glad when term got over. We teachers have done what we had to, and now it is the turn of the girls to get down to it. I have had six exam invigilation duties. Only two are left, and I shall be done for the summer. The two invigilations are for afternoon exams. Imagine how hot it will be — both for us invigilating and for the students writing the exams! But it is like this every year.

Sahayata is doing well. Now that the summer vacations are upon us, I can spend more time there. Ma is fine. And so is Ahmer. He too will have holidays soon, and I will have to juggle my time at Sahayata with his summer activities. I wish I could come to Cairo again, and this time with Ahmer. He would love coming on such a trip. But of course that is not possible.

Thinking of Cairo, I have much to tell you. David Winters did finally come to New Delhi. He was here a full ten days. That was far more time spent in this city than planned. He came over quite often, and I helped him as much as I could with travel agents, and airline offices planning tours in India. He is serious about selling India as a rest-and-recreation destination for the executives of companies in the USA. You may remember, we talked vaguely of this when together on the Nile Cruise.

He has got to know Ahmer quite well. He was very patient, and spent a lot of time doing things with him. Ahmer has also taken to him, and talks about him a lot. In fact, this has got us both into trouble with Bhasker. When Ahmer went for a weekend to his father, he mentioned David Winters often. My dear ex-husband did not like it! Can you imagine? He called me one afternoon at Sahayata (I should be getting my own phone line soon. Shall let you know the number as soon as I get it) and yelled at me, saying that there was no need for me to expose his son — his son, mind you! — to another potential father-figure. I was so furious that I banged the phone down on him. The cheek of the man. He thinks he owns me!

David did ask, though, whether I had ever thought of going to the USA to work on a Ph.D degree. I said that I had not, so far. He thought that I was ready for it, and that he would help me seek admission in some university in the USA. He, of course, suggested Wisconsin, which is where he lives. I am seriously thinking about it. My college would give me sabbatical leave, I know. And it would be a good break for me too. A good break from college, and Sahayata, and Bhasker, and from everybody-and-everything here in New Delhi. And David said there would be no problem about Ahmer. He could come along, and be like any other single-parent graduate student's child.

He really is being very sweet and helpful about it. What do you think, Nalini? Shall I give this David Winter and his suggestions serious thought?

I shall not ask you news about Rattan. I know that you have already made up your mind. You did not tell me anything about what you discovered about him in your trips to Vasant Vihar and the ashram in Old Delhi before you left for Cairo. In fact, you did not even call to say good-bye before you left India. I was a little hurt about all this. But I guess, since I made my views about your Rattan abundantly clear, you could not have wanted to do so.

But some day — and soon — I would like to talk about all these things. We have known each other too well, and too long, to let some man/men come between us, don't you think?

How is everyone at Bharat Bhavan? Please give my love to Ajay and Minti, and regards to your father. Tell Aji, I remember her wise words often. It is she who has always fended for herself. Maybe I should learn more from her.

Love to yourself, and write soon.

Love,

Maneka

P.S. I really miss the Nile. People here cannot believe that I lived on its banks for a month. They are green with envy. Thanks again!

Her friend's letter brought a sober smile to Nalini's face. Maneka was Maneka still, although somewhat less strident than before. But this was a Maneka she liked better. Nalini re-read the letter quickly, noting that Maneka had not hesitated to express her sense of being let down by her. Nalini felt badly about this. It had also been hard for her to leave New Delhi without saying good-bye. But she had done so deliberately, knowing instinctively that her dear old friend had still not been ready to hear about an altered view of Rattan and, anyway, she had too many secrets to keep.

Thus, the way things turned out, what Maneka had feared had happened. 'A man – and his love – *has* come between us,' thought Nalini, folding the letter in her hands and pushing it back into its envelope. But wasn't that the way it had to be? Nalini smiled, sure that before long Maneka herself would also discover the truth about this. Already 73 Hauz Khas and *Sahayata*, Bhasker and the Indira Gandhi Memorial College for Women seemed to have become less prominent in her mind. Other, newer concerns were taking their place. It was obvious that David Winters and the USA were going to loom larger and larger on her horizon. There would be secrets there, and newer personal arrangements too.

But Nalini knew better than to ask about them. She would be told the details as and when Maneka thought it necessary.

In the meantime, she had her own life to think about. And Rattan to wait for.

When Rattan returned from India, his mood was darkly pensive. Nalini was apprehensive too, for she wondered what had been his family's reaction to his wanting to marry again. She was particularly curious about how Pammi Malhotra had behaved, and what she had told her son. When Rattan picked up Nalini after work and drove her to his apartment, he did not at first speak much on the way.

When he did at last, his voice was low and brooding. 'I am worried about my mother, she's not herself, she is completely changed ... She's become so thin, like a ghost. All the time she was with me, she was incoherent, saying all kinds of mad and crazy things ...'

Nalini kept quite still in her seat, watching silently as Rattan negotiated his car through the rush-hour traffic. She wanted to ask questions, to say what she knew, but kept silent.

'Did you meet her at Panna the Fakir's?' asked Nalini at last, for his silence had gone on long enough.

'Yes. I had to go there all over again! I don't like that place ... I don't like it at all,' said Rattan vehemently even as he braked suddenly to stop for the red light. 'It is creepy enough to make you go quite insane ... in fact, I think it has got to my mother. Her white saris, and her old, bare *chappals* were so unlike her. And she said all these strange things ...'

There was silence again. Nalini waited for him to continue.

'She kept talking of Tanvi,' he said, looking accusingly at Nalini. 'Like you always do ... she drove me crazy ... Sometimes she said Tanvi committed suicide; at other times she said she was killed ... by "evil powers in female form", or something like that. "What evil powers are you talking about?" I asked her. But she would only say: "They all knew. All the servants knew, especially Ram Singh" ...'

Nalini remained silent. A knot tightened in her stomach, even as the deep growl of the car reverberated under her.

This was the time – come at last – to tell him all she knew. Inside her heart she felt that Rattan ought to know, for their own sakes, and for the sake of Tanvi.

He had to know, didn't he, what had happened?

But the words stuck in her throat, and she could not speak. She groped wildly for determination, telling herself that if *she* were in his place, she would have liked to know.

But she remembered her promise to Pammi, and said nothing.

Silence reverberated in the small interior of the car. Outside, the lights had turned green. As the vehicle ahead of them began to move, Rattan shifted gears roughly, and the car lurched forward. Nalini wanted to run away to escape the hard facts of knowing and telling. When she heard Rattan speak again, it seemed as if his voice came to her over a great distance. She had to force her mind to attend to his words.

'In the end she got quite hysterical, and went on talking about the card party, and Ram Singh ... You haven't met Ram Singh. He used to be the second servant in our house. But my mother fired him for some odd reason after I left for Cairo. I don't know why she is so obsessed with him! She just went on and on, I had to tell her to stop, and not talk any more ...'

Nalini sat still, clenching her hands and keeping them out of sight by her sides. She might well have been one of Egypt's carven statues, stone-like in her concentration not to do or say anything that would disturb the chain of Rattan's thoughts, or the mood in the car.

She was immensely thankful when their short journey to Tahrir Square was over. Rattan's mouth was darkly set, and his body rigid with the anxiety of responsibility, and the unwanted memories of foggy truths.

'Somehow, it was very hard to leave my mother this time,' he said at last, holding on to the steering wheel of the car and resting his head on it for a few seconds. 'She is not well ... She is not well at all.' His voice, when he finished speaking was low and despairing.

Above them the *muezzin* called the faithful for evening prayers.

Allahu Akbar; Allahu Akbar.

As they stepped out of the car, a breeze swirled the trash at the edges of the street around their ankles. Two alley cats scrabbled for scraps. The *bawab*, who had now come to recognise Nalini and Rattan, felt the need to clear the way for them. Flapping the wide sleeves of his flowing cotton *gallabeya*, he shooed the pocked felines away. They ran off, uttering meows of disgust.

Not well at all . . . not well at all . . . not well at all . . .

Rattan's words echoed in Nalini's ears, seemingly bent on eliciting a reply, a statement, *anything* . . . from her. All the way up to the ninth floor, she did not say a word, willing herself to stay firmly away from him, on one side of the elevator car in which they were enclosed.

She so wanted to hold him, and tell him all. To remove, once and for all, the searing white blankness of ignorance. Knowledge is power, someone had said. But knowledge was also danger and hurt . . . an unhealable, debilitating, perpetually oozing hurt. Human beings did sometimes spare each other, didn't they? Couldn't Rattan also be spared from knowing the truth? What would he really gain by knowing what she knew? What would *she* gain by adding to the millstone of his memories?

And so she didn't say anything . . . deciding then, that there were some things that would − at least for now − remain unspoken between them.

She would speak of them later.

Glossary of Indian Words

adrak – fresh ginger root; essential in Indian cooking for its sharp taste and aroma.

agarbatti – thin sticks of fragrant incense, often sold by beggar women at traffic lights on the streets of New Delhi.

Aji – literally 'grandmother' in Marathi. Here used affectionately for an old maid-servant of the family.

The Al-Ahram Weekly – well-known Egyptian weekly newspaper published in English.

'Allahu Akbar' – literally 'God is great' in Arabic. The phrase forms an essential beginning to the muezzin's call for prayer five times a day.

almirah – anglicised version of *almari* in Hindi, meaning cupboard.

alu methi – a popular dish in north Indian cuisine in which potatoes and fenugreek leaves are cooked together.

anars – a variety of firework shaped like a pomegranate and lighted in open spaces during Diwali. When ignited it sends up sparks which are supposed to resemble the red grains of the pomegranate.

angrez – Englishman/foreigner, sometimes used pejoratively.

'Arre baap re!' – literally 'Oh, my father!' in Hindi.

'Arre bhai!' – literally 'Come on, brother!' in Hindi.

arti – the concluding, thanksgiving part of any ritual Hindu prayer ceremony. It consists of a lighted flame in a metal *thali* (or plate), which is waved in circles in front of the presiding deity to the accompaniment of a prescribed chant/hymn.

ashram – hermitage or retreat where men and women withdraw from worldly life to one of prayer and meditation.

ayah – maid-servant employed in middle-class Indian households with the specific charge of looking after the children of the family.

Ayodhya – believed to be the birthplace of Lord Rama located in the state of Uttar Pradesh. It has been in the forefront of national politics since the coming to power of the Bharatiya Janata Party (BJP) in the 1990s.

'Ayya khidma' – literally 'At your service' in Arabic.

baba – affectionate term for male child, used by servants. It implies both affection and respect.

Babri Masjid – a mosque built in Ayodhya in 1532 by Mir Baqi, a famous general in the court of Babur, the first Mughal emperor. Claimed by some to have been built over a temple marking the site of the birthplace of Lord Rama, it became controversial in the 1980s when a section of right-wing Hindus demanded its destruction. Its demolition in 1992, amidst much publicity, caused political unrest and also gave rise to the Bharatiya Janata Party, in power today. The demand to rebuild a larger temple is on hold at the time of writing, but remains a live and emotive issue in national politics.

bachpan – literally 'childhood', or the first (nurture) phase in Hinduism's traditional divisions of the life of human beings.

bahu – daughter-in-law.

'Bahut zaroori kaam hai.' – '(I) have some important work (with them).'

band gala – literally 'closed-neck coat', often given as a uniform to servants in middle-class Indian families. Also known as the Nehru jacket.

bandhej – tied-and-dyed fabric (cotton or chiffon) native to the states of Rajasthan and Gujarat; often used as a *dupatta* with *salwar kameez*, or made into saris.

bania – the local grocer who would traditionally be of the shopkeeper (or *bania*) class. From the Sanskrit *vanija*, or merchant.

banyan tree – Indian fig tree with aerial roots growing downwards from the branches into the soil, forming additional trunks over the years. Its wide spread often makes its surroundings a desirable location for temples and ashrams.

barsati – literally 'rain room', usually located on the top of a house and used to take in the washing when it rains, especially during the monsoon. Today barsatis consist of two or three rooms (including a small kitchen and bathroom), often rented out by house-owners to people looking for cheaper accommodation in the heart of town.

bawab – literally 'he who looks after the door' or (*bab*) in Arabic, i.e. doorman.

'*Bechara beta*' – 'The poor son (of the family).'

'*Bechari nari, mari gayi, mari gayi*' – literally 'Poor woman, she got killed, she got killed.' The phrase is sometimes repeated like a chant by protestors outside the house where a suspected dowry death has occurred.

behenji – literally 'sister'. The 'ji' at the end lends deference.

beta – literally 'son'. Used as a term of endearment.

beti – literally 'daughter'. Used as a term of endearment.

bhabi – sister-in-law; with specific reference to a brother's wife.

bhai; bhaiya – literally 'brother'. Also implies deference.

'*bheegi billi*' – literally 'drenched cat', used metaphorically to suggest a chastened/subdued persona which could also be feigned.

bindi – red (now even fashionably coloured) dot commonly applied in the middle of the forehead by Indian women. Traditionally, it was made of red powder (*kumkum*) and signified that the woman was married.

biryani – a gourmet dish in which meat (chicken or mutton) and rice (usually *basmati*) are cooked in layers, and flavoured with saffron and other spices.

black lentils – the more popular (in the north) of the eight different varieties of Indian *dals* or lentils.

Bollywood – colloquial Indian term (cf. Hollywood) to describe India's huge Hindi film industry located in Bombay.

brahmacharya – literally 'bachelorhood', the second (preparatory) phase in Hinduism's traditional divisions in the life of human beings.

chakras – a variety of firework which spins in circles on the ground releasing fiery sparks.

chapatis – Indian bread rounds made of unleavened flour, cooked fresh at every meal.

chappals – slippers.

charpai – literally 'four-legged', used to signify a (portable) bed.

chautha – literally 'fourth', used to signify the fourth day after the cremation of a person. It is usually marked by religious ceremonies and a memorial service which includes the singing of hymns.

chiq – door or window blinds made with slatted wicker strips.

choti – literally 'small'; often used as a pet name for the youngest daughter in the family.

chowkidar – security guard or doorman.

chunni – short for *chuneri*, or long scarf, worn as the third part of a *salwar kameez* ensemble.

'chup raho' – literally 'keep quiet'.

coir mat – floor covering made of knotted jute or coconut husk.

curry – literally 'gravy', traditionally flavoured with heavy spices. Used in vegetarian and non-vegetarian Indian cooking.

daadima – literally 'grandmother'; used specifically to signify father's mother, as distinct from *naanima*, which signifies mother's mother.

dahej – dowry.

dahi – yoghurt, usually home-made.

dal – lentils; any one of the eight varieties is essential to the Indian meal.

dal-chawal – literally 'lentils and rice', basic Indian meal.

deodar – a variety of fir tree found in the lower Himalayas. Often used as a Christmas tree.

'Desh se bahar hain' – literally 'They are outside the country', i.e. abroad.

devi – goddess, with connotations of ethical purity; used here to describe someone who fears experience and makes a virtue of shunning it.

dhaba – cheap roadside eating house serving traditional Indian food (often delicious, though spicy).

dharna – a mode of peaceful protest, made popular by Mahatma Gandhi, in which those with a grievance sit outside a home/ office/factory/ to convey their displeasure publicly.

dholak – elongated drum. A percussion instrument commonly used in popular and folk music.

dhols – large percussion instrument used on ceremonial occasions.

dhoti – ankle-length loin cloth (often in fine cotton) worn by men in India.

didi – elder sister; used by younger siblings as a mark of deference.

Diwali – also known as 'the festival of lights', this is the most popular festival in India. Occurring sometime in November, it marks the triumphant return of Lord Rama to his throne in Ayodhya and is celebrated with fireworks, the lighting of *diyas* (oil lamps) or candles, and the distribution of traditional sweets among friends and family.

diyas – oil lamps.

dupatta – literally 'two-edged', or veil, the third part of a *salwar kameez* ensemble. The word is often interchanged with *chunni*.

durrie – floor covering or carpet.

elaichi – green cardamom.

Epics – the *Ramayana* and the *Mahabharata*, whose stories are referred to by all classes of Indians in the course of daily life.

fakir – ascetic mendicant or holy wise man.

felfela – literally a fried patty made of ground fava beans, coriander, leeks and spices. Generally served with tahina sauce, chopped onions, tomatoes and cucumbers, in a pitta bread.

felucca – early Egyptian sail boat still in use. It is also popular among Cairenes for revels on the Nile.

Femina – glossy weekly magazine in English with a wide readership among middle-class Indian women.

Filmfare – one of the earliest weekly magazines in English about the Indian film industry.

fuul – fava beans, a staple in Egyptian diet.

gallabeya – long flowing robe worn by traditional Egyptian men and women.

ghagra – ankle-length voluminous cotton skirt with decorated edging worn traditionally by village women in Rajasthan and Gujarat.

'Ghar me koi hai?' – literally 'Is anyone at home?'

Godrej cupboard – strong *almirah* made of steel, popularised by the Godrej manufacturing company.

goondas – hoodlums.

graha – literally planet; in this context a malefic planet auguring a temporary period of disaster.

grihastha – literally 'household' or family life; the third (and most meaningful) phase in Hinduism's traditional divisions in the life of human beings.

gulabjamuns – deep-fried milk and flour dumplings in a thick syrup. A popular north Indian sweet.

gulmohur – tree with bright red flowers which bloom in the heat of summer. It lines the streets of many neighbourhoods in New Delhi. Also known as flamboyant, or flame-tree.

guru – religious or spiritual leader giving personal guidance to disciples.

'*Hamme Mrs Malhotra se milna hai.*' – 'We want to meet Mrs Malhotra.'

'*Hari Om, Narayan*' – Hindu religious chant, often used colloquially to express shock or amazement.

havan – sacred ritual conducted around a fire on important occasions, for example a marriage, a naming ceremony, death.

haveli – traditionally styled home with living quarters designed around a central courtyard.

hijab – scarf or hair covering still worn by traditional Egyptian women.

Holi – colourful north Indian spring festival (marked by revelry and good food) celebrated sometime in March, in which everyone throws coloured water/powders at each other. It also marks the coming of summer.

jadu – magic.

'*jaldi aao*' – literally 'come quickly' in Hindi.

janaeu – holy string worn over the right shoulder by men of the Brahmin caste.

janam patri – literally 'parchment of birth' or horoscope, written out by astrologer or seer.

jayamala – ceremonial garland (usually made of flowers) exchanged by a bride and groom before the wedding ceremony.

jhuggi – a slum dwelling.

'*Ji, zaroor*' – 'Yes, of course'. The *Ji* suggests deference.

joora – long hair coiled in a low bun at the back of the head, traditionally worn by Indian women.

Jumma – literally 'Friday' in Arabic.

kadahi – traditional Indian cooking utensil shaped like a Chinese *wok* and used for stir-fry cooking.

kajal – cosmetic black *kohl* used to line eyes in Asian and Middle Eastern countries.

'*kakaji* ' – literally 'boy', with the *ji* at the end adding deference. Here used pejoratively to suggest a spoilt and cosseted young man.

Kalyug – the last, 'dark' age in the mythical four-phased Hindu cosmic cycle of life, the first three being *Satyayug, Tretayug* and *Dwaperyug*.

kanyadan — literally 'the giving away of the daughter'. In Hindu belief, a daughter's rightful place is in her husband's home. The moment of her being formally handed over to her husband's family (*kanyadan*) is an important part of the Hindu wedding ceremony.

karma — a collection of a human being's good and bad actions believed to have a bearing on one's fate in the next life.

katha — literally 'story'. Here it refers to regular sermons based on tales (often from the *Mahabharata* and the *Ramayana*) given by a wise man (or woman) in an ashram.

kebabs — spiced pieces of meat cooked on a skewer in a *tandoor* or clay oven. Flattened round patties made of minced mutton and deep fried are also known as *kebabs*.

kebab mein haddi — literally the unexpected bone in a kebab. Used metaphorically to suggest the presence of an unwelcome third in a twosome.

keekar tree — ubiquitous Indian bush-like tree with spines. It needs very little water for survival.

keema-mattar — a popular north Indian dish in which minced mutton is cooked with green peas.

khaddar/khadi — homespun cotton cloth made famous by Mahatma Gandhi during the Freedom Movement.

khandan/khandani — literally family, including the generations that have gone before. When used as an adjective (i.e. *khandani*), it suggests a 'high' (or a 'well-known') family.

khana — literally food or meal.

kismet — fate.

kofta — meat balls, usually cooked in a thick *curry* or gravy.

kohl-lined — lined with *kohl* or *kajal*. See *kajal*.

'*Koi nahi hai ghar mein. Sab bahar gaye hain.*' — 'Nobody is at home. Everyone is out.'

kolhapuris/chappals — popular leather slippers, traditionally made in Kolhapur, and making a basic Indian fashion statement.

korma – meat cooked in a heavily spiced thick sauce.

koshari – Egyptian mashed-rice dish cooked with meat.

kumkum bindi – red powder used traditionally to make red dot or *bindi* in the middle of a woman's forehead, as distinct from a stick-on modern one.

kurta/pyjama – loose knee-length shirt without a collar worn over the ankle-length *pyjama* (or the looser *salwar*) worn by men.

lathi charge – literally 'the charge of sticks (*lathis*)' typically used by Indian police to disperse unruly crowds.

lehaaz – allowance; or 'to make allowance for'.

lehenga – ornate ankle-length skirt usually in silk. It is worn with a small waist-length shirt (or *kurti*) or a *choli* (short blouse) and an *odhni* (or veil). Being made of expensive material, it is usually worn on special occasions.

'loo' breezes – dry hot winds blowing eastwards into the plains of north India from over the Thar desert.

'Maar diya, hai mere Ram, maar diya.' – literally 'Oh! They have killed her, oh my dear Rama, they have killed her.'

maharaj – '*maha*' in Hindi means great or supreme. Here, literally 'great king' or 'great person'. Used deferentially to address any person (especially *gurus* and *seers*) with respect, as distinct from *maharaja*, or king.

maharaja – Hindi word which literally means 'great king', often with special reference to any of the rulers of native Indian states.

maharani – Hindi word which literally means 'great queen'.

Majnu ka Tila – a mound (*tila*) off the Ring Road in Old Delhi, around which an ashram exists even today. However, the one in this story is purely fictional.

mala – a garland of flowers, or a necklace of beads. Also hand-held rosary-like circlet of beads used to count the number of prayers in a cycle.

mandir – Hindu or Jain temple. Also refers to small room or niche in a home housing statues of the Gods worshipped every day.

mantra – incantation (Hindu or Buddhist) used in prayer and suggesting loving devotion to God.

mashrabia – elaborate Egyptian wooden latticework outside windows and balconies allowing women to look out (and below) and yet prevent them from being seen.

masjid – literally 'place of prostration' or mosque in which believers of Islam kneel down to pray.

maun – decision, often voluntary, to maintain silence (i.e. not speak).

maun-vrat – literally a voluntary 'fast' (*vrat*) of words (i.e. self-imposed silence).

mausi – literally aunt; but with specific reference to mother's sisters.

maya – illusion or delusion. Refers to essential Hindu doctrine that the world and all in it is unreal, and that the only reality is Brahma, the Creator.

memsahib – the term used to describe Europeans was 'sahib'. *Memsahib* is a contraction of the words 'madam sahib' and refers to the woman, or the mistress, of the house. The term is still used by servants in westernised homes, although it is often regarded as an affectation.

mithai pink – bright Indian pink, often the colour of a particular kind of Indian sweet.

money order – a method of sending money by means of the postal system to villages unlikely to have a bank.

moti elaichi – black cardamom. It is known for its strong flavour and used in rice and curry preparations.

muezzin – an Arabic word which refers to an official in a mosque who calls the faithful to prayer from the minaret.

Mughals, The – famous dynasty of Muslim rulers (1526–1857) which ruled India from Delhi for almost three hundred years. Its fifth emperor, Shahjahan, built the Taj Mahal in memory of his dead wife, Mumtaz Mahal. The Babri

Masjid (1832) was built in the reign of the first king, Babur.

Mujhe memsahib se milna tha.' – 'I wanted to meet the *memsahib.'*

mul-mul – Indian muslin, or fine cotton.

'Mr ya Mrs Malhotra? ... inmay se ek to hoga?' – 'Mr or Mrs Malhotra? ... at least one of them must be here?'

naanima – literally 'grandmother', but with special reference to mother's mother.

Namaskar; namaste – the typically Indian form of greeting which calls for hands held palms-together under the chin.

'Nari hatya nahi chalegi ... nahi chalegi.' – 'The murder of women will not pass ... will not pass.' A refrain often chanted by men and women protesting against dowry deaths.

neem tree – A ubiquitous Indian tree (*Azadirachta indica*) whose leaves are known for their medicinal, antiseptic, and disinfectant qualities.

newar – sturdy cotton fabric, approximately four inches wide, sold in rolls and woven in a basket-weave around a wooden bed or chair frame.

nimbu pani – literally 'lime water' in which the juice of one lime is squeezed into a glass of chilled water and served either salted or sweetened. Known for its cooling effect, it is especially popular with those who dislike aerated drinks.

odhni – ornate, slightly larger-sized veil or scarf. The third, flowing part of a *salwar kameez* or *lehenga-choli* ensemble.

Om – a mystic syllable, representing, some believe, the glory of the Sun, as also Lord Vishnu. *Om* chanting is an important part of most Hindu religious ceremonies.

Om pendant – the distinctive *Om* shape is often made into 22-carat gold pendants worn on a chain around the neck by both men and women.

pakoras – fritters made by coating chopped vegetable pieces (potatoes, cauliflowers, aubergines, onions, green chillies, etc.), with a chickpea-flour batter before deep-frying in hot oil.

pallav, or *palla* – the flowing end of a sari, often with a distinctive design.

paratha – a layered unleavened flour *chapati* brushed with ghee and containing a mashed vegetable or minced meat filling. Cooked on a hot griddle, it is eaten with butter, yoghurt, or pickles. It is a favourite (often breakfast) dish with Indians from the north, especially Punjabis.

pashmina – from *pashm*, or the fine soft under-wool of a breed of goat found in the higher altitudes of Kashmir, Ladakh, and Tibet. Also known as 'Cashmere' or 'Kashmir'. Popularly woven into (expensive) *shawls* (warm length of fabric worn around the shoulders or wrapped around a baby).

patakas – fireworks, especially the noisy ones.

phool jhari – a hand-held, pencil-thin firework whose lighted tip sheds sparks in the shape of a flower. Popular with younger children and the timid during Diwali celebrations.

phukni – hollow, metal tube (about 12 inches long) used by village housewives to blow life into their kitchen fires, usually lighted in a grate on the ground.

pranam – reverential salutation from a lesser/junior to a superior/senior friend, family member, or acquaintance, which could involve a low bow and the *namaste*, or even the touching of feet. The obeisance to a deity or seer could be more profound with knees and forehead touching the ground, or a prostration.

Public Sector – the part of the economy which consists of state-owned institutions, including nationalised industries and services provided by governmental authorities. After Independence in 1947, India's first prime minister, Jawahar Lal Nehru, chose to give a socialist orientation to the economy, with public sector institutions awarded a prominent place, especially in the development of infrastructure.

puja/s – literally 'adoration' or prayer. It involves the worship of Hindu deities and includes all the complementary rituals and offerings (flowers, kumkum, incense, and a fire in the form of a small flame from a *diya* or lamp). A *puja* can be a personal (often lengthy) devotional activity performed at home, or one in a temple performed with the help of the local priest or *pujari*.

pukka — strong/permanent (cf. structure or road) as opposed to 'kuchcha'.

purdah — the custom in some Muslim and Hindu communities of keeping women in seclusion, with clothing (often a dark cloak with a hood which also covers the face) that conceals them completely when they step out of the house.

puris — rounds of unleavened bread deep-fried in oil.

rajah — king.

Rajdhani, The — a super-fast train leaving westwards from New Delhi to Bombay, or eastwards to Calcutta.

rajnigandha — tuberose; cream-coloured highly scented flowers on long stalks, mostly used during weddings.

Rama, Lord — the central character of the great Indian epic, the *Ramayana*, and the epitome of goodness.

rangoli — Indian traditional art of decorating the floor at the entrance of homes or temples to welcome guests on festive occasions. Geometric designs are made with coloured powders, lentils or flower petals.

ration card — an important civic document which gives proof of residence and identity as a citizen of the city, and authorises access to subsidised food stuffs.

rickshaw — a means of public transport that could be of two or three wheels. The latter are motorised and a popular option for those finding taxis too expensive.

Ring Road — four-laned highway that circles the city and is known for its heavy traffic.

roti — rounds of unleavened flour roasted on a griddle and prepared fresh before every meal.

sabzi — literally 'greens'. Also refers to a dish in which any seasonal vegetable is cooked with special spices to go with the main dish of the meal.

sadhu — mendicant.

Sahayata — literally 'help'. In the novel, it is the chosen name for the organisation set up by Maneka Saxena and her friends to help women in distress.

sahib – literally 'Lord' in Arabic. In India, it is a term of deference used by servants for their employers. The word is also used to convey respect to one's interlocutor.

'*Sahib kahan hain?*' – 'Where is *sahib*?'

salwar kameez – three-piece ensemble (ankle-length loose trousers tied at the waist with a drawstring or *salwar*; knee-length shirt with side slits or *kameez*; and a veil-like scarf of finer material or *chunni / dupatta / odhni*) native to north India but now worn all over the country.

samosa – a three-cornered patty made of *maida* or white flour and stuffed with spicy vegetables or meat and deep-fried in hot oil.

sanyas / sanyasi – literally 'renunciation' of all worldly ties; the last phase in Hinduism's traditional divisions in the life of human beings.

sardarni – *sardar* literally means 'leader', or *sir-dar* in Persian. Title given to all followers of the *Khalsa* (Sikhs) by Guru Gobind Singh. *Sardarni* is the feminine form of the word (Sikhs only).

sari – traditional dress native to the Indian sub-continent. It consists of six yards of fabric wrapped over an ankle-length petticoat and worn with a short blouse or *choli*.

shawl – warm length of fabric worn around the shoulders by Indian women (and sometimes men) or wrapped around a baby. Many varieties and designs are available in India, the most desired (and expensive) of which are those made of *pashm* or the under-wool of the mountain goat found in the higher altitudes of Kashmir, Ladakh, and Tibet.

shehnai – Indian wind instrument played at weddings and other auspicious occasions.

shukriya – literally 'thank you'.

Stardust – popular weekly magazine which details the ups and downs of film stars and the film industry in Bombay.

'*Sukhi raho, beti*' – 'May you remain happy, daughter'.

'*Suniye, bhaiya*' – literally 'listen, brother'.

supari – small pieces of betel nut chewed on as a digestive after a meal.

tabla – a pair of percussion instruments usually played together.

tahina – a paste/thick cold sauce made of ground sesame seeds, popular in Egypt and the Middle East and used as a dip to eat with bread and raw vegetables.

tamayya – green/brown patties made of the *fava* bean ground with green onions and coriander, and fried in hot oil. A popular dish in Egypt.

tandoori – from *tandoor*, or traditional Indian clay oven, in which meat and bread are roasted in dry heat. The spicy marinades (for the meat) and the smoked flavour make for its distinctive gourmet taste.

tava – stone or iron griddle used for making *rotis* or *chappatis*.

teen patti – a popular card game, much like Poker.

thali – traditional Indian plate (slightly larger than the dinner plate) made of brass, stainless steel, or silver, in which the different dishes in the menu are served in small *katoris* (bowls). The portions served in a *thali* are meant for one person.

tiffin – traditionally, a light mid-day meal carried in a box or container to be eaten outside the home, in the office or workplace.

trishul – trident-shaped staff associated with Lord Shiva. Its replica in pendants and charms is considered auspicious.

vanaprastha – literally 'retirement to the forest' or *vana*; the fourth phase in Hinduism's traditional divisions in the life of human beings. The period asks for detachment from worldly life in preparation for the last phase of life or *sanyas*.

Vividh Bharati – popular radio programme (running almost throughout the day) which broadcasts Hindi film songs on request.